Cassandra
NYWENING

Hidden Grace Trilogy - Book One

THE
MASK

A Novel

THE MASK

ISBN-13: 978-1-926676-81-4

Printed in Canada.

Printed by Word Alive Press
131 Cordite Road, Winnipeg, MB R3W 1S1
www.wordalivepress.ca

WORD ALIVE PRESS
Just Write!

FOR MOM AND DAD.

You have been patient with me,

you have encouraged me,

but most of all you have loved me

and allowed me to take a risk.

To the Hoekstra
Family,
I hope you enjoy!
God bless.
Cassly

ACKNOWLEDGEMENTS

There are no words to describe the thankfulness I feel toward those people who have helped me publish my book. To Mrs. Wahn for taking the time to read and give suggestions for my novel when I first brought it to her, even though she had so many other things to do. To Uncle Jake, who has gone above and beyond in editing *The Mask*. The two of you have truly been a blessing from God.

Finally, I would like to thank all those who encouraged me through the long process of editing and publishing. I would never have gotten this far without your support and prayers. You guys are great.

PROLOGUE

ROSE TIPTOED THROUGH THE HOUSE trying to avoid the cricks and cracks of the old structure. It was late at night and she did not want to wake her aunt and uncle over a glass of water; her aunt especially. Rose continued to move along when the sound of muffled voices stopped her dead in her tracks. They were coming from the dining room.

She eased herself toward the door, straining to hear what the voices were saying. Her aunt's rough tenor berated Uncle Murdoch, who would reply as calmly as a sick man could while being harassed in such a manner. Rose's curiosity was piqued by the strange meeting at such a late hour, and though she knew she was not supposed to, she leaned in a little closer to hear their words.

"I will not have it, Murdoch. I simply cannot put up with her in my house for another month. She is of the age where she can marry and it would not be considered a scandal. We shall simply find a suitable husband for her and send her off in marital bliss with none the wiser."

"Surely Agatha, you cannot be suggesting such a rash thing," wheezed her uncle. "There is no reason why Rose should not stay within our care, and I cannot see how it would cause you any stress to have her remain with us. She is just a slight girl, sure to be married off soon enough of her own accord without our assistance. I say we leave it up to her to find her own husband in good time."

"I won't put up with this. Murdoch, I know you care for the girl as you would your own daughter, but you should also know that I detest the girl with every nuance of my being. She's despicable; an eyesore to this entire world. I hate her, and you know exactly why. So, either we find a husband for her now, or I will send her out to live on the streets as soon as you breathe your last."

"Very well, I see that you have left very little room for choice. You may look for a husband for Rose, but do not think that she will consent with your wishes. She is very headstrong and more intelligent than most girls. John will also be against you, seeing as he and Rose have been close since they were children."

"There should be no problem from our son, seeing as I shall not tell either party of my intentions. I will get my way, and Rose will be married off within a month or two. Maybe you will still be alive for the wedding," mocked Agatha.

"You are a wicked woman. If it weren't for Rose's sake, I would not mind one wit if death came a little early, but because of Rose, I hope I am around for many more years."

THE MASK

Rose inhaled deep, short breaths trying to hold back her panic. This could not be happening. How could her uncle allow such a thing? She couldn't marry! She was only seventeen. All thoughts of caution disappeared as Rose raced upstairs and burrowed under the covers of her bed. The quilted comfort nearly suffocated her as she gasped for breath.

Of course, she had known that her aunt hated her. It had been a constant battle between the two of them since the day Rose had come to live with them. This new scheme of her aunt's just marked the beginning of yet another battle, and Rose was determined to win.

ONE

THE DINNER TABLE REMAINED SILENT save for the clinking of silverware on the dishes and the loud inhaling of Rose's neighbour. Mr. Darmouth was a portly fellow with a round head and beady black eyes. He seemed to have trouble breathing, and when he ate, perspiration built up on his brow. The very sight of him made Rose gag, and the reason for his presence was enough to make her wish she was the type of lady that condoned swooning.

Her aunt hadn't taken long to choose a suitor for her despised niece, and Rose feared that if her uncle Murdoch had not been present she would already be married off to this ogre of a man. John sat across the table from Rose, a questioning look in his eyes. She had not yet told him about his mother's schemes, but she had every intention of explaining in full detail as soon as the evening ended. For now, she must act the ever gracious hostess.

"How is your meal, Mr. Darmouth?" Rose asked in the sweetest voice she could muster. "I hope everything is to your pleasure."

"It is most delicious, Miss Wooden. I have not tasted such exemplary food in what seems like ages. You must pass my compliments on to the cook," Mr. Darmouth announced around bites and loud breaths.

"I most certainly will."

With that, the room fell silent. The evening passed by agonizingly slowly. Mr. Darmouth seemed more concerned with his food than conversation, and every female present cringed as each morsel was shoved into the man's flabby mouth.

When dinner was over, Mr. Darmouth left immediately, once again complimenting the cook as he clambered up into his carriage. As soon as it had disappeared down the lane, Rose retreated back into the house. She wished her aunt and uncle goodnight, and as she passed her cousin John to go up the stairs, she tapped him twice quickly on the shoulder. He acknowledged her slightly. Once in her room, Rose dressed quickly in a pair of loose-fitting men's pants, known as inexpressibles, grabbed her sword and mask from the confines of the closet, dove under the covers of her bed, and waited. It wasn't until the latest hours of the night that John knocked three times on her door, waited two seconds, and then knocked three more times. Rose bound out of bed and slipped out of her room to where John waited in the hall. Neither of them spoke as they walked to the back pasture. There, Rose donned her mask, and they began to duel.

THE MASK

John, who was five years older than Rose, had been teaching her to duel since she had come to live with them seven years ago. Though it was not socially accepted for women to wield a sword, it helped Rose relieve her stress after her parents' deaths, and John considered fighting with a sword more useful knowledge than sewing. The two would, therefore, spend many late nights out in the pasture fencing, and when they grew tired, they would talk.

Rose had become exceptional at sword fighting, and she had an unnatural drive to learn more than what John could teach her. It had taken a while and a lot of persuasion, but John had finally been convinced to bring in someone more experienced to train her. She could remember whooping with victory when John had told her this, while he only groaned. He had thought her reputation would be ruined for sure, but Rose hadn't cared. She had little need for society. John disagreed. He bought her a mask to wear when she duelled, so that she would not be found out by her opponent.

The teacher was hired to come once a week to the pasture for lessons, and John and Rose made sure it remained their closely guarded secret. Rose had been taught to fight alongside John, and the teacher had never once discovered that he had taught a woman to fight so well.

Now as the two duelled, they pushed each other to the extreme, testing the other's limits and allowing the stress of the long evening to roll off their shoulders. An hour passed before John called a halt to their competition and asked Rose quietly what the matter was. It took all of Rose's self-control to reply without shouting. "Your mother is the matter," she ground out. "She has schemed to marry me off within the next month or two, or, if her plan fails, to throw me out on the street. Tonight was her first candidate for my matrimonial bliss. How did you like him?"

John laughed at her sarcasm. "Surely cousin, you must be jesting. My mother would never be able to plan such a thing. Besides, my father would not allow it. He would fight it even so far as the courts to keep you living with us."

"John," Rose continued softly now, "your father doesn't have much longer to live, and your mother will have full control once he is gone. I am truly scared of what she may accomplish once he is taken from us."

"Don't speak that way, Rose," John whispered hoarsely. He shook his head and cleared his throat slightly. "There is a good chance that my father will live for many more years to come. You have heard the doctor's reports. He seems to be improving. He has even been walking around the house the past few days. Besides, even if something did happen to Father, I would never allow my mother to do you any harm." John's frustration was evident by the terse way he spat out the last few words.

"And what would you do to oppose your mother?" Rose's voice rose, her anger again piqued by the manner in which John responded. "She would throw you out of the house just as quickly as she would do away with me. She is unreasonable, and slightly insane, if you ask me. She hates me, and I haven't any idea why. She will turn her anger towards you if you get in her way."

"Well then, what would you have me do? Should I challenge my mother to a duel, storm the gates of my own home to rescue you from your evil aunt? All that would be nothing but a fairy's tale. What would I do after that? The government would be after me, and you would be in just as much trouble as before." He let out a growl of frustration. "The only thing I can promise you is that I will not allow my mother to marry you off to someone who will treat you less kindly than you deserve."

"And who do you know that deserves me? Mr. Darmouth? Would he suit your standards? Or should I wait and hope that your mother sets me up with the curate. I hear he is a fine fellow – even for someone of fifty-two years. I know of no man that your mother could possibly contrive to set me up with that isn't double my age or detestable to any sane being."

Rose was sick of the conversation. She began to walk away. It was obvious that John did not have any solutions. It would be better for her to get some sleep instead of wasting her time arguing with him.

"Rose, I would go to great lengths to find the Prince himself for you to marry, but you must give me time to find a suitable match for you."

Rose spun on the spot and glared at him. "I would rather marry a pauper than the Prince," she spat. "The Prince would only marry for money and prestige. The whole royal family looks for nothing save expanding the empire. I, on the other hand, do not wish to marry at all, no matter the benefit." She turned and resumed walking.

"Is that really so? You don't wish to marry at all?" said John. He was following her now. "What then do you plan to do with your life? Being a spinster really isn't all that easy either, especially when you don't have a mother and father to support you. And it is not very likely that I will be able to support you. That would create a bigger scandal than all this fuss is worth."

"I'll find a way to survive," replied Rose saucily. "It's not like I am completely incapable. I have many talents. Perhaps I will become a seamstress, and if that gets too odious, I will join the army. Fighting would be great fun, and if I died, at least I wouldn't be married to Mr. Darmouth."

"Yes," said John flatly, "that would be much better. No one would mourn your passing except for your loved ones, but what do they matter? I mean, I don't mind attending funerals, and tears can only last so long."

Rose stopped in her tracks and let her head fall. "What do you want from me, John?" she asked quietly. "I am seventeen, and I am a slave to my aunt. I have no independence. Can you not understand that?" Rose turned pleading eyes to her cousin. "I hate living under her. I hate having to watch my every step, making sure that I don't offend her."

"I don't know, Rose. I really don't," John groaned as he rubbed his hand across his face. "If I had the answers I would give them to you, but I don't. If you could just have some patience, perhaps I could work this out." He stopped to take a deep breath. "No man in his right mind would make you marry him. You at least have that going for you. As for now, my mother will not have you marry

Mr. Darmouth. I don't think she could make it through any more visits from him. He is quite a horrendous beast of a man. Anyway, it will be at least another week before she can have another suitor come calling. Give me until then to think, okay?"

"I don't like it, John." Rose whispered. "What are the chances that your mother gives up on this plan? And what if she doesn't? John, I don't think I could stand being married if she chose my husband. Every morning when I woke, I would see his face, and I would know that she had won. Every time when I am called by his name, I will know that I am her slave. Every single second that I am in his presence, I will loath her, and she will laugh. If she chooses, she wins, and I can't live with that." Rose wiped at her eyes. She didn't want to cry. She refused to cry.

"Then I will have to find a way to buy you time, and you had best work on choosing your own husband, or at least finding someone you can tolerate. As of now, I can only promise you two months before you must wed, or be on the way to being wed," John replied gently. "Now, come my dear cousin, it is nearing dawn, and we must return to the house before we are missed." He pulled her into a brief embrace and they continued to walk.

"Do not fret yourself so much over this matter. I will keep my eyes and ears open, and maybe this matter will clear up of its own accord. You never know," he said with false cheer. Rose sighed and slumped her shoulders. What else was there to do? She dragged her feet as she walked slowly beside John. Her eyelids fluttered slightly as she fought off sleep. John picked her up when she began to stumble, but before she let unconsciousness take hold, she sent up a hasty prayer to the heavens that her cousin just might be right.

TWO

HENRY LOOKED AT THE YOUNG LADY sitting across from him. Miss Kayla Beton was a beautiful girl who batted her eyelashes and swooned with the best of the ladies of the court. She seemed to know all the tricks in the book and was intent upon making the young prince fall madly in love with her. Unfortunately for her, Prince Henry cared little for the pettish ways of the women of the court.

Supper passed by agonizingly slowly as the king and queen attempted to make conversation about something other than politics with Sir Arthur and Lady Beton. It seemed they had little to talk about, and Henry had no intention of adding to the dead conversation. He was furious with his father, who had arranged the whole supper, the third of its kind, and he didn't feel like talking to anyone about anything at the moment.

The king's intent was so blatantly obvious to Henry, and it only made him angry. His father wished him to marry one of the ladies, but Henry could not put up with their whimpering and whining. They were pathetic, and he would not tolerate them. When he had explained this to his father, the king had retaliated by arranging these dinner dates.

Henry let out a quiet sigh and tried to keep himself from rolling his eyes as Miss Beton made an attempt at conversation, only to blurt out the latest court gossip. Such things were far from Prince Henry's interest, and he could come up with no reply other than, "How lovely to know that Miss Smith will be marrying Mr. Ferris. I'm sure they will lead a happy life." This reply did not seem to satisfy Miss Beton, who continued on her ramble about court life.

Henry kept his face moulded into an expression of interest, but it felt stiff and forced. There was no possible way that Miss Beton could believe that he found her conversation amusing, yet she ploughed on and on. It seemed like ages had passed before he was able to retire to his room and reminisce over the last few evenings.

The first dinner had been with the Grey family. Lord Grey was a good man, but he had a very silly daughter who knew nothing of etiquette and laughed more than was suitable for a lady of her age. Then there had been the MacTaven family. Miss MacTaven was in no way similar to Miss Grey; rather, her disposition was so severe, she would not be prevailed upon to wear any colour besides a sombre black. The thought of Miss MacTaven laughing was a joke in itself. Last, but not least, there had been the Beton family. Henry could not decide whom he liked the least of the three ladies, and he could not bear to imagine whom his father would thrust in front of him next.

A loud knock on his door brought Henry out of his reverie just as his father barged into his room. King James Arden of Samaya was a big man with a good heart, but a quick temper. He did not appreciate those who got in his way, and he especially would not tolerate those who mistreated his guests. "How dare you!" he shouted. "Miss Beton is a perfectly respectable young lady with a lot to offer. There was no need for you to shirk her off the way you did at dinner this evening. What could you possibly be thinking?"

"I was thinking," grumbled Henry, "that I do not want to be married off to a silly girl who has no aspirations other than to serve tea everyday in the palace courtyard. Surely Father, there must be more intelligent ladies in the court." Henry's tone of nonchalance did not sit well with the king.

"Miss MacTaven is an intelligent girl, but you seemed to object to her so severely. Honestly Henry, I cannot determine what you are looking for in a lady."

"What I want most in a lady," said Henry angrily, "is for her to be chosen by myself, not chosen by my father based on her family and wealth. Wealth is only looking for more wealth, Father. I want someone who will marry me because of my character, my likes and dislikes. Not because of my title and large treasury. Is that so hard to understand?" Henry pleaded.

faces he didn't know. He would see his country, and do his searching away from the court and away from the life he had always known. While he was away, he would learn about the people he would someday rule. Perhaps it would make him independent. Perhaps it would make him care.

James did not care if his son should come back with a wife. The law which stated that he needed a wife to rule was easily changed. But if he did find a girl, the king would be that much more thankful.

He laughed again. Who would have known that Jasper's plan would have worked so well? The Betons were appeased of their visit, the Greys had shown their daughter to the prince, the prince was on his way to happiness, and the whole kingdom was content. Yes, Jasper was a wise man. The king would surely have to reward him, but first he had another task for the young man.

The king continued on his way, whistling down the hall. Life was beautiful. It was going to be an eventful year, and he couldn't wait to see what would happen next.

The curate sat across the table from Rose. He was handsome for his age, rather tall and lean with black hair that contained flecks of gray. He had a soft face, almost a baby face, but he was fifty-two. The conversation around the dinner table was light, mainly led by Rose's aunt, who had the audacity to mention weddings in one manner or another at least every five minutes.

Rose's temper was just below the boiling point when her Aunt Agatha said to the curate, "Good sir, how long has it been since your dear wife passed away? It must be nearly five years already."

"Six years, Mrs. Borden. It will be six years this coming Sunday," replied the curate calmly.

"My, that is a long time to be a widower. You must be awfully lonely in that old house of yours. I'm sure you wish that you still had a wife to keep your house nice and homey, do you not?" Her aunt's voice was honey-sweet, and Rose could not control herself anymore. She threw her napkin down on the table, stood, and quickly excused herself. When she had left the dining room, she raced out of doors to the pasture to wait out the curate's visit.

She sat there with her knees pulled to her chest for nearly two hours when her cousin John came out to get her. "My mother wishes to see you in the house immediately," he said with little emotion. "She was quite perplexed when you left the table, and she is not in a good humour. I dare say you best keep your temper in check when you speak with her."

"Thank you for the warning, John. I will do my best," Rose said politely as she headed toward the house. She walked immediately to her aunt's office and closed the door behind her. Agatha Borden rose gracefully from her chair and stared coldly at her niece.

"How dare you embarrass me the way you did today," she spat. "The curate is an admirable man, and he is deserving of your respect. It was in no way necessary for you to leave the dinner table in such a manner."

"Forgive me, Aunt. I will try to do better next time," Rose said through gritted teeth. "*Try* to do better next time? My dear child, the next time the curate is over, which may in fact be very soon, you will apologize profusely for your actions and in every way make up for your attitude by being an ever gracious hostess. Do you understand me? There is too much at stake for you to run off in a temper that way."

"What would you like from me, Aunt?" Rose yelled. "I have had enough of your games. Is it your intention for me to marry the curate? For I most certainly will not. He is triple my age and closer to death than my dear uncle. Now, speak clearly to me your intentions and I will choose for myself what I will do."

"You silly child. You think you have a choice in the matter? No, the curate will come again on Sunday. You will persuade him of your affections, and the two of you will marry. If you refuse, you will find yourself out on the streets as soon as your uncle breathes his last."

John slipped into the room and closed the door with a thud. He looked at his mother with a pained expression. "You cannot do this to her," he whispered softly. "Rose has done you no wrong, and does not deserve your loathing. I cannot allow you to marry her off to the curate. Please, Mother, just let her be."

"Aunt, I beg of you," Rose pleaded. She was playing for time, searching for any scheme that might save her. "Give me at least a year to find my own husband. If I do not find a husband within that time, I will marry the curate as you desire," she cried out in desperation.

Agatha looked at her to see if she was serious. "That will never do. A year is a long length of time, and the curate may very well be dead before your year is up," she mused.

Rose allowed her to continue to think it out.

"But, then again, it is unlikely that Murdoch will allow you to marry so soon. It will have to wait some time." Her aunt looked her up and down. "I no longer want you in my house, or anywhere near Thespane. I am sick of you and your pettish ways. You are despicable, just as your mother was despicable. I will give you a year on one condition: I do not want to see your face for the entirety of it. You can live with my sister-in-law in Emriville. She is a nice enough lady and she will care well enough for you. You will return after a year's time. If you do not have a husband, you will marry the curate and not make any objections. If he is dead, other suitable arrangements will be made. Am I understood?"

Rose glared at her aunt. "Perfectly well, and I agree to your terms. I will have my year of freedom, and then I shall become your slave. I should consider myself blessed. At least I won't have to live out the remainder of my freedom in your presence!"

"Quit it, Rose!" exclaimed John. "Mother, you cannot be serious. This is madness. You honestly cannot expect Rose to live with strangers for a year, and then you would have her marry the curate on top of that? I will not stand for this. It is pure insanity."

"Quiet, boy," shouted Agatha. John cringed slightly. "This is not your battle. You had no right to intrude on our discussion in the first place. Rose has agreed to my deal, and now you must abide by it as well. Even your father cannot object."

"You are insane, woman."

With a sorrowful shake of his head, John left the room. Rose followed close behind, leaving her aunt to stew in her own anger.

Rose sat weeping by her uncle's sick bed. "She cannot do this, Uncle, she simply cannot do this. It's not fair. How can she force me to wed in a year? I simply do not understand."

"My dear, dear Rose," Murdoch breathed slowly. "It disturbs me greatly to hear of what my wife has decided, but I fear there is nothing I can do about it. You made a deal with her, it was your decision, and if I try to stand up to it, she will simply use the same logic with me as she did with John. I fear you are the only one who will be able to stop this mess." He reached out and patted her head gently.

"Don't worry yourself so much, Rose. You have a year. Who is to say you won't find a husband of your own in that time? It wouldn't be that shocking if you did. Who knows, maybe I will be around to see your wedding. A beautiful bride you will make, and I will walk you down the aisle." Rose smiled sadly at her uncle's sick form. He was wasting away before her eyes and there was nothing anyone could do.

"I only have one question, Uncle," Rose sighed as she wiped the tears from her eyes. "Why does Aunt Agatha hate me so much? Is there something I have done wrong, something that I have done to offend her?" she asked.

"There is nothing you did wrong," he murmured softly, "save being the daughter of your mother." He closed his eyes and let out a sad sigh. "I believe it is time that you know the truth, Rose. Your aunt, my wife, hated your mother for a very long time. It started when your mother was seventeen and your aunt sixteen. Agatha at that time was a beautiful young girl, innocent and very carefree." He let out a groan as the past painted a vivid image in his mind. "Being as she was, she was quick to give her heart away to a young farmer, your father. Poor Agatha did everything she could to catch the farmer's eye, but your father had eyes only for your mother, and they were soon wed.

"Agatha has hated your mother ever since that wedding day. When your mother died, and you were given into our care, your aunt's loathing of your mother turned onto you, for you were in every way similar to your mother in appearance." He opened his eyes and looked directly at her. "In fact, you still look shockingly similar to your mother. The only differences are your eyes. You have your father's eyes. That is why, my child, your aunt detests you so passionately."

"Why then, Uncle, did you marry her? Was she not still in love with my father?"

"Yes she was," he replied sadly. "But I was foolish. I loved Agatha so much, and I believed I had enough love within me for the two of us, and so we were wed. Only now have I realized how foolish I was." The light of nostalgia left Murdoch's eyes and he looked sorrowfully at Rose. "Now, my dear, as to your predicament, I suggest that you search very hard for a husband, for a year is a very short time."

THREE

ROSE'S TWISTED AND KNOTTED STOMACH told the state of her emotions as the coach carried her steadily closer to the Monks' home, the place at which her destiny lay. She sat fidgeting with her hands when the coach stopped in front of a small cottage. The front door swung wide open, and a heavyset, kind-looking woman poured out of the entrance. She ran up to the coach and ripped Rose out of her seat and onto the dirt road. "My my, look at you!" seemed to be the only words she could spit out. An older gentleman rolled his eyes at her as he took up a position in the doorway of his home.

"My dear, I believe our guest is quite startled by your actions. You must remember that we have never met this particular young lady before, and it would be much more proper to introduce ourselves before we go sweeping her off her feet."

Mrs. Monks turned bright red at her husband's remark, but appeared to be in better control of her tongue. "You mustn't speak in such a way, Mr. Monks. This is Rose Wooden, the niece to my dear brother. Surely no introduction is required, for we are practically related. Oh, but she is a beauty. Wouldn't you agree now, Mr. Monks?"

Mr. Monks rolled his eyes once more at the audacity of his wife, and said to Rose, "I am Jeremy Monks, at your service." He bowed politely. "I believe you are Miss Rose Wooden, and if that be so, I would be much obliged to carry in your bags. You will be sharing a room with our daughter Katherine, who is away at the moment, or I fear she would be oohing and ahhing just as much as her mother at your arrival."

Rose held back a laugh as all her qualms turned into useless mush, and she was able to calmly reply, "Thank you for your hospitality, Mr. Monks. I am indeed Rose Wooden, and I am very much looking forward to spending my time in your home. Your house appears very charming, and if I had the choice, I would live in such a building for the rest of my days."

"Oh, you are too kind," blubbered Mrs. Monks. "Our home is just a simple cottage. I am sure you are used to a much grander dwelling than this, and you will soon regret your words, but I will gladly accept the compliment anyway."

"Why, Mrs. Monks!" Rose exclaimed politely. "I do not speak only of the appearance of the house, but also the company I shall find inside. For I see already that you and Mr. Monks are a charming couple through and through, and I would expect nothing less of your daughter, either."

Mr. Monks, who had just hefted one of Rose's trunks onto his shoulder, nearly dropped it as he coughed extensively to cover up the laughter that would have offended his wife.

Rose slowly unpacked some of her belongings into the small closet that she now shared with Katherine Monks. Katherine had obviously prepared for her coming, for Rose found half the closet emptied of its contents and left for her use. The thought of the work that the young girl would have had to go through to decide which dresses to leave hanging and which to fold up for another date put a smile on Rose's lips. She was very much enchanted by the small family and wished to do anything in her power to show her appreciation.

Rose quickly filled up her side of the closet and made sure to leave enough clothes on the bottom of her trunk to safely hide her sword and mask. She pulled one last dress out of her trunk to air and, with it, a scrap of paper fluttered to the ground. Rose picked it up and studied it curiously. It was a quickly penned letter from her cousin John. She smiled to herself and was just about to read it when a young girl came bounding into the room.

"Oh, Mother was right, you are downright adorable. The girls at the church are going to be right jealous of your hair and... Oh my, my manners have run right away with me. Father would be so horrified." She stopped briefly to calm herself. With a note of forced politeness, she began again. "I am Katherine Monks, your friend and roommate for the next year. Though I do wish that we will stay friends longer than that. You do not have to tell me your name, for I know very well that you are Rose Wooden, the niece to my mother's brother. How do you do?"

Rose laughed at the girl's wavering self-control. She could be no more than fifteen years, and it was evident she wasn't used to being polite. "I am quite well, thank you, Miss Monks, and I wish to thank you for the closet space you have provided for me; it was much unexpected, but very welcome. You must have spent hours deciding how to create that much room for me, and I fear that I was an imposition to you before I even arrived."

Katherine's face broke into a grin. "Please, call me Katy, all my friends do, and I will forgive you for any impositions as long as you allow me to call you Rose. It is such a lovely name."

"Then feel free to call me Rose, for it is my given name, and there is nothing wrong with putting it to use, don't you not agree?" Rose said, laughing.

"I do, I do, and I can tell already that we are going to be such good friends," Katy replied with a shrill giggle of delight. Rose cringed and wondered if first impressions were always completely accurate.

The time that Rose spent at the Monks' place was going by very quickly. The household fell into an easy routine, which allowed Rose a lot of freedom. Early in the morning she would go to the post office to look for any letters from her cousin, and throughout the day, she would help in the kitchen and in the gardens. On Sundays, the whole family would head to the church for two services and Rose would keep her eye open for any eligible young men.

Unfortunately, the town in which the Monks resided was a military town; the only eligible man just so happened to be the curate. So it happened that one month passed without Rose noticing, and she was left with only eleven months to find a husband.

This thought weighed on Rose's mind late one night as she practiced with her sword out in a pasture she had found. She practiced her thrusts and rolls and anything else she could think of. She even practiced some kicks and punches that John had been teaching her, all to relieve the stress of one month passing by. She practiced long into the night, going over in her mind everything that she had done and everything that she could do, and it wasn't until early dawn that she finally crawled back into bed.

Because she had stayed out so late, it wasn't until noon that Rose awakened, and by then it was too late for her to take her solitary walk to the post office. It had been quite some time since she had received a letter from John, and she was expecting one to arrive that very day, so she patiently waited until Katy had eaten her lunch and could accompany her into town.

"It is such a wonderful day, is it not? I love the sunshine, and the exercise is so refreshing. I am so glad you could join me today,

Rose. I do not see how you can stand to walk each morning to the post, when it is so much more delightful to go when the sun is higher in the sky." Katy continued her steady stream of words as Rose's mind began to wander to the things around her.

It was because of this senseless wandering of her mind that Rose did not notice the man snoozing under a tree while his horse drank from the stream. Katy glared at the man whose legs stuck out into the road. Rose kept walking, oblivious to the obstacle in her way until much too late. She felt herself tripping and couldn't help but let out a little squeal as she fell to the ground. The knock on the leg startled the man into wakefulness and he jumped to his feet, nearly tripping, in turn, over Rose, who was trying to pick herself up off the road.

"Why, Rose," Katy gasped as she saw the incident unfold in front of her, "are you all right? Oh my, you are limping." Katy went white, and Rose glared at her. "We must return home at once," Katy murmured. "Such a spill will have hurt your ankle horrendously."

"Katy, I am quite all right. Just a little sore spot, that is all. Besides, it was my own fault, for I was lost in my thoughts," Rose said through clenched teeth. She could feel the stranger staring at her back, but she didn't want to look at him; she was quite embarrassed by her clumsiness. Slowly she turned to the gentleman, who stepped back with a shocked expression on his face. "I apologize profusely, sir, for I believe that I have wakened you from a much appreciated rest, and I hope you will forgive me."

The man open and closed his mouth as if trying to speak but was unable. He cleared his throat and tried again. "Mademoiselle, I believe I am the one who should be apologizing, for I am the one who tripped you," he murmured. "And I think your companion is right in saying that you should have at least a sore ankle after such a stumble. I would feel much better if you would allow me to escort you back home so that I know for sure that you are all right." He bowed kindly, and Rose felt heat flood her cheeks as her embarrassment intensified.

She was about to politely object when Katy cut in, "Your offer is very much appreciated, good sir, and if you take one of Rose's arms, I will take the other arm, and in that way she will put as little pressure as possible on her ankle." Rose glared at Katy, who seemed much recovered from her bout of faintness. She tried to protest the young girl's plan, but before she could get out a word from her mouth, the stranger had cut in.

"I have a better idea. Why doesn't the young lady ride my horse back, and in that way, she won't put any pressure on her ankle at all." Without further ado, the man hoisted her in the air and seated her on his horse.

When they reached the Monks' front door, Katy invited the stranger in and he gladly accepted. The threesome therefore proceeded to move indoors to the small parlour where Mrs. Monks sat. Mrs. Monks gave the stranger a questioning look, but before a word could leave her lips, her daughter explained the whole situation with many exaggerations and large hand gestures that blew the story out of all proportion. According to Katy, the stranger was a hero and Rose a damsel in distress. Mrs. Monks was shocked by the events of the day, and it took Rose many minutes to persuade her that her ankle did not hurt one mite.

When all the explaining had been done, Mrs. Monks turned to the young man with a look of awe. "You are such a gentleman, and I thank you for the service that you have done our dear friend. I only ask, what is your name, so that I may thank you properly for your service?"

"My name, Madame, is James Hyden. At your service." With that, he gave a very courtly bow that was nearly enough to make Katy cheer and Mrs. Monks swoon at its graciousness. Rose rolled her eyes.

"Well," said Mrs. Monks, "thank you very much, Mr. Hyden, for your service to my daughter and her friend. Please, stay for a little while longer and have some cake and tea. It is the least I can offer in return for all you have done."

"Thank you, Madame. I believe I will stay, for I am sure that you make the most delicious cake."

Mr. Hyden smiled politely at Mrs. Monks, who blushed very much at the compliment and began serving the tea. The conversation went on for quite some time. Rose spoke barely a word, but distracted herself by making sure that all teacups were full and that all cake was replenished if need be. Katy and Mrs. Monks asked question after question of Mr. Hyden, and it was soon discovered that he was a traveler with no real trade but with a lust to see the country before he settled down.

The sun was getting lower in the sky. Rose let out a frustrated sigh. "My dear Mrs. Monks, I hope you will not be offended, but I had wished to visit the post today, and, as the hour is getting late, I fear I will be too late. Please excuse me as I go about my errand." The older lady started at Rose's words, and nearly spilled her tea.

"I fear that I also have imposed greatly on your hospitality," said Mr. Hyden, rising along with Rose, "and I must find a place of lodging for my horse and I before it is too late in the evening." There was a flurry of motion as the Monks set down their cups and plates and got to their feet. "So, I thank you for the cake and tea, and hope that I will see you again in the near future, for I plan to spend some time in this particular town."

"Why, Mr. Hyden, there is a nice little inn on the way to the post, and it is right next to the livery. I believe Rose will have no problem showing you the way, if you wouldn't mind walking with her. In this way, I will have no fear of harm coming to our dear Rose with her sore ankle," chimed Mrs. Monks.

Rose clenched her teeth at this announcement, for she had wished to walk by herself. Now she would have to escort this mysterious Mr. Hyden. She left the room quickly, but Mr. Hyden followed close behind her. There would be no escaping him.

They began their walk into town quite silently. It wasn't until they were out of the sight of the house that Mr. Hyden spoke, "Are you still angry with me for the incident on the road this morning, or is there another reason for your silence, Mademoiselle?"

"I was never angry at you for my own clumsiness. But I do wish that you would not call me Mademoiselle," Rose replied tersely.

"Forgive me, for I do not know how else to address you, for I only know your given name. I do believe, though, that you are quite angry with me for some reason, and I am completely oblivious to it if it has nothing to do with me tripping you."

"You may address me as Miss Wooden, if that pleases you, and I am not angry with you. It is only your imagination that has you believing that. I am only angry with myself," Rose replied as she picked up her pace ever so slightly.

"Surely, Miss Wooden, you must be terribly angry with me, for what other reason could you have for refusing to speak in conversation with the Monks and me this afternoon? And as we left the house you seemed to be grinding your teeth at me. Please, Mademoiselle, tell me the truth if you are angry with me." He was practically begging, which Rose found absolutely pathetic.

"If I was grinding my teeth at you, Mr. Hyden, it was because I was looking forward to a walk to the post by myself, but you have intruded greatly," Rose said angrily. "I chose not to join in the conversation this afternoon because I do not make it my habit to speak with liars, and I believe, good sir, that I have asked you not to call me Mademoiselle."

"Now, who would you call a liar in our conversation, Miss Wooden? Surely, Mrs. Monks and Miss Monks are not liars?" Mr. Hyden asked, quite shocked at the turn in the conversation.

"The Monks are perfectly good company. It is you who I referred to when I spoke of liars, and don't pretend with me that this is not the truth," quipped Rose, who was now in more control of her emotions.

"I do not pretend with you, Miss Wooden. I am not a liar, and I would very much like to know why you would charge me with such a crime," Mr. Hyden said quite seriously.

Rose turned on him and glared. His steps faltered. "First of all, you said your name was James Hyden, and then you said that you were a man of no trade traveling around the country. These I know for sure are lies. What was truth and what was a lie beyond that, I do not know," Rose replied.

"And what makes you conjecture that I am lying on these accounts? Surely, there must be a reason for your accusations," Mr. Hyden replied, a bit angry himself.

"Your boots are what give you away, sir. If you wanted to pass as a simple peasant, you should have discarded your boots." Rose turned and began to walk again. Mr. Hyden remained frozen on the spot.

"My boots?" Mr. Hyden questioned, nearly laughing now at the silliness of the situation. "Is that all that you have to mark me as a liar? A pair of boots that were given to me as a gift from my father?"

Rose stopped once more. "Are you mocking me, Mr. Hyden?" she asked, her anger again rising. She turned slowly toward him. "I will have you know that a simple peasant, or even a middle class tradesman for that matter, could never afford such fine boots unless they were stolen, which again makes you a liar, if you are as you say you are. But I do not believe you are just a traveler. I believe you are a nobleman, and that leads us to your name. If you are a nobleman, you have given us a false name in hopes that you will not be recognized for who you really are. Now do you understand my accusations, Mr. Hyden?"

Mr. Hyden took a step back, his mouth agape in shock at the insightfulness of the young lady standing in front of him. He shook his head. Who would have thought that a simple pair of boots could say so much? "What would you like of me, Miss Wooden?" he asked, a bit exasperated.

"Your name, Mr. Hyden. No lies, just the simple truth," Rose replied frankly.

Mr. Hyden let out a sigh and thought about the pros and cons of telling her his name. He let out a groan before he replied. "My name is Henry. I can tell you no more, for if I do I am surely ruined. I can only hope that my given name will satisfy you."

Rose thought about it for a while and replied, "Very well, Henry. If that is all you can give me, I will be satisfied. But do not think that I will trust any information you give to me or to my friends. That would be stupidity in the simplest form." She paused to think for a moment. "I will keep your secret for now, but if I detect another lie coming from you, I shall spill your secret to the entire town. Do you understand?" She gave him a pointed look until he nodded his head. She nodded back, then continued, "The inn is right down the road there. You will find clean lodging and good meals. The livery is right next door. Goodbye, Henry." And with that, she walked away.

FOUR

PRINCE HENRY ARDEN WATCHED THE SLIGHT figure of Miss Rose Wooden disappear down the road. He would have to be careful what he said around her, for she was very intelligent and would pick up on any inconsistencies. He sighed and turned toward the inn down the road.

It had been three months since he had made the deal with his father and six weeks since his year had begun. He had spent two weeks in Helton, the first town he had visited, attending church and keeping his eyes open for any eligible young ladies, but none had stood out. He had then gone on to Lowry, staying for three weeks because there was to be a ball at the end of the third week. At the ball, Henry had danced with lady after lady, and he was shocked to discover that many of these young ladies were just as silly as the ladies of the court. All they lacked was the money to get dressed up in all the baubles and such. Henry had left quite quickly after the ball and traveled for some days until he reached the town of Tarrant. There he was mistaken for some perpetrator who had been stealing chickens, and was forced to flee nearly immediately lest he be put on trial.

He shook his head at the memory. Maybe he would stay in the area for a while. The Monks were interesting people, very hospitable and welcoming, and Miss Wooden was quite beautiful and intriguing. Surely there were more women such as them around this small town.

Rose walked stiffly to the post office, never once looking back at Henry. She could feel his eyes on her back, and the thought made her scowl. She did not like liars, and she especially did not like liars who could hurt someone with their dishonesty. And that was exactly what Mr. Hyden had the ability to do.

As she had expected, there was a letter waiting for her from her cousin. Rose thanked Miss Mede, who worked at the counter, and started her walk back to the Monks' house. She read the letter as she walked.

> *My dearest Rose,*
>
> *How are you? I hope you are doing better than all those present at home. These past few weeks have been miserable. Father has fallen ill again and will not leave his bed, and Mother has been in the worst of*

tempers. She snaps at all the servants, and one must watch what they say in her presence lest she sends you to bed without your dinner. It seems rather childish, but I fear this has already happened to me on more than one occasion. The picture I paint may appear to be one to laugh at, but please have some compassion, for it is utter misery. Father sends his love and he says he misses you very much. We all miss you, including the servants. Come home soon, Rose. Forgive me, that is not fair to you. I know how much you hate this entire mess, but there is nothing to do about it. I wish you all the best in your exploits.

Your Loving Cousin

John Borden

Rose nearly started crying at the miserable state that John appeared to be in. He seemed to detest the fact that she was gone, yet he did not wish her to feel discomfort in her own situation. It was all so unfair.

She stepped into the Monks' house and tried to put on a smile for them. "And how have things been going at the Borden house? I hope things are looking up, though I'm sure every soul misses your sweet face. But that always happens when someone leaves a house. They are always well missed."

"I fear, Mrs. Monks, that everything is not well at the Borden house, for my uncle has fallen terribly ill and cannot rise from his bed. The whole house is miserable with the state of his health being so low," Rose replied. It wasn't exactly the truth, but it wasn't a lie either, and no harm could possibly come of it.

"That is not good at all. I will have to write and inquire about the health of my brother. It has been a long time since I have seen him. I hope he isn't too poorly. Perhaps we could visit him sometime soon. That would be nice, don't you think, Rose?" asked Mrs. Monks.

"That would be just wonderful. I think the whole family would appreciate such a visit," Rose said, and then excused herself to go freshen up for dinner.

At dinner that evening, Katy and Mrs. Monks replayed the entire afternoon to Mr. Monks with many exclamations and large hand gestures. Mr. Monks appeared to be interested in their tale, but when they were done speaking he turned to Rose and said, "What is your opinion of this Mr. Hyden, Miss Wooden? You are a sensible woman, and I am sure that you have a sensible opinion about this man. So, with little exaggeration, would you please tell me a little about this man's character?"

"I have only this to say, Mr. Monks," replied Rose. "Mr. Hyden is not the hero that your wife and daughter make him out to be, but he seems to have a decent character and he carried himself very well. For any other insight on his character, I cannot as of yet say. We will simply have to wait and see."

Sunday came faster than usual, and Rose was quite shocked to run into Mr. Hyden on the way into church. He bowed politely to the ladies and then introduced himself to Mr. Monks. "So this is the great Mr. Hyden." said Mr. Monks. "I have heard much about your heroism, but have seen little of your person. It is a pleasure to finally have a face to a name that is being circulated amongst the members of my household. Will you be joining us for church this morning?"

"Certainly, sir. I hear that your pastor is one of the best in the region," replied Mr. Hyden.

"Mr. Taylor is a very good curate, but he is also very young and very single. I believe he is getting tired of running from all the young ladies of the community and their mothers. He will be overjoyed to see the face of another young eligible man in the church." The two men laughed at this comment and made their way into the church building.

Rose sat in the pew and listened intently throughout the entire service. She very much enjoyed Mr. Taylor's sermons, for they were so full of passion and meaning that they drew the audience in and held them captive for the whole hour. After the sermon, as she walked past the curate and shook his hand, she couldn't help but say what a wonderful message he had prepared for that particular day.

"I am glad you enjoyed the message so much, Miss Wooden. It is always a pleasure to preach in front of this congregation, and it's such a blessing when I receive compliments such as these."

At that moment, Mr. Monks walked up behind Rose and said to the curate, "If compliments are such a blessing to you, sir, please come to our house for dinner and receive compliment after compliment from the ladies of the house, for they are sure to have many words to say about such a wonderful sermon."

Rose watched as the young pastor tried to cover a slight cringe before he replied, "Certainly, sir. I wouldn't miss it for the world, and I thank you for the invitation."

"We shall see you at dinner then, Mr. Taylor." With that, Mr. Monks and Miss Wooden walked on to go and find Mrs. and Miss Monks. When the two were found, they were just finishing up a conversation with Mr. Hyden, but, when he was distracted by other church members offering him their welcomes, the two female Monks came rushing over.

"We must be on our way home very soon, Mr. Monks," said Mrs. Monks. "For I have invited Mr. Hyden for dinner, and he has accepted, and I wish to prepare a most delightful meal."

"You will have to prepare a little more than normal for our noonday meal then, my dear Mrs. Monks. For I have also invited the curate over for dinner and he also has accepted," said Mr. Monks.

"Oh dear!" exclaimed Mrs. Monks. "I don't think we have enough room for two extra people. It will be a tight squeeze, and we must return home immediately so that I can see to the seating arrangement for tonight's dinner. It will be a delightful dinner if I can plan it all in time. Oh my. We do not have much time at all."

Rose stared across the dinner table at the two gentlemen sitting across from her and Katy. She couldn't stop herself from comparing the two. Mr. Hyden was quite tall with reckless brown hair that looked unkempt even when it was combed. His eyes were a dark blue with green specks and his skin was tanned from spending so much time out in the sun.

Mr. Taylor was very different from Mr. Hyden, almost a complete opposite. He had fair hair and pale blue eyes. He was not tall, but he was in no way short either, and though he did not look unhealthy, he was quite pale, for he spent most of his time among his books instead of outdoors. Both men were very handsome, and very eligible.

The conversation around the table consisted of small talk. No one quite knew what to say with the two very different gentlemen at their table, so it was left to Mr. Hyden to start the conversation. "Mr. Monks, I believe this is a military town with occupants very well aware of the happenings in the war between our Samaya and those Isbetans. Because of this, I would value your opinion of the goings-on."

"That is hard to say, Mr. Hyden. It has been a very long war, over ten years now. I believe I am a little biased in saying that it is getting a little tiring seeing all the young men coming back wounded. It's also been difficult to see all the young ladies about without a suitor for any of them, but this may not be the case in other vicinities," replied Mr. Monks.

"It has been going on for quite some time, but don't you believe that there could be a just cause for the war? I mean to say that there has to be a reason for the king to send out our soldiers. With this in mind, is it not possible to forgive the war its casualties?" questioned Mr. Hyden.

"This may be so," replied Mr. Monks, "but I have yet to hear a just reason for this war. I believe it would be much better to end the whole mess and bring our boys home for a while. People are really starting to miss their sons, and I know of one particular lady who said she would marry her beau at the end of the war, but these ten years have come and gone and they have not yet been able to wed."

"That is quite shocking, but one shocking story does not mean the war is unjust. It is possible that justice is taking longer to accomplish than originally planned. In that way, the war could still be considered just. What do you think, Mr. Taylor?"

"I think," the curate replied slowly, "that Mr. Monks is very accurate. The war has been going on for so long that I think people have forgotten what they are fighting for, but they continue fighting because that is the way it has been for as long as they can remember. It is no longer a matter of justice but habit, and it will continue this way until the king calls a halt to the fighting."

"Oh, enough about politics," Mrs. Monks cut in. "There has been talk about the war for much too long. I dare say we should all be sick of it." She then proceeded to direct the conversation to simpler topics that all could enjoy without much thought or effort.

Mr. Hyden took this time to turn and watch Miss Wooden. She had not joined in the conversation about the war, but he could tell that she had been very interested by the way she leaned in and listened carefully to every word the men had spoken. Now, as the conversation progressed towards simpler topics, her interest faded and she seemed more concerned with making sure everybody was satisfied and cared for.

Mr. Hyden watched as she filled empty cups, served those who wished to have more, and at one point as she even cleared the table of the dinner dishes and brought out a dessert. All the while, Mrs. Monks remained oblivious to the service her guest did her. If Miss Wooden had not dined with the family, Mr. Hyden would have believed her to be a serving girl.

When the dinner was finally over, Mr. Monks asked the curate to close with grace, and then the family moved toward the parlour. Mr. Hyden chose to stay behind in the dining room along with Miss Wooden, who immediately began to clean up the various dishes on the table and bring them to the kitchen to be cleaned. Though he had never done such a task in his life, Mr. Hyden picked up some dishes and followed her.

"What are you doing, Henry?" Rose asked. "You should be in the parlour enjoying your visit with the Monks. You are, after all, their guest."

"Are you not their guest as well? For, if you are, you have just as much right to be enjoying yourself in the parlour as I do. Besides, I am very much interested in helping with the dishes. You may call me a lazy oaf if you wish, but I have never performed such a duty before, and it has me very much intrigued." This declaration brought a smile to Rose's face as she began to fill a tub with hot, soapy water.

"You must have ulterior motives for coming to the kitchen, for no one can find washing the dishes that interesting. If I knew you better, I might even be able to assume that you are hiding in here, but seeing as I don't know you that well, I will have to ask what your real motives are."

"If you must know, I am quite curious as to your opinion about the conversation that took place at the dinner table. The conversation about the war, that is. You seemed interested, but you would not make a comment in front of everyone, so I was hoping you would give me your opinion now."

"I don't think you will find that my opinion varies all that much from that of the curate and Mr. Monks," Rose replied slowly. "I believe the war has gone on for far too long with no real motive save for habit."

"Is that all you have to say on the topic? You are an intelligent young woman, Miss Wooden, and I wouldn't be surprised if you had much more to say, but you are holding back for some reason. If you think you may offend me by your words, do not hold back. I will take any words you speak in good humour," prodded Mr. Hyden.

"Very well, because you asked me to. I believe the war is an excuse to cover up the king's greed. There is no justice in his war. He only fights to gain land and territory. He plunders at the cost of many lives. Lifeblood wasted, all for naught. One only to look at a military town such as this to understand my view. The only eligible young man is the curate, and he has been asked on more than one occasion to join the war. I hear people say many times that the men will be back when the war ends, but then I hear of another young man coming back in a pine box and I wonder, if the war does end, will we really get our men back, or will we just get pieces of them?"

"You feel quite strongly about this, don't you?" asked Henry, trying to hide his offense. "Don't you think there could be some justice in the war? Surely, there must be one reason or another that the king is fighting, that will make this war just."

"To have justice in a war, there has to be an offense first given," replied Rose passionately. "Now, if the king was going to war to protect our country, or to protect a lesser country, I would consider it a just war, but no offense has been made against our country. In this way, the king has made himself a murderer through his greed, for who else is there to blame for the senseless slaughter of so many young men?"

"The way you speak is treason. If someone heard you speak that way about the king, they could report you and you could hang for it," Henry replied stiffly. "I myself do find offense in the way you speak of our king."

"Forgive me," Rose replied softly. "My emotions ran away with me, and I believe I spoke rather rashly. Our king is wise in most matters, but I cannot agree on his wisdom in the matter of the war. I will try to restrain myself from speaking so quickly in the company of others, but in all fairness, you did ask me for my opinion."

Henry could not restrain the laugh that spilled out with Rose's last comment. On a whim, he dipped his hand in the dishwater and flicked it in her face, saying, "You're forgiven, I guess." What Henry had not expected was for Rose to retaliate to his actions. Before he could respond, she had taken a cup of the soapy water and dumped it on his head. He sputtered through the drips of water and was about to yell in defiance, but the sound of Rose's laugh stopped him, and he couldn't help but laugh along.

That night, as Prince Henry sat in his room at the inn, he couldn't help but ponder the words of Miss Wooden. She had called his father a murderer for sending soldiers to fight a pointless war, but that seemed hardly fair. It wasn't as if his father held the sword that killed these men. No, if anything, it was the enemy that was the murderer. But then again, his father had instigated the whole war, and what was the reason for it all? He had never really been told why his father fought, just that it would benefit him in the future.

These thoughts weighed heavily on Henry's mind, so he decided to write a letter to his father and inquire about these matters.

> *Dear Father,*
>
> *I have recently been informed about the people's discontent with the war, and it has raised some questions in my mind about the cause and result of it. First*

of all, why are we fighting? It seems that every time I ask this question, I am told that it will benefit me in the future, but how will it benefit me? I do not understand. If I am to take the throne in the near future, I should understand the affairs of the land. How am I supposed to be king if I don't even know why our country is involved in a ten-year war? Is the war we are fighting really a just war? I have been led to believe it is, but upon further examination, I am filled with some doubts that must be answered to. If this is not a just war we fight, why do we not desist and bring the men back before it is too late? I hope to hear some answers soon. As to news of my goings on, I believe I am going to stay where I am for a while. I have met two very intriguing ladies, one especially who has caught my attention. Anything other than that, I cannot say. Send my greetings to Mother, and tell her I miss her incredibly much.

Your Son,
Henry

With the letter written, Henry set it aside to post early the next morning. It would take some time for the letter to reach the palace, and a bit more time for him to get a reply. He would wait anxiously until that time to hear what his father had to say.

pasture where she usually practiced with her sword, when a sound stopped her dead in her tracks. Ahead of her in the middle of the clearing sat a boy weeping.

The boy wasn't really that much of a boy. He was about Rose's age, maybe a bit younger, with sandy blond hair. He was somewhat tall and willowy. Freckles brushed across his nose, giving him a very boyish look, and his eyes were the saddest puppy dog brown. On his lap lay a sword. "It's no use," he wept. "No use at all." Rose's curiosity was piqued by the young boy's plight and she stepped forward. The boy jumped to his feet at the sound of her steps, and held out his sword. "What do you want?" he asked, a look of terror upon his face.

"What is your name, boy? I will not harm you," replied Rose quietly. "Why are you so sad? Why do you weep?"

"It's none of your business. Why do you ask so many questions?" the boy retorted.

"I might be able to help you, if you wish it."

"No one can help me unless they know how to wield a sword and can teach me to do the same."

"I know how to fight quite well, and I will teach you if you answer my original questions," replied Rose calmly.

The boy hesitated slightly, not sure if he should answer. With a frustrated sigh, he finally spoke, "Fine. My name is Josh Deplin, and I wasn't weeping. I was just frustrated because John Read challenged me to a swordfight today, and I lost miserably. He lorded it over me for the rest of the day, and all I could think of was how ashamed my father would be. He's in the military, you see. He wants me to be a military man when I grow up, just like him."

"I see," replied Rose. "We best get started then. We will start with a duel so that I can take note of your form and your other strengths and weaknesses. Take your position."

With that, the two began to duel. It did not take Rose long to notice that young Josh had a lot to learn. His form was horrible, and he left his left side wide open to attack. It took her only a few minutes to disarm him. It would have taken less time had she not wanted to observe more of his skill.

Rose practiced duelling with Josh until early dawn. She wanted to go on for a lot longer, but she needed to return to the Monks before they noticed she was missing. She informed Josh that she must be going, but would return every Tuesday night to help him improve on his fencing. Josh thanked her profusely, then asked, "You are quite amazing with the sword, sir. Why aren't you in the military like everyone else?"

Rose gaped at Josh through her mask. Couldn't Josh tell she was a woman? She wasn't allowed in the army, but if he thought her a male instructor, it was best that he remained thinking so. "I am an outcast," she replied. "I'm not allowed into the army."

"Oh," Josh replied a bit dejectedly, "I think that I am going to go into the military if I can make it. It's what my dad wants. But I best be going before my mom misses me. Thanks again, sir."

Rose slipped back into the Monks' house. She again dressed in her nightgown and hid her sword and inexpressibles in her trunk. She fell onto her bed exhausted, yet she could not sleep. The good. If Christ did not love, he would not have hurt so terribly bad. Why he chose pain and sorrow, I will never understand," Rose said sadly.

"I think that Christ chose to love, not because it would be easy, but to set an example for us, and to show us how to love others. He was, after all, the greatest example of love." Henry sighed, "I do not have all the answers, but I do know that if I could love someone, even if it was the most painful experience, I would take hold of it."

"You are a brave soul then," replied Rose. "That, or you have never lost someone you loved. I do not think that I could ever be brave enough to hold onto a love that would hurt me indefinitely. It would cost me too much."

"But isn't love about sacrifice? Wouldn't it be selfish to hold back from love just because it would cost you too much? Don't get me wrong, and think that I call you selfish, but I do believe that love should be self-sacrificing."

They drew close to the Monks' drive. Rose turned to Henry and said, "If you really believe this, I leave you with one question: What are you willing to give up for love?" With that, she walked into the house.

SIX

ENRY WALKED SLOWLY BACK TO HIS ROOM at the inn, all the while pondering the conversation he had had with Miss Wooden. When he got back to his room, he found a scrap of paper and wrote down her questions. They seemed to stare up at him from the paper. "*What are you willing to give up for love?*" and "*Why did Christ choose to love?*" The questions bothered him, so he grabbed the slip of paper and tucked it into his diary, which rested next to his bed. The diary shut with a thud, and all thoughts of the conversation disappeared.

He walked out into the lounge and sat at the bar where he would be served his breakfast. Mrs. Hefton, the innkeeper, placed a bowl of hot porridge in front of him, and he dug in. The food was thick and tasty and settled pleasantly in his stomach. Mr. Hyden complimented Mrs. Hefton on the wonderful meal, and headed out to the street.

On a normal day, Mr. Hyden would walk to the livery, check on his horse, maybe ride him around for a bit, and then spend the rest of the day going about the town doing whatever he pleased. But on this particular day, he was rather bored. There was no need for him to check on his horse, for it was well cared for. He had walked the streets many times over and there seemed no other occupation for his time.

Mr. Hyden was contemplating his circumstances when an idea came to him. He was not in need of money, but neither was he lazy, so it was very much possible that he could find work somewhere as a volunteer. This was a military town after all, and many of the young men were away, so surely there was a need for a strong back and willing hands somewhere.

His first stop was the livery. He knew the most about horses, and he figured he would be the most help in that particular area. When he asked to speak to the owner about such matters, the stable boy laughed at him. "I'm sorry, sir," he said, "but you won't find a single soul in need of labour, especially volunteer work." He walked away laughing.

Mr. Hyden could not believe that there would be no place in need of workers, so he spent the day walking about town looking for a job. He went to the stores and shops, he went to the blacksmith and the tailor, he went to every shop or store or trade of any kind to find work, but the answers were all the same. "I'm sorry, sir, but we have all the help we need."

Surely, this was an impossibility, for there were no men to do the labour. Mr. Hyden, getting a bit frustrated in his search, asked the cobbler about the lack of jobs. He replied, "There are plenty of lads about to do the work. Many of 'em will do the work for free as long as you provide a sword lesson for 'em every now an' again. I myself got John Read workin' for me. Bright young lad he is an' mighty fine with the sword. He'll be a military man one of these days, I tell ya."

Mr. Hyden found this hard to believe, but he got the same response everywhere he asked, so it was that later on that night he returned to the inn with no job to be found. He sat down at the bar in the lounge, and Mrs. Hefton served him his supper. The pork and potatoes did not taste near as good this evening as the porridge had that morning, for his spirits were that much more glum.

Mrs. Hefton watched as he fiddled with his food. Normally he was so lively and complimented every morsel she placed in front of him, but on this evening he made no comments, just stared at his plate and every now and then let out a frustrated sigh. Being the good Christian woman that she was, Mrs. Hefton asked, "Why, Mr. Hyden, whatever is the matter this evening? You look absolutely miserable."

Mr. Hyden let out another sigh before replying, "I do not know, Mrs. Hefton. All day long I have been looking for a job to keep me occupied, but everywhere I stop, there are no jobs available. It seems as if there are enough young lads in the community to do all the hard work for as little pay as a sword lesson every now and then."

"Are you looking to pocket some money? Because you won't find that kind of work in our town, but if you wish to volunteer some, I'm sure the curate will have some odd jobs that you can do. Go to him tomorrow and he should be able to give you a task."

"Is that so?" said Henry. "Because if it is, then I should go immediately, so that I will be able to start whatever task is laid out for me first thing in the morning."

"Hold your horses, son. Mr. Taylor won't be able to give you any task right off hand, and it is better that you wait to go visit him in the morning instead of disturbing his supper hour. There will be plenty of time to accomplish all you wish in the morning. Now, eat up. I won't have anyone starving while they stay at my inn."

Mr. Hyden woke up early the next morning. He was very excited about possibly working for a change, and he paced back and forth in his room waiting for a proper hour to come for him to go speak with the curate. It seemed to take hours for the sun to rise higher in the sky, and even longer for him to eat breakfast. As soon as the last drop of porridge was down his throat and he had thanked Mrs. Hefton, he bolted out of the door and headed toward the rectory.

Mr. Taylor answered on the third knock. Sleep held the corners of his eyes down, and his blond hair had yet to be combed. His voice still held the sound of a sleep talker when he said, "Good morning, Mr. Hyden. Please, come in. I have a pot of coffee just made on the stove if you would like some."

"Thanks for the offer, Mr. Taylor, but I really only have a question to ask you and then I will be on my way. Do you by any chance know of any person needing assistance in some chore or another? I looked around the town all day yesterday, and I have not found a single soul who is in need of volunteer help."

"I must admit, Mr. Hyden, that I was not expecting such a question this early in the morning. I can understand your frustration in trying to find a job, especially as a volunteer. But if you are sincere in wishing to help some person, I would suggest you go to Mrs. Jennings' place down the road. She is always in need of assistance." Before the words had left the curate's mouth, Mr. Hyden was already moving down the road, letting his thanks trail behind him.

It did not take long for Mr. Hyden to find the Jennings' place. It was three doors down from the curate's home and stood out from all the other houses. The front yard was littered with the remains of a child's playthings, an old tin can here and a broken doll lying in the grass there. The front door sat crookedly on its hinges and its red paint was peeling quite dramatically. One of the windows on the bottom floor was cracked, and an old piece of wood behind the pane held the weather outside.

But the one thing that made the house stand out amongst the others was the noise. The sound of children laughing and playing, and the occasional scream of a baby spilled from the house and out into the street. Mr. Hyden hesitated as he walked up to the front porch, but he knew what he had come here to do. He grabbed the rusty knocker on the door and tapped three times.

A disgruntled redhead answered the door and in a thick Irish brogue said, "If your comin' to pick out a kid, give me five minutes and I'll line them all up nice and pretty for you. If you're droppin' off another one, fill out the form on the table and leave it with the kid before you leave. If you're here to help, well, my goodness, why weren't you here fifteen minutes ago?!"

Mr. Hyden looked at the woman, a shocked expression on his face. Mrs. Jennings looked at him expectantly, waiting for him to speak up. When Mr. Hyden finally reclaimed his voice, he spit out, "I think I was supposed to be here fifteen minutes ago." Mrs. Jennings looked at him quizzically and then burst out laughing.

"Come on in, lad," she sputtered through her laughter. "I have coffee on the stove that'll waken you up, then we can discuss what you're here for." With that, she led him through the house toward the kitchen.

The inside of the house was in much better condition than the outside, but children ran wild within it. Toys lay everywhere, and two young boys bolted past them as they walked. "Och, Jeremy, Tyler, watch yourselves, boys. We have a guest with us today. We don't want him thinking that we all run rampant, now do we?" The boys laughed as their mistress playfully swatted at them and then ran along with their game. "Boys!" Mrs. Jennings muttered under her breath.

When they finally reached the kitchen, Mr. Hyden was seated at a large table and served hot coffee right off the stove. Some other children played in the corners quietly, and one little girl stared with big round eyes at him as if in awe of his presence. When Mrs. Jennings sat down at the table, Mr. Hyden told her of his plan to work as a volunteer for whoever needed help, and that Mr. Taylor had suggested coming here offer his services.

Mrs. Jennings gave him a good hard look and said, "Mr. Hyden, I really appreciate the thought, and I would very much like the help, but you need to understand something. I have twenty-six children in this orphanage of sorts. Sixteen of these children are waiting for their fathers to come home from the war and take them back to the farm where they can live happily. Five of these children don't know where their fathers are, and their mothers have abandoned them to go search for their fathers, and five of these children are actual orphans who have lost both their parents, or don't know who their parents are. Now, I do whatever I can to take care of them, but since my husband has died, it is hard to do that. But it is not just their physical needs that I try to tend to.

"Most of these children are suffering from the feeling of abandonment. Most think that their parents must hate them, and that is why they are here. Others don't know why their mommas all of a sudden up and left them in this strange place, and some think that they must not have been good enough and that is why their parents left." Mrs. Jennings sighed. "I can give you a job working on the outside of this building fixing things up, but what I really need help with, Mr. Hyden, is mending all these broken souls."

Mr. Hyden looked at Mrs. Jennings' sad face. "I don't know, Mrs. Jennings," he said. "I may not be cut out for this job, but I will try. I can't promise you that I will be any good at it. I might be really bad, in fact, but if you draw up a list of things that you would like me to do, I will start working on them, and maybe I will be able to get some of the older boys to help me out."

Mrs. Jennings gave a small smile. "That would be great, Mr. Hyden. How about you go look in the back shed for some nails and supplies, and I will start making that list."

King James Arden read and reread his son's letter. The words stared up from the page like the condemning glare of a judge. He tried to find answers to all the questions, but none were forthcoming. *"Why are we fighting?"* Was greed a good enough answer? *"Is the war we are fighting really a just war?"* Pah, if this was a just war, then he did not know what justice was.

He let out a soft groan as he determined how to reply to his son. For many years, he had struggled with the war and whether to continue it, but he had never had the gumption to own up to his greed and end it. How could he tell his people that their men had gone off to fight a war just because their king was greedy and land hungry? He wouldn't be surprised if he should lose possession of the crown for such a thing.

His wife came up behind him and began to massage his shoulders. "What did our son have to say for himself this time? Has he met a girl yet? I hope he has, because I would greatly appreciate a daughter-in-law. James, would you really make Henry marry one of the ladies of the court if he went over his year? All those girls are so dreadfully silly."

King Arden sighed as he leaned into his wife's massage. "I don't know, my lady. He says he has met two women that are *intriguing*—whatever that is supposed to mean, and he says one of those two ladies has especially caught his eye. If he does go over his year, I may be forced to make him marry one of the ladies of the court. There just doesn't seem to be any other option. He is, after all, twenty-one."

"It just doesn't seem fair, that's all. I love him dearly, and I don't want to see him live out the rest of his life miserably with a wife that he detests. We weren't forced to wed. We had options. Why can't we give our son the same freedoms we experienced?"

"Because, my dear wife, I was in love with you from the day I set eyes on you, and would not rest until I married you. Our son has not yet found a girl that he would even consider pursuing, and marriage hadn't even entered his thoughts until I pressed it on him. It is time that he got married, for then he can take the throne."

"Very well, Your Highness. I only hope you know what you are doing." With that, the queen ended her massage and headed out of the room. The king sighed again and looked at the letter in front of him. There was no need to tell the queen what she could not possibly understand. He would not make Henry wed. Such a thing would be barbaric. But he needed his son to grow and to learn before he took on the throne, and unfortunately that was not going to occur at home.

He finished the letter quickly and sat staring at it for a while. After a goodly time, he crumpled it, tossed it in the fireplace, and headed off to bed with a very heavy heart.

Mr. Hyden worked hard at the orphanage for the next few weeks. There were lots of things to do, and he was plenty busy fixing the door, replacing windows, patching holes in the roof, and going about various other small tasks. It was rare that he had any help as he worked, for as soon as the boys reached an age where they could do anything useful, they were apprenticed at various locations in the town. The two oldest boys were Jeremy and Tyler, who seemed determined to continually and vanished every time work appeared.

The only company that Mr. Hyden seemed to keep was that of little Lisa, the round-eyed toddler who never spoke a word. She would follow him around and sit and watch his every move. If he was working at some height, she would sit at the bottom of the ladder, and wait until he came down, then follow him to his next destination. He estimated that she was two years of age, yet she never once spoke.

On one particular Tuesday, Mr. Hyden was out fixing a broken windowsill, when Mrs. Jennings came running outside. "Och, it's glad I am to see you, Mr. Hyden. I'm in need of some supplies uptown, and I was hoping you would watch the children for a while. I shan't be long, I promise. If they give you any trouble, you can punish them any way you wish."

Before he could think what he was doing, Mr. Hyden accepted the task at hand, and Mrs. Jennings was off down the road on her way to town. Thinking that it would be better if he could see all the children at once, Mr. Hyden rounded up all twenty-six little ones and had them come out and play in the front yard where he could keep an eye on them while he worked.

Things went well for all of two minutes. Mr. Hyden turned his back for a short while when a piercing scream came from behind him. When he turned around, one of the little girls was on the ground crying, claiming Jeremy had pulled on one of her braids, and that it hurt so bad. Mr. Hyden tried to comfort the girl as he looked around to find Jeremy and reprimand him. At the same time, two boys began to holler and scream at one another, and it wasn't long before they were rolling on the ground, fighting.

Mr. Hyden tried to disengage himself from the little girl to stop the fighting, when he noticed Jeremy and Tyler preying on the braids of another poor young girl. He hollered at them to stop, and raced over to pull the two wrestlers apart. His little shadow followed close behind him, and when he got close enough to pull the two apart, a stray foot reached out and kicked the little girl in the stomach. Tears welled up in her eyes and a soft hiccup came out before she wailed. Mr. Hyden scooped her up into his arms and awkwardly rocked her back and forth in his arms, making hushing sounds.

That's when he heard light laughter behind him. He turned to find Miss Wooden standing in the road, dressed in a beautiful new dress. Her beauty made him think only of how ridiculous he must look, and he felt himself flush with embarrassment. He quit his swaying in hopes of looking more controlled, but the small hiccupping girl in his arms took this as her cue to reach up and latch her small hand onto his nose.

Rose couldn't help but burst out laughing, and she continued to laugh as she walked up the drive and into the yard. She looked around and asked, "Do you need any help, sir, or do you have everything under control?" She tried to hold back her laughter, but she was having a lot of trouble, and if he didn't say something soon, she would be totally lost.

"I thought I was doing quite well," replied Henry. "I have all twenty-six children in one tiny yard, and most of them look miserable. I think this is an accomplishment in itself. Why? Were you looking for a job? I'm sure I could find one for you here somewhere."

His pert reply caused Miss Wooden to break out into another burst of laughter, and when she finally had control of herself, she said to Mr. Hyden, "You hold onto that little angel that you have there, and I will have the rest of the kids productively occupied within the next few minutes."

Mr. Hyden breathed his thanks and followed Miss Wooden around as she organized the children. She started with the girl who had suffered from the attack on her braids. She neatly fixed the braid, kissed the crown of the girl's head, and sent her to go play with a doll with some other girls around her age. She then moved onto the boys who were wrestling earlier, and were now standing sheepishly to the side of the lawn. She reprimanded them for their behaviour and sent them on their way to play a game together.

Miss Wooden then proceeded to speak with each of the children, asking them what they would like to do, and setting it up so that all of them were playing peacefully in some part of the yard, or in the house. She then walked over to Mr. Hyden and the child he held. "Now Mr. Hyden, you must tell me who this darling child is and how you happened upon the job of taking care of twenty-odd children all by yourself."

Mr. Hyden groaned. "If you come with me to the kitchen, I will tell you the tale over a cup of hot tea."

In the kitchen, Henry tried to put down little Lisa, but she would have none of it. Apologizing profusely, he asked Miss Wooden to serve the tea. She quietly did so, and when they were both settled, he proceeded to tell his story.

It did not take long to tell, and when he finished, he said, "I do not know how you did it, Miss Wooden. You seemed to be in total control, and the children listened to you even though you have never met them before. Even Jeremy and Tyler seem to be staying away from mischief. How do that?"

Miss Wooden laughed softly and replied, "If you must know, Mr. Hyden, I think children smell fear. They knew you were scared of a total disaster, and took control. All they really need is something to occupy their time and energy. If you do not have that, they run rampant. You ask me how I did it. My trick is to allow them to do what they want within limits, and they will be content."

"You are a wise woman, Miss Wooden. I don't think that I could ever have that much control over a group of children. They all seemed to turn wild after Mrs. Jennings left. It's a good thing that you came along when you did, or I would certainly have been lost."

"I'm sure you would have figured it out. You seem to have this little one smitten. Whatever did you do to get her to cling to you so? It seems as if she will never depart from your side."

"I don't know if she ever will. She has been my shadow ever since I came here. She refuses to leave my side, yet she never speaks a word. All I know of her is that her name is Lisa and she is one of the five true orphans that occupy this building," replied Henry softly.

Mrs. Jennings bustled through the door. "Och, lad, what have you done with all the children? I thought something tragic must have occurred, for the place was much too quiet, but you don't seem in the slightest bit disturbed. So I ask myself again, where could the children be?"

"The children are all fine, Mrs. Jennings. They're all occupied peacefully thanks to Miss Wooden here, who came just in the nick of time to save my life. Without her, I fear the children would all have turned savage by this time. We were just enjoying a cup of tea, if you would like to join us. I would get up to serve you, but I fear Lisa here will not detach herself from me."

Mrs. Jennings turned an appraising eye on Miss Wooden. She seemed shocked that such a slight girl could take charge of so many children, and still seem poised and unruffled. "I may just be getting old, Miss Wooden, but I am no longer capable of taking care of all these children by myself. If you really did handle the children as well as Mr. Hyden claims, I would greatly appreciate your help in the future. That is, if it's not too much to ask of you."

"That would be just wonderful," replied Rose. "I do not know when I can come to help, but whenever I have a chance, I will come. As for now, I really must go. Mrs. Monks is expecting me home soon, and I still have to go to the market to pick up some meat for tonight's dinner."

"That is not a problem, dear," replied Mrs. Jennings. She watched Mr. Hyden, who was staring intently at the beautiful young Miss Wooden. "Mr. Hyden, lad, why don't you escort Miss Wooden along her way? I'm sure I can handle the children by myself for the rest of the day, and I'm sure Miss Wooden would enjoy the company."

Mr. Hyden jumped and blushed when he noticed that he was caught staring, but he didn't mind the idea of escorting Miss Wooden through town. At this moment, he would have done almost anything to spend more time with the attractive young woman before him. He handed Lisa over to Mrs. Jennings, and she hardly made a fuss, then held out his arm to Miss Wooden who accepted it with a slight blush. Mrs. Jennings followed them to the door, and when Mr. Hyden went to close it, he had to hold back a laugh when Mrs. Jennings gave him a quick wink.

SEVEN

ROSE WALKED SHYLY BESIDE MR. HYDEN. She wasn't used to being escorted through town by a gentleman, and she feared the rumours that would be started by such a display. "You do not have to walk with me, Henry. I am quite capable of getting about town on my own."

"But that would defeat the purpose, Miss Wooden," replied Henry. "For if I allowed you to walk about town all by yourself, I would not be able to spend this extra time with such a beautiful young woman." Rose blushed at the compliment and disengaged herself from his arm. She began to walk a little faster.

Henry's long legs allowed him to keep up with Rose with little trouble, and they continued at the quick pace for quite some time before he spoke. "Is there a reason why we are walking so fast? Or are you trying to lose me in the crowd?" Henry's humour was lost on the empty streets.

"I am enjoying the exercise, Mr. Hyden," Rose replied tersely. She was not in the mood to be flirted with, and she had not the spirit to jest with any person, for she had received a letter just that morning from her cousin saying that her uncle's condition was deteriorating. She had not told a falsehood in saying that she was going to the market to pick up meat for Mrs. Monks, but she had not been totally honest, leaving out the fact that she was headed to the post to send a letter to her cousin.

They finally entered the market, where the bustle kept Rose from walking as fast as she would have liked. Henry again offered his arm, and, not wanting to be overly rude, she accepted it with a sigh. A small smile played at the corners of his mouth as he escorted her to the butcher's stand.

"Good afternoon, Miss Wooden," beamed Mr. Riley, the butcher. "What can I get for you today? We have a fine haunch of porch in the back, and you are welcome to it; or maybe just a few steaks for now?"

"Good afternoon, Mr. Riley," Rose replied. "I think we'll stick with the steaks today. The last ones we had were absolutely delicious, and I'm sure that Mrs. Monks will be delighted to have some more. Oh, and I believe I will also take a ham for tomorrow night's dinner."

Mr. Riley wrapped up the meats and handed them over to Rose, who thanked him sincerely. She placed them in a basket she was carrying, and then she and Henry were again on their way. As soon as they were out of the crowds, Rose disengaged herself from Henry's arm, but when she said she would be fine walking by herself, he would have none of it and insisted on walking her all the way home.

As they walked past the post office, Rose stopped and told Mr. Hyden that if he would hold her basket, she would just be a minute. Before he could respond, she took out her letter, placed the basket in his hands, and entered the post office. Mr. Hyden held the basket awkwardly. Thankfully, Rose did not take long in the post office and she was soon back to rescue the basket from his hands.

"Thank you," was all she said before she started walking toward the Monks' home. Again they walked in silence. It was starting to become an oppressive quiet, when Rose finally spoke. "How have you enjoyed your stay at the inn so far? I hear they have very good meals there, and that its caretaker is very kind. Is this true?"

Henry noted her attempt at small talk and proceeded to tell her about the wonderful meals he had had, and how the rooms were very comfortable, but that in truth he really longed to have a house to share with a person that he knew. "You know, Miss Wooden, it gets awfully lonely away from home. I was not expecting that at all."

"I know what you mean, Henry," Rose replied. "There's many a time that I wish I could go home for just a while and see my family, even if it were just for a day or two." She sighed, then added, "But that would never be possible, so I shan't even think on it much longer. Can you tell me a bit about where you grew up? I know you wish to keep your identity a secret, but perhaps it would help pass some of the homesickness if you could tell me something about your family or your home life."

"That would be nice," Henry replied, and then began to tell Rose a little about his life. He told her about his pony named Horse, on which he had learned to ride, and about the many times he had fallen off. He recalled to her the time that his father had to gently coax him back onto the pony after one big spill that had hurt him just a little too much.

He told her about pestering the cook, picking apples and pears and peaches and all sorts of fruit in the orchards that they had. He talked about his youth, fishing in the ponds and driving his mother crazy with his continual untidy appearance. And finally, he told her about all the grand ladies he had met and their silliness, and how they swooned and batted their eyelashes.

The two of them were laughing and enjoying each others' company, and before they knew it, they were at the Monks' house. Rose found that at some point she had taken hold of Henry's arm again and she stepped back shyly. "Thank you for escorting me home, Henry. I very much enjoyed your stories."

"It was a pleasure to tell them, and I think they took away the sting of homesickness after all. I feel so much better after telling them. In that respect, it is my turn to thank you." Rose blushed again, and Henry continued, "I hope that we will be able to talk again soon. I am sure that you have lots of stories to tell about your own life."

Rose shied away from this topic. "Maybe someday," she said. She was just about to enter the house when the door opened from the inside. Mrs. Monks and Katy spilled out and looked just a little bit shocked at seeing them both standing there.

"My! I was just about to go looking for you, Rose," Mrs. Monks said, a bit perplexed. "We were all wondering what could be taking you so long, and being the worrier that I am, I feared that something dreadful had befallen you. So I said to Katy that we should go look for you. Katy didn't seem in the least bit worried at that time, though, and she took some persuading, but here we are about to look for you, and you show up at the door on the arm of Mr. Hyden."

Rose tried to assure Mrs. Monks that nothing dreadful had befallen her; she had just been distracted. She was having difficulty explaining everything to Mrs. Monks when Mr. Hyden stepped in. "If you will, Madame, it was my fault that Miss Wooden was late. I was in a bind with several children, and she came to my rescue just in time. I don't know what I would have done without her."

"Why, this does sound like an interesting story. Why don't you stay for dinner, and in that way we'll be able to hear the whole story from both yours and Rose's perspective? I'm sure we would all enjoy that, and it would be such a pleasure to have you around. I'm sure that Mr. Monks would enjoy your company as well."

"Thank you for the invitation, Mrs. Monks," replied Mr. Hyden. "But I wouldn't want to impose on you in any such way. Your family has already shared much hospitality with me, and I wouldn't want to wear out my welcome."

"Wear out your welcome? Whoever heard of such a thing?" replied Mrs. Monks in a tone that said that the whole notion was preposterous. "If that is your only excuse, Mr. Hyden, then I will have none of it, and I will have to be very upset if you do not stay for dinner. I therefore insist that you come in and join us."

"If this is true, Madame, then I fear I have no choice but to come in and enjoy a wonderful evening with you and your family. But if I am at any point an imposition, I expect you to kick me out of your house and send me on my way immediately."

Mrs. Monks laughed at Mr. Hyden's good-natured humour, and they all walked into the house. Rose watched from the back of the group. She especially watched Katy, who seemed unable to take her eyes off Mr. Hyden. The girl looked absolutely smitten with the man, and Rose began to worry just a little.

The conversation at dinner was light and cheerful for the most part. Rose told her part of the story of the afternoon's events and participated in the chatter, but she always kept a close eye on Katy. Katy did very little talking. She fawned over Mr. Hyden, batting her eyelashes and doing everything in her power to grab his attention without making it too obvious.

The thought that Katy might really like Mr. Hyden scared Rose because she didn't trust him; at least, that is what she told herself. She didn't want Katy to get hurt, and Mr. Hyden would be the one to hurt her. It would be best if Rose could somehow dissuade Katy from these intentions.

Through the rest of dinner, she thought about how she could accomplish this, and it wasn't until the end of dinner that she noticed the foolishness of her thoughts. Who was she to say who Katy should like or dislike? It was not her place to dissuade her of anything. If Mr. Hyden liked Katy, then maybe it would be good for the two of them. She would inform Mr. Hyden of Katy's admiration, and if he did not return the sentiments, he would be better prepared to dissuade the girl's flirtations on his own. In that way, no one would get hurt.

These thoughts rolled through Rose's head as she cleared the dishes from the table, and she was so much preoccupied with them that she did not notice Mr. Hyden carrying dishes to the kitchen behind her until she began to prepare the dishwater. When she saw him, she jumped a little and said, "Oh! I did not see you there... you scared me a little. Thank you for carrying in those dishes. It is greatly appreciated."

Mr. Hyden nodded and began to help her with the dishwater and the dishes. "You don't have to help with that. I am perfectly capable of washing dishes myself. Why don't you go and enjoy the company of the Monks out in the parlour? They very much enjoy your company."

"I enjoy washing dishes, believe it or not. I have never had the opportunity to do it before, and it is something I will not have much opportunity to do when I go back to my other life. Why do you insist upon washing dishes and cleaning up the dinner dishes for the Monks when they are perfectly capable of doing it themselves?"

Rose shook her head, thinking of a similar conversation they had had. "I have a question for you as well: Is there a reason that you stay in our town and do not move on? Or maybe a certain person?" It was a rather bold question for Rose to ask, but she thought she could use it to lead up to questions about him and Katy.

Henry's reply was hesitant and noncommittal. "I have thought of leaving, but I think I may stay a while because I am enjoying the company that I have been keeping. As to any particular reason why I stay, I would have to say that it is just a feeling that this is where I am supposed to be."

Rose thought about this for a while, and then said, "Would you stay if there was a particular girl that you liked?" It would be hard to say whose face was more shocked. Rose, because she surprised herself with how bold she was being to ask such a thing, or Mr. Hyden, who was thinking about the girl that was the reason for his staying. "Forgive me," Rose said quickly. "I did not intend to be so bold, but I must address you on something I have observed over dinner tonight."

Henry was curious as to what Miss Wooden could be talking about, and asked her to continue. "Mr. Hyden, Henry, I don't know if you have noticed, but Katy has feelings for you that surpass those of a friend. I do not know what your opinion of her is, but if you do indeed like her, then I give you my blessing; but if you look on her only as a friend, then I suggest you be careful of what you say in her presence. She is still very young and apt to have her heart broken. I would have to be very upset if she were hurt in any manner."

Henry tried to keep from laughing. "Surely, you must be jesting, Miss Wooden. How could it have become evident to you over dinner that Miss Monks likes me? I would have noticed if she had done anything to suggest she might like me. I therefore believe that your worries are unfounded."

"Do you mean to tell me," Rose said sternly, "that you did not see her batting her eyelashes and trying to catch your attention the whole night? She watched your every move intently. It was so blatantly obvious that I am surprised anyone could have missed it. I am very certain that she likes you, Mr. Hyden, and you had better be careful, or else someone might get hurt."

Henry sobered at the serious note in Rose's voice. "You're serious then, aren't you." It was more of a statement then a question. "But I did nothing to encourage affection. I don't even think I paid that much attention to her. I thought it was obvious that I thought of her no more highly than a friend."

"Mr. Hyden, she is fifteen years old. Girls at that age do not need encouragement. If they see a man that they like or find agreeable, they will pursue him. They do not think of social class or etiquette, they think only of finding a husband who is handsome, tolerable, and conveniently rich."

"Are all fifteen-year-old girls like this? Because I cannot picture you looking for a husband in the same manner as that. In fact, I cannot picture you fawning over any man, or batting your eyelashes, or swooning, as is the social norm."

"I did not say that all fifteen-year-old girls were like that, and I was not looking for a husband when I was fifteen. At that age, I had better things to occupy my mind." Rose thought of her sword upstairs and continued. "Besides, I am not the type of girl who likes to fawn over men and bat my eyelashes and swoon, as is the social norm."

"I ask you then, what would occupy the time of a girl such as yourself at the age of fifteen?" Rose was thinking about how best to avoid Mr. Hyden's question when Katy walked into the kitchen. She seemed to have a knack for showing up when the dishes were just being finished, and Rose had to bite back the comment that she wished to make. She quietly reprimanded herself, for the Monks had been very gracious hosts, and it did not bother her any to wash a few dishes for them.

Katy looked at the two washing dishes and exclaimed, "My, Mr. Hyden! What are you doing washing the dishes? Why don't you join us out in the parlour for some tea? I'm sure that Miss Wooden wouldn't mind finishing up the dishes, now would you, Rose?" Her eyes batted in the direction of Rose with an expression of complete innocence.

Rose was about to reply and encourage Henry to go to the parlour when he cut in. "Miss Monks, I am sure that Miss Wooden wouldn't mind finishing the dishes at all, because she is a kind soul and doesn't mind doing a service for another person, but I do not wish for her to over exert herself, and I believe that she has just as much right to participate in the activities of the evening as I do. That being as it is, I will continue to help Miss Wooden with the dishes until they are finished, so that we may all enjoy the evening together." Mr. Hyden seemed to emphasize the word together as if to make it evident to Katy that he wanted to spend time with all of them, but the notion seemed to fly right over her pretty head.

"We can spend time together. Rose is almost finished and it shan't take her long to do the rest by herself. I insist that you come and join us immediately, or I will have to be very upset." With that, Katy gave a very pretty pout that had no effect on the persons present.

Henry tried to keep his temper under control, but Katy was making it very hard. Who in their right mind would allow their guest to be treated in such a way? It was against all social norms to have a guest do the dishes, and it was downright rude to have one's friend do one's dishes while one sat in the parlour sipping tea. "I believe, Miss Monks, that I will finish the dishes with Miss Wooden and join you and your family in the parlour for tea in a while so that we can all enjoy time together." Henry spoke through his teeth in an even tone.

Katy, seeing that he could not be dissuaded, flounced from the kitchen, leaving them to their peace. They continued to work in silence for some time before Henry spoke. "They should not treat you as they do. It is very wrong of them. They say you are their guest, but they treat you as a servant."

"Do not speak so," Rose cut in. "I willingly work for them, because they have been so generous to me. I admit sometimes I am a bit annoyed with Katy's attitudes and childishness, but she is still young and will have to grow up eventually. It is nothing that I can't put up with, really. But I thank you for your concern. It is very considerate of you."

"Why are you so quick to defend others' actions? Don't you believe in standing up for yourself and possibly doing something for yourself instead of always giving to others? When is the last time you have done something of your own accord without any other opinion or any other need motivating you?"

Rose stiffened at his words. "What you describe seems rather selfish, don't you think?" she said sharply. "My needs are met quite sufficiently. I do many things for myself that you know nothing about. Are you saying that just because I am not as self-seeking as others may be, I am a doormat to everyone?"

"What was the last thing that you did for yourself? I wouldn't be surprised if you couldn't remember," Henry shot back.

Rose thought about telling him of sword fighting with young Joshua, but thought better of it. Instead, she thought of the many morning walks she took. "I went for a walk today. I enjoyed it immensely, and there was no demand or need for me to go. It was just my pleasure to go for a walk."

"Does that happen to be the walk where you rescued me from the children? For if it is, it does not count. You helped me during that walk, and it was not a *selfish* walk."

Rose let out a frustrated sigh. "I picked some wild flowers before I went on my walk. They are in the vase over on the table." Henry gave a shake of his head as if to say that that was not a good enough response either. "I made myself a new dress then. That should be considered selfish, for I really didn't need it."

"Very well, I guess that can count. Though I think that the work you put into it would outweigh the selfishness of the deed.

Don't you see, Miss Wooden? Selfless people like you have no problem working hard, which is a good quality to have until people like Katy come along. These people are selfish and think only of their needs before others and they tend to use people such as you as a doormat."

"That's enough," Rose said angrily. "I will have no more of it. Now, if you will be so kind as to make my excuses to those sitting in the parlour, the dishes are done, and I would selfishly like to take a walk." Henry was about to ask to come along when Rose continued. "You are not welcome to come along, Mr. Hyden. This is one thing that I will not be swayed on. Why don't you spend the rest of the evening persuading Katy of your intentions?" With that, she left through the back door.

Mr. Hyden went to the parlour where he informed the Monks of Miss Wooden's whereabouts, and then excused himself from their company, claiming that he was tired after a busy day. He would never admit the truth to the Monks, that he was frustrated by his conversation with Rose, and he wanted some time to think through what had been said. He went to his room in the inn and began to pace back and forth.

As soon as Rose left the house, she began to run. She didn't know where she would go, she just wanted out and away. She didn't want to be around people anymore. When she finally ran out of breath, she found that she was in the pasture out back. It was dark outside now, and the stars winked and sparkled in the sky above.

Rose sat down on a boulder and pulled out a letter from her pocket. Her hands began to shake as she read the now familiar words.

> *My dearest cousin:*
>
> *It is with a heavy heart that I write these words. I fear that my father's condition deteriorates with every passing day, and the doctor says he will not live much longer. Sometimes I wake up in the night hearing him cry out in pain. He misses you very much, and there seems to be nothing that any of us can do to comfort him. The other day, I walked in and found him holding the portrait of your mother. He looked up when I walked in and said to me, "Isn't Rose a beautiful girl, son?" Oh Rose, how I fear he is losing his mind from the pain. Even mother has given up on him, it seems. She no longer shares a room with him, for he stirs so much in his sleep from the pain. We all miss you incredibly.*
>
> *With love,*
> *John Borden*

The words on the page began to blur as tears fell from Rose's eyes. She set the letter back in her pocket and lay down in the grass. She wept for fear that she would never get to see her uncle again. She wept for herself and what would become of her when her uncle did die. And she wept for her cousin, who was miserable just because his mother detested Rose.

When the tears finally subsided, she began to walk around the pasture. There were spring flowers all around, and their pollen filled the air with a heady scent. She walked around for some time, hoping that the red puffiness would leave her eyes before she returned to the Monks. When at last she thought that all signs of her tears had disappeared, she walked calmly back to the small cottage.

The whole house was dark, so she tried to be as quiet as possible. She was just about to step up the stairs to bed when a noise from behind her startled her. She spun around to find Mr. Monks sitting in a chair in the dining room. "Do you have a minute to spare, Miss Wooden, before you sneak off to bed? I have some important issues to discuss with you."

EIGHT

ROSE NERVOUSLY FOLLOWED MR. MONKS into the parlour. She took a seat on the sofa, her back stiff and straight. Was it possible that he had found out about her fencing? Was he upset with her for staying out so late? She looked around the room. A vase held a bouquet of wild flowers on the coffee table, and chairs and couches rested comfortable distances from the table. The walls were a bland white that turned to a ghostly gray in the candlelight.

Mr. Monks let out a sigh as he sat down in his favourite chair. "Tell me, Miss Wooden, are you enjoying your stay here? Be totally honest with me please. I do not have time for any lies."

Rose hesitated, then replied, "I very much like it in your home, and the town is just delightful. There are so many interesting people that I have met. But I do admit that I have suffered from bouts of homesickness. I would therefore say that I am very much enjoying my stay here."

"That is good," Mr. Monks said thoughtfully. "If this is the truth, then I have nothing further to say, and you may be off to bed, if you wish. It is getting quite late, and you must be tired."

Rose was quite shocked by the abrupt termination of the conversation, but thought it best not to ask too many questions. She turned to leave when Mr. Monks again called out, "Miss Wooden, I asked you this question for a very specific reason. I have recognized the service that you have done for my family in small areas such as washing dishes, tidying up a room, mending clothing, and such things as that, and I can't help but feel that we are treating you more closely to a servant than a guest. I therefore asked if you were enjoying your stay, for fear that we are putting too much of a strain on you personally."

Rose slowly turned around and smiled at Mr. Monks. "Believe me, Mr. Monks, I feel no such strain on my person, and I rather enjoy helping out around the house. I am glad that I can do some small things for your family in return for the hospitality that you have shown to me."

"That is very generous of you, Miss Wooden, and I hope that you continue to enjoy your stay here. Now, I say once and for all, off to bed with you. I will not be the cause of you falling ill from lack of sleep. That would never do."

Rose bestowed another smile on the kind Mr. Monks and hurried up the stairs to the room she shared with Katy. When she reached the room, she quickly changed into her nightgown and burrowed under the covers, where she thought about the events of the day. A smile came to her face when she thought of her conversation with Mr. Monks. She wondered if Henry could have been the motivator behind this episode.

Sunday came quickly, and with it the rain. It was a downright dreary day that would have persuaded many to stay indoors had there not been a church service to attend. Rose busily prepared herself for the service, looking for a suitable dress that would not be ruined by the rain. Seeing that her search was hopeless, she decided to wear her least favourite dress and, therefore, not feel regret at the loss of it.

She walked down the stairs to the dining room where the Monks were eating their breakfast. She was shocked to find that none of them were dressed for church, but were rather dressed in modest everyday clothes. "Will you not be attending the service today?" she asked.

"Attend services? On a day like today?" Mrs. Monks asked incredulously. "Surely you are not suggesting we go out in such weather and be ill for the next week. I will not have it. Not for any person in my care. You weren't planning on going to the service, were you? For I shan't allow it."

"Mrs. Monks," replied Rose, "I would very much like to go to the service. It is only but a little rain, and it shall do me no harm. I have no fear of becoming ill, for I cannot remember the last time that I was ill. This being as it is, I would like your permission to go off to church by myself. In this way, we will not endanger any members of your family, and if I become ill, it will be of my own doing."

Mrs. Monks hesitated before replying. She did not like to have her opinion contradicted, but she knew that Rose was stubborn, and would not be easily persuaded from her intent. "Very well, Rose, you may go to service, but if you fall ill, do not cast the blame on me, for I tried to warn you." Rose did not reply; she just sat down to eat her breakfast with a smile on her face.

Mr. Taylor stood before his church. Most of the pews were empty, the rain dissuading many members from joining them this morning. Only those with carriages and a few members who lived quite near the church seemed to have made it out. He was just about to start the service when the door at the back opened and Miss Wooden walked in, dripping from head to toe. Mr. Taylor smiled to himself as she, even in her state of dress, walked elegantly to the pew she normally shared with the Monks, and took her seat.

It wasn't very often that a young lady would venture out to service in weather such as this, and it was even more uncommon for one to show up unaccompanied on these days. Another smile played at the corners of his mouth as he welcomed the small congregation to worship and began the service.

When it was time for him to give his sermon, he could not help but watch Miss Wooden's reaction. The text of his sermon was Micah 6:8, where the prophet said, "He has showed you, o man, what is good. And what does the Lord require of you? To act justly and to love mercy and to walk humbly with your God."

He started with a discourse on justice. He spoke of the need for justice, and the world's duty to deliver justice to all persons whether they be of high standing, or whether they be orphaned. Miss Wooden appeared to be interested and enjoying the sermon until he changed to the topic of mercy.

"I believe that many of us understand what it means to show justice to others, especially when it benefits us. We show no qualms about administering justice to those who have harmed or hurt us in one manner or another, but when it is our own person deserving a just punishment, we tend to believe that we should be shown mercy." Miss Wooden turned her head away from the curate as if trying to ignore what he was saying.

"Mercy is a gift given to a person who is undeserving of it. We witness mercy when we forgive someone of their wrongdoings against us without exacting any punishment or penalty. We understand mercy by the gift of Christ on the cross, who gave up his life willingly so that we might not die but have eternal life.

"In the passage from Micah, we are commissioned not only to act in justice, but to act in mercy. The two coincide with each other. This may seem like an impossible task, to show mercy while administering justice, for how can one give out a just punishment yet still be merciful in his actions? When we justify an action, we believe that the offender must pay the full offense. If this were true, we would be a lost people, for we have come nowhere close to paying for our full offense. Through mercy, we can allow some of the weight of the offense to lie on our own shoulders. In this way, justice is shown and mercy is given.

"We are not always called to show mercy. There are times when justice must be delivered in full to the offender..." The rest of Curate Taylor's words slipped away as Rose contemplated this new view on mercy and justice. She had always believed that justice should be served to the full extent. Could it really be true that she was just as much called to show mercy as she was called to show justice? These thoughts plagued Rose through the rest of the service.

She sat in her bench far longer than normal, and was about to rise when Mr. Taylor stepped toward her. "Are you all right, Miss Wooden? You look a little bit disturbed. I hope I did not offend you by anything that I said in my sermon," he asked gently.

"Not at all, Curate," replied Rose. "I was just contemplating your view of showing mercy while also acting justly. I must admit, I have always considered justice to be the higher road, and I have not put that much thought into the need for mercy to coincide with justice. I believe I would be one of the people who would want justice to rest completely on the offender."

"I understand that completely, Miss Wooden. It is much easier to seek justice when the offense is done against us, but when we think of the mercy that was shown us on the cross, and the justice that we deserved, how can we not show mercy to others as well?

God is just, and God is merciful. If he is both of these things, then how can we ourselves as his followers not also be these things?"

Mr. Taylor watched Miss Wooden contemplate these ideas, but before she could ask any further questions, he had to excuse himself, for he had just noticed Mr. Hyden walk by, and he needed to discuss a matter with him before he left. He walked toward the gentleman, trying to keep Miss Wooden in his eyesight, but she soon disappeared in the crowd.

"Mr. Hyden, how good to see you today," the curate said when he reached the other young man. "I have a proposition to set before you. I was hoping you would take some of your time to hear me out."

"I have all the time in the world, sir," replied Mr. Hyden. "Whatever your proposition is, please take your time in explaining it to me."

"Very well then," replied the reverend. "I shall start at the beginning. I have noticed that you have been staying at the inn for the past few weeks and do not have a place of your own to stay while you are visiting amongst us. I have been thinking on this for the past few nights, and I came to the conclusion that you may very well like to have a place to reside other than the inn. In short, I was wondering if you would like to come live at the rectory with me. There is plenty of room there for you to stay, and I figured you would be much more comfortable in a house than in a room at the inn."

"That is very considerate of you, Curate, but I wouldn't want to be an imposition on you in any way. I fear that if I do join you at the rectory, I will be a bother to the peace and quiet that you have so long been accustomed to."

"I do not know if you know this, Mr. Hyden, but I grew up in a home with two brothers and left that house a mere ten years ago. I do not believe that you could make so much noise as to bother me. In fact, I think I would very much enjoy your company as opposed to the dreary silence."

"If this is truly how you feel, then I will bring my possessions by tomorrow, and I am very grateful to you, sir. The truth is that I was getting very tired of the inn; no matter how well it is kept, it is not a home."

"Then I shall see you tomorrow, but I do have one request of you. If you are to stay with me, would you please call me Caleb and allow me to call you James? For these formalities would cause me much grief if I were to use them consistently even at home."

Mr. Hyden laughed at the honesty in the curate's voice. "Very well, Caleb. I will see you tomorrow, and I look forward to getting to know you better." With that, Mr. Hyden slipped out into the rain and ran to a waiting carriage.

Caleb turned to look for Rose. He had hoped to continue his conversation with her. She was an insightful and honest young lady. She was also very beautiful, which Caleb had noted long ago. He was twenty-eight years old, and was very much thinking of marriage. If Miss Wooden happened to be the woman that God had chosen for him, then he would be forever grateful, but if not, he would keep searching.

He continued to look around the church, but she appeared to have left already. He looked outside and watched the rain fall down in torrents. He wondered if she would walk all the way home in the rain, and he began to worry about her health, but there was nothing he could do about it now; he would have to visit the Monks' home on the morrow to inquire about Rose's health.

Rose walked slowly through the rain. Her heart felt nearly, as heavy as her rain-soaked dress. In her mind, she could still remember how she felt when she was ten years old, and the more she tried to push the memory from her mind, the more it invaded her thoughts.

It was her birthday, and there was a cake on the table, but there was no one to celebrate with her except for Meggy, the housekeeper. Mom was sick in her bed, and Dad was away. At least, that was what they told Rose. They didn't know that she knew the truth about where he was. They had tried to protect her, but she had found out the truth.

There had been a knock at the door. She answered it in her most polite voice. The man on the other side just stared at her sadly. She knew he was sad because his eyes were red and droopy, just like her mom's when she was crying about Dad being away. He gave her a letter to give to her mom and left. She didn't give the letter to her mom, because then she wouldn't know the truth about why the man was sad. Her mom was always trying to hide sad things from her.

She opened the letter slowly and began to read. Some of the words were big and hard to understand, but the main message stood out. *"Mrs. Wooden, we regret to inform you that your husband has passed away..."* Rose didn't want to believe it. It was a lie, and her mom shouldn't see this lie. She was too sick, and this lie might kill her. Tears poured down her face as she stuffed the letter back in the envelope and hid it under her mattress.

She didn't tell anyone about the lie until two weeks later when Dr. Macey came. He always tried to keep sad stuff from her as well, but this time he didn't. He had sat her down like an adult and told her all about her momma's sickness, and then he had said really sadly, "I'm sorry, Rose, but I couldn't save your mother, and she has gone home to be with her Lord."

She had run out of the room screaming that it was a lie, but it hadn't been. Later that day, she had heard Meggy talking with Dr. Macey about what they should do with her until her father came home. She had thought about the letter under her mattress and wondered if it really was a lie. She had run upstairs, taken out the letter, and with tears in her eyes had given it to Meggy...

Rose felt the tears roll down her face and add to the puddles forming on the rain drenched ground. She remembered the unfairness of it all, and her need for justice, but she was never given justice. In place of justice, she was dealt more pain, and the fault of her pain all resided on the shoulders of one man. The pastor may have spoken of mercy that morning, but the need for justice rose stronger and higher within her, far outweighing the goodness of mercy.

Caleb helped James move his few belongings into one of the rooms at the parsonage. He had a few changes of clothes, a diary, a flute-like instrument, and a sword. All other things he had left at home. When all his things were put away, Caleb showed him around the house, and told him to make himself at home. The housekeeper would take care of cleaning the house, and he should feel free to help himself to meals.

By noon, James was well-established in the parsonage and headed out to go help Mrs. Jennings at the orphanage. Caleb took this time to go call on Miss Wooden and the Monks family. He walked up the drive to their small cottage and knocked at the door. It was soon opened by Rose herself.

"Rose!" Caleb said, quite shocked that she would be the one to answer the door. He cleared his throat. "I mean, Miss Wooden, how glad I am to see you. I came to inquire about your health, since you made the journey to church and back in the pouring rain. I had hoped you hadn't fallen ill."

"I am quite all right, Mr. Taylor, and I thank you for the time that you took to stop by, but I must admit that now is not the best time to visit. It is the oddest thing, but all the Monks have fallen ill, every one of them. I am quite busy tending to them as of now."

"All ill, you say? Were they also out in the rain yesterday? I would think that Mrs. Monks and Miss Monks would be the type of ladies who do not wish to harm their clothing by exposing it to such harsh weather."

"Not one of them stepped out of doors during the rain. That is why I am quite shocked at the outcome, for Mrs. Monks, who was so concerned about my health because of the rain, is now quite ill despite the rain. It perplexes me so."

"Me as well," replied Mr. Taylor. "But I insist on staying and assisting you with the invalids. You must be quite tired after taking care of them all morning, and I am sure that I can be of assistance." Rose tried to object to this, but Mr. Taylor would have none of it. She was finally left with no choice but to succumb to his wishes.

She allowed him into the house just as Mrs. Monks began to call out, before the door was even closed. "Rose! Oh Rose, please come and assist me at once. I am in great need of something for my head. Oh, how it aches." Rose gave the curate a knowing look and then raced off to Mrs. Monks' side, where she placed a cool damp towel over her eyes and forehead.

Miss Wooden and Mr. Taylor spent the rest of the day running at the beckoning of the three invalids. Mrs. Monks complained consistently of a sore head and an aching stomach, which Rose treated with a damp cloth and herbal teas. Katy could not make up her mind about what hurt the most. Sometimes her head hurt, and other times it was her back or her stomach, but one thing was for certain—if Mr. Taylor came with a remedy, it was sure to work. Rose laughed when the poor curate brought a steaming cup of awful smelling tea to Katy, who thanked him pleasantly then dumped it in the chamber pot when he was not looking.

Of the three, Mr. Monks was the most pleasurable to be around. He coughed a lot and needed help moving, but he was quite content to sit in his rocking chair reading a book with an occasional cup of tea. He never once complained, and was always overly thankful for any small task that was done for him.

No matter how pleasant a sick person Mr. Monks was, Rose was quite thankful when all three sufferers were sound asleep. She tiptoed around the kitchen preparing a cup of tea for herself and Mr. Taylor, as well as a plate of food for each of them. She brought them to the dining room where the two of them started a whispered conversation.

"I want to thank you very much for your assistance today, Mr. Taylor. I don't know what I would have done without you coming along as you did. I fear that I would have been run into the ground trying to keep Mrs. Monks and Katy both comfortable. You truly were a life saver."

"It really was no problem at all, Miss Wooden," replied the curate. "But I do ask one small favour in return. I would like it very much if you would call me Caleb instead of Mr. Taylor. There are very few people who feel comfortable using my given name, and I fear I will forget it altogether unless someone uses it."

Rose laughed softly at Caleb's humour. "I will only use your given name on one condition. You must call me Rose, for I am quite tired of formalities. It takes much too long to give title to every name. We were blessed with beautiful given names that should be used on the rare occasion in place of our surnames."

"I like your conditions, Rose," replied Caleb, "and I appreciate your disregard for formalities. It is… refreshing, to say the least." The two enjoyed each other's company over their meal when Caleb finally said, "I fear I must go. I have invited Mr. Hyden to live with me while he stays in our small town, and I don't think he knows of my whereabouts as of now, for I left while he was at the orphanage. I thank you for the meal, and I will stop by tomorrow to see how the Monks are doing."

Rose got up from the table and escorted Caleb to the door. "Thank you once again for all the help you have given me in caring for the Monks. I will not forget your kindness."

Caleb turned toward her, and a smile spread across his face. "It is always a pleasure to be of assistance, Rose." She didn't know for sure, but Rose was almost positive that the good reverend winked at her as he turned to leave.

Caleb met up with Mr. Hyden on his way back home. He looked tired and was quite filthy. They walked in silence to the house where Mr. Hyden immediately fell onto a couch and let out a groan, followed by the growl of his stomach. "What happened to you?" Caleb couldn't help but ask.

"Did you know there are twenty-six children at that orphanage, most of them under the age of eleven?"

"Yes, I was quite aware of that, James. What of it? I did not know that that was a bother to you before. You seemed to enjoy your work there. I can only imagine what was so different about today, that you return so bedraggled," replied Caleb hesitantly.

"Nearly half of them were ill with some sort of sickness. I spent the day running around with Mrs. Jennings trying to care for all the sick while also keeping track of the healthy. Worst of all, Lisa was sick, and half the time she would refuse to let go of me, and Jeremy and Tyler seemed unaffected by the illness. Rather, they were quite full of energy and up to as much mischief as before."

Caleb couldn't help but feel compassion for the poor fellow. He knew that adults could be trying when they were ill, but children were near impossible. He walked into the kitchen and prepared a plate of food for James. He brought it back into the living room, and found the gentleman fast asleep on the couch.

He walked over to him and gently shook him awake, telling him it would be better for him to eat before he slept. James looked up into his eyes and sincerely said, "Thank you. You have been a blessing to me already. I don't know what I would have done if I had gone back to the inn after such a day."

"God works in mysterious ways sometimes," replied Caleb with a slight smile on his lips.

James let out a laugh. "That he does, that he does. But I must admit that I am a bit appalled with myself, for here I am in your house complaining about a bad day and having you serve me, while I don't even know what occurred in your day. For all I know, your day could have been much worse than mine, yet you offer no complaint."

It was Caleb's turn to laugh at this. "Believe me, James, your day was far worse than mine. I had the pleasure of assisting Rose Wooden in caring for the ill Monks family. I fear this illness is not isolated to the orphanage, but has affected other families as well. Though I do not think that the Monks caused as much trouble as your orphans."

James grew quiet at this. He seemed to have something on his mind, but was hesitant to share his thoughts. "Miss Wooden is a wonderful young woman who is very caring of other people. Would you not agree with this?"

Caleb noted the sensitivity of the conversation before he replied, "I believe that Miss Wooden is a very wonderful young woman. She is compassionate, and she goes out of her way to help others in their time of need. So yes, I would agree with you."

James took this in and seemed to ponder it for a while. "Caleb, I am not known to beat around the bush, and I really do hate some of the polite formalities, so I hope you will not be offended by my being very blunt. I would like to know if you have feelings for Miss Wooden. You do not have to reply if you are offended by my question, but it would help me to know your feelings for her, so that I will not step on any toes in future conversations."

Caleb was a bit shocked at the bluntness of the question, but was quite glad that it was in the open. "As I said before, Miss Wooden is a very wonderful young woman. She is everything that a man would look for in a wife. She is beautiful, intelligent, and she genuinely cares for others. To answer your question, I would have to say yes, I do have feelings for her. I like Miss Wooden quite a bit, but I do not know her feelings toward me or any other man."

James didn't respond at first. He cleaned off his plate and finished chewing. When he swallowed, he finally answered. "Thank you, Caleb, for your honesty, and also for the meal. I am very grateful."

With that, he stood up from the couch, walked to the kitchen, cleaned up his dishes, and went to bed.

Caleb at first thought James' behaviour a bit peculiar, but he did not wish to dwell on it too long. He himself was quite tired and wished for some sleep. He headed up the stairs to his bedroom, and before his head hit the pillow he was fast asleep, his dreams filled with the beautiful Miss Wooden.

In the room below him, Henry stirred restlessly on his bed. Caleb liked Miss Wooden. Miss Wooden may very well like Caleb. The thought shouldn't have bothered him as much as it did, but no matter how much he tried to put it out of his mind, the bigger it got. It filled his thoughts, pushing the need for sleep into the back recesses of his brain. If he had been thinking clearly, he would have been able to pinpoint his concern with this topic, but he was in no shape to think clearly, so he spent the rest of the night tossing and turning.

NINE

THE EPIDEMIC SPREAD QUICKLY throughout the town, making many ill for a time, and then moving on. It did not seem to be fatal, but made life miserable for the houses that were infected. The Monks did not remain sick for long, and much to the dismay of Katy, as soon as they were well enough to care for themselves, Caleb and Rose went to help out at the orphanage. Katy had very much enjoyed the company of Mr. Taylor, and did not want to see him leave, but she refused to go to the orphanage amongst the sick children.

The work at the orphanage was hard, but enjoyable. Rose found that she spent much of her time with Caleb and Henry, as she had now come to call Mr. Hyden. They worked side by side caring for the children and for Mrs. Jennings, who had also fallen ill. The only time that Rose was separated from the two was when she went to the kitchen to bake and cook, or when someone needed to go to the market to buy more food. She found that the more time she spent with them, the more a feeling akin to friendship grew within her, but she did not give this much thought.

Two weeks after the epidemic struck, Rose walked to the orphanage and found all the children playing outside, and Mrs. Jennings busily cooking in the kitchen. No matter where she looked, she could not find the two men. When she asked Mrs. Jennings about this, she said that they had not yet showed up that morning. Rose found this odd, and seeing that Mrs. Jennings had the children well in hand, she walked down the three doors to the rectory.

She knocked lightly on the door, and it was soon answered by a rather frazzled Mrs. Meps, the housekeeper. "How nice to see you, Miss Wooden," she said. "But I fear you must not come in unless you have had the epidemic, for both Mr. Hyden and Mr. Taylor have come down with it, and they do not want it to spread any farther."

"Mrs. Meps," replied Rose, "I have been working with children who have been infected by the disease for the past two weeks right alongside those two men. Now the children are better, and I would like to continue my service to others, so I would greatly appreciate if you would allow me to come in and assist you, seeing as you look so tired already."

Mrs. Meps looked at her sternly, as if sizing her up to see if she was actually capable of the task, or if she only wished to look good in front of the two most eligible men that the town supplied. "Very well. You may come in, but if you get sick, do not put the blame on me, for I tried to warn you."

Rose walked in behind Mrs. Meps, who was walking quickly towards the upstairs. She did not slow her pace, but called behind her, "You may tend to Mr. Hyden. He is in the room down the hall. He is near burning with fever, so you will need to bathe the sweat off him." Rose was quite familiar with this task after doing it for sick children all week, and it did not take her long to gather the cool water and a cloth and walk down to Mr. Hyden's room.

The inside of his room was quite dark, for the curtains were closed. The smell of the illness filled every corner. The room's furnishings were sparse, the bed being its dominant feature. On the bed, a prone figure lay amongst a tangle of blankets that had been tossed around during a restless night's sleep.

Rose swallowed when she recognized that the prone figure was in fact Mr. Hyden, and that he had already shed his shirt in the struggle against the illness. As she came closer, her hands began to shake. She realized that she had never washed the feverish sweat from a grown man before—only young children, the oldest being eleven. She took a deep breath to calm her nerves, then dipped the cloth in the water and began her task.

She first placed a wet cloth across his forehead, and then dipped a second cloth in the water and began to bathe him. As soon as the cool water touched his chest, Henry let out a moan, and Rose almost lost her nerve, but she bit her tongue and continued to work. She soon had to change the cloth on his forehead for a cooler one, and when she went to place the new cloth on his head, his eyes opened.

He looked at her for a while and then, with a scratchy voice, he said, "I'm sick, aren't I? What about Caleb, is he okay? And the children at the orphanage, what about them? Mrs. Jennings should have some help caring for them."

"Shhhh now," replied Rose. "Yes, Caleb is sick as well, but I haven't gone to see him yet. I'm sure he is doing fine. As for Mrs. Jennings and the orphanage, everyone is quite all right. It seems that the epidemic has passed through the worst of it, and there are only a few more people that are ill. Now, you rest yourself and get better. The more rest you get, the faster you'll get well."

"You shouldn't be here," continued Henry through a yawn. "You haven't been sick as of yet, and you are more susceptible to the disease. Mrs. Meps can care for us. We'll be all right."

"Nonsense. I will have none of that," said Rose. "I have been caring for the children right alongside you and Caleb, and I will not leave you two now that you have fallen ill. I will be perfectly safe caring for you. Now, please rest so that I can tend to you more easily."

"Yes, Mademoiselle," Henry said with a smile on his face as he closed his eyes. He slept all the while that Rose tended to him. She quickly washed all the sweat off of him, and tried to cool him down. She fixed the tangled covers and pulled them up over his legs and chest. She found his discarded shirt and hung it up. She was about to leave when she remembered the cloth she had left on his head.

She slipped the warm cloth off his forehead, and a lock of his tangled hair fell onto his face. She gently picked it up and put it back in place. His hair was soft with a slight curl to it, and so dark—like all his other features. A slight smile tipped the corners of her mouth as she looked at his sick person, but she soon turned and walked quickly out of the room.

She worked with Mrs. Meps all day and quite long into the night. As the hours went by, Mrs. Meps seemed to become more and more drained. At first Rose thought it was because of her age, and that she was unaccustomed to such strenuous work, but as the day progressed, she began to fear the worst. It was later that night, when Rose caught Mrs. Meps just leaving the curate's room, that she asked her, "Mrs. Meps, are you all right? You look quite ill."

"No, not at all, dear," she said. "I think I'm sick." With that, she fainted onto the hall floor. Rose was unable to carry the elderly lady too far, and she didn't know where her room was, so she decided to place her in the spare room right next to Caleb's. In this way, she would be able to keep an eye on all the invalids quite easily as she cared for them.

When all three were comfortable, Rose slipped out of the house. She did not intend to be gone long, so she raced back to the Monks' house where she found all the residents fast asleep. She left a note explaining her whereabouts, and asked Katy to come in the morning with fresh food and some clean cloths. She also grabbed a fresh pair of clothes and some other necessities in case she stayed a couple of nights. She then rushed back to the rectory where the sick needed tending to.

Rose did not sleep much that night. She spent much of her time bathing the sweat off those who burned with fever, and placing blankets on top of those who shivered. She was able to take a few quick naps when all three were comfortable, but it didn't take long for her to wake up to the soft moaning of one or another of the sick persons.

By the morning, Rose was quite exhausted, but thankfully Henry's fever had broken, and it didn't look like it would take long for Mrs. Meps' fever to follow suit. She had not been attacked nearly as hard as the men, who had been working with sick children for quite some time, and she would not take long to heal.

Katy came later in the morning, but she refused to step inside the house. She remembered how awful it had been to be sick, and she did not wish to become ill once again, so Rose was forced to gather the fresh supplies from the door and go back to work. By noon, Mrs. Meps' fever had broken, and Henry was able to sit up and eat some broth on his own. The only person Rose feared for was Caleb, who continued to shiver and burn despite her diligent attention.

She spent much of her time by his bedside caring for him. She bathed him with cold water when he sweated, and she covered him with thick heavy blankets when he shivered, but the fever persisted. Her second night at the parish was spent mostly in Caleb's room, for Mrs. Meps and Henry both slept peacefully.

On the third day, Henry was able to get out of bed, and Rose walked with him about the house. He looked at her worriedly, and said she looked tired. She made nothing of it, and soon returned him to his bed so that she could again tend to Caleb. The third night was much like the second, but by the fourth morning Henry was walking around by himself, though he tired easily and slept often. Mrs. Meps still remained in her bed.

The fourth night provided the greatest amount of trouble for Rose. She was quite tired from lack of sleep the past three nights, and Caleb's fever kept getting progressively worse. By the middle of the night, he was in such a state that his whole body shook with the illness. Rose wept beside his bed because she did not know what to do for him. She bathed him continuously, but the sweat continued to pour off his body no matter how fast she worked.

Long into the night this continued, until Rose's tears ran out. As dawn broke, so did Caleb's fever. With one final shudder, it left him, and Rose collapsed exhausted with her head resting on the bed. She didn't stir until later that morning, when she felt herself being picked up from the chair she was sitting in, and carried to a spare bedroom where she was lain down on a bed to rest.

She opened her eyes and tried to protest, claiming that she had work to do, but Henry would have none of it. "It is your turn to rest now, Rose. You have worked long enough, and you are tired. Caleb is quite safe now, thanks to your tending, and I can care for the rest of us while you sleep."

The look on his face told Rose that he would bear no arguments, so she closed her eyes and was soon asleep. She did not wake till later that evening from a growling stomach. She got up, and found that she had lost some of the pins from her hair. She found them among the blankets and hastily pushed them back in place.

She walked down the hall and into the kitchen where she found Henry making something that smelled absolutely delectable. Her face turned red when her stomach growled quite loudly, but Henry just laughed and continued to cook his meal. "Why don't you sit down at the table there?" he said. "I'll serve you when I'm all finished."

Rose smiled and took a seat. She didn't say anything, because she was still too tired to talk and feared if she opened her mouth only gibberish would come out. Henry soon placed a plate of flat round pancakes in front of her with molasses drizzled all over the top. She took one bite and sighed with contentment.

When she finished her meal, she finally spoke. "How are Caleb and Mrs. Meps? Have they much recovered since I last saw them? I have slept so terribly long that I fear I have not been much of a help to you. You yourself should be resting, for you don't want to take ill again now, do you?"

Henry patiently listened to her spiel, then replied, "Caleb is much better. He is awake and you can see him very shortly. He is still very tired, but he should recover soon enough. As for Mrs. Meps, she is quite old and tired. The illness took a toll on her, and she is content to stay in her small apartment behind the parish until she is fully recovered. There, she can easily take care of herself. While you were taking your much needed rest, I have been relaxing. I spent some time talking with Caleb and helping him drink some broth. Katy stopped by to make sure you were all right.

She stayed for about an hour, but the sick smell in the air seemed to scare her off. She is to return later this evening with Mr. Monks to retrieve you. Now, if you are ready, you may go speak with Caleb."

Rose got up eagerly from her chair and raced up the stairs to Caleb's room. She knocked quietly on the door and entered. The room was much brighter than before. The curtains were drawn, and a light breeze blew through the open window. A chair sat beside the bed, and Rose went to sit in it. Caleb looked sickly and pale, but he was not sweating and shivering, which was a very good sign.

He smiled at Rose and said, "I think that I may very well owe you my life. I hear from James that you tended me quite tirelessly while I was sick, even to the point of utter exhaustion, and I thank you for that."

Rose smiled back. "I would prefer it, Caleb, if you would not do such a thing again. You were quite ill and scared me severely." She looked at him seriously and continued, "You were very sick. At one point, your whole body shook with the fever, and I thought for sure you were going to die. I felt so helpless."

A tear slipped out of the corner of her eye, and Caleb lifted his hand to wipe it away. "There, there now, Rose. I am quite all right now, and I shall be my normal healthy self in no time at all. Now, don't fret about the things of the past, but let us think about how God has blessed us so that we still have a future to look forward to." He gently took Rose's hand and squeezed it. She gripped it back, and the two sat for a while in companionable silence.

It didn't seem long before there was another light knock on the door, and Henry entered. "Your entourage awaits, Mademoiselle," he said with a smile on his face. "I fear you must leave this horrid place behind you. We will miss you terribly, but do not come back until you are well rested and in better spirits. We therefore wait in misery for your return."

Rose laughed lightly at Henry's dramatic speech. She did not want to go, but she understood that she must. She said goodbye to Caleb and was escorted down the stairs by Henry to the parlour where Katy and Mr. Monks waited.

Katy paced around the room as if the epidemic would jump out at her from any corner, and Mr. Monks sat quietly in the cushioned chair by the door. When Rose entered the room, Katy stepped back with a look of horror on her face. "Why, Rose, you look absolutely terrible. Have you had no time for sleep, or to do your hair or anything like that? You look as if you were up the entire time caring for invalids."

Rose was just about to respond that she had had some sleep, when Henry cut in rather harshly. "Miss Wooden has been quite busy taking care of all of us while we were ill. If it were not for her help, I fear that Mr. Taylor would not be with us anymore. If she looks a little tired, it is because she would not rest until she saw to the needs of those around her."

The tension in the room escalated as Henry spat out these words in Rose's defence. Rose could almost see the hackles rise on his neck. She gently placed a hand on his arm, and he calmed down quickly. A slow smile spread across his face and he said with a lighter tone, "Of course, she does look a lot better when she isn't so tired, and she has been in a horrible mood all day. She wouldn't even talk with me."

Katy turned an understanding look toward Rose and a glare at Mr. Hyden. Rose had to fight back a laugh. If only Katy knew that she had spent nearly the whole day sleeping, but she did wonder at the difference in the girl. Only a few weeks ago, she had been afraid that she was falling hard for Mr. Hyden, but now she seemed determined to dislike him. Rose would have to ask her about this on the way back home.

"Well, we should be leaving," Mr. Monks said, his voice cutting into Rose's thoughts. "It is getting dark, and I believe that Mrs. Monks has a wonderful meal waiting for us at home. Send our regards to the curate, and tell him that we hope to see him well soon." Rose followed the two Monks out of the door and into the street.

Mr. Monks walked at a fast clip, and the two girls were content to stroll at a slower pace behind him. Rose took this as her opportunity to talk with Katy about what had happened inside. "I must admit, Katy, that you took me by surprise at the rectory. You seemed quite cold toward Mr. Hyden, when I had believed you to have feelings for him."

"Don't be silly, Rose," replied Katy. "I may have had feelings for him, but that was weeks ago. I've talked with May Evans since then, and she has warned me against him. She says that her daddy wouldn't allow her to go after him because nothing good can ever come from a traveler like him. For all we know, he could be running from the law, or he may be a liar and a cheat. None of the girls will go after him anymore, after May warned us about that. We've decided that if he was of any interest to us, he would have come with money to spend, and he wouldn't wear those dingy traveling clothes."

Rose fought the urge to laugh again at the pettiness of Katy and the "girls," as she called them. They based their knowledge of Mr. Hyden on appearance and gossip spread by a loose-lipped child, for what other word could describe such a girl at the age of fifteen? They did not consider his character, which denied the possibility of him being a thief or a liar or a cheat. No, Mr. Hyden was deserving of a better analysis than what was given him. "It seems rather harsh to judge Mr. Hyden without knowing who he really is. For all we know he could be a noble, or even the Prince himself traveling in disguise."

Katy threw Rose a disgusted look. "You can't be serious, can you? Why in the world would the Prince or a noble travel in disguise? It would be much easier to travel in style, and to have all sorts of servants, and the best of rooms that could be supplied. Don't you think?"

"It may be more beneficial to travel in style, but don't you think that you would get sick of all the people staring at you, and all the people pretending to be your friend to get benefits from you? Besides, if you travel in disguise, you wouldn't have to worry about people trying to steal your money, or the possibility of dishonest servants. No, I think that it would be much easier to travel without servants and other 'benefits,' as you call them."

"You're strange, Rose," said Katy, turning her attention back to the road ahead. "Even if he was a noble, which is very unlikely, there are better men to mark for conquest than a boring noble who likes to travel. There are men who are already settled with a good profession that is respected wherever they go. They would not be ashamed to tell people who they are."

"I will admit, you have me interested," replied Rose. "I only know of two single men in this community, and you have already knocked one off your list of eligible men. You seriously cannot be considering a conquest of Mr. Taylor? He is much too old for you, is he not?"

"Mr. Taylor is not all that old, Rose," Katy said almost dreamily. "He's only twenty-eight—and very handsome. Now that he has been ill, many of the girls will be attempting a conquest, but I shall be the first in line tomorrow morning. I shall have the very first chance at him."

"Now you have me very confused. Why would all the girls suddenly take a fancy to the curate now that he has been ill, and how will you be the first in line tomorrow? I cannot picture a line of girls outside the door of the rectory very well now."

"Why, you are silly. Of course there will be no line of girls. I was speaking figuratively when I spoke of the line, like what they do in good literature. This isn't an all-of-a-sudden fancy as you say, but many of the girls have had their eyes on the curate since he has come to our town. He has turned down every single one of us in one way or another, but now that he has been sick, we hope that he will see the need he has for a good wife. All the girls will be vying for his attention, for this time he is certain to choose a wife."

"You cannot be serious. Surely the ladies of the parish will not allow their daughters to throw themselves at Mr. Taylor in hopes that he will choose one of them as his wife. What if he doesn't choose any of them? What will occur then? For there will be many a broken heart in the community."

"What is so terribly wrong with trying to catch the curate's eye? Just wait until Sunday. Nearly every eligible female will be wearing a new bonnet, dress, or jewel. I myself have already picked out some fabric for a new dress. Mother promised to sew it for me by Sunday, but I was hoping that you would add some extra embroidery. You are so handy with a needle."

Rose ignored this remark and went on with her questioning. "You still haven't answered me on how you are planning to be first in line to the curate's heart come tomorrow morning. You cannot plan to walk up to the rectory, knock on his bedroom door, enter, and have him fall instantly in love with you, can you?"

"I am not that silly, Rose. I have thought this through quite thoroughly. You are sure to travel to the rectory tomorrow to check on your patients, and I will come with you. I will help you around the kitchen and with whatever Mr. Taylor needs, and then I will travel back with you at night. The curate will see what a kind, caring person I am, and already I will be a step ahead of all the other girls."

Rose didn't know how to respond to this claim, but she was left without need to, for they had arrived home and Katy was already skipping up the stairs and through the front door. Rose did not doubt the girl's words, but she feared for poor Caleb, who would not only have to concentrate on getting better, but also fending off the man-hungry females.

TEN

A S SOON AS ROSE LEFT, Henry went back up the stairs to Caleb's room. He opened the door quietly and walked over to the bed. He sat in the chair that Rose had just vacated and looked at Caleb. He was still quite pale, but there was some colour coming back into his cheeks. "How are you, Caleb? The honest truth. No lies."

Caleb let out a soft sigh and looked at Henry. "I don't know, James. I am better than what I was before, that is for sure. But I feel very tired, and I don't think that I have the strength yet to stand. I still ache all over, and my head pounds every time I try to raise myself more than what I am already at."

"Have patience, my friend," replied Henry. "It will take time. I myself still feel some effects from the illness, and I did not suffer near as badly as you did. This disease does not appear to take lives, but it does sap the energy of those who fall ill enough. Before you know it, you will be well again."

Caleb laughed softly. "That is what I told Rose, but she is a smart girl, and I don't think she believed it. I think she fears that I will never be as well as I once was. It scared her when I was sick. She said that at one point the fever so consumed me that I shook, and she did not know what to do." Caleb looked at Henry seriously. "I honestly think that I almost died."

"You are here now, and that is all that matters. Rose will see to it that you heal. I found her asleep in this chair this morning. She seemed to have passed out from fatigue, but she still persisted in helping you heal when I woke her. If I had not insisted upon her sleeping, she would have been by your side all of today."

Another smile spread across Caleb's face. "She is a wonderful woman. She is so wise and caring, yet so young. Do you know how old she is? I do not believe that she is as young as Miss Monks, but neither is she as old as you are. I have never heard anyone speak of her age…"

"I would not be able to guess at her age, but I can agree to her wisdom. She is the only one who was able to find me out. The only person to question my identity…" Henry seemed to ponder this thought for a moment, and Caleb looked at him quite confused.

"What do you mean, James? How was she able to find you out? And why would she have any reason to question your identity? Have I missed something while I was ill, or are you speaking of things unknown to me."

Henry turned beet-red when he realized he had spoken of his identity. He was so comfortable with Caleb that he sometimes forgot that his friend did not know who he was. Well, if they were to be friends, it was best that he told the truth to him. "I guess it is time that I am perfectly honest with you Caleb. James Hyden is not my real name. I have been traveling under a false identity for the past three months or so, but it is for a very good reason."

Caleb looked at him questioningly, but he didn't seem to raise any fences or barriers as Henry had feared. "So, you have been traveling under a false name, and Rose was able to find a falsehood in your story and weed it out. I knew she was smart, but what could have possibly given you away?"

"Rose is a very observant woman. When I first met her, I was resting by the road, and she tripped over my feet. She did not speak with me while I visited with the Monks, and I feared that she was angry with me. I walked with her to the post office that evening and asked her about her behaviour, and she pinned me as a liar. She said that my boots gave me away, for no person but a noble could afford such boots. I will admit that I was so shocked by her observation that I admitted that she was right."

"So you admitted your identity, and Rose was satisfied enough with it that she concealed the truth from everyone?"

"Not exactly," replied Henry. "I told her my given name and asked her to leave it at that, for if I gave her any more information, I would be ruined. She seemed to allow this. I think she recognized that even if she knew exactly who I was, no one else would believe her if she told them."

"That is very true, but now there are two of us who know you are not who you say you are. How do you know that we will not give you away? It is biblical to have two witnesses against a person in a trial. With both Rose and I as witnesses, you could easily be convicted."

"Yes, you could, but I pray that my true identity and a little begging on my part will keep you from speaking against me. I assure you that I have good reason for keeping my identity hidden, and you may very well understand when I explain."

"Well then, please continue and reveal your identity, for I am tired of waiting in suspense, and I do not believe my patience will last much longer if you do not speak." Henry could tell from his voice that Caleb was getting very tired.

"Very well," Henry began hesitantly. "My name is Henry Arden, Prince Henry Arden." Understanding slowly dawned on the curate's face, but before Henry could determine any reaction to this news, he turned his expression to one of stone, so unreadable that Henry feared he might be quite angry.

"I believe that your claim comes with some sort of proof, for it is not every day that the Prince travels around with a false name."

Henry left the room and soon came back with a note from his father with the King's seal. The note attested to the true identity of James Hyden, and in it the king claimed him as his own son. Along with the note, Henry also carried a signet ring of his own that his father had given him for his twentieth birthday.

A slow smile spread across Caleb's face. "You truly are the Prince, aren't you?" Caleb blew a heavy breath out, as he looked through the note again. He let out a slow chuckle. "I think, Prince Henry, that you are going to have to tell me this again in the morning, for I will think that it is a hallucination caused by the disease, or a most splendid dream."

Henry let out a sigh of relief. "I will repeat this all to you in the morning on one condition. You do not refer to me as Prince Henry, and you continue to address me as James in public. Oh, and you also treat me as you did before. Believe me, it gets quite tiring being treated as a prince."

Caleb let out a hearty laugh that caused him to start coughing. Between gasps for breath, he said, "I think that I can handle your conditions. It shouldn't be hard to treat you as a brother, as long as you continue to act as annoying as one. Now, be gone with you. I need my sleep if I am to get better."

A huge smile crossed Henry's face as he left the room. A brother. He liked being called a brother. He had always been an only child very much in need of a sibling, but that wish had never been granted to him. Yes, he could continue to act as a brother towards Caleb.

Rose woke up early Saturday morning, ready to head to the rectory and visit with Caleb. She would have left immediately, but she feared that Katy would be quite upset with her if she left without taking her, so she satisfied herself with going to the post to check for letters. It did not take her long to travel the distance, and she was back in what seemed like no time at all. There had been no letter from John.

She opened the door and Katy ran down the stairs. "How could you?" she trilled. "I made myself perfectly clear that I wanted to go with you to the rectory this morning, and you went without me. I thought we were friends, and now you do this to me. One would think that you have your own designs on the curate."

"Katy!" exclaimed Rose. "Do not vex yourself so. I have not as of yet gone to the rectory. I was up early and decided to make a trip to the post to see if I had a letter from my cousin. We will walk over to the rectory after breakfast is done. You may come with me then, if you like."

"Oh," was the only word that came out of Katy's mouth as she flounced back up the stairs to prepare herself for the day. Rose went into the kitchen and began to work on some breakfast—a task Mrs. Monks would tend to, but she was still in bed. She was just about finished with the preparation when Katy came down the stairs.

Rose looked at her in exasperation. She was wearing one of her best gowns festooned with an abundance of ribbon and lace. Though it was very pretty and made Katy look very beautiful, Rose could not see how she planned to be of much service in such a dress. It was very possible that it would get very dirty and even ruined if Katy were to attempt any work in it.

Rose was just about to suggest she change when Katy began to speak. "Oh Rose, do you like my dress? I have had it for some time now, but there has never been an occasion to wear it, save for today. Oh, I do hope that the curate will like it." Rose did not respond. She placed the eggs on the small table along with some bread and some cheese and sat down.

They ate their small breakfast quietly and then headed out the door toward the rectory. The dress was very difficult for Katy to walk a distance in, so it took them quite some time to reach the rectory. When they finally arrived, Katy was tired and wished to straighten herself out before they knocked. She patted down her dress and pinched her cheeks. After about a minute of preening, they knocked on the door.

Henry opened the door, and a look of shock covered his face. Before him stood two very different ladies. Katy, in her finest apparel, looked very pretty, but out of place at the modest rectory. Rose, on the other hand, was dressed very modestly. Her simple blue frock was serviceable, and easy to work in. It also accentuated her character and gentle manner, making her look even more beautiful than the silly girl who stood behind her.

"Please, come in," said Henry, and he opened the door wider.

Katy charged in and headed directly to the parlour, where she could rest on one of the chairs. Rose walked slowly behind her, and as she passed Henry, she gave him a look as if to say "Don't ask," and he certainly would not.

Rose and Henry entered the parlour together, and Katy scowled at the poor Mr. Hyden. "Well, aren't you going to offer me a glass of water or a cup of tea?" she demanded. "I am quite thirsty after such a long trek to this place."

Rose was horrified at Katy's behaviour, but Henry seemed to be trying to hold back a laugh.

"Of course, Mademoiselle. Which would you prefer? The tea may take a while to brew, but I can have a glass of water for you within minutes if that is what would please you the best." There seemed to be a twinkle in his eye as he said this, and Rose wondered what kind a mischief he could be up to, but she had no way of asking.

"I guess a glass of water will have to do, but be quick about it. I don't think that I could wait a couple of minutes. It is so insufferably hot these days."

Now both Rose and Henry were fighting back laughter.

"As you wish, Mademoiselle," replied Henry. Then he turned to Rose. "Would you like anything? Perhaps a glass of water, or a cup of tea?"

"I am quite all right, thank you. Do not exert yourself on my behalf, but I would like to know about Mr. Taylor. Has his health improved much overnight? I would like to visit him if that would be all right, but if he is too tired, do not disturb him."

"Mr. Taylor is doing quite well, and he should be back on his feet within the next week. I was just about to bring him his breakfast tray, but if you will wait but a minute, I will bring Katy her glass of water, and then we can go to Caleb's room together. I think that he would very much enjoy your company."

"I would like to visit with the curate as well," burst in Katy angrily. "So let's just forget all this silliness about a glass of water and visit him immediately. He's bound to be awful lonesome for company, and he will also need someone to care for his needs. I am perfectly capable of helping in that area."

"But, Katy," Rose said, rather surprised, "I thought you were dreadfully thirsty. Wouldn't you like to have your glass of water first, before you tend to the curate? It would be much to your benefit, don't you think?"

"Nonsense, Rose. I never said I was dreadfully thirsty, and I will survive quite well. Now, the curate is waiting for his breakfast. We shouldn't keep him waiting any longer than need be." She turned accusing eyes toward Mr. Hyden, then began up the stairs. Rose and Henry followed a way behind after collecting the breakfast tray.

When she had the chance, Rose turned to Henry and asked, "How can you find Katy's behaviour so amusing? It is rude, and she has not considered that her station is more than likely lower than yours. She has treated you with impertinence, yet you laugh."

Henry let out a low chuckle at this observation. "I fear, Miss Wooden, that young Katy does not have the intelligence you have acquired. To her, I am in a lower rank because I have not told her of my permanent place of residence. I can laugh at her behaviour toward myself because she reminds me so much of home. There, the ladies act in much the same way to the servants who are taught to ignore the taunts, and to fulfill whatever command as quickly as possible. I will admit that I used to dismiss servants in that manner as well, but now that I have been put in their situation, I can't help but find it humorous."

Rose gave a slight smile at the thought of many ladies acting as Katy did. "You must be very rich then. You speak of ladies and servants as if they are a common occurrence in your life. It makes me wonder what family you come from. Unfortunately, I do not know the noble families all that well, and there are far too many with sons named Henry."

"You wonder out loud to me, yet you do not ask me what my title is. You seem content with the name Henry. Why do you not ask? You wonder, but do you really want to know the truth, or are you refraining from asking so as to avoid the truth?" Henry asked curiously.

"I have decided that you will tell me your identity when you are ready, once you know you can trust me. Until then, your secret is safe, and I hold onto the truth of your first name."

He thought about telling her his full name then, for he did trust her explicitly. But they had come to Caleb's room, and Katy was waiting impatiently in the hall for them.

Her eyes shot daggers at both Rose and Henry, but she took out her fury on Henry. "You are much too tardy. For all you know, Mr. Taylor could be famished in there, and you are taking your time dallying on the stairs before you serve him his meal. Have you no compassion for his health? Now, be quick with you." Henry threw a look over his shoulder at Rose that made her laugh, then entered the room.

Katy followed closely behind Mr. Hyden, but she stopped in the doorway as if unsure of where to go or what to do. Rose made her way past the stunned girl and raced to the curate's bedside.

"How are you, Caleb? I hope you are feeling much better today. The sickness took its toll on you, but you are strong and I hope that you will be able to get up very soon."

Katy seemed to unfreeze from her spot at the sound of Caleb's laugh and she moved forward just in time to see the look on his face when he turned to Rose and said, "I am doing much better, thank you, Rose. I do not feel that tired at all, and I hope to get out of this bed very soon. I did have a very lovely conversation with James last night, and it has seemed to heal my soul a very little bit."

"Now, what could you and James be talking about late at night that would cause your spirits to heal a little bit, as you say? Let me guess. You spoke of politics and the war. But, of course, that would never do, for such talk would probably make you wish you were ill again."

Caleb laughed heartily and replied, "Politics, Rose? You would surely get along with James here. He seems to enjoy politics greatly. No, we talked nothing of politics at all. Rather, we spoke of truth and honesty. A conversation that only a pastor would enjoy, but it did me much good, and I think that it may be the very reason for my bolstered spirits."

Katy seethed as Rose, James, and Caleb bantered with each other. How could Rose be so selfish? Why couldn't she have just told Katy that "Caleb" was already in love with her. It would have saved Katy the trip to the rectory and the time she had spent preparing the dress that no one would take note of. It wasn't fair, and Katy wanted justice.

She sidled up to the bed that the curate rested on, and with a pretty pout on her face and the batting of her eyelashes, she said, "Why, Mr. Taylor, these two have no compassion for your health. They came to bring you breakfast, and instead of serving you the meal, they banter with you until you are near famished. And look at this tray. There is not one thing to drink."

Henry looked a little sheepish at the remark about the tray, for he had done his best, but the curate's face grew quite solemn and cold at Katy's remark. "Thank you for your concern, Miss Monks, but my friends' banter does me no harm. As for a beverage, I am quite thirsty and glad that you have noticed the absence of liquid. Would you mind terribly bringing me a cup of tea that would quench my thirst?"

Katy's anger burned within, but she could not object to the pastor's request. She quickly consented and slipped out of the room. She muttered her loathing under her breath as she headed to the kitchen. It did not take her long to return to the room where she found the three talking again, the breakfast tray forgotten.

The morning passed by agonizingly slowly for Katy and much too quickly for Rose. On their way home, a smile resided on Rose's face. She had enjoyed her time greatly, and she had only been persuaded to leave when Caleb's stomach had growled, and she realized that he would not eat until she left. He was a very good friend, and had shown her many kindnesses. She hoped that she could visit him again tomorrow, but it would be Sunday, and many people would be going out to visit the young pastor.

The rest of the day passed slowly for Rose. Katy left to visit with her friend May Evans as soon as she was able to change out of her overly extravagant dress, and Rose was left with little to do around the house. She found some odd jobs to do, but they did not last long. She was not in the humour to read her book, so she finally decided to sew out in the back yard.

The dress she was sewing was simple but elegant, and it didn't take her long to finish. She was just putting the last stitch in as the hour struck six. She placed the new dress in her trunk and went to help with dinner. Katy came in while the food was being prepared with a smile on her face.

"You seem to be in a much better mood. One would think that your time at the Evans' was more favourably spent then the time at the rectory," Rose remarked as she watched Katy dawdle about the kitchen. She seemed unaware of the pots boiling and the work that Rose and Mrs. Monks were doing for the dinner that would be served later on.

"May and I had a wonderful time. She is a true friend. I know I can trust her with all my secrets, and she won't backstab me like some of the other girls might. Plus, her father is quite rich and can afford so many luxuries. He was a colonel, you know." Katy continued to prattle, but Rose ignored her. It was useless information that would not benefit her in any way.

"May wanted to go down to the rectory, but I told her it was no use, because the curate already has designs on a girl. She couldn't believe this, but I persuaded her of it."

Katy now had Rose's full attention.

"What do you mean that Mr. Taylor already 'has designs' on a girl? Which girl? I have heard nothing about this, and you seemed determined to catch his attention this morning. Surely no girl could have caught his attention between the time we left the rectory and you walked to the Evans' house."

"Don't be silly, Rose," replied Katy. "You know exactly who I'm talking about, and don't try to deny it."

Rose was shocked at the venom in Katy's tone, and feared what would happen if she asked another question, so she allowed Katy to continue her gossip as she finished up dinner, all the while wondering who Caleb could have feelings for.

ELEVEN

S UNDAY PASSED QUICKLY. Rose was unable to visit with Caleb, because the rectory was quite swamped with visitors, and when she arrived again on Monday, the house seemed just as occupied. When she entered the parlour, she saw heads turn and some old biddies begin to whisper. She ignored the change in the atmosphere, and looked for Henry.

She found him in the kitchen trying to make an escape through the back door. It appeared as if all the eligible women had taken it upon themselves to visit the poor, sick curate, and nearly all of them had shown some form of resentment toward the traveler, Mr. Hyden. He didn't understand the reason for it, but he was determined to leave the house to Mrs. Meps' care.

Rose slipped out of the house with Henry, and when they were on the street, she was better able to ask him questions. "So, how is Caleb? He must be exhausted with all this company coming through. Wouldn't the ladies understand the need for him to rest and get better?"

Henry laughed. "You would think they would understand this, but they seemed most determined to sway the minister while he is so weak. As to his health, it is much improved. He seems to thrive on the company of others, and he was even out of his bed and walking around yesterday. His recovery shouldn't take much longer. As you have said many times before, he is strong."

"Good," replied Rose. "But that brings me to another question. On Saturday evening, Katy suggested that Caleb has feelings for a particular girl, and she would not say who the girl was, because she was certain that I already knew. I must admit that she has piqued my curiosity, for I know of no such girl."

Henry thought about this for a while, then replied, "I know of the girl you speak of, Rose, but I honestly do not think that I should be sharing this information with you. If you ask Caleb, he will be sure to tell you."

Rose and Henry entered the town, where people were going about their business. As they walked past the tailor's shop, Rose heard two ladies whispering, and turned very pink when she recognized what they were speaking of. She determined to ignore them. She straightened her shoulders and continued walking. She had just about gotten over the comments made by the elderly ladies when they passed a group of young, giggling girls.

As they walked by, the girls' conversation turned to quick whispers, but no matter how softly they spoke, Rose could still hear what they were talking about, and again she flushed pink. She made her shoulders even straighter and continued to walk.

Henry noted the change in Rose's posture, but remained oblivious to the whispers of the gossiping women. He was just about to ask Rose what the matter was when a gentleman from the church stepped up. "Why, isn't this a pretty sight? Miss Rose Wooden, you should be ashamed of yourself. You are only here for three months, and already you put a mark on our community. You are a fast one, aren't you? It's no wonder they sent you from home."

Henry stiffened at these words, and he stepped in to defend Rose from the maliciousness of the man's words. "What is your quarrel with Miss Wooden that you would speak of her so cruelly? I have not seen a single mar on her character that you would accuse her so."

The man seemed to sneer at him. "No, you would not see any harm in Miss Wooden's character, would you? My quarrel with Miss Wooden is in the way she has defiled the curate's house and turned it into a harlot's den."

Henry was about ready to smash his fist into the pompous face of the man before him when Rose gently placed her hand on his arm, and with fire in her voice retaliated against the man before him.

"Your accusation is harsh and unfounded, sir. The sins which you claim are mine have not been committed, and not only mar my name, but also the curate's good name. I believe it would be best if you discontinued these rumours and think about the truth-fulness of the next piece of gossip that you plan to act on."

The man laughed at her. "The curate has done nothing sinful or dishonest. I do not mar his name in any way, and I have good reason to believe that the piece of gossip that was given to me is very truthful. By the way you deny it, I would have to assume that what the whole town is speaking of is the truth."

"What is the whole town speaking of, sir?" cut in Henry. "I have heard nothing of these accusations against Miss Wooden's character, and I would like to set these rumours straight if at all possible, so that as little damage as is possible can be done by thoughtless words."

"I guess I must speak plainly, for the two of you are deter-mined to deny the truth of your sinful actions. The two of you should very well know that the truth has been let out about your relationship, and all that took place the nights that Mr. Taylor and Mrs. Meps were sick. The elders of the church have not yet de-cided how you should be punished for such actions and are going to talk with the curate about it as soon as possible."

Rose stepped back in shock at the implication of the man's words. Henry's fury rose up within him, and it wasn't long before he had wrestled the man to the ground and had begun to beat him. Rose quickly came to her senses and stepped up to Henry to stop him as some men from the neighbouring shops stepped in to help their fallen comrade.

She was knocked roughly to the ground as the men began to brawl with Mr. Hyden. Fear filled her and she had to fight to keep herself from screaming. "Stop it!" she screamed. "Just, stop it." The men looked at her with shock written over their faces.

Tears poured down Rose's face as she continued. "You accuse me of a crime which I have not committed, without first talking with Mr. Taylor or myself or Mr. Hyden. You do not think of how your actions have harmed me or the other parties involved. Instead, you brawl like a bunch of mad dogs in the town square, fighting to defend their territory. What crime have I committed save that of being the victim of gossip? You all ought to be ashamed of yourselves. You say you are men of the church, but you are so concerned with justice that you do not first seek evidence of guilt. I am innocent of all you have accused me of. While I was at the rectory, I worked to heal those who were within. I did not leave until there was one well enough to care for the other two ailing."

"How do we know you didn't do more than just physical healing while you were there? Rumour has it that you were pretty comfortable with Mr. Hyden. How do we know that you are as innocent as you claim?" spat out the man who had first approached Rose.

Fire built up within Rose as she turned toward him. "What you are insinuating, sir, is vulgar, and I choose to ignore it. If you are determined of my guilt then, I will not be able to persuade you otherwise, but for all the rest of you, I would expect you to trust my honour, the honour of Mr. Hyden and Mrs. Meps, and the honour of the curate himself. I have nothing further to say." With one last meaningful glare at the men, Rose dusted off her skirt, and walked away, tears pouring down her face.

All the men watched her slight figure disappear. Some turned away in disgust, while others had a new look of respect on their face for her. Henry stood in place the longest. His lip bled from where it had been ripped open, and his eye was beginning to swell, but all he could think about was Miss Rose Wooden. He had retaliated against these men with his fists, and lost miserably. She had retaliated with truth, and won at least some over. Either way, her method had been much more effective.

Mr. Taylor sat in stony-faced silence as he listened to the elders make their accusations against Mr. Hyden and Miss Wooden. He heard them speak lies as truth and watched as they shred to pieces the reputation of Miss Wooden. By the time they were done, he had to fight to hide his fury. "We therefore ask you, Curate," said Mr. Walters, one of the elders, "what would be the best method of punishment for these two sinners?"

Caleb could not answer for quite some time, and the silence in the room grew stiff and uncomfortable. When he finally had control over his emotions, he spoke.

"Good men of the church, I do not know why you come and bother me with gossip and lies. If your accusations against Miss Wooden and Mr. Hyden were anywhere close to being valid, I would have notified you immediately. Instead, you have come to me, and I have allowed you to destroy the names of a brother and a sister in Christ without any evidence.

"While Miss Wooden resided at the rectory in the past week, she spent her entire time caring for the ill. On her first day present, she worked with our housekeeper Mrs. Meps, caring for both Mr. Hyden and myself, for we were both ill. Mrs. Meps fell ill that evening, and Miss Wooden stayed the night caring for all members of the household. The next day, Mr. Hyden's and Mrs. Meps' fever broke, but both were still too ill to leave their beds. The third and fourth day were much the same as the first two. Both Mr. Hyden and Mrs. Meps were past the worst of the disease, but still too weak to move far from their beds.

"On the fourth night, I nearly died. The fever ravaged my body, and if it weren't for Miss Wooden, I would have perished while the other two slept. My fever broke early the fifth morning. Miss Wooden was exhausted from the previous sleepless nights, and she slept the whole day through with Mrs. Meps attending to her when needed. That evening, the Monks came to take Miss Wooden home."

The elders sat in silence, not knowing how to respond. Finally, Mr. Walters, the most vocal of the elders spoke up. "If this is true, then who would start such a malicious rumour, for surely justice must be served for slighting someone's name to this degree."

Caleb let out a groan. "Good sirs, listen to yourselves. You were just asking that justice be served against Miss Wooden for a wrong she did not commit. Now that your accusations have been proven false, you seek justice in another area. I believe the proper course of action at this time would be to show mercy to the gossiper and take some of the responsibility on ourselves, for we were all privy to the harm done to Miss Wooden and Mr. Hyden by our own words and actions. Now, I could really use some rest, for I plan to be ready to give a sermon on Sunday, and I still need time to heal."

The elders of the church mumbled their goodbyes and apologies as they left the room. Most of them looked shamed for their part in the day's events, and others still sought justice, but nothing could be done for it. Caleb sank into his bed and prayed a quick prayer that Rose would not have to deal with a confrontation such as the one he had just experienced, for gossip spread quickly in a small town, and it could do a lot of damage on the way through.

He was just falling asleep when there was a knock on the door. He called for the visitor to enter, and in walked Henry. One look at his bruised and bloodied face told Caleb that he may have prayed his prayer a little too late, and he quickly gave up another prayer for an abundance of mercy and compassion to be given to Henry and Rose so that they would be able to deal with the public stares and false accusations that would be made against them for the next little while.

Henry sat down on the chair by the bed and let out a sigh. "You are not surprised by my appearance, so I am assuming that you have had a meeting with the elders of the church already. Do you also believe their accusations? Or are you the only one in this small town who does not believe all the gossip he hears?"

Caleb heard the venom in Henry's voice and took his time to respond. "I have had a meeting with the elders, and I take it you have had a confrontation with one of the townspeople. I am sorry about their accusations. They do not know what they speak of, and they do not consider others' feelings before they speak. I ask on behalf of the church that you forgive all those who have wronged you."

Henry groaned. "How I wish it were that easy, Caleb. At first I thought that I could hold my temper in check, but when they spoke of Miss Wooden in that manner... I guess I could no longer contain my anger. They called her a harlot! Can you believe that? To degrade her to such a name when they have no evidence of her guilt. And it was her they degraded. They said nothing of my actions, but placed all the blame on her. They were despicable, yet she handled it all like a lady."

Caleb stiffened. "What do you mean, she handled it? Was Rose present when these accusations were made against her? Would men be so crude as to talk to her in such a manner? She is a lady! Such things are not supposed to be mentioned in front of a lady!"

Henry let out another groan. "We were walking toward town to escape the melee of eligible young females who came to visit you. A man from the church came up to us and made the accusation. I pummelled him to the ground and then was beaten by half a dozen other men. Rose then proceeded to shame us all with a couple words."

The silence in the room burned as hot as coals as the men raked through their anger at the injustice done to their friend. Caleb thought of the tears on Rose's face when she spoke of how ill he had been. Her kind compassion had caused her to care for all members of the rectory at her own risk, and it had nearly cost her

her reputation. He longed to go to her and comfort her, but he knew that it was impossible at this time. He would have to find a way to make it up to her as soon as possible.

Rose wiped her tears as she walked. She would not give in to them. Whoever had started the rumour had been out to hurt her, but she would not give them that victory. Lies held no weight and would not stand against truth. She continued to tell herself this as she walked, but she could not hold back her cry to God. *Why, oh Lord? Why did you let this happen? Have I not suffered enough? I am without home and family because you have willed it so, but is it also your will to take my reputation and my respect?*

For the first time in a long time, Rose had the urge to scream, but she couldn't, because people were watching. Instead, she went back in her memory to the last time she had felt so abandoned by God.

Aunt Agatha looked her up and down. A sneer curled her lips, and dislike for the child in front of her filled her eyes. "So, you are my niece, the daughter of my poor, dead sister." Her sneer seemed to increase. "Well, come along. We don't want to keep your uncle waiting." She walked away, and the scared ten-year-old Rose was left to fall in step behind her.

They came up to the carriage and Aunt Agatha entered. Rose followed behind and the two sat silently. Rose did not wish to speak, and she was glad that she wasn't asked any questions, but she hated the way her new aunt glared at her as if she were a mark on a beautiful day. Those piercing eyes made her squirm and fidget.

"Sit still." The order came from the sneering lips that were nearly as dangerous as the eyes. "I will have you know, Rose Wooden, that I do not appreciate your presence in my house, but your uncle could not say no when we heard about the death of your parents. If you do anything that disturbs me or causes trouble for me or my family, you will be out in the streets before you can say boo. Do you understand me?" Rose nodded. "Answer me respectfully, girl!"

"Yes, Madame," replied Rose, and she tilted her head down toward her toes. She didn't dare look up into those eyes, and she feared what other remarks might come out of her aunt's mouth if she did something wrong. It would be best if she made a supreme effort not to offend anyone by her actions.

The weeks passed by agonizingly slowly. Uncle Murdoch was busy working and was rarely seen. Her cousin John was fifteen years old and liked to spend time with his friends. Rose remembered passing the time with the servants trying to please her aunt. She rarely spoke, and often cried herself to sleep at night.

On one particular night as Rose was crying, she remembered something her mom had told her. She had been crying when she was little, and her mom had told her when she was sad that she could just talk with Jesus and he would make it all right. So, slowly got down on her knees and said a sad prayer to Jesus. When she was finished, she felt a little bit better, but nothing seemed to have changed, so she crawled back up into her bed and went to sleep.

The next day, Aunt Agatha was in a very bad mood. Uncle Murdoch was away on business, and she was very frustrated with some of the servants who would not obey. She took out her wrath on Rose. "What are you doing, child!" she yelled as Rose slipped into the kitchen. Rose didn't know how to answer, so she just looked up into those eyes.

"Are you stupid? Answer me, girl. I am not in the mood to trifle with you." Rose just kept looking up into those eyes, and she began to tremble. "Enough." She grabbed Rose by the ear, dragged her to a chair, and told her to sit there until she could come up with a reply.

Rose sat there for the rest of the day until her aunt sent her to bed with no dinner. She lay there crying until she heard a knock on the door. She held her breath, hoping that if she didn't reply the person at the other side of the door would think she was asleep. It didn't work. The door cracked slightly open, and John walked in with a plate of food.

That had been the start to her relationship with John. He had taught her everything she needed to know in life, and he had helped her get over the death of her parents. Slowly she had regained some of her confidence, and she was able to live with her aunt. She learned to be independent and do things for herself. She never asked for anything, but she took it all in stride. And when the stress became too much, there was always John.

Rose wept when she realized that John wasn't there this time to bring her a plate of food. He wasn't there to tell her it would be all right, and he wouldn't be able to comfort her from so far away. She quickly brushed away the tears, for tears were a sign of weakness. She quickened her strides to get back to the Monks. She thought of her mother's long lost words again.

Did Jesus really make things all better when she prayed her sad prayers? She was tempted to get down on her knees in the middle of the road and pray, but her anger at the situation got in the way. How could God allow such a thing to happen? It would take awhile for her to be able to pray to the God that seemed to have abandoned her.

As Rose walked up the drive to the Monks' house, she spotted Katy and May Evans looking at her mischievously. She could only imagine the sight she must be, for crying was not a benefit to one's appearance. She walked quickly past them, her shoulders held high. She would not let others degrade her any more than they already had. They could laugh, but she was stronger than that. She had to be stronger than that.

"I told you it would work," whispered May to Katy as Rose walked past. "Her reputation is pretty much ruined already, and Mr. Taylor cannot have a wife with a ruined reputation. All we had to do was somehow let it slip to Mrs. Avol that all was not as it seemed, and now the whole town knows."

"Are you sure about this?" replied Katy hesitantly. "I mean, will it really work? What if the curate finds out it was us who started the rumour? Won't he be really mad? A minister cannot have a liar as a wife, either."

"Don't be silly, Katy," said May. "The Curate will never find out that we slipped the news to Mrs. Avol. Besides, we never really lied. We just planted ideas. Mrs. Avol is the one that did all the lying, and now Miss Wooden's reputation is ruined, and the curate is sure to fall in love with you."

Katy's eye lit up when May mentioned love and her voice took on a dreamy note. "Do you really think that he will fall in love with me? He is so terribly handsome," she sighed. "To love a man like the curate would be wonderful." May rolled her eyes at her friend, but Katy didn't notice.

The truth was, May had no designs on the pastor at all. He was much too old for her liking. But she did detest Miss Rose Wooden. She burned with jealousy. Since Miss Wooden had come, the town had talked of nothing else. Even her father had mentioned how pretty the little Miss Wooden was. It wasn't fair. *She* was to be the belle of the town, not Rose.

May had wished to seek revenge on Miss Wooden, but had never come across an opportunity. That was, until Katy had come over on Saturday. Katy was so much in love with the minister, and wished to marry him, but he was already in love with Miss Wooden, or at least according to Katy he was. May had used the information Katy had given her about Rose to plant a rumour that would be enough to exact her revenge.

Rose would pay. Of that, May was certain. She turned her attention back to Katy, who was still mooning over the curate. She listened to her talk for a while longer, then made her excuses and walked home where she could revel in her victory.

TWELVE

ROSE WOKE EARLY THE NEXT MORNING. She felt like hiding under the covers for shame, but she was determined not to be harmed by the malicious lies being spread about her. She dressed quickly, and made her way to the post. Miss Mede waited by the counter sorting letters. When Rose entered, the young girl blushed and tried to hide it.

Rose bit her lip to stop the words that wanted to spew from her mouth. The young girl could not be expected to know what was the truth and what wasn't. Rose walked up to the counter and cheerfully asked for the mail. The young girl didn't respond at first, but then, with big round eyes, she looked up at Rose and asked quietly, "Is it true, Miss Wooden? Can it really be true what they are saying about you and Mr. Hyden? Because I just can't believe it. Mr. Walters was talking about you so meanly, and I just couldn't believe what he said."

Rose saw the tears that built in the girl's eyes and her heart swelled with compassion. "Thank you for your trust in my integrity, Miss Mede. I can assure you that it is well founded, and that I did not do any of the things that people have been suggesting I have done. Both Mr. Hyden and I are modest persons with nothing of disrespect between us."

Miss Mede seemed assured by her words. She nodded and then looked back up with a small smile on her face. "He's falling in love with you, you know. He won't admit it, but he really is—quite quickly, too, I think."

"What do you mean? Are you speaking of Mr. Hyden?" Rose was quite confused. What would posses Miss Mede to say such a thing? There was no way that Henry was falling in love with her. He was much too noble, and she was much too simple. But, of course, Miss Mede would not know that he was a noble. She would think him a common traveler, which would make the two of them seem much better suited than reality dictated.

"He speaks of you quite often when he comes in asking for his mail, and he always says such nice things about you. He is such a handsome fellow. The two of you would be perfect for each other." Miss Mede blushed at the bluntness of her words. "Forgive me. I should not have spoken so plainly. It was not my place."

"It is quite all right," replied Rose. "Mr. Hyden is a very nice man, and he is sure to make some woman very happy some day, but I do not think that I am that woman. The two of us are good friends, but I don't think that he sees me as any more than that. Neither do I see him as any more than a friend."

"You are probably right." Miss Mede went back to her work, looking for letters addressed to the Monks' household. She handed over one letter addressed to Mr. Monks and Rose bid her farewell, thanking her again for her kindness toward her and Mr. Hyden.

Rose returned to the Monks' house, but she soon grew restless and headed out to go back to town. She wished to miss as many people as possible with their judgmental glares and their scathing whispers, so she walked toward the orphanage. There she would find many innocent persons who would not understand the gossip that passed from stranger to stranger. She also would not have to look at Mr. Hyden, who was sure to be at the rectory with Caleb.

When she arrived, she found the house quite still. Most of the children still suffered from fatigue after the epidemic, and most were not in the mood to be rowdy or at play. Rose didn't see much that she could do, so she headed to the kitchen where she baked cookies and various pastries. It did not take long for the smell of the delicate treats to fill the air, and the sweet aroma put Rose at ease. She began to hum as she worked.

The music rose within her and soon spilled out in words and song. It was a familiar tune and reminded her of home and John. She wished he would write soon. She missed him terribly. Her song finished, and someone started clapping behind her. She jumped and spun around, brandishing a batter-covered wooden spoon.

Henry stood there with Lisa clinging to his leg. He turned to the small child, picking her up in his arms. "That was a beautiful song, wasn't it, Lisa girl? We should persuade Miss Wooden here to sing more often, don't you think?" The little girl giggled and Rose blushed. "But I don't think she will be easily persuaded, so maybe we should just leave her be on that note, and beg her for one of those delicious smelling pastries."

The little girl clapped her hands and dove from Henry's arms to reach for a pastry. She toppled to the ground and started to cry. Rose rushed to pick her up and cradle her in her arms. "Shhh there, babe. It is all right now. Just a little bump on the floor, that's all. Now, now, you are all right. I've got you."

Lisa quieted and snuggled into Rose's shoulder. Henry watched the two quietly. A smile lifted the corners of his mouth as he watched the gentle manner in which Rose treated Lisa, and the look of pleasure that crossed her face when Lisa snuggled her head into her shoulder. Rose would make a good mother some day; of that, he was certain.

Reality kicked in when Rose turned away from him and tried to ignore his presence. She had been hurt badly yesterday, and he needed to apologize for the behaviour of other people and make things right between them again. How he would make things right, he had no idea.

"Rose, I would like to apologize to you for yesterday. The people in the streets were uncommonly cruel and very much misguided. Caleb says that he has straightened things out with the elders, and that the rumour should be silent within a few days. I hope that you will be able to forgive the people of this town, for they really didn't know what they were speaking of."

Rose sighed, but she did not turn to face him. "Why do you apologize for them, Henry? You are not the one who did anything wrong. In fact, you were probably wronged as much as I was by their accusations. Shouldn't the townspeople be asking our forgiveness themselves instead of sending the innocent to do their duty?"

"Maybe they should, but it is unlikely that any person will venture so far as to ask your forgiveness, and that is why I ask on their behalf. I also hope that by asking you to forgive them, you will be able to be comfortable around me again. I would very much like to have back in place the friendship we had before."

Rose grabbed a pastry from the tray, and handed it to the child in her arms. Slowly she turned to Henry. "Very well, Henry. I will forgive the people of the town their false accusations, if that is what you desire, but I do not know if I will be able to walk in front of Caleb again, for the shame that would fill me would be much too great. He is sure to loathe me for bringing him all this trouble."

Henry laughed lightly. "I believe that is as far from the truth as you can get, dear Rose. Caleb was quite peeved when the elders came to visit, and he was still blowing off steam when I returned home. He was hoping that you would stop by today so that he could apologize to you personally and ask you to come to dinner at the rectory this Sunday along with the Monks."

Relief swept through Rose and she smiled up at Henry. "Thank you for bringing me this news. I think that I would have been most uncomfortable attending service on Sunday if you had not told me this. I almost did not make my trip to the post this morning for shame, but Miss Mede was very polite and assured me of her support."

"You still attend the post every morning? I have visited the post quite often, but I have not been for the past few days, because no matter how often I go, it seems that my father has not written. He has not even responded to my first letter which I sent out, which is very odd indeed. Perhaps I will visit again tomorrow. There is sure to be a letter there by now."

Rose smiled at Henry's musings, and placing the child on the floor she went back to work. Henry took a seat at the counter, and Lisa climbed into his lap. The two of them munched on pastries while Rose worked. The silence was comfortable, but Rose soon became unnerved by the thought that Henry was watching her.

She glared at him. "Don't you have something you're supposed to be doing? Maybe helping Mrs. Jennings, or doing something at the rectory to help Mrs. Meps and Caleb. You should do something, don't you think?" Henry laughed and consented to her wishes. He placed Lisa on the floor and went to find Mrs. Jennings.

Rose lay in her bed until late that night. Once Katy was sleeping soundly, she slipped into her mask and a pair of inexpressibles, and grabbing her sword, she headed toward the pasture. Josh was waiting for her, and he looked miserable. "Why weren't you here the past two weeks?" he asked angrily. "I waited and I waited, and you never showed up. Where were you?"

"Forgive me, Josh," Rose replied calmly. "The epidemic kept me busy, so that I was unable to come and practice with you. Next time, I will find a way to send a message to you so that you will not wait so terribly long for me."

Josh seemed to take this in. "Well, I guess I can forgive you for this, but it wasn't really fair to leave me like that. I thought that maybe you had forgotten about me and weren't going to come and teach me anymore."

"I agree that it wasn't very fair of me, but you must remember that the world is not very fair at all. There will be times when you will be treated unfairly, and there will be times when you are treated unjustly. When you are treated unfairly, you must seek to look beyond it, and extend easy forgiveness. When you are treated unjustly, you must seek justice, but never forget to be merciful as well."

"Very well. I can do that, but can we practice now? I think I am far behind in my training, and it is very important that I keep up the effort." Josh was anxious to keep going and it showed in his features, but Rose was not ready to give up the topic.

"Justice has a lot to do with practicing with the sword, Josh. If you are unjust in wielding a sword, it would have been better for you to have never learned to fight. Justice is key to all acts of aggression. If you act violently without justice, you become cold-hearted and a criminal in many senses. I would therefore have you learn both the knowledge and the skill in this area, so that someday you will become great."

Josh's reply was hesitant. "I guess I could listen to what you have to say for a while. But I would really, really like to fight tonight. If that is all right with you, of course." Josh looked at her hopefully, and she couldn't help but give in. They spent the rest of the night working on Josh's fighting skills.

Rose woke with a start. By the placing of the sun, she could tell it was late in the day and she had overslept. It wasn't like her to oversleep, and it annoyed her. She liked the quiet morning hours, but her lesson with Josh had kept her out very late. She could feel the bags under her eyes. She would have to find a way to get enough sleep before the lesson so that she would be more refreshed the next day.

She dressed slowly, feeling all the aches and pains of overworked muscles. She was out of shape as well. She would have to work on that some more. She walked over to the mirror to brush her hair. In the corner, Katy always had a slip of paper that she kept track of the date on. Rose looked over at it and nearly jumped.

It was the thirtieth of August. It was her birthday! She was eighteen. It was odd to think that she had passed so much time here at the Monks already without even noticing it. Three months had passed, in fact, and she was not anywhere closer to accomplishing her goal. She would have to work on that as well.

She looked in the mirror again and began to fiddle with her hair. She pulled it up and pinned it fancily in the back. Why not celebrate her birthday by looking extra pretty? For there would be no other celebration. She looked at the trunk where she had placed her new dress. Slowly she took it out and put it on. She looked in the mirror with a half-hearted smile, then left the room. There was no use becoming vain.

She walked into the kitchen, but the Monks had already finished their breakfast and were about other tasks. She prepared herself a plate, and sat down to eat. She was eighteen. This was the proper age for marriage, yet she felt much too young to marry. She didn't want to marry at all, if possible, but of course that wasn't possible. She would have to make an effort to find a husband who was tolerable.

She sighed. Mr. Taylor would be a good husband, but he deserved someone who would love him. Caleb was the sort of man who would love with all his heart, and he deserved that type of love in return, which she could never give. No, she could never marry Caleb. She would have to think of someone else.

She could marry Henry. He didn't look like the type to be seeking love, but he was a nobleman. Noblemen were supposed to marry noblewomen, however, and she was far from being a noblewoman. She was an orphan, after all. Henry would therefore have to remain a friend, and she shouldn't think of him anything more than that until she knew his true identity.

She sighed again. Such thoughts were depressing on one's birthday. She should be celebrating, but she hadn't celebrated her birthday since she was ten years old. Her uncle and cousin had tried to persuade her to celebrate her birth, but this was also the anniversary of her father's death, and that she could not celebrate. Remembrance of death and life should not coincide on the same day, she reflected.

Rose cleaned up her dishes, determined to be rid of the overwhelming thoughts. She left the house and walked to the post. Perhaps she would have a letter from John. Miss Mede greeted her kindly and immediately reached for a letter. "This one is addressed to you, Miss Wooden, and it is very heavy. It must have something inside besides the paper."

Rose accepted the letter and felt the weight of money inside. It would have to be from John, for only John would be daft enough to send money through the mail. He was altogether too trusting, and he was most certain that if someone was so desperate as to steal, they must have more need for it than he had. A smile played on Rose's lips as she left the post. She could hardly wait to see what John had to say.

She walked and hummed lightly to herself. She was in a much better mood than she had been when she left, and it seemed as if nothing could make her happier. "Miss Wooden... Rose!" she heard someone call behind her, and she wheeled around to see who it could be.

"Good day, Henry. How are you this fine morning?"

Henry was trying very hard to catch his breath. A smile covered his entire face and lit up his eyes.

"It is the most wonderful news," he said breathlessly. "I have received a letter from my father, and it contains the best of news, and I knew you would be the most blessed by it, so I came as fast as I could to find you."

"Well then, spit it out," Rose said impatiently. His words made her anxious, and she didn't know if she could stand waiting all that long.

Henry took in another deep breath. "The war is over. The king has ended the war, and the soldiers will be back within a month. There is no more fighting, no more death. It is done at last!"

Rose stepped back, stunned. Her mouth gaped open. Could it really be possible? Could the war really be over? "Do you know this for sure? I mean, can your father be certain that what he heard is true? Is the war really over?"

A slow smile crossed Henry's face. "I am as sure as if the king had said it to me himself. My father is very well connected and usually knows things as soon as the king decides on them. Come, Rose. Celebrate with me, and let us go tell Caleb the good news together. He is sure to rejoice over it."

Rose was finally able to smile, and it spread across her entire face, chasing away the last traces of the morning's depression. "Give me a bit of time to bring a letter back to the Monks' house. I do not wish to carry it with me, for I fear I may lose it and that would be very dreadful indeed."

"Then let me walk with you, so that I will not be tempted to share my good news with Caleb while I wait for you." The two began to walk. Rose was so happy, and a smile rested on her lips. This day, which had started out so horribly, had become so good. She turned her face toward the heavens and she said a quick prayer of thanks to the God that now seemed to remember her.

The walk back to the Monks did not take long, and they were soon on their way to the rectory. Henry and Rose made small talk, but neither of them really felt like talking about anything pertinent. They both wanted to run to the rectory and speak to Caleb, but decorum would not allow them to do such a thing. Instead, they walked quickly and concentrated on the task at hand.

When the rectory was in sight, Rose could not handle it anymore. She hiked up her skirts and began to run. She barged in the front door only to find four ladies from the church sitting with Caleb, who had a look of polite calm on his face. Rose blushed bright pink and straightened out her skirts. She was just about to turn and leave when the door opened and in walked Henry.

Rose did not think she could be any more embarrassed. What would people think of her after they heard about her running into the rectory with Henry following close behind? The rumours were sure to start up again in full force. She tried to make excuses, but Caleb asked her and Henry to stay, and she knew she had no choice.

The two of them sat and listened to the polite conversation that took place around them. "As I was saying before, Curate," said Mrs. Jamison with a pointed look at Rose, who blushed, "we all miss your sermons terribly much, and we are hoping that you will be able to lead us again come Sunday. Is that not right, Jane?"

Jane Jamison was twenty years old, and the only child of Mr. and Mrs. Jamison. She was tall, petite, and terribly shy. She blushed at being acknowledged, and responded with her head down. "I very much enjoy the curate's sermons. He speaks very well on all matters of the Bible." Caleb kindly acknowledged the girl's words, and she blushed even more.

Rose fidgeted. She wanted to cut in and send everyone away, for surely this petty small talk was not worth it. Wasn't it clear to them that Caleb would not fall in love with any of them if they chased after him in such a manner? She was about to let out a soft sigh when she saw Caleb's face. He was politely responding to Mrs. and Miss Cummings, and though he did not particularly like all the women chasing after him, he had a look of compassion about his face. He would not turn any of them away, and the thought of it shamed Rose.

She turned to hide her blush, and she determined to patiently wait out the visit. The Jamisons did not take long to leave, but the Cummings seemed determined to stay. Mrs. Cummings talked on and on about the goings on at the church, and reported all the town gossip. She nearly mentioned the rumour, about Henry and Rose but then remembered that the two were present and contained herself.

It took some time, but Mrs. Cummings finally ran out of topics, and the room fell deadly silent. No one spoke a word, and no one moved. Rose fidgeted again, because she wanted to give Caleb her news, but she didn't dare speak in the presence of the other ladies. Finally, Mrs. Cummings stood. "Well, we best be on our way. Miss Wooden, we will be walking toward the Monks' house. Would you like to join us."

Rose finally understood why the ladies would not leave. They did not want to leave her with the two men unattended. Rose nearly laughed at the thought, but replied politely, "No thank you, Mrs. Cummings. I believe I will stay for a while longer. I would like to talk with Mr. Taylor and Mr. Hyden for a while longer."

Mrs. Cummings gave her a cold stare, but she left quietly with her daughter. When the room was finally empty, Rose let out a heavy sigh. "At last," she said. "We have so much to tell you, Caleb, that I didn't think I could make it through such a visit. It seemed to go on terribly long."

Caleb chuckled lightly. "You did very well waiting then. And might I add that you looked very pretty while you waited. Your dress is new and does you justice. Is there an occasion for such dress? Perhaps that is what your news is about."

"My news had nothing to do with the way I dress, but if I had been given this news this morning, I certainly would have chosen a more festive dress. I would like to share the news immediately, but I fear it is more Henry's news to share." Rose stopped cold. She had just used Henry's real name. She looked at him worriedly, but he seemed relaxed enough. She turned to Caleb, who laughed again.

"Then, Henry," he said, "tell us the news, and do not hold me in suspense any longer. What could have possibly brought the two of you here in such a rush?"

166

"I have received a letter from my father. It appears the war is over. The soldiers shall make it back home in a month's time. Things will go back to normal, as they should." A smile lit across Caleb's face and he began to laugh. Tears of joy began to roll down his face, and Rose couldn't help but laugh along. This was such good news, and so refreshing to hear on her birthday.

When Caleb finally finished laughing, he turned to Rose. "This is indeed wonderful news, but it does not explain the occasion for your dress. I am still very curious."

Rose blushed and replied, "I will tell you why I dressed so, if you will tell me how you knew Henry's name. I thought I was the only one to know the truth, and I felt horrible just then for slipping up so."

"Very well. I know Henry's name because he slipped up one night and made mention that he was not who he appeared to be. I questioned him about it, and he told me who he was. That is how I know his name."

"You know his full name? Henry, why haven't you told me your full name if you have trusted Caleb with it? Surely you can trust me." Henry looked cornered by Rose's words, and he clearly did not want to respond, so Caleb cut in.

"Quit deferring the point, Rose. You are supposed to be telling me about your dress, if I recall correctly. Now out with it, for I will not wait any longer."

Rose let out an exaggerated sigh. "Very well then. I did not think that a girl would draw so much attention for dressing up on her birthday. It was just a small thing to trifle with. I did not think that anyone would take notice." She let out another nonchalant sigh.

Henry and Caleb both responded with the same passion. They were both disappointed that she had not told them it would be her birthday, and determined there should be a celebration as soon as possible so that they could wish her the best in years to come. She tried to dissuade them, explaining that she had not celebrated her birthday since she was ten years of age, but they would not be dissuaded.

"Surely, you must have celebrated your birthday many times since you were ten. No girl can go without celebrating the year she comes of age, or commemorating her first ball. You must be jesting that you haven't celebrated in that much time," said Henry. He had a look of shock on his face that emphasized his disbelief.

"I am speaking the utter truth," replied Rose. "My last celebration was on my tenth birthday, and my last seven birthdays have passed without much notice. It has never been a matter of much importance to me. What is the day but just that, another day?"

"It is a special day, for it is a day that marks a milestone, another page turned, another year passed. We would truly like to celebrate with you, but if you do not wish it, at least come tomorrow evening with the Monks family so that we can celebrate with you privately. I'm sure that Mrs. Meps will make a marvellous meal," encouraged Caleb.

Rose hesitated. "All right. I guess it would do me no harm to come tomorrow evening with the Monks to celebrate my birthday, but you must promise me you will not make any mention of birthdays. If they ask why you have invited them, tell them of the war ending instead, for that certainly is what I will be celebrating."

Henry and Caleb both gave her a smile as she stood. It was time for her to go. She did not want gossip spreading, as it surely would if she spent too much time under the curate's roof again. Besides, she had a letter from her cousin waiting for her at home. She would see the two of them tomorrow. Now it was time for her to return home.

THIRTEEN

ROSE SMILED TO HERSELF AS SHE WALKED back to the Monks. The two men had acted exactly as her cousin acted every year. He always insisted on a celebration, but Rose never would have any of it. John would always succumb to her wishes, but buy her some extravagant gift.

She recalled the time that he had bought her the sword she now used. He had been anxious that whole day, and when night finally came, he had brought it to her. Her shriek of joy nearly woke the whole house, and he had to tackle her to keep her quiet. The two had spent the rest of the night talking and laughing, trying their very best to keep quiet.

Other times, John had brought her a hair clip or some fabric for a dress or a book that she would enjoy. He always seemed to know what she would like, and she loved him for it. Such thoughts brought a longing for home, and she quickened her steps so that she could read his letter as soon as possible.

She ripped into the envelope as soon as she was alone in her room. Some coins fell out, but she did not take the time to count them. She was more concerned with the words on the parchment.

My Dearest Rose,

Happy birthday! It distresses me that I cannot be there to celebrate with you, so I sent some coins so that you will be able to buy a new dress, or at least some fabric. Promise me you will buy something that you will enjoy. I hope you have friends who will celebrate with you, but if not, we will celebrate when you come home.

Now that the birthday salutations are done, I have other news that you may have heard, but I believe it will bring as much joy a second time through. The king has signed a decree that has marked the end of the war! When I heard the news, I couldn't help but think of the joy you would experience from it.

The soldiers will be home within one month's time, and while we wait for their return, the king has commissioned towns to set up hospitals for the injured to return to. Those that require doctors' attention will remain at the hospitals already in service, but those who only need tending and care can go to the hospitals close to home to be tended to by the locals.

There will be traveling doctors to visit each local hospital once every two weeks.

Oh Rose, this news is so wonderful that it has put everyone at home into good spirits. Father is improving and moving about. He also sends his regards to you and many birthday wishes. I think I may have even caught mother singing the other day. I cannot remember the last time I heard her sing!

I miss you dreadfully, and I wish that you were here to celebrate with me. There is to be a ball held here when the soldiers arrive home. I wouldn't be surprised if you attend many of your own balls this coming autumn and winter. I hope you will have many dance partners. As for me, I will be dancing with Emily Drake. She is a very pretty girl.

All the best in your conquest,

Your loving cousin,

John Borden

Rose looked at the coins in her lap and finally decided to count them. Her eyes grew big and round when she realized there was more than enough money to buy two dresses. She would buy enough fabric for one dress for now, and she would decide what to do with the rest of the money later. She smiled again, then went to find the Monks to tell them of the curate's invitation to dinner the following evening.

Henry and Caleb sat in the parlour that Rose had just vacated. Neither spoke, and the slight ticking of a clock was the only sound to be heard. A small smile rested on Henry's lips as he thought of the disregard that Rose treated her birthday with. He never would have guessed that someone could care so little about the passing of one year of life. The thought was inconceivable.

He turned to Caleb to share his thoughts. The curate's face was dark and saddened. His eyebrows creased together as he mulled over the thoughts flying through his head. A scowl marred his normally boyishly handsome face, and a storm brewed in his pale eyes.

"A penny for your thoughts," quipped Henry. Caleb jumped from his seat, but sat quickly down again when he realized it was only Henry. He covered his face with his hands and let out a deep agonizing groan.

"She is so young, isn't she, Henry?" he asked sadly. His eyes pleaded with Henry for a favourable answer, but Henry didn't know what to say. He was rather confused as to what Caleb was talking about, and why it was causing him such distress.

"I haven't a clue what you are talking about, Caleb. You act as if the end of the world has come, then you speak of age. I really do not understand."

Caleb threw him a disgusted look, as if to say he should pay more attention. "I was speaking of Miss Wooden, of Rose. She is so terribly young, only eighteen years. Eighteen very, very short years." He let out another moan that could be compared to the moan of a dying animal. This only confused Henry more, for he could not understand such distress over something as trifling as a woman's age.

"What does Rose's age matter to you? Yes, she is eighteen years, and eighteen years is not a long time, but I myself am only one and twenty years. This did not cause you distress, so why should her age cause you any?" Henry was given the disgusted look again.

"Rose's age does not matter so much as it does when compared to my age."

Henry looked at him with confusion, so he continued. "I like Rose, very much, but I am ten years her senior. I am much too old to even be considering marrying her, especially while she is yet so young."

Caleb's words brought a mixture of feelings to Henry. He wanted to encourage Caleb and tell him that ten years was not much to be considered in matrimony. Many men of the time married women twenty or thirty years their junior. But another feeling swelled in him as well. This feeling encouraged him to deter Caleb from pursuing a match with Miss Wooden, for surely the two of them would never get along.

The former feeling won out. "Surely Caleb, you jest. You cannot consider yourself so old that Rose would not consider you. Eight and twenty years is still quite young, and you are nowhere near death. It is only a fool who despairs over ten short years of difference." Caleb looked at him, renewed hope shining in his eyes. A tentative smile touched the corners of his mouth.

"This is your opinion, Henry, but I don't know if I share it. I would love to think that ten years is not a large gap, but what if Rose does not agree with that? I would set myself up for worse despair if I allowed myself to hope. And even if she does not consider ten years such a large gap, what if she does not care for me in the way that I care for her? No, I can hold no hope until I am sure of her feelings."

"Are you always such a pessimist?" asked Henry incredulously. "One would think from your point of view that it is better to believe that the sun will not rise tomorrow, for if it doesn't you will not have had false hope, but if it does you will be pleasantly surprised. Such thinking is barbaric and terribly depressing."

Caleb's eyes widened in shock at such a statement. He blinked a couple times as if to clear his vision of the accusing form before him. "Do you really believe me to be so pessimistic? I assure you that I am not. I was entirely optimistic about a relationship with Rose until she spoke of her age. Now I have lost all hope, for surely such an age difference would distress her greatly in a relationship."

"Have you consulted Rose on this matter?" asked Henry indignantly. "Do you know for certain that this is her opinion? Or is this your own biased conjecture based on your opinion of age?"

Caleb didn't know how to reply, so he sat there quietly, hoping that if he did not respond the subject matter would be dropped and he could return to his misery. Henry remained staring at him until he had no choice but to respond. "Well, I guess it is a bit biased, because I have not yet spoken to Rose on the matter, but…"

"So you admit it!" cut in Henry. "Rose may very well have feelings for you, but you are so pessimistic that you have found a fault in the possibility in order that you will not accumulate false hope!"

"I have admitted no such thing," responded Caleb angrily. "I have only admitted that my opinion is biased and that Rose may very well have feelings for me, but it is unlikely." He did not much appreciate the attitude of the younger person toward him. "She is more likely to fall for you than me because of the age difference, though I admit I hate the thought of it."

"Do you know nothing of love, Caleb? Love does not look at age. Besides, there could be a far greater age difference. You could be nine and forty years old and be desperately in love with the young Miss Wooden. If that were the case, then I believe I would say your position was hopeless, but with only ten years difference? You are a pessimist to believe you cannot have her."

Caleb was getting annoyed. What Henry was saying made sense, but he didn't know if he could bring himself to hope. Hope left room for hurt, and he didn't want to be hurt. "Enough, Henry. I have had enough of this conversation for today. We can discuss it further at another time." He stomped out of the parlour and did not turn, even when Henry called out to him.

Henry sat in his room reading and rereading his father's letter. It was a brief letter that explained his delay in writing and the reason for the end of the war. Nothing further was said about life at the castle, but the king did ask about his son's activities and the new people he had met, especially those of the female gender.

Henry didn't know where to start. He could speak about Caleb and Rose, but his father would read too much into that and think he had feelings for Rose. He could write about the townspeople and their apparent dislike for him, but that would only cause his father to wonder why he stayed. Or he could speak about the epidemic, but then his mother would worry about his health.

Henry blew out a breath of frustration. No matter how he started the letter, he would cause discontent for one of his parents. He dipped his pen into the inkwell and raised it over the paper. A drop of ink splattered onto the page, leaving a dark smudge that could not be erased. Henry laid the pen to the side, crumpled up the paper and tossed it in the wastebasket. He grabbed a new sheet.

Dear Father,

> *Over a month ago, I started to work as a volunteer at a local orphanage. The orphanage has twenty-six children, but with the end of the war, I believe the numbers will decrease dramatically. Mrs. Jennings is the proprietor of the place. She loves the children, but she is old and cannot care for all the children on her own.*

As of late, Rose Wooden, a young lady from Thespane, has been helping with the children as well. She is kind and compassionate and very giving with her time. A week after she had begun work at the orphanage, an epidemic swept through the town, and after she and the curate had finished caring for the Monks family (the home at which Rose resides), the two of them came to help at the orphanage.

I can't begin to express how miserable the work was. When Mrs. Jennings fell ill, Rose, Caleb and I were left to tend to all twenty-six children. I do not know what we would have done if Rose had not been there to cook meals and help us two men with the children. She worked tirelessly, and it is amazing she never fell ill, but the same cannot be said for Caleb and I.

Before I go on, I should make it clear that Caleb Taylor is the curate here in Emriville, and he has provided a place for me to stay in his house. The two of us fell ill, and when we did not show up at the orphanage one day, Rose came to the rectory to help the housekeeper Mrs. Meps tend to us.

When Mrs. Meps fell ill, Rose stayed five days straight to care for us, with little sleep. If it weren't for her, Caleb would surely have died, for on the fourth night he burned with such a fever that his whole body shook. Rose stayed with him the entire night trying to break the fever, and wasn't successful until the early morning hours.

I speak highly of Rose because she is a wonderful woman who is sure to make Caleb a good wife someday. She is my friend, and though any man would be lucky to take her as a wife, I fear it shall never be so for the two of us. She does not trust me and knows me to be a noble. If you are ever in the neighbourhood of Emriville, I would suggest that you stop by and visit the intriguing Rose Wooden, and the kind and considerate Curate Caleb Taylor.

These have been the acquaintances and friends that I have made while staying in this town. I have not yet found a female friend that I would take as my wife, but I do not give up hope. I fear, though, that I will not be able to leave this town without causing a tear in my heart, for these people have become very dear to me. I will consider moving on after the soldiers have returned, but until then I will remain.

Send my regards to Mother and tell her I miss her dreadfully. While I was ill, all I could think of was her gentle tending while I was a child. Assure her that I am in fine health now, and that I will write again soon.

I am proceeding as if my identity is still safe, but if this ever changes, please notify me immediately.

Your loving son,
Henry Arden

Katy was all aflutter. She couldn't decide which dress to wear, and she had Rose redo her hair three times. Each time she found a fault with the style, whether it be that Caleb liked women to wear their hair up, or ringlets should be worn around the face, and they should not be pulled back so tight. She was starting to get on Rose's nerves.

Rose was not looking forward to tonight's celebration. She feared it would slip out that it had been her birthday yesterday, and she would be expected to celebrate. Any direct celebration of her birthday she must refuse. She decided that the best way to deflect attention given towards her was to wear a simple dress and hair-style. With Katy's fancy outfit, there were sure to be no eyes on her.

She chose to wear an older blue frock. It was simple and elegant, and it would suit for the evening's activities. She pulled her hair back tightly to her head, but let some strands hang loose in the back. The look was pleasing but modest, nothing that would attract attention. She chose to wear no jewellery, save for a small necklace that John had bought her for her eleventh birthday.

As she walked down the stairs, there was a smug look on Katy's face. She looked overdressed and somewhat gaudy in her pink gown with puffed sleeves. Her hair was pulled up in the back, but some curls hung loose in the front, and she was bedecked in so much jewellery that it was a miracle she could still walk. Rose thought the look extravagant, but made no comment.

Mr. Monks was in a festive mood. He openly rejoiced over the news of the returning soldiers, and to show his joy, he had ordered a carriage to carry them the short distance to the rectory. Rose thought the notion silly, but she wasn't going to object. The Monks and Rose piled into the carriage and were off.

It took all of five minutes to reach the rectory, but more time was needed to stable down the horses. The women entered the parlour while Mr. Monks tended to this matter. The parlour was neat and in good order, but it looked as if Mrs. Meps had done some extra cleaning in this room before the guests arrived.

Caleb greeted each person individually and Henry followed suit. When he came to Katy, he looked her over carefully, and said in a measured tone, "Why, Miss Monks, you look stunning this evening." Katy blushed and turned to see if the curate had noticed. Caleb took no note of the conversation, because his eyes were held fast to Miss Wooden, who stood back and watched the whole charade with a suppressed smile on her face.

Katy glared at Rose, who had to bite her tongue to keep from laughing. Henry, feeling no qualms at all, chuckled softly, which cost him a petulant glare from the girl in pink. This of course made it impossible for Rose to keep from laughing, and a giggle escaped before she could clasp a hand over her mouth.

Caleb and Mrs. Monks both looked very confused, and Katy looked furious. She let out a huffy breath and said, "Very well then," and took a seat. Mrs. Monks followed suit, and Rose, seeing that she could no longer remain standing, took a seat on one of the sofas. Caleb sat next to her, and Henry settled into one of the corner chairs overlooking the room.

The room fell into an awkward silence. Caleb peeked at Rose from the corner of his eye whenever possible, which made her very uncomfortable. She tried to deflect his attention, but she didn't know how. Thoughts of various conversations she could start up buzzed through her head, but none seemed to suit the occasion. Katy saved her.

"Mr. Taylor, I was wondering how you've been fairing since the epidemic. From my understanding, you were quite ill, and I have been praying quite earnestly that you suffer no more effects from being sick."

Caleb had no other choice but to respond to Katy politely, and though he answered bluntly so as to sever this thread of conversation, Katy was persistent and kept the topic alive for quite some time. She talked about how the epidemic had harmed some, and how other families were faring. Caleb paid polite attention, though his thoughts were obviously not on the subject at hand.

Katy kept the conversation going until Mr. Monks entered, and the party was able to move over to the dining room, where dinner would be served. Henry was very interested in how Rose would act in a formal setting. She had proven herself to be an experienced hostess, but would she be able to play the part of a refined guest?

Henry watched her as the meal was served. She never once left her seat to help with removing old dishes and placing new dishes, but she allowed the host to provide. She waited patiently when Caleb got a bit distracted and forgot to cue Mrs. Meps to bring the next course, and she even allowed another to serve her.

Yes, Miss Rose Wooden played the part of the perfect guest. She allowed herself to be pampered, but did not take offense at the small mess ups of the host. She would do well in an upper class society, and Henry wondered where she had learned her manners, for surely they were impeccable.

If it weren't for the sparse settings, Henry would have thought himself in the presence of nobles, for all members of the party were polite and refined, and Katy kept up a constant dialogue of gossip. It seemed there was nothing that separated the two social classes save for the store of wealth. The thought made him groan, because if all societies were similar to that of the nobles, then he would fail miserably at his attempt to find a wife outside the social norm of the court.

Caleb took note of Henry's discomfort and took it as his cue to bring in the dessert. He waved at Mrs. Meps, who disappeared into the kitchen and came back loaded with plates of cake for every person present. "I hope you will not mind the informal dessert," said Caleb softly to the members of the room. "I could not help but have cake tonight on a night of celebration, for it is what my family would always eat when we were celebrating a birthday or other occasion." Caleb looked at Rose, who blushed slightly and gave him a slight nod of approval. He beamed at her assent.

"Oh, how wonderful!" exclaimed Katy. "I don't think that it is informal in any way. And to think, it is my birthday in a few days.

The fifth of September to be exact. I shall be sixteen years." This was news to Rose, and she began to think of a gift that she could buy for Katy. Maybe she could make her a dress.

Caleb cleared his throat. "That is wonderful, Miss Monks. I wish you every blessing on your birthday. May God give you many more to celebrate." He didn't look at Katy when he said these words. Rather, he looked directly at Rose, who had disappeared in her thoughts and did not take note of what was taking place.

The table was again silent as everyone enjoyed their cake. It was not an uncomfortable silence, but rather a companionable one, as every person retreated into their own thoughts. Caleb thought about how beautiful Rose looked in her dress tonight. It was simple and modest and very pretty. Rose thought about a gift for Katy. Katy thought of how to capture the curate's attention. Henry thought about the current condition of his mission. And the elder Monks thought about how delightful the party was.

When the cake was finished, Mr. Taylor closed with a prayer. As he said amen, the whole attitude of the party changed. Katy jumped to her feet and offered to help wash the dishes in the kitchen. She claimed she did not want to leave all the work to his housekeeper. Rose stepped out of sight to the side, where little attention would be drawn to herself, and Caleb tried to encourage everyone toward the parlour where they could enjoy a card game.

The elder Monks easily made their way to the parlour. They were not used to such extravagant evenings, and they were tiring quickly. Katy insisted upon seeing the kitchen in order to better understand the state of the elderly housekeeper. Caleb was obliged to escort her. Henry was left with Rose, who seemed ready to disappear into a crack in the floor.

He held out his arm to her, and she accepted. They started to walk toward the parlour. "Tell me," said Henry, "how is it that a lady of your social class learns such impeccable manners as a guest, as well as a host? You played both roles to near perfection."

Rose's answer was blunt and quick. "One escapes reprimand if one works at perfection. I am not one who takes reprimands lightly, and I will go to great lengths to avoid them."

Henry pondered this. "Does it not say in the book of Proverbs that the wise love reprimands, for they can learn from them and better their ways?"

"That may be so," replied Rose a little slower. "But if there is no reprimand to be given, even the wise would detest the false saying of one."

They entered the parlour, where they joined in the conversation with the elder Monks and waited the return of Katy and Caleb. It seemed to be taking them quite some time to return and Henry was about to rescue Caleb from the young girl when there was a loud crash from the kitchen area.

Rose stood up quickly and hurried toward the sound. Henry and Mr. Monks didn't even have time to leave their chairs before she was out the door. A few minutes later, Rose came back to the parlour supporting a very pale Katy, who had the start of a goose egg growing on her forehead. Mrs. Monks raced to the aid of her daughter as Caleb entered the room.

"Mrs. Meps sliced her finger on a sliver of glass. Miss Monks fainted at the sight of blood and knocked her head as she fell down," explained Caleb, his voice dripping with disdain. "She should be quite all right after a good night's sleep and a cool cloth placed on her forehead."

Mr. Monks left to go prepare the carriage, and Rose helped Katy rest in one of the chairs. She looked absolutely miserable. Her dress was dirtied and her jewellery was all askew. Some pins had come loose and knocked some of her hair out of place, and her ringlets seemed to have deflated with her fall. There was nothing Rose could do about her appearance, but she could do everything possible to make her comfortable.

Caleb handed her a damp cloth and she gently applied it to Katy's forehead. She let out a soft moan and sank farther into the couch cushions. Rose cooed to her softly, telling her everything would be all right, and Katy seemed to relax. "My head hurts so badly," Katy moaned again and again.

It didn't take long for Mr. Monks to return with the carriage. He lifted his daughter and carried her out the door. Mrs. Monks followed close behind. Rose turned to the two men left standing bewildered in the parlour. She gave a slight shrug of her shoulders, said her goodbyes, and headed out the door.

Katy moaned the whole way home. Her head was hurting immensely. Rose tried to quiet her, but nothing seemed to work. She was in pain and she wanted a cure. Rose was glad when they rounded the corner to the cottage. She let out a sigh of relief, but she couldn't stop herself from laughing when she heard Katy softly mumble, "And he didn't even catch me!"

FOURTEEN

ROSE TENDED TO KATY THROUGH THE NIGHT, and did not come out of their room until Katy was ready to go with her. By that time, it was already late in the afternoon, and Mr. Monks sat reading the newspaper at the dining table. "Well ladies," he said, "it appears that our humble town will have a hospital in the next little while."

"Who would care about a hospital?" Katy asked incredulously.

"It would have to be a temporary hospital," replied Rose thoughtfully. "My guess is that it is for the men returning from the war. That way, the injured can stay close to home while they mend. Seeing as we are in a military town, it would make sense that they erect a temporary hospital around this area. Will it be run by the locals?"

Rose knew very well that the hospital would be run by locals, but she didn't want to steal all the news away from Mr. Monks, who enjoyed telling them what he learned in the newspaper. "Yes, yes, indeed it will be run by locals. They shall need lots of volunteers, but they shall have them." Mr. Monks voice trailed off as he returned to his paper.

Rose and Katy took a seat, waiting to see what other tidbit of news they might pick up. "Ah," said Mr. Monks, "this is a piece of information you might find interesting, Katy. There is to be a ball when the soldiers return. That is in a month's time, you know, and the entire town is invited to come and share in the festivities."

Katy let out a squeal. "You mean that I am allowed to go to this ball? I won't be forced to sit and wait at home?"

Mr. Monks looked up at his daughter with an appearance of questioning shock. "You will be sixteen years by then. Plenty old enough to attend a ball, I would think."

Katy let out another squeal, but her exuberance soon died. "Oh, that will never do, it will never do at all."

"Whatever is the matter, dear?" Rose asked sympathetically. "Don't you want to go to the ball and dance with all the eligible young men?"

Katy let out a moan. "That is the problem. I would love to dance the whole night through, but I have never learned to dance! What opportunity have I had to dance? There has always been one thing or another to keep me from learning, and now I shall miss my chance at my first ball."

Rose laughed softly at the girl's distress, which cost her an evil glare. "Forgive me, Katy, but I did not learn to dance until before my first ball either. It was my cousin who taught me to dance, and

I'm sure that you can get a grasp of the basic steps in a month's time."

"And who would teach me?" Katy replied a bit bitterly. "You?"

Rose shrugged her shoulders. "Unless you have someone else in mind who is willing to teach you. If not, I can start your lessons this afternoon."

"How do I know you won't be horrible at dancing? You can't be good at everything, you know."

Rose bit down on her lip to avoid retaliating in kind. "I guess you can't know unless you come to one of my lessons. So, will we practice this afternoon?"

Katy crossed her arms and sighed. "I suppose so. But if you teach me any wrong steps, I will never forgive you."

Rose ignored her last comment.

Rose walked toward the orphanage after her lesson with Katy. She laughed quietly to herself and shook her head. Katy was clumsy and didn't know where to put her feet, but she could learn, hopefully.

Rose took in a deep breath of air and exhaled it slowly. She couldn't help but overflow with joy. It was a wonderful day, and she was at peace with all that was around her. She twirled on the spot, enjoying the way that her skirt filled with air and twirled with her. She did a little hop skip like a young girl and nearly fell when she heard a voice behind her.

"So that is how a young woman acts when she is by herself. It is rather amusing."

Rose spun around, but she broke into a grin when she saw who it was. "Caleb!" she shouted and raced toward him. On a whim, she embraced him. Shocked, he stepped back. Rose turned red when she realized what she had done. "I am so sorry, Caleb. I really did not mean to do that; it's just that I am in such good spirits that I let impulse lead me and, well…"

Caleb started laughing at this explanation. He walked toward her and gently hugged her and held her for a while. When he finally let go, Rose had turned two shades redder and could not bear to look him in the eye. He tipped her chin up. "There is no shame in embracing someone in a friendly manner. I have often heard it said that a hug is good for the health. You just took me by surprise, that's all."

Rose looked at him with pleading eyes. Her lip trembled as if she feared his wrath, and he had to fight the urge to kiss her gently. There may be nothing wrong with a good natured hug, but kissing a person who may not have feelings for him was out of the question, especially when she was so vulnerable.

He let go of her chin and gave her another quick embrace. "Now, where were you going before I interrupted you?"

Rose cleared her throat before she responded. "Well, I was making my way toward the orphanage. I was going to see if Mrs. Jennings needed any help with the children or in the kitchen."

"I am sure she would enjoy your help. I, on the other hand, am headed toward the site of the new hospital. They are looking for volunteers, and I was thinking that I should donate some of my time toward that cause."

"They are already setting up the new hospital? Where will it be? I think that I would like to help out if at all possible. Do you think they will allow the women of the town to help with the wounded?"

"I think they were hoping that the women would do most of the work, for the men have not seen their women in a long time. It will benefit them to be in the company of sophisticated young females."

"Then please let whoever is supervisor of the hospital know that I am very interested in helping out."

"Your services will be greatly appreciated," replied Caleb as they came to the orphanage. They said their farewells, and Rose skipped up the steps as Caleb walked on down the street.

Caleb walked slowly down the street, his head full of thoughts of the beautiful Miss Wooden. He could still feel her embrace that had shocked him so, and how good she had felt in his arms when he had hugged her back. He let out a soft sigh. He had to stop this. If he wasn't careful, he would find himself in love with a woman who would never love him back.

Love? Could he truly love Rose? Yes, he could very easily love Rose, and he could very easily greedily take her home to be his wife. But that wouldn't be fair to her. He would never marry her if she did not love him. Every person deserved a chance at love, and even if she would marry him without love, he could not marry her unless she loved him back.

He shook his head. What was all this thought about love? He had only known her for a short while. There was no possible way that he could love her already. Love took time to grow and bloom. No, it was infatuation that he felt for Rose, and it would be better for him to cut it out before it grew into something he could not control.

He rubbed his jaw hard, but nothing could take away the memory of how she had looked up at him with those deep, innocent eyes. He reflected on this for a moment, then with a snort of disgust he began to go over his Sunday sermon in his head as he walked on.

Rose slipped into the orphanage house. She could hear the gentle sound of kids laughing and their gleeful shouts of joy. It seemed as if all occupants were content. She headed toward the kitchen in hopes of finding Mrs. Jennings. As she drew near the room, she heard the soft shudders of someone weeping. She picked up the pace of her steps.

When she entered, she found Mrs. Jennings sitting by the table weeping softly over a cup of tea. Rose didn't ask any questions. She drew the older lady into her arms, and gently reassured her. Mrs.

Jennings continued to weep, but she seemed at least a little assured.

When she was finally calm, Rose helped her rest at the table and went to prepare more tea. She brought back a steaming cup for herself and replaced the cold contents of the cup sitting in front of Mrs. Jennings. "Now, tell me," she said, "what is the matter?"

Mrs. Jennings sniffed slightly. "Oh, it is nothing of real importance, just the trifling of an old lonely woman. It is nothing that you should concern yourself with, Rose."

"Please, Mrs. Jennings," begged Rose. "Please tell me what is the matter. I would take great concern even in the smallest of your trifling."

Mrs. Jennings gave her a small smile and patted her hand. "You are a good girl, Rose. You truly are. I am glad you came to the orphanage. But I fear that my weeping is unfounded. I was just bemoaning the fact that the war has ended. It is really selfish on my part actually."

Rose stepped back, shocked. "Why in the world would you bemoan the end of the war? I thought everyone would be pleased with the end of the senseless slaughter of men's lives."

"Do not get me wrong," said Mrs. Jennings. "I am quite glad that the killing will end. It's just that, well, you see, now that the men are coming home, many of my children will go back home to their families, and I will be left without children, and well…" Tears welled up in her eyes again, and Rose drew her into another hug.

"I understand perfectly well, Mrs. Jennings. You have cared for these children so long, it is as if they are your own. To now have them taken from you is just mean, in a way. I do not think you selfish in any way for thinking this. It makes perfect sense to me."

"You are too kind, my dear," said Mrs. Jennings. "I will miss your company as well, for surely I will no longer need your assistance, and you will most likely be enjoying your time at the balls and other social events that are sure to take place." She let out a sigh.

"My dear Mrs. Jennings," replied Rose, "do not think that I will forget you now that the soldiers are returning. I will come to visit you often, if that is all right. I enjoy your company, and I look forward to conversation with you. It may be a little more difficult to arrange time with you, but do not think that the presence of a few handsome men will keep me from the company of a very wise woman."

"Och, that's a bunch of posh. Now you are just flattering me. Calling me wise. Ha, I am no more wise than I am rich. You should know that," Mrs. Jennings said with a blush on her cheeks.

"In my estimation," said Rose, "you are the richest, wisest lady that I have ever known. I would be blessed to call you my friend." The two embraced, and thus began a very sturdy friendship.

Rose looked at the material that was presented before her. There were blues and greens and reds and colors of all sorts. There were velvets and silks and fabrics of various kinds. There were so many options, and she couldn't make up her mind. She could go with the green velvet, which would make her eyes look wonderful, but it wouldn't be nearly as comfortable as the blue silk, but the blue silk wouldn't go nearly as well with her eyes, or would it?

She sighed in frustration. She never picked out the material for her dresses. The clerk at the store in Thespane had always helped her make these decisions. She could sew well enough and pick out a dress for another, but when it came to dressing herself, she never seemed able to choose the right fabric.

The clerk from Emriville looked at her with annoyance. She had already sat there for nearly ten minutes pulling out different fabrics and putting others away. It seemed that the task at hand was near impossible. Rose looked at the young lady apologetically as she asked her to take down one more bolt of fabric. The clerk looked ready to bite her head off.

Rose felt the fabrics and decided against two that didn't feel nice to the touch. She looked at the price of two others and decided that they were more than she cared to pay, and another was of a colour that was very undesirable. She was therefore left with two options: the blue silk or the green velvet.

Rose continued to contemplate the pros and cons of each piece of fabric when the clerk excused herself to go help another customer.

"Staring at them won't make anything about them change."

Rose jumped at the nearness of the voice and nearly lost her footing, but a hand from behind caught her before she could fall.

"Careful there. You would think I was a ghost to scare you in such a manner as I did." Rose glared at Henry and the big goofy grin that he insisted on wearing on his face. She gave him a scowl and turned again to contemplate the two fabrics.

"Come now, Rose. By the way you are treating me, one would think you are angry with me. Have I done something to offend you, or does looking at fabric put you in a sour mood? Most women I meet would love to look at fabrics all day long."

"I am not most women, Mr. Hyden," Rose retorted. "Fabric is an enigma to me. How am I supposed to know which will look best, and which will best suit the purpose that I am putting it to? It is infuriating, if you ask me."

"Well then, Miss Wooden," Henry said, slipping into a formal tone, "allow me to offer my observations." He made a courtly bow. "If you are looking to make an everyday dress, I wouldn't go with either of the fabrics you have chosen, for they wear out all too easily. But I don't think that you are looking for fabric for an everyday dress. If my assumptions are right, you are looking for fabric for a ball gown.

"This of course does cause a dilemma, for ball gowns are to be very fancy indeed. The two fabrics would suit a ball gown wonderfully, though I do warn you that velvet can get quite warm, though you may be too cool in a silk gown if the evening turns a bit chilly. The green in the velvet would match your eyes wonderfully, but I must say you look stunning in blue. Therefore, if in fact you are looking for a ball gown, and if you trust my opinion, I would go with the blue silk, for it is clearly the better option of the two."

Rose gave another scowl as she looked at the fabric. "I don't see how the blue can be any better than the green. You didn't make my choice any easier. If anything, you have made my choice hard by giving me more pros and cons than I had before."

Henry let out a sigh. "Would you take my advice then, without weighing the pros and cons?"

Rose looked at him hesitantly, then with an overwhelming sense of frustration said, "Very well, I will take your advice. Which fabric do you think I should buy?"

Henry slipped behind the counter. He put both the blue and green away, and pulled out a rich turquoise-coloured fabric. It was made out of a soft material that Rose had never felt before, and it was more exquisite than any of her other options. She liked it very much, but she shook her head. "It's too much. I will never be able to afford it, though it is very beautiful."

"How much money do you have?" Henry asked. Rose placed her coins on the counter for him to see. "And how much fabric will you need?" Rose calculated the amount and gave it to Henry. He sat there pondering for a while, then dug into his pocket and pulled out a few more coins, placing them next to hers.

Rose gasped in astonishment. "Henry, you can't do that. How could I ever accept money from you? It's, it's—"

"A gift," Henry said, cutting in. "It is a gift for your birthday, and I hope that you will make the most spectacular ball gown and put all the young girls of the community to shame."

Rose blushed slightly, then said, "I was going to say that it is unheard of for a young man such as yourself to give money to a young woman such as myself."

Henry laughed. "Well, then do not tell anyone about the money, and it shall still be unheard of. Please, Rose," he said with gentle insistence, "let me do this for you."

She looked up at him and a smile covered her face. "Thank you, Henry. I really appreciate it. This is the most beautiful fabric I have ever seen, and I look forward to making a dress with it."

"And I look forward to seeing what type of dress you will create."

Rose laughed and swatted at him playfully. He stepped out from behind the counter, and after saying his goodbyes disappeared out the shop door. Rose continued to smile as the annoyed store clerk looked at her fabric choice and deepened the scowl on her face.

Rose hadn't lied to Henry when she told him that she only had those coins to spend on her dress, but neither had she told him the full truth. The full truth was that she had a few more coins, but they were not to be spent on the dress. Rather, she had set them aside to buy a gift for Katy. What she would buy for Katy, she had no idea.

At first she had thought to buy Katy a dress, but Katy already had so many that it didn't seem worthwhile. Rose had then thought that she would get something for the girl's apparel at the ball, but what should she get her? She could buy her a hair clip, or maybe some gloves, but would that suffice? She didn't know.

She walked back to the shop where she had bought her fabric. The clerk looked at her warily and disappeared into the back room. Rose didn't mind. She walked to the hair clips and began looking through them. They were nice, but none seemed to suit as a birthday gift. She turned to the gloves, but the options were sparse, and none would match Katy's dress.

Rose looked around in frustration for anything that would work as a birthday gift. There were brushes and bonnets. There were soaps and perfumes, but there seemed to be nothing that Rose would even consider buying for the young girl. That was when she saw them.

Standing in the corner next to the thread were a pair of white slippers. They were dainty and very pretty, but they were also very plain. Rose looked them over with a smile of appreciation. She thought of Katy's dress, then she picked up the slippers and some thread. She would have to go home immediately if the slippers were to be ready for tomorrow.

As she walked back to the Monks', the design formed in her head, and she knew exactly what the finished product would look like. It would be hard to finish in one night, but that would be the price she would pay for procrastinating so much. Besides, the outcome would far outweigh any cost.

Rose groaned when Katy excitedly bounced from her bed early the next morning and began noisily preparing her attire for the day. It had been a late night, and Rose was tired. She wished she could sleep a little longer, but now that Katy was up, sleep would evade her.

She wished Katy a happy birthday and headed downstairs for breakfast. By Katy's plate there were two packets. When her parents were seated and she was given permission, Katy opened them greedily. One of the packages contained a pretty clip that would go nicely with Katy's ball gown, and the other was a pair of long white gloves. They were from Mrs. Monks, a treasure from her own ball-going days.

Katy loved each of the gifts and couldn't wait to use them. After exclaiming over them for some time, she turned to Rose and asked if they could work on the dance lessons they had practiced. Rose readily conceded.

The two always met in the parlour, and when the breakfast dishes were put away, Rose went up to their room where she found her gift for Katy, then made her way toward the young lass who would be waiting eagerly for her dance lesson. Rose held the package behind her back as she entered the room. "Now Katy," she said, "I have something that I want to give you before we start our lesson."

Katy looked up at her expectantly, and Rose handed over the package. Katy opened it hesitantly, but she let out an exclamation when she saw what rested inside. "Why, Rose, they're beautiful." Inside the paper were the white shoes which Rose had embroidered. Across the toe and heal were tiny stitches that formed the image of a beautiful flower with delicate leaves and silky looking blossoms.

"I hope you like them," Rose said. "I figured you could start breaking them in for the dance. That way, your feet will not hurt so much after dancing the night away." Katy let out a squeal of delight and hugged Rose, saying her thanks over and over again. Rose laughed at the exuberance of the young girl, but she cut it short and began the dance lesson.

Josh looked around for his teacher. He was at the right place at the right time, but his teacher wasn't there. He let out a frustrated sigh. He was learning a lot, but the lessons were rather unpredictable, as was his teacher.

His teacher was short and very small. He wielded the sword with power and cunning, and he was quicker than anyone Josh had ever met. He also knew how to punch, kick, and roll. The strange thing about his teacher was that he hardly ever talked. Every now and then he would give a curt instruction about his form, but then they would go on fighting. The only other time his teacher spoke was when he lectured on the topic of justice. And his teacher wore a mask.

Josh had no clue as to his teacher's identity. He felt sometimes that he was caught up in a myth with a legendary knight from the past who was teaching him how to fight and act justly. Maybe he should ask the mysterious knight how to treat a damsel in distress, for he definitely did not know how to talk to a girl yet.

Girls were a mystery to Josh. They giggled a lot and batted their eyelashes, too. They blushed easily and talked about marrying some rich man, even though they were only fifteen and sixteen years. And they always acted as if they were more mature and knew more than his seventeen-year-old mind could comprehend. He just didn't get it. He would ask the knight—if he ever showed up.

Josh sat on a rock and swatted at some grass at his feet. He continued to mull over his thoughts, and the more he did, the angrier he got. Why did he have to be who he was? Why couldn't he be someone like John Read, someone who had everything in life? John could fight well with the sword, and he was old enough that the girls treated him kindly. And no one ever called him Stick or String Bean, for John was muscular and well built.

The grass crunched, and Josh looked up to find his teacher standing before him. Instead of getting into the ready position as he normally did when the knight arrived, Josh stayed sitting on the rock. The knight lowered his sword and waited.

"I have a question," Josh said. The knight continued to wait. Josh cleared his throat. "Do you by chance know how to talk with a girl? I mean, of course, you know how to talk, but when you try to speak to a girl and they start to giggle and…" Josh turned red and the knight just stood there.

Josh waited and waited. Finally the teacher answered. "I don't think I am the best person to ask this question of, Josh. I do not have much experience talking with girls."

Josh continued to whack the ground with his sword.

The knight let out a sigh. "When a girl giggles, do not take offense. They are just being silly. When you are talking to a girl, be sure to treat her with the utmost respect. If she does not treat you with respect back, she is not worthy of you."

The knight stood in the ready position and waited. Josh knew that that was his cue to stand himself. He had hoped for a better answer, but it didn't appear that he was going to get one. Instead, he stood and got ready to fight.

FIFTEEN

OW DO YOU TALK WITH A GIRL? How was Rose supposed to answer that question? She was a girl! It was Wednesday morning, and Rose was still fuming over Josh's question. When he had said he had a question, she had been expecting something about sword fighting, not anything to do with girls. She scowled at nothing in particular.

She was all alone on the road that led into town, and it was a perfect time for her to brood over the previous night's escapades. She was headed toward the new hospital to offer her services in any fashion that was needed, though she felt more like crawling back into bed and sleeping away the day. Instead, she was headed to the one place where she knew she could escape the frustrating giggles of two very obnoxious girls.

Rose loved Katy, but her tolerance had its limits, especially when she was tired. Today she was especially tired, and maybe a tad grumpy. It wasn't because she had stayed out to all hours teaching Josh, but rather because she had stayed up till early morning thinking about Josh's question. When she woke up and discovered that Katy was hosting May, she was again brought back to Josh's question of how to talk to giggling girls.

Her mood had been sour all morning, and it showed no signs of clearing up, even as she came to the building that was to be the hospital. It was a large brick building that had at one time been a school for the children of the town, but had been out of use for many years. Now men were crawling all over the place trying to piece together a temporary hospital in a matter of weeks.

Rose pasted a smile on her face and walked down the path to the front porch. She tried to ignore the lewd comments coming from the less reputable men working, but she could not keep her ears from turning bright red at some of the snarling words that suggested she was less than a reputable woman. Apparently the rumour about her and Mr. Hyden still held some weight in different crowds.

She walked up to a kindly looking older gentleman and asked where she could find the supervisor. He had a look of bewilderment on his face. "Now lady," he said, "I don't know what yer at comin' down here, but I don' think that you will be of any use to the supervisor, as you call him. Unless you are what some of these men suggest you might be, I suggest you do what all the other young ladies are doing, and that is keepin' a wide berth between here and them. You understand?"

The red reached beyond Rose's neck and began to touch her ears and cheeks. "I understand perfectly well what you are saying, sir, but I would still like to talk with your supervisor if it is at all possible. It is important that I discuss a certain matter with him immediately."

The man looked at her sceptically, and Rose had to fight to keep control of the anger that would have her lash out at him. Finally, he turned and whistled at a man named Joe, who walked over. Joe was a decent looking man, but he wasn't someone Rose would ever put much confidence in. He eyed Rose up and down, and her blush crawled farther onto her face. This only brought a smug grin to his face which displayed his yellow, crooked teeth.

"Are you the supervisor?" asked Rose. The puffed out chest and the prideful glitter in his eyes were enough to convince her of his position, so she continued. "I would like to know in what ways I and the other ladies of the community could help with the hospital as of now."

The steam that seemed to be inflating the man's chest appeared to deflate a little. "I'm sorry, lady, but there is no way you and some ladies group of sorts can help out. Everything is taken care of."

Rose was in a horrible mood by this time, and she was determined not to be sent away without a fight. "Is that so, sir? Have you taken care of the medicine that will be needed, or the bedding that the men will rest in, and the food they will eat? Have you covered all these areas in your preparation?"

The man named Joe was becoming angry. "Look here, lady," he said, "don't make me out to be incompetent. Food and medicine are being brought with the soldiers for at least the first two months, and my men are making the beds the day after tomorrow. The soldiers will be well looked after."

"And what," continued Rose, now blind with rage, "will your men be making these beds out of? Slats of wood and some nails? I can definitely see then how our soldiers will be well looked after. Have you even considered bedding, like blankets and quilts? It will be winter soon, and they will need blankets to keep them warm at night."

The raised voices were starting to draw attention. Joe had turned a dark red with a purple tinge. If Rose wasn't so angry herself, she would have had a mind to be at least a little bit scared, but fury had a way of keeping common sense from the forefront of one's thoughts. Joe began to sputter. Spittle flew out of his mouth and landed in various areas in close proximity to Rose's face. "Well?" she demanded.

When Joe could finally speak, his words came out in a snarl similar to that of a wild beast. "Get your blankets then, lady. See if I care. Just get your stinkin' self out of my hospital." He raised his fist at her, slowly extending his index finger. "If I see you here again, I'll have the mind to call the authorities to drag your sorry rear to jail before you can say mercy."

"Fine!" Rose shouted as she spun around and walked back down the drive. She would collect her blankets and bedding, and she would have someone deliver them to the hospital. She would be sure that there were plenty there to keep all the soldiers good and warm in the wintertime and enough to be a nuisance to Joe the Supervisor as he worked.

Rose stomped to the rectory, where she hoped to find support for her cause. Caleb was the unlucky person to answer the door, and shock was the worst possible expression that he just happened to be wearing. "Rose, what are you doing here?" She scowled at him. "I mean, it's always a pleasure to see you, it just took me by surprise to see you here today." Nothing he said seemed to appease her, so he finally settled with inviting her in.

When they were settled in the parlour, Rose finally let her anger burst out. "How could they! Didn't you tell them that I wanted to help with the hospital? And they had the nerve to suggest that the ladies of this community should just give it a wide berth. And the comments that they made... Why, I would have to say they are not gentlemen at all!"

Caleb looked at her in bewilderment, then burst out laughing. "You can't be serious, Rose," he said. "Those men there know little about hospitals and the running of them. They were just there to do construction. If you wanted to do something for the hospital before there were occupants in it, you should have come talked with me. I have a whole list of things that the women of the community can easily participate in."

This did nothing to settle Rose's anger. Instead, she scowled again at Caleb and started on another rant. "You had a list of things to do, and you didn't tell me? What were you thinking? I would have been very willing to help out and give whatever time I could to the hospital. You should have known to tell me."

Caleb chuckled softly. "Rose, settle yourself down. I would have told you right away if I had known it was that important to you, but I thought you were so busy with the orphanage that you would not have time to work with the hospital till all the men returned. So, please forgive me."

Rose turned her back to him and bit her tongue. She wanted to forgive him, but her anger and embarrassment wouldn't let her turn and face him. Gently, he reached out to her. Touching her arm, he softly turned her toward him and pulled her into a hug. At first she resisted, then with a shudder she gave up. Tears poured down her cheeks, and she tried to hide them.

This was silly. Only petty females used tears to get their way, but Caleb didn't seem to mind. He wiped his thumb under her eyes and whispered reassuringly to her. She turned red and began to apologize for the tears, but he quieted her. He held her for another couple minutes while she quieted down, and Rose began to think about how inappropriate their actions were. They were alone in a house with no chaperone, and he was holding her quite close.

Caleb appeared to be thinking the same thing, because he gently detached himself from her. His face was red as he moved to another couch, and Rose felt the urge to apologize again, but Caleb beat her to it. "I'm sorry, Rose. I shouldn't have…" His face turned redder.

Rose let a slight smile touch her lips to try and cover the blush. "It was my fault. I shouldn't have come here. I was just angry and, well..."

The room hung in painful silence. Both occupants were embarrassed over what had happened, and neither knew how to move on with the conversation. It was a great relief when Henry walked in. He carried with him such an aura of cheer that the two could not help but feel their spirits lift. It did not take them long to return to easy conversation, and for Rose to make her excuses and head home.

Henry had been in the back of the house when Rose had come calling. He had been polishing his sword, and had stopped what he was doing to see who the visitor was. He had opened the door just in time to see Caleb gently reach to embrace Rose. He had kept the door cracked open as the two sat in each other's arms.

The sight still made him sick to his stomach. Why it did, he didn't know. He had been the one to encourage Caleb, the one to tell him to talk to Rose about his feelings and move forward with them, hadn't he? Then why did the thought of the two of them together make him feel like he needed to vomit?

He tried to think of his feelings on the day that Caleb had bemoaned the fact that he would never have Rose. He tried to think of every thought, every feeling that had entered into his head as he had responded, but none of them betrayed the reason for his sudden illness.

Rose had looked so comfortable in the curate's arms. She had looked so innocent and so content, and Henry had looked away, for the sight was too much for him. He should have been delighted that Caleb had found someone so special for himself, and he should be wishing Caleb every happiness, but he couldn't bring himself to do it.

Maybe he was jealous of Caleb. That could very much be the case. Caleb had a beautiful girl who probably loved him with all her heart, and he, who was supposed to be finding love in a year's time, couldn't convince himself to leave a town that held no opportunities for him to fulfill his goal. Yes, he was most likely jealous of Caleb.

With this decision made, Henry felt awful for interrupting the two. With his feelings unknown as they were, he had closed the door for a couple of minutes, then re-entered the room with a sense of false cheer. It had been rude of him, and he now regretted his actions. It would be necessary for him to apologize to Caleb later.

In the meantime, Henry began to ponder his jealousy and the best way to deal with it. He could ignore it and go on with his life in Emriville, or he could run from it. There were plenty more towns to visit in the kingdom of Samaya. Perhaps he would go to Thespane next. Rose was sure to have kin there, and he wanted to meet them.

Henry let out a sigh. There was no possible way that he could leave Emriville. There was too much that he loved here. He had to stay at least until the end of the ball. He owed that to Caleb and Rose. He only hoped that he could keep his jealousy contained until that time.

Caleb sat in the parlour in silent mortification. How could he have done such a thing? How could he have put his feelings for Rose above her feelings and her reputation? Was he so selfish that he couldn't keep some space between him and a girl? No, not a girl, a woman, a very beautiful woman.

Caleb continued to sit there, piling abuse after abuse upon himself for his thoughtlessness. It was in this state that Henry found him. If he had the chance to describe him later on, Henry would have described Caleb as a dejected puppy who had just been thrown to the streets, but that chance never came.

Henry cleared his throat and tried to think of a way to start the conversation he knew they had to have. Caleb didn't look at him. He just sat there looking into nothingness. Henry was left with no choice. "Caleb, I would like to speak to you about something that occurred this afternoon."

At these words, Caleb looked up at him. In seconds, the expression in his eyes changed from sad puppy to more-scared-than-a-man-ought-to-be. His voice was hoarse when he spoke. "You saw us, didn't you? You saw Rose and me, and now you are here to punish me for my inappropriate actions."

To say that Henry was shocked would be an understatement. "No, not at all. I mean, yes, but no." Henry let out a frustrated sigh. "What I mean to say is that I did see you and Rose today, and no, I do not wish to punish you for your actions. Quite on the contrary, actually. Why you would think that I would punish you; I don't understand."

Caleb looked at Henry again, and new hope shone in his wispy eyes. His voice was full of unbelief when he asked, "You mean to say that you were not disgusted with me when you saw Rose? When you saw me..." Embarrassment took over, and Caleb was not able to finish his sentence, but Henry caught the gist of it.

With as truthful a voice that he could muster, Henry responded to Caleb. "I don't have a clue what was so disgusting about the affection you showed to Rose. I started this conversation with the express purpose of apologizing for stepping in when I should have allowed you your privacy. With this said, I hope that you can forgive me."

Caleb was hesitant to believe what Henry said. It seemed impossible that a person such as Henry, who was in fact the Prince of Samaya, would find little harm in the lack of propriety shown by the curate of a small town. A war as vicious as the one between Samaya and Isbetan was going on in Caleb's head. Samaya seemed to say that it was all right to accept Henry's apology, while Isbetan told him he should ignore the apology and continue to heap guilt on himself. In the end, Isbetan won.

"I am a horrible person, Henry. I ignored all propriety. I allowed her to come into the parlour, and I sat with her with no chaperone. I held her in my arms while she was so vulnerable, knowing my feelings for her while she lacked knowledge or an opinion in our relationship. How could I have done such a horrid thing?"

"Horrid thing, indeed! Do you repent of having feelings for Rose? Is it so horrible that you love her and she may not love you? What is with you, man? Rose is a beautiful young woman with a good head on her shoulders. For all you know, she may be very well aware of your feelings for her and is just waiting for you to speak up a little. Now, will you stop groaning and moaning and tell me once and for all if you will forgive me for intruding?"

Caleb blinked a few times to clear the shocked fuzz that left him speechless. "Of course I forgive you Henry. I did not think it that important to you that I forgive you for something as trifling as interrupting something that was inappropriate." At the word inappropriate, Henry stiffened and gave Caleb a look that said if he used the word one more time Henry would not be responsible for his actions.

"Good," Henry said. "Now, to move on to other matters, I think that it is time you tell Rose how you feel. It is quite obvious that you are in love with her, and the longer you take to admit it, the more likely you are to get hurt. So I suggest that you find a time to speak with Miss Wooden about this."

"I agree that I should talk to Rose about how I feel about her, but I do not agree that I love her. How could I love her? I have only known her for, what? Three months? Maybe a tad longer, but the time has been much too short for love to be a relevant consideration."

Henry looked at him like he was an Isbetan soldier in a Samayan army camp. "Do you mean to tell me that you do not believe in such things as love at first sight? That is odd. You have worked with Rose at the orphanage, you have spoken with her in private, she has tended you while you are ill, and still you don't think you could be in love with her?"

Caleb didn't understand what was so shocking about this revelation. "As I said before, I do not think that I could be in love with Rose. Too little time has passed since I met her. Surely that makes sense to you."

"Not one bit," Henry responded and turned to leave the room.

"Wait!" cried Caleb. "Why doesn't that make sense to you? Do you believe in love at first sight and all that crazy nonsense?"

"Crazy nonsense!" Henry exclaimed indignantly. "How can you call it crazy nonsense? Tell me what you felt when you first saw Rose. I will tell you my first thoughts. I thought she was beautiful. She probably had good character, and I felt that she was determined. She is exactly the kind of person I will be looking for in a wife someday. It may not be love at first sight, but first impressions have a lasting impact, and who's to say that it can't be love?"

"I think that it's infatuation, if you ask me. A man can lust over a beautiful girl when he sees one, but he cannot say he loves her, for he doesn't actually know her. He knows a little about her appearance, but what else does he know? For all the man knows, she could be a very unpleasant woman. She may be demanding or very nagging. Then his love was proven to be lust and nothing more."

"Believe me," said Henry, "a demanding woman is very evident when you see one. On first encounter, she will bat her eyelashes at you, and maybe throw in a few swoons or two. If the woman is very good at being demanding, she will have mastered the art of tears. She will use the dreadful things to make you feel like a worm, mean and insensitive." Henry shook himself to get off that particular train of thought. "Besides, even if a man lusts over one woman, it does not mean that he will not fall immediately in love with the woman he is to marry when he sets his eyes on her."

"You are a romantic, Henry, and I don't think there can be a cure for you. Maybe when you fall in love someday, you will realize that love is not just an easy romantic feeling. Even the Bible mentions that love is always giving of itself."

"Maybe someday I will change my opinion, but as of now, I will continue in my beliefs. Do you think that you can live with that, Caleb?" Henry asked.

"What, live with a hopeless romantic?" Caleb asked teasingly. "Of course I could never put up with you with such beliefs. Now, you best change them before I take you to the elders of the church. They still aren't very fond of you, you know." The two men laughed at the joke, and the conversation turned to a lighter topic, leaving all thoughts of love at the back of both men's minds.

SIXTEEN

ROSE LOOKED DOWN AT THE FABRIC ON HER LAP. It shimmered slightly in the light and flowed smoothly over her hand. Her fingers worried the edges, moving it back and forth from one appendage to the next. Her thoughts were far from the dress design that she should have been contemplating.

In her mind, she was again fifteen. She was dressing for her first ball, and she was terrified. John said she would be fine, and that she was a natural at dancing, but she didn't think so. She knew for a fact that John had many sore toes from the days of practicing each dance with their many different steps.

She slipped into her gown, pulling it over her corset, bloomers and petticoats. The material was lovely, and she had sewn the dress together herself. Her aunt could never afford a seamstress for such a trifling matter as a ball. The cut accentuated her small waistline, and hopefully made her look taller, for she was much too short for her age.

When she was finally ready, she stepped out of her room and walked down the stairs where her cousin would be waiting with her aunt and uncle. The first face she saw was her aunt's, and the sneer on her lips nearly made her turn and hide in her room, but she kept walking. When John came into view, he let out a gut wrenching groan. "What, what is it?" asked the young Rose frantic- ally. "Is the dress inappropriate? I will go upstairs and change im- mediately."

She turned to leave, but John stopped her. "Settle yourself, my dear cousin," said John. "I was only bemoaning the fact that I will be spending the entire night fighting off nagging brats who do not deserve to dance with you. You look absolutely marvellous, and the dress is stunning. There is no need for you to change your cos- tume."

Rose blushed at her cousin's compliment and tried to hide her discomfort. It did not take long for her feelings of unease to leave, for one look at her aunt's scowl ceased all emotions. All that was left of her joy vanished, and embarrassment and discomfort turned to annoyance and edginess. All desire to attend the ball disap- peared. She would rather restrain from all merriment if it would mean that her aunt would at least smile.

Her uncle held open the carriage door, and John helped her in. She sat bolt straight, and refused to let her shoulders slouch in any manner. Her face was blank of any emotion as the carriage took off down the road. It bounced over ruts and potholes, but she kept her straight demeanour. When they arrived at their destination, she was again assisted out of the carriage by her cousin.

As Rose entered the ballroom, she determined not to participate in the gaiety all around her. She was going to refuse to dance as well, but John would not have it. Associating her refusal with nerves, he took it upon himself to lead her in the first dance, and by the time the last note had been played, her frigidity had melted ever so slightly.

An eligible young man came up to her and asked her to dance, but she tried to deter him, saying she would probably harm one of his toes, and that it would be better for him to ask her later on in the evening when he did not wish to dance anymore. The giddy young man would not believe that she was less than an excellent dancer, and she was forced out onto the floor once more.

Thus the evening went. Rose would complete one dance only to be asked by another young sir if she would accompany him in the next. She tried to refuse each time, but as the evening continued, her excuses became idle chatter and often fell on deaf ears. She danced long into the night, until she was out of breath and needed a drink for fear she might faint.

She slept in the carriage on the way home, and did not care that her aunt appeared to be furious. She would worry about her aunt's dark mood in the morning. In the time that she had then and there, she dreamed. She allowed herself to join in the gaiety of the ball with no reserve and to enjoy every last morsel of rich goodness. She did not hold back any emotion, but allowed herself to love every bit of it. At least, as she dreamed, she could imagine it so, for when she woke in the morning, it would all have vanished with the darkness of the night.

Rose let out a sigh as the last traces of the memory disappeared from her mind. That had been one of the happier times. It was a time when her uncle was still healthy, and her aunt only had the chance to make her life partially miserable. Soon after that day, her uncle had fallen ill, and all that had changed.

Her aunt had taken rule of the house, and Rose learned that it would go better for her if she submitted without a fight to her aunt's will. She had once tried to defy her aunt. She had refused to sit through another tea at the curate's house, but she found the only result of this was a sore back end while she sat sipping tea politely. From that day on, she had lived in quiet defiance of her aunt's deeds.

If her aunt wanted her to go to tea with the curate, she would sit through the tea, but she would refuse to say a word. She would later bear the punishment, but would not let her aunt see the harm that the punishment did. She refused to feel the pain of a belt on her back end, and the rigors of difficult chores held an appeal to her that her aunt found uncanny. When Aunt Agatha noticed that her force of will held no effect over Rose, their bitter squabbles turned into a silent battle.

They went back and forth, tit for tat, using whatever they had in their power to exact pain or grievance upon the other. Her aunt had delivered the last blow when she had determined that Rose would marry the curate in one year's time. The only way that Rose could defy her aunt in this would be to marry someone else against her wishes. Then, and only then, Rose would be free of her aunt's tyranny.

If the incentive wasn't already there, to be free of her aunt would be reason enough for Rose to marry. This thought brought a renewed vigour to Rose as she thought of her potential candidates for matrimony. So far, Caleb and Henry were her only choices, but that would soon change. When the soldiers returned, she would have many more options, and she would be able to make a reasonable choice.

With this in mind, Rose began to picture her ball gown. If she was to find a suitable husband, it would have to look spectacular. It did not take her long to come up with an idea, and she began to work slowly, carefully. Every mark, every stitch, every cut would have to be exact. If it was done just right, her dress could be something very exquisite.

"Step to the right, Katy! Quickly!" Rose cried as she played the piece on the piano. Katy let out a gasp as she made the quick step and tried to get back into the flow that the dance required. She stumbled, but she caught herself and continued on with the steps. "Good, keep up that pace," encouraged Rose as she continued to play.

Sweat began to collect on Katy's brow as the music resumed at a faster tempo. She tried to move her feet with the music, but it got too fast for her. With a sigh of exaggerated frustration, Katy gave up altogether on the dance and took an unladylike seat on the sofa. "It's no use," she moaned. "How am I ever going to learn the steps if I cannot see a partner across from me? It is nearly impossible to dance by myself, but in a whole group of people! How terribly awful that will be."

"Nonsense," replied Rose. "You are doing marvellously well. You are just having a little trouble keeping up with the tempo. Here, let us try a slower piece." With that, Rose sat down at the piano and began to play a slower melody. Katy stood up and began making the correct steps.

Rose hadn't been totally lying when she had said Katy was doing marvellously. She was doing wonderful at remembering the steps, but she lacked any appearance of grace. Her steps were heavy and her feet clumsy. Each move she made was stiff and formal and lacked any of the fluid motion that made the dance a work of art.

When the piano lilted the last notes of the sorrowful, soft tune, Rose congratulated Katy on her success of completing the dance without a single misstep. Katy beamed at her praise. "Now," said Rose, "let us try the quicker dance." At Katy's hesitation, she continued, "I will act the part of your partner, and we will slowly go faster and faster. You will get the hang of it, I am certain of that."

Katy wasn't so sure about this new development, but she took her place and curtsied to Rose, who returned with a very well practiced bow. Rose began to hum softly, and slowly the two began the steps. Katy had no qualms with the slower pace, and soon grew confident with the motion of the dance. Rose picked up the tempo.

The two continued. Rose acted the part of a handsome suitor escorting Katy around the dance floor of the parlour, and Katy did a marvellous job of playing the ever-blushing maiden. As Katy's confidence grew, Rose would pick up the tempo, and they moved faster and faster around the room. Rose quit her humming for a quick second to compliment Katy on her success and noticed too late the fatal mistake in this.

When the music stopped, Katy misstepped onto the hem of Rose's dress. Rose, who continued the flowing motion of the dance, tripped and fell into Katy. The two of them went crashing to the floor amid many squeals and screams. The terror of the moment quickly passed and turned into silly giggling at the mishap.

Rose clutched her sides laughing on the floor. Katy laughed as well, but her exuberance was cut short. Rose looked to see what the cause for Katy's lack of merriment was. The smile slipped from Rose's face when she saw the two figures standing in the door, one bewildered, the other very disapproving.

Caleb and Henry walked slowly back from the Cummings' house. Caleb had been invited to come last Sunday, and had accepted on the one condition that Henry could join him. The whole visit had been awkward and stiff. The Cummings were still quite miffed with Henry, and the young Miss Cummings wished only to catch the eye of the curate.

The two young men had escaped the grasp of the family as soon as was politely possible. "To think that I thought the ladies of the court bad," mumbled Henry to himself. Then to Caleb he said more clearly, "I do not know how you do it. I would not be able to make those types of visits whenever it was asked of me."

Caleb mulled this over for a minute. "Do you not make the same visits that I do? I mean, you certainly do not visit the sick and the ailing, but when you are home, people are always vying for your attention and asking to be in your presence for at least a little while. I would think that you would even have to put up with the fawning daughter every now and then."

"Ha!" exclaimed Henry. "People do not vie for my attention. What favour can the Prince give that does not first proceed from the king? It is my father that people would like to see, and as for the young women, they only seek a crown and their own type of glory."

"You speak as if you are bitter toward your lot in life. This cannot be the case, can it?"

"The life of a prince isn't all they make it out to be, Caleb. Can you imagine a life where no one cares for you except for the power that you can bestow on them one day? Or, even worse, they hate you because your ancestors did something they disagreed with. Everywhere I go, I am prejudged. No one looks at me and sees Henry. What they see is Prince Henry, the giver of gifts and the upcoming power of a nation."

"And when one looks at me, they see not Caleb, but the curate, the one who can give a blessing from God and can offer a better position in life to the one I choose to marry. Honestly Henry, there are benefits and downfalls to each position a person holds. It is best that you do whatever you can to uphold the power you have been given, and do nothing to disgrace your name."

Henry could see that Caleb would not understand, so the two walked on in silence.

It wasn't long before they came to the Monks' cottage, and Caleb suggested that they stop in for a visit. Henry had no misgivings about this, so the two went to knock on the door. Mrs. Monks answered the door and greeted the two pleasantly and invited them in for tea. Upon entering the room, Caleb and Henry were met with feminine screams of terror.

Henry, being the better trained of the two, bolted toward the sound of distress, reaching for the sword that did not hang at his side. Caleb followed not far behind with a quiet prayer on his lips. The sight that met Henry when he entered the parlour both amused and bewildered him.

Rose and Katy lay on the floor laughing. Their dresses were askew, and their hair tumbled about their shoulders. There was a slight tear in the hem of Rose's dress, and Katy's shoe had slipped off her foot. The guilty shoe rested across the room where it had landed after being flung from the owner's foot in the tumble.

Caleb entered the room wearing a look of severe disapproval. All merriment left with his chilled appearance. Rose stood quickly, straightened her skirts, and tried to match Caleb's stern demeanour. It was hard to take her seriously when her hair fell about her shoulders in such a manner, but Henry gave it his best shot, biting his lip to hide his smile.

"Mr. Taylor, Mr. Hyden, how wonderful to see the two of you. Please forgive Katy and me. We were just preparing for the ball, and we had a little misstep that sent us to the floor. Please, have a seat." Rose turned to help Katy up, and together they went to sit on the couch.

"Forgive me," said Caleb, "but I must be going. I only stopped by to give a quick salutation, but I must be on my way. There is still much work I must attend to, to prepare the hospital for our soldiers." His face was beet red and scrunched from the foul taste of the lie. Henry did not know how to react to the sudden change in Caleb.

"I had no idea that you were planning on leaving so soon, Caleb," said Henry, forgetting all decorum. "If I knew you were so busy, I would have suggested we keep walking past the Monks' house, for now that I am here, I find it hard to leave. I would much rather stay and converse with the present company."

Caleb knew that Henry had seen through his lie, but he persisted. "You may stay, Mr. Hyden," he said, emphasizing the formal name, "but I fear that I must go. So, if you will excuse me." With that, he took his leave of the room. Rose and Katy sat stiffly and Henry slouched in his chair until all signs of the cold curate had evaporated.

Henry was the first to break the silence. "I believe I interrupted a dance practice?" he said. Both girls groaned and let the stiffness out of their backs. Smiles appeared again on all the faces, and Katy couldn't hold back a giggle.

"We must look a mess!" exclaimed Rose. "It really was just a simple misstep. You see, I am teaching Katy to dance so that she will be prepared for the ball, and we were going through a faster reel, and I stopped humming, and you saw the result."

"A dance lesson, you say!" exclaimed Henry. "Then maybe I can be of assistance. I love to dance, and I would not mind being the partner to either of the beautiful women in this room, seeing as it is a training session, of course. I would not want to pressure you to dance with me." He directed these final words at Katy, who blushed slightly and turned her face away.

"That is a wonderful idea, Mr. Hyden," Rose said. "You and Katy can dance while I play the piano. That way, Katy can get used to the music and the timing, and she can know what it is like to dance with a partner. I fear I do not play the part of a male suitor that well."

Henry laughed at the picture of Rose playing the smitten suitor of a young maiden. Standing, he offered a hand to both of the ladies. He escorted them to their various places in the room, then took his place across from Katy. He bowed handsomely and smiled at Katy's clumsy curtsy. The music began, and he fell into the familiar steps that now came second nature to him.

Katy had a little more trouble with the steps and often relied on Rose for coaching from the piano. Even when she had the steps right, Katy was stiff and lacked grace. It would take her time to grasp the finer details of the dance. It was best now that she just learn the steps.

The song ended and Henry again bowed to his young partner. "You did very well, Katy," he complimented earnestly. She blushed and tried to hide her face. She begged Rose to start the next dance, and Rose allowed her fingers to fly across the piano in a fast-paced Quadrille. Henry loved the song and felt his spirits lift with the music.

Katy stumbled her way through the dance. Henry couldn't count the times that she stepped on his toes, but he was patient and helped her finish. She beamed when the song ended and she realized she had made it through the whole thing without falling or quitting. "I did it, Rose!" she exclaimed. "I really did it!"

Rose laughed softly. "You did wonderfully, Katy," she encouraged. "You will do wonderfully at the ball, and I am sure that you will have many a suitor waiting to dance with you."

Katy smiled dreamily at the picture of a line of suitors. She could think of one face that she would long to see in that line ready to dance with her, but that was sure to never happen.

Cold reality snapped her out of her dream, and she turned to Rose. "I have yet to see you dance, Rose. You have taught me so well, but I have only seen you dance as my partner. How about you dance with Mr. Hyden, while I play a song on the piano? It would be good for me to observe another dance so that I can apply it to my own steps." Rose was hesitant, but when Mr. Hyden held out his hand to her, she had little choice.

Henry bowed, and Rose curtsied. Katy began the slow melody of a simple country dance on the piano. The song was delicate and graceful. Of all the dances that the land of Samaya possessed, this had to be the most intimate of them all.

Rose followed Henry's lead, matching his steps, steps that brought them side by side, face to face, and then far away again. She used the grace that she had learned while fencing, allowing it to bring her gliding around the room. Most of all, she watched Henry. He moved with adept motions. His grace was beyond that of most men, and was stunning to look at.

While Rose watched Henry, he watched her. He watched the way she moved into every step, and swayed with the gentle beat of the music. He watched her come close to him, then step away. He felt her hand in his, and he hung on tightly. He felt the music encompass them, and they were alone for the briefest of moments.

The music stopped, and Rose looked up at him. Her eyes seemed to pierce his very soul, and he knew he must be undone before her. He looked away with shame, but her eyes burned on him hotter than the flush in his cheeks. Slowly he turned back to her. He looked again at her eyes expecting judgment, but all he found there was acceptance. He couldn't explain it, and he didn't understand it himself, but he knew that she had accepted him for whom he was, and the notion thrilled him.

"Oh!" squealed Katy. "That was marvellous. The two of you danced so wonderfully. I don't think I have ever witnessed such wonderful dancing. It was as if... as if... Why, I don't know how to describe it. It was almost as if you two were meant to dance with each other, you were so well matched. I hope you will dance again at the ball. That would be a treat."

Rose cleared her throat and the spell was broken. "I think, Katy, what you witnessed was the grace of a man well practiced in the sword. When a man has learned to fight well, his talent spills over into the rest of his life. You will see it in the way he walks, the way he stands, and in the simple grace that he possesses while he dances."

Henry turned to Katy. "Miss Wooden is, of course, correct in her assumptions. I have been well trained in the sword, and it does affect my grace while I dance." He let out a soft chuckle. "One would almost assume that Miss Wooden wields a sword by the grace that she herself possesses while dancing."

Rose's flushed face turned ghostly white at the light-hearted jest, and she began to sway as if she was about to faint. Henry reached out a hand to steady her. "Are you all right, Miss Wooden?" Henry asked, alarmed. He helped her to a chair where she sat waxen faced.

Slowly, colour came back to her cheeks, and she looked up with a faint smile on her lips at the worried faces above her. "Forgive me," she said lightly, "I am a trifle tired from the dancing, and I became a little lightheaded. A glass of water will heal all my ailments." Those words were enough to send Katy to the pump, and Henry was left in the room to worry over Rose.

"I am quite alright," she said to Henry as he kept inquiring about her health. She even managed a slight chuckle when he wouldn't let up. She again blamed her slight illness on the over exertion caused by the dancing. When he was finally satisfied that she was alright, Henry took a seat beside her.

The two sat in companionable silence for a while before Henry spoke. "Rose, I would like to speak about the dance. You are an amazing dancer…"

Rose, not liking where the conversation was going, cut in. "Let us not talk about the dance. It was a joy to dance with you, but that joy shall not be repeated again… until the ball, perhaps." With the conversation cut short, the two were again left to sit in silence until Katy returned with the water, and Henry took his leave.

Henry walked into the rectory to find Caleb sulking in his chair in the parlour. "What is the matter with you?" he demanded. "Why in the world did you act as if you had swallowed a June bug at the Monks? You were positively cold." Caleb looked up at Henry sourly. Instead of replying to Henry's questions, he returned to his sulking. It was a miserable sight to behold, and Henry wanted to leave the room in disgust, but he needed answers. "Well?" he asked again. "What have you to say?"

"Did you not see the way they comported themselves?" asked Caleb angrily. "It was absolutely disgraceful to see two grown ladies act like children, rolling and laughing on the floor. I was embarrassed, and I did not want to take any part in their levity." Caleb, assuming his answer made perfect sense, resumed his position of dire misery.

"Levity? Surely, Caleb, you speak as if the two of them acted in disrespect toward an important matter. There was nothing amiss with their heightened spirits. They were simply enjoying a wonderful afternoon. They took pleasure in the joy of being around each other. Now, tell me what is so wrong with that."

"Did you not hear me?" asked Caleb, bewildered. "The two of them were sprawled on the floor like little children. My goodness, Rose's skirt was raised clear up to her knee." Caleb blushed and scrunched his face when he realized what he had said. "Of course, I do not blame Rose for the unscrupulous way in which they presented themselves."

Henry felt anger rise up in him. "Are you so daft? I would not think you that cold and that heartless. Rose had been teaching Katy to dance for the ball when the two of them took a spill. They were on the way to mending themselves when we barged in."

Caleb raised his voice when he replied. "Sophisticated young females do not giggle on the floor of the parlour after a spill. They collect themselves, putting everything to rights, and they continue about their business. I am not daft in saying this. It is the proper thing in society. What would the elders of the church say if they saw the two of them sprawled in the room with their hair dishevelled and their skirts hiked to their knees?"

"The elders would be daft as you are if they did anything other than help the young ladies off the floor. I am ashamed to think that I myself forgot my manners and watched as they picked themselves up," Henry shouted back.

Caleb sputtered over his next words. "Image is everything for a young lady, they should have been aware of this..."

"Is that what this is about?" yelled Henry even louder. "Are you worried that your precious Rose won't live up to the standards of a minister's wife? If that is what you are afraid of, then you were right all along. You don't deserve her. You would have better luck finding a perfect minister's wife in the petty Miss Cummings."

Caleb's face turned a deep burgundy as anger took hold of him. "None of this was Rose's fault! I only blame that senseless Miss Monks. She would be the one to instigate such an atrocity. She is a silly, petty female."

"Go stick your blame where it belongs, Caleb. Neither Katy nor Rose is to be blamed for falling. It is just a fact of life that we do not always stand as securely as we would like to. If their mishaps caused them joy, then I will not be the one to stand in the way of it."

If Caleb responded to his words, Henry did not hear it. He walked to his bedroom, where he grabbed a purse full of money, his diary, and his sword and headed out the door. He would not bother with the irksome curate this evening. Instead, he walked down the road toward the inn. There would be a bed and a good meal waiting him when he got there. Caleb could mull over what he had said, and maybe by the morning, the two of them could be on a better note. If not, Henry had plenty of money to stay at the inn, or perhaps it would be his time to move on.

SEVENTEEN

Henry sat in his room at the inn brooding over what had happened at the rectory. He was angry with Caleb, and he needed some way to vent that anger. He paced back and forth, kicking at whatever got in his way. Finally, he grabbed his sword, walked down to the livery, saddled his horse, and took off.

He rode on for quite some time, till he came to a pasture where he dismounted. It was quite late, and a young man stood in the clearing. When Henry stepped closer to get a better look, the boy swung around and defiantly took up the ready position with his sword.

"Who are you?" the boy demanded.

"Cool yourself, boy. I only came here to practice my sport," Henry said, calmly holding up his own sword. The words did nothing to change the boy's posture. Instead, he seemed to tense more and better prepare himself for a fight.

He licked his lips before he spoke. "Did the teacher send you? It would be like the knight to send someone to test me unexpectedly. Were you told to test me?"

Henry was becoming more and more confused as the conversation went on. The boy made no sense to him at all. "Teacher? Knight? I do not know what you speak of. I came here of my own accord, and I definitely was not expecting to meet up with the likes of you."

The boy scowled and dropped his sword dejectedly. "Then he did not come, or he won't come 'cause you are here. I best be going then. There's no use in me sticking around if you are going to." Slowly the boy man slumped away.

"Wait!" called out Henry. "Would you stay for a while? You are here now, and it would help me greatly relieve my anger if I could fight against a real foe instead of the air." Henry looked at the lad hopefully.

The boy's eyes brightened as he turned and got into his ready position again. Henry followed suit, and the two began to duel. Henry eased into the fighting not knowing what to expect from the boy. He watched intently as the lad took careful but practiced steps. His form was excellent; he was just a bit slow yet. With the proper training, the boy could be an amazing fighter.

Henry began to press harder and harder. The boy grunted when he was stressed, but Henry was shocked to find he never spoke. He remained oddly silent throughout the duel. Henry tried to start up some conversation, but the boy did not reply. Instead, he concentrated on what he was doing. The silence was a bit eerie.

When he had enough of the fencing, and his anger was sufficiently vented, Henry intensified his fighting and disarmed the boy. He then sheathed his sword and rolled onto his back on the grass. "You are a good fighter, young sir," Henry said to his opponent, who had joined him.

"But you disarmed me, sir! You could have easily disarmed me at any moment. How then can you call me a good fighter?"

"Your form was good and you paid attention to your steps. You didn't lose your cool when I pressed you. This is all a mark of a good swordsman. You must have a very good teacher," Henry said matter-of-factly. "Who is your teacher, anyway? You mentioned a knight? The last I heard, all the knights were in Silidon with the king."

The boy blushed slightly and turned away. "Well, that's the thing. I don't know who my teacher is. He meets me at nights and we practice till the early morning. He doesn't speak much, and he's never told me his name, but I have never seen anyone fight like he does. He even kicks and throws fists like an expert, though he claims he only knows a little of that stuff. I call him 'knight' because I have no other name."

"Hmm," Henry muttered under his breath. "That is very interesting. And you do not recognize this man? You have never seen him around the town or at service? Have you not seen him anywhere?"

The boy blushed again. "I don't know if I have seen him anywhere else. I guess it could be possible, but I would never know."

"What do you mean, you would never know? I would think that you would be able to recognize your own teacher."

"He wears a mask," said the boy, his frustration evident in his words. "Besides, he says that he cannot identify himself, out of fear of being revealed. He will explain no further than that."

Henry could tell that the boy was tiring of the topic, so he decided to change it. "The sun is coming up, and I am tired. Do you live near here? I will escort you home, then be off myself."

"I can make it home by myself easily enough. My place is just through that patch of trees. I will be fine. You can head home. Thank you for fighting with me. I never know if the knight is going to show, and it is good to keep practicing with the soldiers returning and all that." The boy's voice trailed off as he headed toward his house, and Henry turned to leave.

Henry came up to his horse and began to untie him. A rustle in the bush startled him, and he turned to see what had made the noise. He peered into the darkness, looking for the disturbance, but he saw nothing. Slowly he turned back to release his horse. A soft sigh escaped the woods, but Henry chose to ignore it—a figment of his imagination that caused him to gallop all the way back to the inn.

Rose let out a soft sigh of relief when Henry turned to go. She had been walking to a lesson with Josh, but had been stopped when she noticed the two already fighting. She hadn't dared disturb them, so she had watched.

As she had guessed at their dance lesson, Henry was an exquisite swordfighter. He would have had to be trained by the finest in the country to be able to move as he did, and the gentle ease with which he held his sword bespoke a comfort with his weapon. If she thought on it, Rose could very easily have been jealous of the freedom he had with his sword. But she didn't think on it.

Rose had taken the time afforded her to sit back in the trees and watch as the two men fought. She enjoyed the show and didn't feel rude at all listening in on their conversation, though she did feel a little foolish gloating over the title bequeathed to her by young Josh. She was tempted to show herself then, but decided that it was too dangerous. Instead, she contented herself listening to them speak.

When Josh finally disappeared and the sun began to rise, Rose had lifted herself to leave. This had been her mistake. Henry had been nearby, and she had had to slink back into the shadows in hopes that he would not see her. He had peered through the branches, seeking the source of the noise. Rose had held her breath, not daring to move. Then he had turned, and she had been able to breathe as he galloped away.

Rose walked with springing steps back to the house as the morning light began to shine. She hadn't seen such good sport in a long time, and it put her in such a good mood she could sing, but she refrained due to the early hour. She slipped back into the

Monks' house, found her bed, and easily fell asleep with a smile on her lips.

Henry slipped into the rectory late Wednesday afternoon hoping to be able to grab his clothes and be gone without being noticed, but such was not to be his fate. As he passed by the parlour to get to his borrowed room, he was met by a very sorrowful Caleb.

"Look, Caleb," he said, "I'm just here to grab my things, then I'll be gone."

The look that Caleb gave him could only be described as pitiful. "Please don't go. I would like it very much if you would stay." His words dripped with pleading. "I am sorry for the things I said yesterday. They were uncalled for, and I could have been a little more understanding."

Henry looked at him suspiciously. It seemed odd that Caleb would be apologizing when yesterday he had felt so strongly about what he had said. It frustrated Henry that he had told Caleb who he was. Now he didn't know if Caleb really wanted him to stay or if he wanted the Prince to show favour to him. "You are forgiven," Henry replied bluntly.

"Then you will stay?" Caleb asked excitedly. "I will order a splendid dinner tonight, and we can celebrate the renewal of our friendship. I think that would be superb."

"Yes," replied Henry stiffly, "that will have to do." He walked away then. He had things to do. He had to grab his things from the inn, prepare for the soldiers' upcoming arrival, and help Mrs. Jennings, who was sure to have a chore for him around the house. Caleb had already disappeared to the kitchen, so Henry left without a farewell, thinking how he would really have rather come to blows to solve the whole ordeal.

The crowd was overwhelming. People pushed in from all sides trying to see the road where the soldiers would be walking. There was shouting and flag waving and an excited flush that rested on the cheeks of all those present. Every person was in good spirits. Today the soldiers were coming home, and tomorrow there would be a ball.

Rose stood in the back of the crowd with Katy, who wanted to push toward the front. It wouldn't be worth it, Rose told her continually. They would just be jostled about and regret it later. It would be much better if they waited near the back. All the soldiers would be in view at the ball tomorrow. There was no need to push to see them today.

Katy soon got too restless to stick with Rose, and when she saw May further up in the crowd, she took off to join her. Rose just shook her head and kept to her spot in the back of the crowd. The crowd was too big for her liking, and she would have much preferred to stay at home, but Katy had insisted upon coming.

Rose was carrying a basket of food that she had insisted on bringing. Katy had been frustrated with her when she had taken the extra ten minutes to pack a lunch. She was terrified that they would miss the army's entrance, but Rose had no such worries. Her fears were of another nature. She feared that the soldiers wouldn't come till later that day, or late into the night. They might even be so much delayed as to come the day of the ball. That was why Rose packed the lunch.

The day passed slowly. It was hot for a fall day, and most people in the crowd were sweating. The soldiers were to come at the stroke of one. When they hadn't come by two o'clock, the tension began to build. Two older gentlemen got into a fight, and if it hadn't been for their wives being present, the fight might well have escalated.

The clock ticked slowly by as drops of sweat continued to water the ground with salty wetness. People peered anxiously down the road. Talking had ceased. A hush fell as people held their breath. A soft whisper of murmured prayers was the only sound. Then they heard it. The practiced *clomp, clomp, clomp* of the foot-soldiers was heard.

Many people rubbed their ears to make sure they were not hearing things. Some leaned forward to peer down the road, but nothing could be seen. "I can see them!" shouted out an excited little boy, and he pointed to a cloud of billowing dust. The crowd again burst into a swarming mass of shouting flag-wavers.

Rose felt a swell of joy rise up in her breast as she watched the first of the soldiers pass. They walked straight on, not once turning to the side to look at the cheering crowds. Rose looked closely at all the faces that passed, seeing if she recognized any of them. She couldn't help but feel a twinge of bitterness when no one familiar stood out. But she still rejoiced in the returning of the troops.

Once the foot-soldiers had passed, five men who had risen in rank passed by on noble looking steeds. They marked the end of the procession, and the people of the town swarmed in behind them. They walked to the center of the town where the soldiers lined up. A man on a white horse, which looked to be the noblest of all the beasts, stepped forward and began to shout at the men. Rose couldn't make out a single word that was uttered except for the final *dismissed!* that sent the men running into the crowd to find families and friends who hadn't been seen in an ever so long time.

Rose felt tears roll down her cheeks as she saw a young man go up to a little girl, sweep her up in his arms, and swing her around and around. She watched the two for quite some time, then turned away from the sight that blessed her and grieved her so much. She walked the opposite way of the procession in hopes of avoiding such encounters, but the new sight that met her was equally as grieving.

Coming up in the distance was a group of scraggily looking men. Their uniforms hung on their skeletal forms, and many of them limped or carried their arms in slings. Others were carried on stretchers piled in carts bumping along behind poorly shod workhorses. Two men with the medic's insignia on their shoulders walked among the injured.

The tears rested on Rose's cheeks as she watched the sorry party walk toward the town. No one took notice of them or cheered their entrance. Instead, they were left to fend for themselves. Rose whispered a prayer for their poor souls and hoped that the family members of these men would soon step up and claim their loved ones, but no one showed pride in men so broken.

Rose felt a gentle nudge on her shoulder and turned to see Henry standing beside her. "It is a sad sight, is it not?" he said slowly. "These men fought bravely, many of them giving up their limbs and lives for the country. When they return, they are not recognized. The heroes are the ones that come back whole and without defect." Tears welled in his eyes. "Little do we know that those who see war never come back whole."

Rose looked at Henry closely. She looked at his strong features and gentle eyes that glittered with unshed tears. "Who are you, Henry?" she asked quietly.

Henry turned and looked her in the eye. He stared down at her for quite some time, and she saw the confusion and discontent that lay behind his calm composure. "I am but a traveler looking for what I have been missing for all my life." He turned away and looked again at the sick. "My father was a war hero, but he never was the same when he returned. He was distant. I missed the old him, the man I knew before he left for war." Henry turned back to her. "Sometimes I see the old him, but he always disappears."

A tear dripped down Rose's cheek at the pain in Henry's voice. She reached out and touched his arm as she said, "I am truly sorry for you, Henry. That must have really hurt you. War is a horrible thing that should be avoided if at all possible. If only those in power could see the negative effect the war has on the people."

Henry gave a weak smile. "I believe those in authority have finally taken notice of the smaller people who are hurt by the war." He began to walk. "Come. Caleb is at the hospital. We can help these soldiers get to their destination and help them get settled. The work will be good to remove our melancholy mood and will also make us more thankful for the ball tomorrow."

Rose laughed and followed Henry's jaunty step toward the men. The medics looked at them warily, but accepted their help. Rose ended up walking with a hobbling young soldier who lost his footing each time he turned to stare at the beautiful angel that had come to his rescue. Rose tried to prevent this from happening, but nothing seemed to work, so she continually prepared for the stumble and helped him back up every time he fell. Henry and an older soldier followed behind her, snickering at the young man's every misstep.

Caleb walked from room to room of the hospital looking at all the neatly made beds and carefully set nightstands. Everything was in place. Only the patients were missing. Caleb kept going over the things in his head that he was supposed to do. He checked and double-checked that there were enough beds and food for the next week. When there was nothing left for him to do, he paced.

He could hear the celebration of the returning soldiers outside, but he knew that the invalids would come after the parade of the well. He tried to go over his Sunday sermon while he waited, but his mind would not settle on the subject for long. He sat down to read a book, but the words in front of him meant nothing. He went back to pacing.

The celebration outside died down as the soldiers moved farther into town toward the square, and the room was filled with silence. Caleb sat and waited and listened. He strained to hear the faint clop of horse hooves on the hard packed dirt road. He listened for the distant moans of the ill as they were jostled about on their stretchers. Quite some time passed before he heard them.

First he heard the horses, then he heard the laughter of men and moans of the sick. The sound drew nearer and nearer until it rested right outside the hospital. He was just about to open the doors and welcome them in when he heard the cheery sound of a female's laughter. Caleb stopped in his tracks and tried to think what female would consider coming to help at the hospital when there were men aplenty whole and healthy in the town square.

"Open up the door, Caleb!" shouted a voice that Caleb very well recognized. He hurried to do as he was bid. He opened the doors with his welcome on his lips, only to have it die before it was spoken. Before him stood Rose and Henry, each supporting a wounded soldier who was growing weary from the walk. Behind them were about forty men either standing, nursing wounds, or lying in the back of a horse-drawn cart. There were only two medics.

"I thought I was supposed to have five," he muttered under his breath. He looked at Rose who smiled up at him, and he scowled back. She looked at him questioningly, but he didn't respond. He was in a bad mood and didn't want to deal with the fact that there were only two medics when there should have been five, and Rose was there at the hospital allowing all the men to stare at her when she should have been celebrating at a safe distance from all men.

"Are you going to allow us in, Caleb?" asked Henry again. Caleb stepped aside and allowed them to walk in. Rose walked in first with a young soldier leaning on her shoulder. She walked into the nearest room and helped him settle on a bed. The man walking behind her hooted at the way the boy stumbled, but quickly sank down into the bed that was offered him. Caleb watched in stunned silence as Rose, Henry, and the two medics made trip after trip helping men into their beds. He didn't come to his senses until he saw Rose helping Henry carry a stretcher with a grown man on it.

"Al-low me," he stuttered as he took the stretcher from Rose's hands and began to walk away with Henry. Rose shrugged her shoulders elegantly and walked outside to help more men. It wasn't a minute later that Caleb saw her walk in again, helping to carry a stretcher with another grown man on it. Henry laughed at the shocked expression that hung on his face.

When all the men were in and settled, Caleb went to find Rose, who was tending to the young soldier she had first carried in. "You should go now, Rose," he said gently. "Most of the work is done for now. You can come back in the morning with the other women of the town to tend to the ill."

"I don't mind," Rose replied. "I'll stay for a little longer if it is all right. I know you were expecting more help. I'm sure an extra pair of hands would be welcome."

"You don't understand, Rose." Caleb said tersely. "You must go. That is an order. You should be out celebrating the return of the soldiers. Now, go find Katy and enjoy a refreshing night at home."

"If you don't mind, *Curate* Taylor, I would much rather stay and care for the patients."

"You must go!" Caleb shouted. "There is no choice in the matter."

"Hush," whispered Rose. "This is a hospital and patients are trying to rest. You should know now that I don't take very well to being ordered around, and I see no reason why I should go. That is why I will stay."

"You must go," replied Caleb in a quieter tone, "because you are the only female present, and these men have not looked at a female for a long time. It is inappropriate for you to stay, and I would not be doing my duty if I allowed you to continue without a female chaperone."

"Tongues will wag, will they?" Rose retorted bitterly. "What will they say? That the silly Miss Wooden helped care for the soldiers and is therefore a less than reputable woman? Have they not already made that accusation against me and been proven false? What is worse, Caleb— that I cared for you by myself for five days with no woman present, or that I remain working in the hospital for the evening where most men present are unable to stand up?"

Caleb's face flamed red. "You will go," he snarled, "or you will not be allowed to return. Do you understand? I can only protect your reputation against so much, and I will not have my name tainted because you would not listen to me."

Rose stood up angrily. She was much shorter than Caleb, so she was forced to look up at him. "I understand completely!" she spat at him. "That you had to resort to threats shows a lack of character in you, Caleb. I am rather disappointed."

Rose spun around on her heals and stormed out of the hospital. All the men watched from their beds, some letting out soft whistles, and the healthier ones releasing a few catcalls. The young soldier on the bed looked up at Caleb with round, cloudy eyes. "If that was your woman, sir, you are in big trouble. When my momma was in a mood like that, she could near spank the pants clean off of me and holler down my poppa while she was at it."

Caleb scowled at the boy with his innocent eyes and stormed away to find someone who hadn't witnessed the whole ordeal.

With a satisfactory crash, the front door opened and young Josh Deplin burst in to rescue the curate. "Curate, you're going to have to come fast. There's nearly five men who are ready to take and wed their brides with or without a pastor, and their mothers-in-law to be are not cooperating." Josh shrugged his shoulders. "Maybe they will listen to you."

With a sigh of relief, Caleb left the hospital to Henry's capable hands and followed Josh to the square where the impatient couples waited.

EIGHTEEN

ROSE WALKED INTO THE HOUSE to be greeted by an overly excited Katy. "Hurry up now!" she exclaimed. "The ball starts in two hours. We must be getting ready immediately. How in the world am I supposed to get dressed in under two hours? And do my hair as well?"

Rose sighed softly. "Don't you fret any, Katy. All will get done, and you have plenty of time to get ready." The young girl didn't look convinced as she raced up the stairs to her room. Rose shook her head as she followed slowly behind her.

It had been a long day. She had worked at the hospital with many older ladies of the town. They had learned how to change bandages, administer medication, and check for signs of gangrene. It was hard work, but very satisfying. She loved to interact with the patients and some of the men's families who had shown up to help with the work.

The only thing that soured Rose's day was the presence of Caleb. She was still quite miffed that he had thrown her out the other day, and she didn't feel like talking with him, so she avoided him. This was easily done because the women had all but kicked him out of the patients' quarters, claiming that the men needed a woman's tending just as much, if not more than a curate's. So Caleb spent most of his time tending to paperwork, only venturing from his office when one of the patients asked for prayer.

It wasn't until Rose was packing up that Caleb found her. She was placing her instruments in their proper place and cleaning up a small mess when he walked in the room. She tried to finish her task quickly and leave, but he came directly toward her. She pretended not to hear him when he addressed her, but he was persistent. When she finally looked at him, he proceeded to apologize for his appalling behaviour the day before, and that he was really only looking out for her best interests.

Rose couldn't help but accept his apology and the first dance of the ball, which he also offered. Now, as she worked her way up the stairs, she couldn't help but scoff at her foolish behaviour all day. If she had sought Caleb out, they could have made amends earlier, and the whole day would have been much more comfortable.

There was nothing she could do about past mistakes, but she could make up for them by looking very elegant at the ball that night. She would have to rush to help Katy get ready, and then she herself could get ready. She picked up her pace as she walked up the stairs, and she nearly ran down the hall to Katy and her room.

Katy sat by the mirror trying to twist her hair this way and that, but she was only tangling it into a bigger mess. "Patience, Katy," said Rose. "First you must get out of your everyday dress. If we do your hair first, it will be mussed up by the time we get you into your gown." Katy quickly undressed as Rose set out the various hair products she would use.

When Katy was ready, she sat down in front of Rose, who began to work with the rags that had tied Katy's hair into tight curls. When all the hair was loose, Rose gently picked up piece after piece and twisted them elegantly into a feminine hairstyle. By the time she was done, some curls hung around Katy's face and others piled atop her head in a most becoming way. Anyone who saw her would recognize her natural beauty.

Rose bent and kissed her cheek. "You are beautiful, and make sure you remember that tonight as bachelor after bachelor asks you to dance." Katy gave her a bright and happy smile, for indeed she did feel beautiful. "Now, go finish getting dressed and present yourself to your mother as I myself get ready."

Katy jumped up from her seat and hugged Rose. "Thank you, thank you, thank you. You have a knack for these things, don't you? You always know just the right touch to make something look exquisite." She let out an excited squeal and ran to finish getting dressed.

Rose began to dress down, and then turned to the mirror and began pulling her hair up in an elegant twist. She pushed the pins in place and let some of her hair fall around her face to cover her ears. She rummaged in her trunk and pulled out a clip that John had given her years ago, and pushed it into the side of the knot in her hair.

By the time she was done with her hair, it was almost time to go. The hall in which the ball was going to be held would be packed, and it would never do to be late, so most families were leaving well in advance. It would not be considered unruly to leave a half hour before the designated beginning.

Rose walked over to the closet where her dress hung. She rescued the shimmering fabric from the dark recesses of the wall and slipped into the layers of material. The dress glimmered in the light of the early setting sun and accentuated the subtle curves of Rose's body. It was by far the most elegant piece of clothing she had ever owned.

She looked at herself in the mirror and felt a little vain for scrutinizing her appearance so. She didn't turn until the beckoning of the party below reached her ears. She grabbed her gloves and slippers which rested on the bed, and left the room behind her. She pulled on her slippers as she walked down the hall, and she was just pulling on her last glove when she turned into the parlour where the Monks family waited.

There was a quick intake of breath as she turned the corner and a look of astonishment on everyone's face. Rose directed a confused look at Mr. Monks, who stepped forward and said, "I do not believe we have met, my lady. My name is Mr. Monks, and this is my family. Anything that we can do to make your stay here more comfortable will be our pleasure."

Rose blushed slightly at the high ranking title that Mr. Monks addressed her with, but returned his banter with the same spirit of gaiety. "I assure you, Sir Monks, that my stay here has been most pleasant and the only thing that I lack is the sight of a young lady enjoying her first ball."

Mr. Monks let out a hardy laugh at her quick wit. "Then we shall be off. We do not want to keep the lady waiting." Mr. Monks opened the front door and escorted the ladies out into the chill evening. They walked briskly to their destination, holding their skirts just above the ground.

On their way, they were greeted by neighbours and friends alike, and as they traveled closer to their destination, the streets became more clustered and crowded. It seemed as if every person from the town would be present, which may in fact have been true. Soldiers dressed in heavily pressed uniforms stood in the doorway of the hall, jabbing their friends in the gut and laughing each time a pretty lady passed by.

As Rose and Katy stepped closer to the door, one of these soldiers let out a catcall, and Rose blushed when she overheard what the man had said to his friend. Apparently Katy heard their words as well, for a dark blush coloured her face and neck. The two walked quickly through the door, where they were greeted by a more respectable party of soldiers.

The soldiers who now stood before them were in fact the high-ranking colonels who had ridden into town on their horses. Rose and Katy approached each member of the party, introducing themselves and curtsying prettily. These men were polite and never let a rude comment pass their lips, but Rose watched as their eyes roamed over her and Katy. These men had been out of sophisticated company for too long, and if it hadn't been for their rank, they would be just as boorish as the men outside.

Rose tried to ignore the extra long looks that she was given, and how Colonel Jasper held onto her hand a little too long. She ignored the catcalls she heard from the men outside as other ladies joined the party. But she could not ignore the way that some of the women present practically drooled over all the men.

They tried not to make it look obvious. They were in every way polite, blushing when a remark was a little too indecorous, and batting their eyelashes when the men looked down at them. It was disgusting the way they threw themselves at the men, flirting and giggling. One would think they would have greater self-respect.

Rose decided to veer away from these bitter thoughts and think of more pleasing things. Caleb would be there soon, and then the dances would start. She would share the first dance with him, and possibly the second. Henry would also be there before long. She wasn't sure if she wanted to dance with him. He was a very good dancer, but it was dangerous. She couldn't help shivering as she remembered how he had looked at her when the two had danced last. It had been much too intimate.

Katy disappeared from her side, so Rose stood on tiptoes to scan the room for familiar faces. "May I assist you?" Rose took in a quick gasp of air as she turned to see Colonel Jasper standing behind her. He was of medium build with a kind face and flat brown eyes. He was the type of man who excelled at what he did not because of passion, but rather out of a need for personal comfort. Everything about him spoke of this inner need.

Rose blushed slightly. "No, thank you, sir. I was just looking for a friend. He is sure to be here soon enough."

The colonel's face turned slightly downcast at this announcement. "Who is your friend?" he asked politely. "Perhaps I can help you find him."

"Perhaps," replied Rose. "I am looking for the curate, Mr. Taylor. He is a very good friend of mine, and I would like to speak with him." Rose again turned to look for Caleb, but she could not see him. The touch of a hand on her elbow startled her and she jerked away, only to stumble into the arms of a man standing to her right.

Mortified, Colonel Jasper looked down at her as she leaned into the arms of a stranger. "Forgive me, my lady," blushed Jasper. "I think I am much out of practice. I was going to tell you that Mr. Taylor was over in the next room, and that I would escort you there, but I seemed to have startled you before a word was out of my mouth."

Rose cleared her throat and tried to stand, discouraging the questioning looks from the ladies around her. The man holding her nearly picked her clean off the floor and placed her back on her feet. She murmured a thank you, then turned to the blushing Colonel Jasper. "I am quite all right, Colonel Jasper. You have merely startled me. No harm was done, thanks to…"

Rose turned to her rescuer, who supplied his name. "Thanks to Mr. Caman, I am quite all right." The colonel seemed to collect himself when he recognized the rescuer and stood up stiffly. He eyed Mr. Caman up and down, glaring at the taller man with a look that would have caused a lesser man to cower.

Mr. Caman did not back down; instead, he returned an equally fierce scowl. Rose was afraid they would come to blows, and was relieved when Caleb stepped in. "Miss Wooden, what is going on here?" he asked sharply.

Rose blushed and was about to explain when Mr. Caman cut in. "It is nothing of importance, Curate," he said politely. "Miss Wooden was just about to offer me a dance as a reward for saving her life, and I was going to gladly accept."

Rose blushed again. "I fear," she said a bit shakily, "that my first dance has already been claimed. You will have to wait for the second." She had gained her confidence by the end of the sentence and was able to look the smooth talking Mr. Caman in the face.

"If I cannot have the first dance, then I shall have the last. Until then." Mr. Caman tipped his hat and turned away from a stunned Rose and a scowling Colonel Jasper and Mr. Taylor.

When Mr. Caman had disappeared, Caleb grabbed Rose by the elbow and said, "A word with you, Miss Wooden." Rose couldn't even object as Caleb began to pull her to a less crowded section of the room. As soon as they were in a private area, Caleb began to scold her for her actions. How could she fall into the arms of a passing soldier? It was far too flirtatious and inappropriate.

Rose listened to his ranting calmly, then with a cold voice she replied, "I am sorry if I have offended you, Caleb, but I was startled when Colonel Jasper touched my elbow, and I stumbled. Mr. Caman kindly caught me before I tumbled to the floor."

Caleb blushed at this revelation. "Oh," was all that he managed to say before the warning note sounded. All the dancers took their place on the floor across from each other. Caleb stood unsmiling across from Rose and bowed stiffly. She curtsied back politely.

The dance began. It was quick paced and required the dancers' feet to move rhythmically. Caleb moved stiffly and woodenly with the music. He was still angry. Rose could see it on his face. Why he was so upset, she didn't know. He seemed very uptight lately. She didn't let his mood bother her and she danced gracefully to the music.

"You should be more aware of your image," Caleb said as they came together to grasp hands. The two parted again, and Rose mulled over what he could mean.

"I think that my image is very beautiful tonight," she said to him pertly, knowing perfectly well that it wasn't what he had meant. "It would have been nice if you had complimented me on my dress. It took hours to make."

Caleb fumed as the two separated, but was ready with a reply as soon as she was back within hearing distance. "You look quite beautiful tonight, but there are those here who would question a person's inner beauty and judge them rather harshly."

"Then I would say that those people should listen more carefully to their curate's sermons. If I recall correctly, you recently gave a sermon on not judging lest you yourself should also be judged harshly." Rose's reply was light and friendly so as to divert from the seriousness of the conversation.

"People are not perfect, Rose," said Caleb, trying to impress upon her the seriousness of the matter. "When they see you falling into the arms of some unsuspecting man, they assume you are quick, and that you are flirting with the man shamelessly. You should be more careful."

Rose spun away and returned with a smile on her face. "If people are going to judge me for a mishap, then perhaps they should look at their own daughters and sons. Many of the young ladies present tonight have been batting their eyelashes and flirting with the men shamelessly. How much more then should they be judged if they judge me? Now, Caleb, do not be so serious. We are at a ball, and we are supposed to be having a good time. Your appearance says you are having a most horrendous time."

There was no use resisting. One look at the smile on Rose's face, and Caleb's shoulders drooped a little, and he began to dance more smoothly. "I knew you would be able to dance marvellously as soon as you had the rod out of your back. You move much more fluently when you are not angry."

Caleb smiled at the beautiful Rose. "Forgive me. I must admit that I was jealous seeing you in the arms of that man. I guess I may have lost my head a little." Rose returned his smile and continued the dance.

They shared lighter conversation through the rest of the dance. She told Caleb about what she had done at the hospital that day, and the smitten look on Private Arnold's face every time Miss Cummings entered the room. He told her about praying with the wounded soldiers and the camaraderie shared between those that fought in the same division. Then the dance was over. The two stepped apart. Caleb bowed and Rose curtsied, and the room burst into clapping.

Caleb escorted Rose off the dance floor to where a nervous looking Colonel Jasper stood. He bowed politely to her and asked if she would like to dance. Rose turned to Caleb to see if he might want to dance again, but he was already waylaid by a group of young females wanting to dance with him. Rose smiled and turned back to the colonel. She accepted his offer and walked once more toward the dance floor.

When the music began, Colonel Jasper bumbled his way about. He obviously knew the steps, but he was rather nervous in the presence of the beautiful, young Miss Wooden. Rose bit her lip each time he stepped on her foot, and pretended she didn't feel it. She liked the colonel despite herself, and couldn't help but feel pity for him.

When the dance finished, he beamed at her, and she smiled back. He took her by the elbow comfortably and led her off the floor. He asked if she wanted to dance again, but Rose was becoming concerned with Katy's wellbeing, so she suggested that he find another partner, and she would rest a little. He took her advice, though unwillingly, and danced with Mrs. Monks, who had joined in the festivities.

Rose watched as Katy stood up to dance with a young soldier. He bowed, and Katy curtsied, and the dance began. Rose could tell that Katy was unsure of her steps, but she made her way through them slowly but surely. She smiled and blushed at her partner and moved more gracefully than she had in any of the dance lessons. By the time the dance was done, there was another young man to take the place of Katy's original suitor.

"Could I have the next dance?" Rose turned to see Henry standing beside her. He was tall and handsome in an expensive looking suit, and he looked very noble indeed with his hair pulled back smartly. She reached out her hand and he took it. He placed it in the crook of his arm and led her to the dance line.

He leaned toward her ear and spoke so only she could hear. "You look very beautiful tonight. Your dress is magnificent. How you ever made it, I shall never know."

Rose blushed and tilted her head upward to respond. "I have been making dresses since I was ten years old. I should be good at it by now." Henry smiled and then left her to take his place in the line across the floor.

The music began softly, slowly. It wasn't the same song that Katy had played for them, but it was similar. Rose bit her lip in an attempt to hide her nerves. There was nothing she should be nervous about. She had done this dance many times before. Perhaps if she talked a little, she would calm down.

"How have you been enjoying the ball? I have not seen you dancing with any of the girls, and I was beginning to wonder if you were really here."

"I ran a bit late. I received a letter from my father, and I wanted to respond to it before I left. I told Caleb to leave without me, and that I would catch up later. I must admit that I have never been to a ball quite like this before. It is much different than the dances that are held at my house."

"The dances are held at your house?" exclaimed Rose. "Your house must be very big indeed to hold so many people. All the dances that I have attended have been held at public halls, or if they have been at someone's home, they have been quite small with only a few people present."

Henry smiled. "You would enjoy the balls at my home. All the ladies dress in their best wares, and they are even more flirtatious than the women present tonight, though I admit it is a much more refined flirting. The men all dance with grace, and there are tables at the side overflowing with food and the choicest of wine."

Rose peered up at him with a look of dreamy wonderment, and he wanted to gloat on about the wealth of the whole affair, but he contained himself.

"It sounds like a marvellous time," replied Rose. "But I doubt that I shall ever be present for such an occasion as that." With the fatal reality of the words, all dreaminess left her eyes, and she was left only with the dancing.

The two moved in time with the music, but it held no spell over them. Their grace was unsurpassed, but it lacked any joyous excitement. Their dance had no life, for Rose's spirits died with reality, and Henry sought to speak truth at a time when lies were safer, and honesty could cost him everything he had gained.

They moved toward each other and then apart again, until the dancing ended and the clapping began. Bows and curtsies followed along with the rest of the evening. Rose gained back her good spirits during the next dance, and Henry milled about the crowd, dancing now and then and talking with the men at other times.

Rose introduced him to Colonel Jasper, whom Henry thought he had met before, but the colonel insisted it was impossible. The two men chatted for awhile as Rose danced with a young soldier. The time passed quickly.

Before Rose knew it, it was the last dance of the night, and Rose was standing across from the smooth talking Mr. Caman. He addressed her politely, but there was a different gleam about his eyes as they began the dance. He acted as if he knew a secret, and the thought of it made him giddy. Rose wondered if he was intoxicated.

He was the first to speak while they danced. "You are in fact the only Miss Wooden in this area, are you not? And you are staying with the Monks for the year?" Rose thought it was an odd question, but she answered in the affirmative. "I hear you are the one to talk to about services offered freely to those who ask."

Rose didn't know what to think of the man standing across from her. She wondered if the soldiers had not been allowed wine or whisky while they were on duty. "I have cared for the sick, and I know how to sew and clean, if you are talking about those services. But I warn you, I refuse to care for those who are inebriated."

Mr. Caman laughed heartily. "I was not talking about those types of services, Miss Wooden, and I assure you, I am not drunk; the wine is far too watered. Rumour has it among the men that a beautiful Miss Wooden who is staying at the Monks spent five days at the rectory, caring for the men within."

Rose was starting to get very confused. If Mr. Caman needed medical attention, he should go to the hospital. There would be plenty of persons there willing to help him. "I cared for Mr. Hyden and Mr. Taylor while they were ill. The epidemic hit them quite hard, and they were sick for quite some time."

"If you wish to call it an epidemic, you may," replied Mr. Caman nonchalantly. "Most men I know call it their need, lust or desire. It is very common among men who have been in the army for some time. Most men will settle for a whore, but I..." His words trailed off as Rose became faint.

She stepped out of the way of dancers toward one of the side walls and tried to take in air. Mr. Caman again came to her assistance, but she pushed him away, resisting the urge to spit on him. She made her way out of the crowded room and into the hall where there was no one to see the tears of embarrassment and shame on her face.

Henry danced the last dance with Katy Monks. He had hoped to dance it with Rose, but her hand was already spoken for, so he satisfied himself with taking glimpses of her. The dress was beautiful on her. She could pass for nobility anywhere in the kingdom. She even danced better than most noblewomen who took lessons.

He watched as she danced with the fellow named Caman. As the music flowed, she had a look on her face that became more and more confused. Caman seemed to be enjoying himself.

Henry's heart nearly stopped when he saw Rose's face go white, and she began to sway. Caman followed her off the dance floor with a feral gleam in his eyes. His lust for the woman in front of him was evident to anyone who took the opportunity to look. Rose pushed him away and walked out toward the backroom. Henry made his apologies to Katy and followed after Rose.

He found her out in the hall, tears pouring down her face, and he cursed Caman for whatever he had said to make her cry. He reached out a hand and wiped a tear from Rose's face. She startled and nearly fell. Her face held a look of terror that almost broke his heart. "Forgive me," he said weakly.

Rose hugged her small frame and tried to hide her tears. "I was so gullible," she whispered. "Caleb was right. I should have been more aware. I should have done something to protect my name, and now this happens, and I am undone."

"Hush now," murmured Henry. "What did the cad say that has upset you so? I promise you that nothing will come of it. You have not done a thing ignoble, and you have never once tarnished your name in any way. The man was a fool, a dog of fools."

Rose blushed and turned away. "He compared me to a whore. He said I was known among the men for providing services. He even suggested that my tending you and Caleb was... was..." she shuddered and didn't continue.

Henry made her turn and face him only to see fresh tears streak down her face. On instinct he opened up his arms and pulled her to him. Her tears wet his shirt, but he did not mind. He held her until she could cry no more. When her tears had ceased, he handed her his kerchief and excused himself. She nodded slightly, so he left her there to redeem some of her pride.

He waltzed back into the ballroom and spotted Caman laughing with some of his goon friends. Henry made his way over to the dog and, placing his hand on the man's shoulder, asked for an audience with him. "Why would I speak with you when I do not even know who you are?" cracked the fool.

"Believe me," replied Henry, "if you knew who I was you would not have made that comment." He pressed his fingers into the base of Caman's neck to emphasize his point. Caman winced slightly, and stood to have an advantage of height. Unfortunately for Mr. Caman, even while standing, Henry was taller than him.

Henry indicated a private spot where the two of them could talk, and Caman headed in that direction. Henry followed close behind. When he was sure that no one would overhear him, Henry began to speak. "You have made some insinuating remarks to a young lady who I highly respect. Now, the damage has already been done and an apology will not repair what havoc your words have wreaked. Therefore, all I ask for is an assurance that this young lady will never hear such things suggested around her again. If she does, I will hold you responsible, and make your life miserable."

"I know who you are," spat Caman. "You are the insufferable Mr. Hyden. I bet she was good bed sport for you, and now you don't want to share. I believe that is up to the lady..." His words were cut off by a quick jab in the throat.

Henry glared at him. Anger told tales of horror in his eyes, and Caman cowered at the sight of it. "You dog," growled Henry. "If you wish to speak again, I suggest you remain civil. Such slanders that you have voiced will only cause you harm and others grief. You are nothing but a worm to be loathed."

"What is it to you what I say of the lady?" wheezed Mr. Caman. "I have heard word myself that she is just a poor orphan."

Rose, an orphan? When did that happen? he wondered, but he didn't let it show in his eyes. "Orphan or not," he continued, "I respect her, and you will show her the same respect which she deserves. Now go." Henry pushed the man away. Such scum was only worthy enough to be walked over.

He turned in time to see Rose walk back into the room. She was much more composed and there were only a few traces of the tears she had shed. She saw Henry looking at her, and she smiled. He smiled back and only hoped that his intervention hadn't been too late.

Jasper watched from the corner of the crowd as Henry spoke with Mr. Caman. The man was a cad and always would be, but Henry was doing a wonderful job of dealing with him. In fact, the colonel was surprised at how well Henry was able to keep the dog under control.

Jasper sighed and began to walk around the room. He was where the king wanted him. He was close to Henry and guarding the woman that Henry was in love with. Yes, though the Prince was too dense to realize it at the moment, it was evident to every other person that he was in love with Miss Rose Wooden.

Jasper shook his head. How he was going to keep his presence a secret, he didn't know. All the king had ordered to do was to keep an eye on his son's love. Unfortunately, the king had not given any suggestions as to how to do so. So it was left to Jasper to be creative.

He had thought himself ingenious when he got a pass into the town as a part of the army. No one would suspect one of the soldiers as being out of place. Then he had greeted the townspeople at the door waiting for the woman that the king had told him to look for. Everything from there had been simple. He played the part of a nervous suitor and had gotten to know Miss Wooden better as they danced. The tricky part would come again tomorrow when he needed to keep an eye on the lady without being noticed. But that was tomorrow's worry. Besides, the ball would have everyone in bed till all hours. It was best he also went to bed to sleep while he still could.

NINETEEN

COLONEL JASPER WALKED SLOWLY BESIDE Rose on the way into town, and Katy followed close behind with a smitten young soldier. The young man looked at her like she was the goddess Hera, but she completely ignored him. He was nothing to her but a minor distraction to pass away the lazy Sunday afternoon.

Rose smiled politely as Colonel Jasper talked about his family. He was quite proud of his younger siblings, as well as his mother, and though he said they lived in town, Rose couldn't recall meeting a single one of them. He rambled on and on about everything and nothing. Rose listened politely and found that she rather did enjoy the colonel's company. Talking with him was comfortable and relaxed. It wasn't pushy or awkward like conversation with a suitor; rather, it was much like talking to a long-time acquaintance.

The walk lasted most of the afternoon, and the two men stayed for dinner as well. All in all, it added up to a very pleasant day to be enjoyed after such a horrendous end to the previous evening. Rose couldn't help but shudder as she thought about the words Mr. Caman had spat at her. They had been cruel, cold-hearted, and uncalled for. She would have to make a point of avoiding such men.

The evening came to a close, and the smitten Colonel Jasper spoke a warm farewell as he made his way down the road to where he lived. Rose smiled as she waved back at him. He was a good man. She could very well grow to like him, and it was time she started thinking of whom to wed. Caleb was out of the question, along with Henry. Colonel Jasper would make a very comfortable choice. She could be very happy with him.

Rose cast these thoughts aside as she headed up the stairs to bed. There was work to be done tomorrow, and she couldn't waste her time fretting over her options with men. It would be much better if she concentrated on sleeping and working. If there was a man to be had, he would propose soon enough.

Rose woke bright and early the next morning and let out a slight groan as she stretched the muscles in her back. She sighed sleepily as she slipped into a modest working dress and made her way silently down the stairs. Her breakfast consisted of cold leftovers from yesterday's meal, and then she was on her way.

Her steps carried her quickly toward the hospital where she knew she would find plenty of work. Sheets always needed to be changed, men needed to be fed, bandages needed to be replaced, but most of all, soldiers needed a woman's presence. The deprivation of the female sex had made many of them crass and unruly, but that did not deter the women. Most believed that within time the men would become gentle and even likable, at least that was what the young marriageable ladies hoped.

Rose hoped this as well. It wasn't because she intended to marry one of the young men. That was as unlikely as the sun not rising with the dawn. But she did not want the war to steal any more than it already had. Enough blood had been shed to quench the soil; men's souls did not need to join in the mixture. She would do everything in her power to prevent that.

Rose kept this in mind as she made beds and washed sheets. There wasn't a set launderer, so everyone took their turn. She also remembered this as she ignored the cusses and catcalls that followed her through the men's rooms. But it took all of her will power to keep this in mind when she fed Private Hepton.

She had been minding her own business, administering medicine and changing bandages, when there was a loud crash from the other room. It wasn't uncommon to hear loud crashes, so Rose ignored it and continued her work. A few minutes later, a teary eyed Miss Cummings burst through the door.

"I can't do it!" she wailed. "I refuse to help him! He is as insolent as a two-year-old and mean as a cock-eyed rooster. He threw his soup at me just because he wanted to, and now he is laughing at me. Of all the insufferable things."

Rose ran to soothe the young girl, who was now weeping at the soup stain on her dress. "There, there," said Rose. "It can't be all that bad. Who threw the soup at you? How about you finish tending to the soldiers in here, and I will go feed the young sir who has acted so rashly."

Miss Cummings nodded her assent with a pretty sniff of her nose. She let out a tiny hiccup as she said, "He's in there. You'll know who he is." Her sad state made Rose pity her, but it also made her curious as to the character of the young man who lay beyond the swinging door.

Rose grabbed a bowl of soup off of a tray that was always filled with provisions for the men. She made sure it was still warm, then hesitantly stepped through the door. Private Hepton was not hard to spot. He wore a glower that would scare most men, and a scar ran down the right side of his head. He sneered at Rose as she walked toward him and muttered when he saw the bowl of soup that rested in her hands.

Guessing that he might intend to send the food flying if it got within his reach, Rose made a wide berth and placed the bowl where it could not be easily accessed by the patient. When the private noticed this, he let out a low growl of anger. He didn't like to be outsmarted by a woman.

"Now, Private Hepton," Rose said calmly and politely, "are you going to behave, or am I going to have to spoon-feed you?" The private let out a strangled chuckle and held up a maimed right hand which lacked the three middle fingers. "Oh," was all that Rose could reply.

"Very well then," continued Rose. "If I must feed you, I would like to know if you will cooperate. I would appreciate staying as clean as possible today. Are you willing to eat and behave yourself?"

Hepton grunted. "I'll behave sure enough as long as you don't send me any of those fluttery-googled eyed looks that them other girls was givin' me. A man don't much appreciate being coddled in that manner. And don't you dare pity me."

"I think I can live with your terms, Private Hepton," replied Rose sternly. "I don't think I am the fluttery-googled eyed girl type."

The private scrutinized her closely, and Rose felt herself blush as his eyes raked up and down her body. "We'll have to see," he said.

Rose picked up the spoon and began to feed him. All was going well and they were about halfway through the bowl. Rose was beginning to wonder what trouble Miss Cummings could have possibly had when the bowl went flying from her hands and landed with a splat on her lap. "Hey, what was that for!" she demanded.

"I didn't much like your look," replied the private. Rose glowered at him and went to grab another bowl of soup. She bit her lip as she thought of all the things she would like to say to him but knew she would regret later. Instead, she plopped down in the chair by his bed and began to feed him again.

A few mouthfuls in, Rose found her lap to be the recipient of another bowl of soup. She held her tongue at all the things she would love to yell, and went and grabbed another bowl. The third bowl lasted shorter than the second, and Rose began to believe that Private Hepton was just trying to antagonize her.

By the fourth bowl, she had had enough. She placed the empty dish by his bed, stood, and grabbed a fifth bowl of soup. She smiled sweetly back at the smirk on his face, and when he was least expecting it, she dumped the bowl of soup over his head. Private Hepton howled with shock, but it soon turned into guffaws of laughter. Rose looked at him incredulously, which only brought more fits of laughter.

"You know, you are somethin', Miss," he said. "You showed me right up." More guffaws escaped him. "Gosh darnit, lady, you have some sass."

Rose glowered at him, and before she could stop herself, she spoke. "And you, sir, are the most miserable patient I have ever had. If you keep this up, I'll pour a bowl of soup on your head every morning. It'll give you a taste of your own medicine."

Private Hepton guffawed again and Rose turned and stalked away. She needed a new dress. Then again, she needed a lot more than a dress; she needed a whole new set of manners, because hers had just been emptied out with that last bowl of soup.

The hospital came alive behind Rose as worried nurses rushed to the side of the soup-soaked private. The private resisted all their attempts to help him and growled at the googly eyed looks he received from the young females. He was quite content to sit with the soup rolling down his face, relishing the memory of the sassy nurse who had put him in his place.

Rose paced back and forth in her room, horrified by her actions at the hospital. How could she ever show her face again? The women were sure to be whispering behind her back about how she was unable to handle herself with esteem and was a bad example for the soldiers. This one act of stupidity was sure to be her downfall.

Rose continued to pace, berating herself with every step. She did not show herself any mercy. Instead, she rained down the justice she knew she deserved. She was even tempted to go so far as to acquire a bowl of soup and pour it on her own head, but such an action would lack all sanity, so she resisted.

Rose did not stop her rampage until she heard a soft knock on the door. Katy stepped in and hesitantly told her that she had a visitor downstairs. She seemed to wear a look of pity as Rose made her first steps toward the stairs, and when Rose turned into the parlour she understood why.

Caleb stood by the piano, his whole posture stiff and angry. He refused to look her in the eye when she entered, and he would not speak until he heard the front door click and Katy's footsteps disappear down the road. When he finally did speak, Rose wished he had never opened his mouth.

"What were you thinking? Do you lack all couth? Or, better yet, do you enjoy the attention that you gather from your mad endeavours? My goodness, Rose! You have the whole town blathering about a bowl of soup. Most normal persons are shocked and dismayed by such an insane action!"

Rose turned away, hot anger turning her cheeks scarlet. "Do you think I have not punished myself for my actions? I run over and over in my memory the moment, trying to find what so possessed me that I would dump a bowl of soup on a soldier's head, but I find no way to justify my actions, and the thought grieves me to no end."

"Then why do you not apologize and set the record straight? Many in town would be willing to forgive you if you returned immediately to seek the forgiveness of the private."

"I will do no such thing," replied Rose sternly.

"And why ever not?" exclaimed Caleb with some exasperation.

"Because," Rose said through clenched teeth, "as much as I grieve my actions, I feel no remorse over them. It may have been wrong of me to do, but Private Hepton deserved each noodle that slipped onto his head!"

"You... you cannot be serious!" sputtered Caleb in clear outrage. "No man deserves treatment such as that under any circumstance. No man! You should apologize immediately."

"Why?" Rose asked defiantly. "Why does it matter to you so much if I apologize? How has this any effect on you or your affairs? For that matter, how does it affect the affairs of the town? As far as I am concerned, this dispute should remain between Private Hepton and myself!"

"Why does this matter to me?!" exclaimed Caleb as he took a step closer. He grabbed her shoulders and she felt terror in his grip. "Surely you must know, woman!" Rose cowered before him, and he grasped her tighter. "Surely you must know how I love you!" He grabbed behind her neck pulling her face towards his and kissing her soundly on the lips.

He released her and she stumbled backward. A look of horror crossed her face, and fear quaked within her chest. She tried to form words on her lips, but could only gasp for air. Caleb also appeared shocked as he looked down upon the trembling Rose and bile rose up in his throat. "Forgive me," he murmured. "Forgive me."

Rose turned away as gentle tears rolled down her face. "I'm so sorry, Caleb," she whispered. "I am so dreadfully sorry." With the words finally released from her lips, she fled from the house out into the pasture, leaving a broken-hearted curate standing in the parlour.

Rose stood looking at herself in the mirror. Her bare arms revealed dark black bruises where Caleb had grasped her, and the sight of them made her sick. She hated what had occurred more than anything else in the world, for she had caused Caleb pain. She had unknowingly made him fall in love with her though she could never return the sentiment, and now she bore the price of that sin on her arms.

She tried to ignore the pain while she dressed, but she knew that she would be hard pressed to conceal it all day. She would have to try. She made her way toward the hospital. The clean air and the warm sun had no effect on her dark spirits. She did not notice the last clinging wild flowers or the crisp, clean snaps of fresh, breathable air. She only noticed her sorrow.

At the hospital, she went about her work quietly, ignoring the stares and glares of the other nurses. She ignored the pain that coursed through her arms as she lifted loads of laundry and used it only as a reminder of how just a punishment for her sins it was. When the pain became too much to bear, tears would fill her eyes, but she would not shed them.

About halfway through the day, she was called into the other room. It appeared that Private Hepton refused to be fed by anyone other than the feisty nurse who had helped him the other day. Rose silently obliged. She carried over a bowl of soup that weighed heavily in her aching arms and began the slow task of dipping in the spoon lifting it and then refilling.

Private Hepton, discerning her dark mood, ate in silence, never once refusing the spoon that touched his lips until the bowl was empty. As Rose turned to leave, he reached out to halt her forward motion. He caught her by the arm and did not miss the quick intake of breath she took before turning to him with tear-filled eyes.

"How may I help you?" Rose asked in a small, sorrowful voice.

The private looked at her with questioning eyes. He studied her and searched for the cause of an ailment, but could discern none. His eyes prodded her, searching for what was amiss, but they came back empty. "I wish to apologize for my actions the other day," he said slowly. "I was very much in the wrong and I think that I may have harmed you far more than I intended."

Rose had to fight back the tears as she responded to his apology. "Do not think yourself at fault for my dark mood. I am the only one to be blamed. I am the cause of all my sorrows and justly take up my punishment."

Private Hepton scowled at her. "Did someone hurt you?" he demanded. "If one of those louts of a soldier hurt you, I swear, I will track him down and bring him all sorts of pain." Rose gave a weak smile at the brave soldier's words and couldn't help but sneak a peek at his stump of a leg.

"No soldier has harmed me," she said sadly. "I have, in one way or another, inflicted my own punishment. I am the only to blame for all my sorrows." A sad smile rested on her lips as the terrible truth escaped her lips. There was no denying that all her pain could have been prevented if she had been more cautious.

"I, too, am responsible for my sorrow," replied the soldier determinedly. "All this could have been prevented if I had made some better choices. I could have kept my foot and my fingers if only I had stayed out of the war. So I am the only one responsible for my sorrow."

Rose looked at him shocked. "How can you say such thing!" exclaimed Rose. "I know your story, and I know that it was the enemy who dismembered your body. How then can you blame yourself for your sorrow?"

"The same way you blame yourself for your own pain. I don't know for sure, but I think I can safely guess that you have some pretty nasty injuries on your arms, and if I am right, those weren't self-inflicted."

Rose turned away in shame. "I am still responsible for them. I could have prevented them if only I had been a bit more careful. I should have been more careful."

"I'm still responsible for my wounds as well. I could have easily prevented them if I had been more careful, instead of racing off into battle. I had a choice, after all. I should have made better ones."

"Don't say such things," replied Rose harshly. "Such thoughts are insanity itself, and they hold no truth. You only harm yourself if you speak them."

"Then listen to my truth!" cried Private Hepton. "You are not responsible for the harm done to you. A man should never harm a woman in such a way, and if he does he deserves death. No matter what the woman did, she does not deserve such treatment."

"How do you know?" asked Rose, tears pouring freely down her face. "You have not seen a woman for many years. How do you know how a woman should be treated? Your words do not hold truth; they only hold what you pertain to be true."

Private Hepton let out a frustrated sigh. "I know these words to be true because before I left for the war, I saw my father beat my mother to death while I stood by and watched. I vowed then and there that I would not let such harm befall a woman again."

"Who are you to speak!" demanded Rose. "Yesterday you poured soup on my dress, yet you do not call this abuse?"

"If you are harmed by the soup, I will ever be sorry for it because it was a careless act meant to test the spirits of the women around me. I meant no harm by it, and I believe that no harm was done. If you still do not believe me, know by my solemn vow that as long as I live, I will never lift a finger to harm a woman, and I will do anything in my power to bring justice to those who do."

Rose believed every word that left his mouth. How could she not believe when he spoke with such fiery passion? Yet she still faltered in the reality of his words. Caleb was not an awful man. He was the curate, for Pete's sake. How then could she blame him with such a crime? It had to be an accident. There was no other way around it.

"I ask you again, who has laid a finger on you that you are hurt?" Private Hepton's question tugged at her, begging a reply, but she bit her tongue and refused to answer with a name, for giving a name would only cause more damage than had already been done. So instead she mulled over her answer before speaking.

"He claimed he loves me, and I believe he does, but he knows now that I will never have him. It is not because he is unsuitable. Rather, he is too suitable. He may love me with all his heart, but I do not love him back, so we will never be a match. That is why I dare say I will never be harmed nor held by him again."

Private Hepton nodded slowly. "It still hurts, though, doesn't it? It still hurts to think of what has occurred, and the thought of it still scares you, doesn't it?" Rose nodded her head slowly. "Good," replied the soldier. "Let it be a reminder, so that you do not fall to hands that would harm you as he has, for his love may be real, but he acted in rage that is only fit on a battlefield."

Private Hepton closed his eyes and turned as if to go to sleep. "Go home and tend to your arms. If it is only bruises, they should heal soon enough, but I expect you back in the morning so that you can serve me breakfast." He did not watch as she stood and left, but a smile played on his lips as he heard the dull click of the front door and her soft footsteps on the dirt path outside.

TWENTY

ROSE MADE HER WAY TOWARD THE PASTURE to meet Josh. She had no intention of fencing tonight, for her arms ached from the labour inflicted upon her bruised muscles. It seemed only fair to tell Josh that she would not be able to practice instead of leaving him there waiting.

She moved slowly, not relishing the task at hand, for how could she tell Josh that she could not fight when she longed to wield a sword and burn off some of the pent-up emotion inside of herself? She was angry at herself for crying today in front of Private Hepton. She was confused over his words regarding how a man should treat a woman. But most of all, she was hurt and sore from the look in Caleb's eyes when he had proclaimed his feelings so ardently.

She bit her lip and moved on. Josh would be waiting for her if she did not speed her steps. As she entered the clearing, Josh rose from the rock he often occupied and stood in the ready position. "At ease, lad," Rose said softly. "As you can see, I am unarmed. We will not be fighting tonight. I came only to tell you that I would be unable to fight for a week or so."

Josh looked at her with a degree of disbelief. He glowered as he asked, "Are you going away?"

"No," replied Rose, "I will be staying at my former place of residence. I just won't be able to fight for a while."

"You're leaving, aren't you?!" demanded Josh. He seemed angry and disturbed by this news. He didn't want to look at her, and Rose wondered if she should push the topic further or just leave him as he was.

"I am not leaving, Josh. I would not leave without bidding you farewell. I do not know why you should accuse me so, when I should be back within a week's time." Josh didn't respond; he just turned his back and swatted at the ground with his sword. "Josh," Rose continued hesitantly, "has something happened that you would speak about?"

"The soldiers came back, but my father did not come back with them."

Rose's heart broke with these words, and she had to fight to hold back the tears.

"That's not the worst of it," continued Josh. "I went to figure out what happened to him by asking about his name at the office. They said there was never a man by such a name signed up for the army. I asked my mom about this and..." Josh hesitated to continue. It was evident he did not want to speak about it, but he felt compelled to go on.

"When I asked my mom about it, she broke right down and cried. She said that my dad had never been in the army. She said he left ten years ago when the war started. She said he had no intention of coming back, and she was glad to be rid of him. And to think, all this time I have remained naive to the whole matter. I should have clued in when we didn't receive any letters." Josh shook his head sadly, fighting back tears.

Rose burned with righteous anger. How could a man abandon his wife and young child like that? It wasn't right or good in any way. If he had died, it would be a different matter, but to just outright leave them was more wrong than anything Rose could think of. She wished to comfort Josh, but feared what would happen if she attempted to do such a thing.

"Do not ever think that I would do anything such as that, Josh," Rose said with a slight quiver in her voice. "If I must leave, I will tell you before I go, and I will explain where I am going and if I am ever coming back. Do you hear me? I will never leave you like a coward as your father did."

"Then why can't you fight tonight?" Josh demanded as tears poured down his face. "There must be a reason that you cannot fight. Why won't you tell me?"

"I do not fight," Rose said calmly, "because I have acquired a slight injury that makes it painful to move my arms. There isn't anything I would rather do than wield a sword at this moment, but it has been suggested that I rest my injury so that I do not make it worse. I have heeded these instructions given to me by a seasoned warrior."

"Oh." Josh's countenance fell as Rose proclaimed her reason for not fighting as if it hurt him to think on the matter. "Will you be okay in a week's time, do you think?" he asked anxiously.

"I suppose I will be. My injury is not all that strenuous, but it does impede the motion of my arms. I should be fit by next Tuesday. Shall I meet you here then?" Josh nodded vigorously. "Good. I will see you then." Seeing her task completed, Rose turned and walked back to the Monks' where a bed was waiting for her.

The weeks went by. Rose spent her time at the hospital mostly, where she got to know Private Mark Hepton better. She received weekends off, so she had lots of free time to visit Mrs. Jennings at the largely diminished orphanage, and to go on walks with the very comfortable Colonel Jasper.

She did not see much of Caleb, because he often kept himself locked in his office, reviewing the hospital's paperwork. The only time they interacted was at worship services. Even there, she tried to avoid him as much as possible. She did not wish him to be in love with her, and she would do anything in her power to make him un-in-love with her. Sadly, this often meant that she avoided Henry as well. This separation caused much frustration, as she had enjoyed both their company. Henry, on the other hand, could not figure out why the separation had occurred. He spoke to Caleb about the matter, but the curate was rather tight-lipped about the ordeal. He then tried to speak to Rose about it, but any mention of the fact was stoutly denied. It was really rather frustrating for the man.

Rose continued to meet with Josh on Tuesday nights, and as time passed, she found that he was more open to talking about all that was going on his life. He had gotten over the initial shock of his father's abandonment, and now he spoke of a job he hoped to get, an apprenticeship of sorts.

With so much to occupy her time, Rose found that the month of October flew by, and it wasn't until the middle of November that time confronted her. Nearly half her year had passed, and she had not found a husband. Sure, there were many potential candidates, but none had as of yet stated intentions of even courting her. How then could she be married in half a year's time?

She mulled this over as she walked to where Josh waited in the clearing. It was getting cold out, and they decided that this would be their last practice until the warmer weather returned. Rose was surprised that they had kept practicing this late in the season without snow preventing them. In Thespane, the first snow usually came with the first of November.

Rose reached up to scratch her face and was startled when she was not met by the comforting impediment of her mask. How could she have been so thoughtless as to forget her mask? What would have happened if she had made it all the way to the clearing without her mask on? How would Josh have reacted?

She reeled around on the spot and was startled again when she heard voices coming toward her. "Oh, it's so cold," squealed a high-pitched girly voice. There was some shuffling and a giggle.

"I know a place where we will be nice and warm," rumbled a male counterpart. This was followed by some more giggles and the dreadful shuffling noise. Rose was sickened by what she knew must be occurring, and she tried to hide before the party appeared. What she wasn't prepared for was who came around the corner.

Mr. Caman was the first person she saw, but following, too close for propriety, was a rather red-cheeked Miss Cummings. Rose burned with anger when she saw the wanton look on the young girl's face. How could she fall so easily into a trap laid by this dog of a man? It was vile and repulsive to think of how many other women he may have seduced.

Before she could think what she was doing, Rose stepped out of hiding, right into the path of the spellbound couple. Mr. Caman was the first one to notice her, and after his initial shock, a sneering grin crossed his face. "Rose! How nice of you to join us. I see you are dressed appropriately for the occasion. Would you like me to take you for a small dally in the woods?"

Rose stared in disgust at the worm before her, and then at the young woman who cowered behind him. "Go home, Miss Cummings," she demanded, "while you still have the chance to keep your virtue. I tell you, this man does not have good intentions for this night. You will only find yourself hurt."

Miss Cummings seemed to gain some gumption and she stood up to Rose. "I will not go. You must go. I am going to spend the night with my love." She gave Caman such a look that Rose would almost believe her to be in love, but such a thing was preposterous. No one could love a man such as Caman. Or could they?

Rose unsheathed her sword and looked at Miss Cummings with fire in her eyes. "Did you not hear your lover's words just spoken to me? Go. Leave us before it is too late for you. If you do not leave, you will force me to talk to the curate about your nightly excursions, and I do not believe he will be as forgiving as I."

Miss Cummings looked at her with horror, then ran off.

"That was a nice touch with the sword," Caman said with a smirk on his face. "Do you always carry it around on late night excursions? I must admit, it did a very good job of scaring off the competition."

Rose lifted the sword and placed the tip at Caman's chin. "This is not a play toy, Mr. Caman. You are a military man and are known to carry a weapon. I suggest you draw it now to fight for your honour, or I will cut you down where you stand."

Caman smirked at Rose and pulled his sword out of the sheath at his side. "Come, Rose. Do you always make men go through this process before they can sleep with you?" Rose struck out with a fury that startled him and put him on his toes.

"Are you ready to fight now, Caman, or do you wish to make more remarks that will only serve to sign your death warrant?" Rose sneered at him and he sneered back. He took up the ready pose and the two began to duel.

Rose's fury caused her to fight harder than she had ever fought before, but Caman was no fool. He knew how to handle himself.

He was well skilled at defence as well as offence, but Rose never gave him a chance on the offensive. She kept pushing him, harder and harder, until his sword flew from his hand, and he landed with a thud on the dirt street.

"Give me one reason not to kill you, and maybe I'll spare your life," snarled Rose. For a moment, fear entered into his eyes, but it was quickly vanquished by pure rage.

"Is that all you can do?" he questioned mockingly. "Then do your worst. Take my life if you wish, but remember yours also will be forfeit to a hangman's noose." Rose pressed the blade harder into his neck as his words hit their mark, and he felt a slight trickle of blood slide down his throat.

A feral gleam entered Rose's eyes as she came up with another idea. Slowly, her blade slipped down his throat, across his chest, and past his stomach to land somewhere in his middle section. Sweat broke out on his forehead as a new terror was set in place. "You may not value your life, but there is one other thing that I could take from you that is sure to be missed," Rose said tersely.

"What do you want from me?" Caman asked hoarsely, his voice filled with the terror of the situation. Rose smirked down at him, and made him wallow in his fear for a while longer.

"I would have you leave town and never return. I wish never to lay eyes on you again, or hear the gossip of your ill deeds. I wish to never see a woman mistreated by you ever again." The passion in Rose's voice crescendoed and made her press her sword a bit. Caman squirmed under its point.

"Am I to be a bandit then?" he asked. "Am I never to have a home, for fear that you will come to the town that I live in, and I will again be forced to leave? Am I never to see my family here again?"

Rose considered his plea for a time before she responded. "I will allow you to come back on one condition. You must first prove yourself worthy. If you ever present to me a wife that you love and cherish and who loves and cherishes you, I will lift this ban from you, and I will no longer terrorize you if you come into my presence. Do you understand these terms?"

Caman groaned. "Yes, I do understand these terms, but I fear that they damn me to life as a nomad, for what you demand is impossible to fulfill."

"If you believe thus, then you are damned, and I wish you good luck. But if you change your ways, perhaps there is still a chance for you, whether you are a nomad or not." Rose lifted her sword and watched as Caman scrambled to his feet. "Now go. I give you till morning to be gone from this place."

Caman picked up his sword, sheathed it, then turned and bowed to Rose. "My lady," he said, then disappeared down the road. He had a long night ahead of him if he was to pack and be gone by the morning sun.

November 16. Henry groaned as he looked at the date. Could it possibly be that late in the year already? Where had all the time

gone? He had wasted six months of his time, and now he had only six months left to find a wife. He needed to leave Emriville, but he just couldn't bring himself to do it.

One night, he had packed his clothes and was ready to say farewell to Caleb when the curate stormed into the house in high dudgeons. Henry tried to bring Caleb out of his mood in order to say his farewells, but the curate remained unmoved. He was angry and refused to speak, and when he did speak it was in a soft moan under his breath, and his whole body shook.

After this failed attempt to leave, Henry hadn't dared try again. Caleb often went about the house in dark moods. His countenance was sour, and he even denied the young ladies tea. If he wasn't careful, he would have the whole town talking about his moods. When Henry asked Rose about this, she blushed and turned away, refusing to speak a word.

Henry would have to be dense not to deduce the truth of the situation. Caleb had most likely proclaimed his love for Rose, and he had been sorely rejected. Henry took the blame for this, and for that very reason he could not leave Caleb. He helped Caleb as much as he could, and when his dark moods hit, Henry would make his escapes to the orphanage, or to the Monks' house where he was able to share conversation with Rose.

It was because of this impromptu dispute between Rose and Caleb that Henry did not notice the passing of time, and found himself in the predicament he was now in. He had six months to find a bride, and found such a task daunting.

Henry looked again at the letter that his father had sent him. It was filled with talk about engagement rings and wedding cakes. Both his father and mother expected him to announce his intentions soon, for surely that could be the only reason why he was staying in one vicinity for so long. Henry was loath to tell them the truth.

Perhaps he could find a wife among the people of Emriville. There were many pleasant young women around, and any one of them could make an excellent wife. Henry let out a groan. That defeated the purpose. There were many ladies of the court who would make excellent wives, but he could not love them. Neither could he love the women of Emriville. Well, at least not most of them. He could very easily love Rose, but that was out of the question. Rose was already spoken for. Anyone who watched the way that Colonel Jasper looked at her while the two of them walked knew that she was spoken for. The man was so besotted with her, it was amazing that he did not convince her to elope, and end his agonized waiting.

Yes, Henry could very easily love Rose, but that was another reason to leave Emriville, for she would never love him back. Henry let out one final groan as he came to his decision. He would leave within a week's time. That would give him enough time to say farewell to all his friends, and to make sure that Caleb was left in good hands.

Chill winter air bit on her nose as Rose walked slowly beside Colonel Jasper. Wispy snowflakes fell gently to the ground where they added to the fluffy piles of new snow. It seemed rather odd to be out walking in such weather, but the colonel had insisted on it. He said walking was good for the soul in any type of weather, so Rose had obliged.

The two walked in silence, and Katy trudged far behind, her face displaying her misery. She detested the cold weather, and she hated even more that she had to act as chaperone. What a silly thing, to have a chaperone on a walk in the middle of winter. What unscrupulous action could occur in such a climate? But Rose had insisted.

Normally Colonel Jasper filled their walk with stories of all sorts, but today he remained silent, as if contemplating something of great importance. It wasn't until they were on their return that he finally spoke. "I do not know what your feelings are, Rose, but I must ask you anyway." His low voice took on a determined, steady tone. "I like you very much, more than I have liked anyone of the female gender, and I wonder if you would consider matrimony?"

The words said, the colonel looked down at his shoes and waited for Rose's reply. Not sure what to say, Rose sputtered about for a minute. "I, I do not know what to say," she replied. "Do not mistake my hesitation. I look upon you with the highest regard, but I did not think that you had feelings for me in this way."

"Then you do not wish to marry me, do you?" His eyes were so sorrowful that Rose wished to say she would, but she held her tongue. She still had six months to consider matrimony. She would not tie any man down to a loveless marriage unless she was desperate. It just wasn't fair to lead the colonel on in such a manner.

"That is what I thought," he continued. "Forgive me, Rose, for intruding so much upon you. This shall be the last of our walks, for I do not wish to put you in an awkward position, now that you know my feelings for you." He lifted her hand, kissed it gently, and placed it back at her side. He was about to turn and continue their walk, when they heard the crunch on the snow behind them.

Both of them turned to see Mr. Hyden standing there with his face devoid of all emotion. How long he had been standing there, Rose couldn't be sure. "Forgive me for intruding," he said politely, "but I would like to say my farewells to Rose before I leave."

"Are you leaving Emriville for good then?" asked the colonel.

"I don't know," replied Henry. "My father has called me away on business for a while, and I don't know how long I'll be occupied. It could be a week or less, or it could be many months." Thoughts reeled in Henry's mind. A week or less? Yes, that had become very much possible when he realized that Rose would not be marrying Colonel Jasper. He would be back in a week or less.

"Very well, then," said the colonel. "I wish you safe journeys, and I hope that you will be restored to us soon. You are a great addition to our small town, and it would be a deprivation to have you gone."

"Thank you, sir," replied Henry. He turned to Rose, bowing deeply and kissing her hand. "I will return as soon as my father's business is done, but until then, Miss Wooden, I bid you farewell."

Rose blushed slightly and curtsied. "Until we meet again, Mr. Hyden. God's blessing on your journey. May it bring you speedily back to this place."

A broad grin covered Henry's face as he stood again. "I am sure that I'll be back with much haste. I'll be back before you even notice I'm gone."

Rose laughed slightly. "Then be gone with you now, so that we will not have to suffer your absence long, and we will not have to draw out these farewells."

Henry gave a jaunty salute, then turned and made his way toward the livery where his horse awaited. Rose and Colonel Jasper continued on their walk. It would be the last they were to have together, and they thought it best to enjoy it to the fullest.

Jasper watched as Henry disappeared. He shook his head slightly and tried to wipe away his stupidity. The whole town had assumed that he had fallen for Miss Wooden. That was not supposed to happen. He was supposed to be protecting Miss Wooden and trying to push her toward Henry, but fool as he was he had messed it all up, and he needed to fix it.

Henry had started to back off when the town started talking about weddings. It had become important for Henry to understand that Rose would not marry Jasper. How could Henry be so foolish to believe that in the first place? Proposing had been a dangerous task, especially since he waited for Henry to be present, but it had been necessary. He didn't actually think that Rose would ever accept him, but she could have, and then he would have had to clean up that mess as well. Oh well, what was done was done. It would be better for him to forget about it. Besides, he had to think of a better way to look after Rose.

TWENTY-ONE

YOU MUST EAT A LITTLE MORE, MARK. You're skin and bones."
pleaded Rose. She looked at the sunken cheeks of Private
Hepton and tried to hide her fear. He wasn't doing well at all.
He had been on the road to recovery when gangrene had set in and
consumed what was left of his leg. They had cleaned the wound
regularly, but it was no use. The infection still took hold.

Mark let out a shallow cough. "That is enough for today, Rose.
I don't think I could eat another bite." He patted Rose's hand
lightly, and she had to fight back the tears. What had happened to
the defiant private she had first met, the private who had dumped
bowl after bowl of soup on her dress? The man on the bed in front
of her was only a skeleton of what he used to be, a mere shadow
compared to his original hearty figure.

Rose set aside the bowl and went about cleaning his bandages.
It had been suggested that he might heal if his leg were further

amputated, but Mark would have none of it. So Rose took up the task of changing his bandages with the hope that he might heal despite what the medics said about his chances of survival with the decaying limb.

Gently she lifted Mark's stub and began unravelling the stench-filled bandages. The smell was overpowering every time the last layer of cloth fell away, but Rose gritted her teeth and pressed forward. She cleaned off the noxious pus and then slowly re-wrapped the useless limb.

Mark let out a groan as his appendage was placed carefully back onto the mattress. No matter how hard he tried to fake it, Rose could tell he was in great pain by the grimace that took hold of his features every time his bandages were changed. It was impossible to keep him comfortable during these ministrations, so Rose decided to try to soothe him afterward.

"So, tell me again why you came to Emriville." Rose tried to keep her voice light and happy. She had heard somewhere that a cheerful attitude could be one of the best medicines for a patient.

Mark let out a sigh and answered the familiar question. "I asked to be brought here because I heard that one of my brothers had been sent here. Now, don't get the wrong idea that me and my brothers were close, but they are family, and family has to stick together when they can."

The conversation was familiar to Rose, because she asked the same questions every time. It seemed to have a hypnotic effect on Mark to talk about his family. Sure, he had a past with an abusive father, but he seemed determined to make it right with his brothers if he could at least find them. "Who are your brothers? I do not know any other Heptons, and I have been in town for quite some time."

"You wouldn't know my brother. At least, I would hope that you don't know my brother. He wasn't the nice sort of person when we lived at home. I always thought that he was like my old man, but then again, he did leave before any of us ever got the nerve to. Maybe he changed, you never know."

Mark closed his eyes and allowed the conversation to comfort him. "My oldest brother was the one that I heard was here. He lives under a different name now, though. He told me that he would change his name if ever he moved out. He didn't want to be associated with the name of his daddy. He wanted to be his own man."

This was a twist to the conversation that Rose had not yet heard. "I thought you said your brother was a lot like your dad. If he was so much like your dad, wouldn't he want to keep the same family name and not bother changing it?"

"Nah, those weren't the ways of Pops. He liked individualism. At least, that's what he called it. He said there would come a day when we would strike out on our own, and we would have to be our own men, men who could handle themselves and their women. That was where Seth was like dad."

Rose heard the bitterness in his voice, and she suppressed the shudder that wanted to crawl down her back. She didn't know what to say, she didn't know what to do, so she just waited. The seconds seemed to tick by agonizingly slowly before Mark spoke again.

"There was one girl, her name was Sarah. I thought for sure that she would change Seth. She was the only one that seemed to calm him a bit. She was a real pretty thing, with blond hair and big blue eyes, and smaller than one of those little tweety birds. She had authority, though. My goodness, did she have authority. She would hear of something Seth did, and she would go right up to him, and she would say, 'Seth boy, did you do what I hear you did? Because if you did, I am real disappointed in you.' I don't know how she did that. All of us boys were afraid to go up to Seth after he had done something, cause that was when he was the meanest. But she wasn't afraid."

Again there was a pause, and Rose waited. She wanted to prod. She wanted to know what had happened to this Sarah girl. She wanted to know what had happened to Seth. But she couldn't ask, so she waited.

"I think Sarah would have changed him had it not been for Bill. Bill was another one of my brothers. He wasn't too smart, and he went and told Pops about Sarah. She didn't have a chance once Dad found out. Dad told Seth that he had to invite Sarah over for dinner. He made it sound like a whole polite ordeal. I don't know why, but Sarah's parents let her go." A tear slipped down Mark's face as he said his next words. "They should have never let her go."

Rose tried to stand and leave. She didn't want to know what had happened to that young girl, but before she could lift herself from her chair, Mark had started talking again, and she could not leave.

"Sarah came for dinner all right, and Pops was ready for her. She didn't even get a friendly hello before she was tied up in the corner crying. Mama was sent out back, so she couldn't hear the cries, but she knew what was going to happen anyway." More tears poured down Mark's face, and he had no control to stop them. "He made us watch as first Seth then he took his turn at her, over and over again. When it was done, Seth took her out back, and we never heard from him again. Pops said he was on his own now because he knew how to handle his woman."

"Oh, Mark!" was all Rose could utter through the tears that poured down her face, but he wasn't done speaking yet.

"It wasn't long after that that mama was killed, and I got the nerve to leave home. In the army, I met up with Bill again. He hadn't changed much. He was still a lousy drunk, but he said he knew where Seth was. He said Seth had come out this way under a different name, so that is why I am here. I have to know what happened to Seth."

A hand fell heavily on Rose's shoulder, startling her. Mark opened his eyes and looked at the man who stood over Rose. She hadn't talked to him in a while, but it would be rude not to make introductions. "Curate, this is Private Mark Hepton. Mr. Hepton, this is the curate, Mr. Caleb Taylor."

The two men stared at each other for quite some time, which Rose found very odd. Both of their faces were blank and showed no emotion, but their eyes were searching, as each was trying to determine the other's fortitude. "It's nice to meet you, Curate," said Mark. His words seemed to hold a challenge, but Caleb didn't engage it.

Instead, Caleb turned to Rose. "It is best that you leave now, Miss Wooden. You have done much already today, and you need your rest if you are to help the patients to the best of your ability."

Mark watched as fire entered into Rose's eyes. "I don't think I would like to leave yet, Caleb. I have not done much today, and there are many more things I would like to accomplish before I leave. Now, will you accept that answer, or are you going to order me out like the last time?"

"I will not order you out, but I would make a strong suggestion that you leave here immediately, Rose." Caleb's voice was terse and angry, but Rose did not care. She was still quite angry with him for the way he had treated her, and her anger was making it hard for her to feel compassion for his needs.

"You don't get it, do you Caleb? I do not wish to leave, and unless you give me a good reason to leave, then I will not. You do not run this hospital, and you do not determine who works here. Most of all, you have no control over my life, no matter how much you seem to think you do."

Caleb didn't even bother arguing. He spun around on the spot and stalked away.

"I'm sorry about that," Rose said to Mark. "He has been like that for the past little while, and I have no clue why. It seems that everything I do upsets him, and yet he claims he loves me. I can feel no compassion for him, though. He is not the man I originally thought he was."

"He was angry when he left," Mark said half to himself. "Didn't that scare you at least a little bit? I was afraid he was going to act out of kind for a minute there because he was so mad."

"Caleb doesn't scare me. He bruised me once, but that was an accident, I think. He would not harm me other than that. He has to worry about his image. If he were to harm me, his work as a minister would be over for good. There is no way he could continue after that."

"You should be careful around him." Mark looked her squarely in the eyes as he said his next words. "Things aren't always what they seem. He may seem incapable of evil, but things can change in the blink of an eye. I know. I have seen it happen on more than one occasion."

Rose nodded, but she turned away. She might have no compassion for Caleb, but she would not think him capable of hurting anyone on purpose. "Do you understand me, Rose?" Mark asked. "You need to understand that. Okay?" Rose nodded her head one last time, then walked away.

It was late. The hospital was dark, and most of the patients were sleeping. Private Mark Hepton tossed and turned on his small mattress, but sleep evaded him. He had asked to be sent to Emriville with the set purpose of finding his brother and making things right. What he hadn't expected was to actually accomplish his goal.

What was he supposed to do now that he knew where Seth was? Was he able to forgive him? Was he able to move on with his life? For so many years, he had thought that if he could only see Seth, he would be able to forgive him, and he would be able to live at peace. He had made himself right with God, and now all he had left to do was make it right with his family.

Billy had been easy. He was the same lousy drunk, but he hadn't done the things that Seth or his dad had done. His dad was long gone in the grave, but Seth, he was still out there, somewhere. Now he knew where.

He tried to ignore the uneasy feeling that came with the thought of his brother. God told him in his word that he needed to forgive him, but was that really possible after witnessing such horrors? Maybe in a couple years, but God hadn't given him a couple years. If Mark was guessing right, he had only a few days to live.

There was a thud at the end of the hall as the front door opened and closed. *It must be the night staff switching up*, thought Mark. There was a creak as the door into his room opened, and a lone figure entered and walked toward him. "Hello, Seth," he said, "or would you rather I call you Curate?"

Seth looked down at the gaunt figure on the bed. The last time he had seen Mark had been years ago. Ever since then, he had been paying penance for his sins. Now, with his brother looking on, Seth felt the rage, the fear, and the hatred well up in him. He cursed the invalid for bringing all this upon him. He had been so close to finding peace, so close to forgetting his past, and now his brother had to show up bringing it all back.

"What are you doing here? You were supposed to stay in the past, along with everyone else."

"The past doesn't seem to want to leave us alone, though, does it? Wherever we go, all we have to do is look in a mirror and we see the past staring us in the face. We both know that we favoured our father in appearance, so why try to hide from the past?"

"You don't get it. I was happy here. I had a life, and God was going to forgive me. I have committed my life to him, and he was going to forgive me," hissed Seth.

"Is that what you are doing as a curate? Paying penance for sins that are freely forgiven? If you want to try to pay for your own sins, be my guest, but know this, you will never pay enough for what you did to Sarah!"

Seth took a step back as if he had been kicked in the stomach. His mouth gaped open, and he looked faint, but he soon regained his feet. "You demon! You think you can understand the guilt of what I did to Sarah? Well, you can't! Every time I see blond hair or blue eyes, I think of her begging me not to, and not being able to stop myself. I am not guilty of what I did! That devil made me do it!"

"Did the devil make you run away, so that Dad was left to beat Mom to death? Did the devil make you turn to rage and violence? Did the devil make you grab Rose and bruise her and hurt her? Can you blame the devil for all your deeds, or are you ready to take some responsibility?"

"I am in charge of my own sin, but who are you to speak? What of your own sins? We both came from the same bastard. Who are you to think that you are any better than I?"

Mark allowed himself time to regain his breath and think before he spoke again. He said a little prayer and then began quietly, confidently. "I am a son of God Most High, who sent his Son, Jesus Christ, to die on the cross for my sins. I am a sinner, but I have been saved wholly and completely by the blood of Christ. Not by what my hands have done can I save myself, but only by the grace of God."

Seth looked down on him with disgust. "Who are you to say these things? Do you think God could really have favour on the likes of us? No, we are too dirty, too vile to even consider such a thought. We must make ourselves right before we can come to God."

"Brother, I pity you, for with such reasoning you can never know the peace of Christ. You may wish to know God, but he will never make himself present to you if you go on your own deeds, because it will never be good enough."

"Get out of my life," Seth whispered hoarsely. "God will see me as I am, and you as you are on the judgment day. We will see who is right then."

"For your sake, Seth, I hope you are, because otherwise I would hate to see your fate on that terrible day." Seth did not hear him, for he had already turned and left. Mark closed his eyes, and, overwhelmed by fatigue, finally slept.

It was the next night that the summons came. Rose was asked to come to the hospital immediately. Private Hepton was dying, and he was asking for her. Rose did not waste any time. She raced toward the hospital and to Mark's side. The poor man was barely hanging on to life when she arrived.

"Mark, Mark, are you still with me?" Rose pleaded. Mark opened his eyes and looked at her hollowly. There was no life left in him, no will to live. Tears began to pour down Rose's cheeks as she tried to keep him with her, but death kept tugging.

She sang songs and hymns to try and brighten his spirits. Sometimes he would close his eyes and smile and seem to mouth the words, but no noise emitted from his mouth except shallow groans of pain.

Rose held his hand, but it was cold, and no life resided in it. She massaged warmth into it, but it wouldn't last. As the hours dragged on, there were fewer and fewer signs of life in Mark, and there were times when Rose thought she had lost him for sure, but he would always open his eyes again and smile, and Rose would again sing.

As the hour drew close to dawn, Mark began to make a desperate effort to speak. He coughed and sputtered, and Rose tried to calm him, but he would not settle down. Finally, Rose leaned toward his mouth and told him to whisper what he wished to say.

The first words that came were hoarse and tickled her ear, but she forced herself to listen. "I am about to leave you now, Rose," he said. "I have to go see my heavenly Father, my one and only true Father. I am not scared. I know he is good, and I know that he has forgiven me. Do not be sad for me when I go." He broke into a fit of coughing and Rose tried to sooth him, but he insisted on speaking some more.

"My Father has forgiven me, and he has given me the chance to forgive those who have done me wrong. Always forgive, Rose. Don't be like I was and wait to forgive. Forgive immediately. It is not worth it to hold on to the bitterness. It eats you."

Rose pulled away at such strong words coming from a dying man. They were not words about himself; rather, they were a commission to her. She was about to speak, but she was not given the chance. "Goodbye, Rose," he whispered as the last breath left his body.

Rose held back the tears as she cut off a lock of Mark's hair and placed it in her handkerchief. She held back the tears as she gently closed his empty eyes, and she held back the tears as she pulled the sheet over his head, marking him as a dead man. She walked slowly, stiffly out of the hospital as the sun rose on a new dawn. No hope lived in this dawn, only tears, tears that remained unshed.

She probably would have stood looking at the thankless dawn for many hours if it weren't for Henry. He came to her on horseback and greeted her with such joy that she couldn't help but weep. He came to her, and held her as the tears flooded out.

She was angry, mad at the world. Had it taken enough now? Had enough lives been ruined, enough blood shed for the earth to be satisfied? How long must she now wait in this curse that left all she loved dead?

She wept for Mark, the young man who never got to live his life. She wept for her parents, the ones she never really got to know. She wept for her uncle, who even now lay dying. And she wept for her bitter self, for how horrendous and despicable her life had become even in her own eyes. And through it all, Henry held her.

TWENTY-TWO

THE TOWN CAME ALIVE AS HENRY AND ROSE walked toward the Monks' house. A remnant of tears still resided in Rose's eyes, but for the time being her weeping had stopped. Every now and then, a shiver went through her body as she tried to throw off the last grasping hands of grief. She was done with tears. They hurt too much.

Henry didn't speak. Instead, he allowed Rose to take the time she needed to collect herself before a conversation was started. So it was that they remained in silence until they had almost reached their destination.

When the house was in sight, Rose finally spoke. "I thought you wouldn't be back for quite some while, but you are here now. How is that so?"

Henry paused thoughtfully before he answered. "There was a slight misunderstanding, and the enterprise fell through. I was not needed after that, so I decided to return to Emriville. Besides, I thought two weeks was long enough to be absent."

Rose nodded slightly. "A lot has happened in two weeks. There was a celebration at the church for the fall harvest. I really think that that was just an excuse to celebrate, because there are not many farmers around this town. Some of the patients were discharged from the hospital, and just last night, Private Mark Hepton passed away from gangrene." Tears filled Rose's eyes once more as she spoke of Mark, but she fought them back. "He was a good man."

"Is that why you were out so late this night?" Henry asked gently. Rose again nodded. "I see. Does Mr. Hepton not have any family hereabouts? It does seem odd that they would send a soldier to a hospital far from his home."

"Mark didn't have much of a family. His father was abusive and his mother died before the war. He came here because he had heard that one of his brothers resided in Emriville. He wished to make things right with him. I don't think he ever found him."

"Hmm, that does make things a bit more difficult doesn't it?" mused Henry.

"Why would that make things more difficult?" Rose asked. "Death is difficult no matter if it is family or not. Even though he did not have family here, that does not mean he won't be mourned!" Rose was indignant by the end of her spiel, and had yanked her hand from where it rested on Henry's arm.

"Settle yourself, Rose," calmed Henry. "I only meant that it would be more difficult to host the funeral. How do you hold a funeral for a deceased man with no family and few connections? Is there anyone we should contact about his death?"

Rose calmed down with the soothing tempo of his voice. She leaned back on his arm. "I suppose that I will be responsible for his funeral." She seemed a little bewildered by this fact. "I was the one who tended him in the hospital, so I suppose I should tend to him now."

"Perhaps," suggested Henry, "you should speak with Caleb first. He will know how to best handle a funeral of this nature. He is, after all, the curate."

Rose stiffened. "I do not wish to speak with Caleb. There must be another that I can speak to."

The steel in her voice told Henry not to push the matter too much. "What if I talked with Caleb, would that suit you?"

Rose turned to him with a look of surprise on her face. Tears welled in her eyes. "Would you really do that for me, Henry? Would you really talk to Caleb about a funeral for Mark?"

"Of course I would do that for you," Henry replied. "Look, Rose," he said. "I don't know what happened between you and Caleb to cause this rift, but one thing I know for sure is that I don't want it to affect our relationship as well. I like you, and I would like to continue to get to know you, if that would be all right with you."

Rose smiled up at him. "I would like that as well, Henry. But I must tell you that I don't think I can speak with Caleb ever again." Rose turned red and turned away as she spoke her next words. "Caleb proposed, and I turned him down. And now I think he is quite angry with me."

To say he was shocked would barely describe the emotions that went through Henry. Caleb had proposed and been turned down. How could such a thing cause such a rift? Rose and Caleb had been such close friends; it only made sense that they would be able to look past this in order to keep that friendship. "Why did you deny him?" Henry asked.

Rose heaved a sigh and turned toward the astounded young sir. "Caleb is a good man—you agree?" Henry nodded. "Yes, he is a good man, but he does have his flaws. One of his biggest flaws is that he is very concerned with image. I could not live with a man who berated me every time I did something outside of the social norm."

Henry groaned. "Now I feel like all sorts of a fool," he mumbled. "I, not thinking, encouraged Caleb to make his feelings clear to you, and now that he has, he has been denied. Forgive me, Rose. This is all my fault."

"Don't blame yourself, Henry. There was a time when I would have accepted Caleb to be my husband, but as the days went on, I saw in him this flaw, and it grew in my mind to such an extent that I could not look on Caleb in the same manner."

"Nevertheless," said Henry, "I still feel horrible for counselling Caleb so. I dare say, he may never forgive me."

"Will you still talk to him?" asked Rose. A look of apprehension tightened the lines of her face, and Henry was momentarily confused.

As they reached the door of the Monks' home, he reached down and gently grasped Rose's arms, where Caleb had grabbed her before. "I will speak with Caleb as soon as possible about the funeral. Every man deserves to have a funeral, especially one who has fought so diligently in the King's army."

The door burst open, and Henry quickly dropped his hands. "There you are, Rose!" exclaimed Mrs. Monks. "You have us all in a flutter. We all thought that something horrible had befallen you when you didn't return last night. It makes me wonder what kept you out so late."

"Forgive me, Mrs. Monks," replied Rose politely. "I was at the hospital all night. Private Hepton has gone on to be with the Lord, though it was a long arduous journey. It wasn't until the crack of dawn that he finally passed on." Tears welled in Rose's eyes, and the over enthusiastic Mrs. Monks took pity on her.

"Oh, forgive me, Rose. I did not think. Of course, that must have been a terrible experience for you. No young lady should have to see a man face death. Posh, what am I saying? No lady, young or old, should have to witness the death of a person. Now, you must be terribly hungry and thirsty."

Mrs. Monks turned to go back into the house, but in so doing, Henry came into her line of sight. "Oh, Mr. Hyden, I did not see you. You should have said something. When did you get back? We all thought you would be on business and would not return for quite some time, if ever."

Henry laughed lightly. "I hope that it does not bother you that I have returned so soon. Business did not go as planned, but it brought me back to Emriville all the sooner, and I am content. It should be some time before I must leave, and I am looking forward to spending Christmas amongst all the delightful members of this town."

"Oh," sputtered Mrs. Monks, "you are a flatterer, aren't you?" She blushed slightly. "Well, we are glad that you are here, and we hope that you will enjoy a splendid Christmas. We, Mr. Monks and I, we enjoy your company so much, which reminds me of my manners. Please, Mr. Hyden, come in for a bite to eat. You have been travelling and must be quite famished."

Henry bowed deeply, and in his most stately voice replied, "Forgive me, Mrs. Monks. I would love to stay, but I fear that I have things to attend to in town. Perhaps I will stop by later to speak with Mr. Monks."

"Perhaps?" exclaimed Mrs. Monks. "My dear Mr. Hyden, I would be insulted if you did not accept an invitation to dinner tonight. In fact, I command you to come. Be here by half-past six. Don't be tardy. Mr. Monks gets quite grumpy when his dinner goes cold."

Henry gave a mock salute. "Yes, Madame. I will report to the table at precisely six-thirty, but I wonder if my presence will be accepted in the parlour at an earlier hour?"

Mrs. Monks swatted at him playfully. "Be gone, you pesky boy. You cause this old woman much grief and make me wish that I had never extended such an invitation. Now, disappear before I change my mind." Henry laughed and took off down the road at a good trot.

Mrs. Monks waved after him, and Rose smiled at their easy banter. It was funny how Henry could be so easy with the exuberant Mrs. Monks, and yet so formal and elegant when occasion demanded. He was a man of many talents, there was no doubt of that.

Rose yawned and turned toward her bedroom as Henry disappeared down the road. If they were to have dinner tonight, she would need some sleep. Her stomach growled, and she grimaced. Sleep would have to wait for a while. Her stomach had taken control and wanted some food. Rose sighed. She looked longingly at the stairs that would take her to bed, then slowly turned toward the kitchen and food.

Caleb stared with horrid fascination at the corpse lying on the bed. Its gaunt form was stiff and cold. The stump of a leg still held the odorous gangrene, rotting away the flesh that no longer lived. Its arms were crossed on top of its chest. The three missing fingers on the right hand gave sick humour to the pose.

If Caleb had been cursed with a weak stomach, he would be retching into a pail, but he wasn't weak. What was a corpse, but a bloated bag of bones? What was this corpse, but his brother?

If tears were supposed to come, Caleb did not know what they would be for. He felt no grief over his brother's death. All he felt was relief. Tears were for weak men and women. He was neither of those, and he would not cry. He would not grieve a brother who had never done anything for him, a brother who represented everything that he had tried to bury.

Caleb walked toward the body and gently reached out his hand. His hand brushed across the dead man's forehead and trailed down the side of Mark's sunken cheek. He had known it was Mark as soon as he had laid eyes on him. Mark had always favoured their mom in appearance. He had the same round eyes and thin frail cheeks. Pops had hated him for that. He looked too much like a woman he always had said.

Caleb was different. He had favoured Pops. He had the same empty eyes, and the same large hands. Caleb had the strong jaw, and the high forehead. And he hated it. When he had left home, it had taken over a year before he could look in a mirror without seeing his father.

Always like his father. That's what people had said when they had seen Caleb. They knew whose son he was, and they cursed him. They had spit on him when he had walked through the streets. They cursed him when he tried to enter their churches. And they had nearly hung him when he brought Sarah home.

Sarah. She had been everything to him. She was the light of day. She was a hand to hold when the beatings got too bad. She was the hope that he never thought possible to have. That was, until Pops made him take her home.

Caleb cursed under his breath. This never would have happened to Mark. All the townspeople believed in him. When people saw Mark, they saw his mother. They saw the helpless young woman whom they had failed, and they were determined not to fail her son. At least, they wouldn't fail the son that favoured her.

Caleb slapped the man on the bed across the face. He cursed him and berated him. "How could you? How could you? Why didn't you stop it? You could have stopped it! You could have stopped me!" Caleb swore again. "You selfish, little beast. You didn't want to stop it. You wanted to see me hurt."

Caleb lifted the corpse by the scruff of the shirt and slammed him back into the bed. His arms uncrossed, and his head lulled to the side. "I hate you," Caleb whispered. "I hate you so much!" Slowly he let go of the dead man. He straightened his posture and he walked out. The hospital remained sleeping.

When Caleb returned to the rectory, he had a guest waiting for him. "Henry! I did not expect to see you again. When you left, you made it sound as if you were not to come back. How glad I am to see you, though."

"I am glad to see you as well, Caleb. I hope things have been going well for you," replied Henry.

"Well enough, I suppose." Caleb's reply was half-hearted, and Henry doubted he was in as good a mood as he suggested. "I just returned from the hospital. I had heard that one of the patients may have been dying. Sadly, I was too late for him. The poor soul has gone on ahead of us."

"Yes, I have heard already the sad fate of Private Hepton," stated Henry bluntly. "I met up with Rose on my way into town.

She was just coming out of the hospital after sitting with the private while he died."

Caleb swallowed hard. "It was Rose who stayed with the private? I had not heard that. I had only heard that it was one of the young ladies of the church." Caleb bit the inside of his cheek to hide his anger, but Henry could feel him tense up.

"Yes, it was Rose. It was quite awful for her. She was very torn up about it, but she wants to hold a funeral for the poor man. He has no family, so she has taken it as her own responsibility to make sure he has a funeral. She was especially hoping that you would help. She thought that you would know how to handle such a funeral." Henry looked at Caleb hopefully.

"I'm sorry," Caleb replied tightly. "I can't do it. It would be inappropriate for me to hold a funeral for this man, when I don't even know who he is. It would be better that he was laid to rest in an unmarked grave somewhere in the woods."

Henry looked at the curate in shock. "You cannot be serious, Caleb. This man fought in the army, and he deserves a proper burial. He may not have any family, but there are those who grieve over him, who would want a proper funeral."

"I cannot do it," replied Caleb. "I simply will not. It would be wrong for me to do a funeral for this man. It would all be a lie. I cannot lie. It is against the law of God."

"Would it be a lie to speak a few words over a man as we lay him in the ground? I don't ask you to preach a sermon on his life. All I ask is that you say a blessing over him as he is buried. Nothing more, nothing less."

Caleb's visage turned to stone at Henry's words. "I will not do it, I tell you. I refuse to do it. Now, get the silly notion out of your head. If you wish for the man to be buried, do it yourself, somewhere away from this town."

Henry scowled at him. "I never thought you to be this selfish, Caleb. I think even Christ would make exceptions from stiff rules for a man without a home." Henry turned and walked away. He didn't want to talk with Caleb anymore. He was angry, hungry, and tired. He needed to get to the inn so he could get cleaned up and rested up before dinner that night.

"Wait, Henry," Caleb called. "Are you not going to stay with me at the rectory? There is still plenty of room here for you."

"I think that I have overstayed my welcome already," Henry called back and kept walking. Caleb slumped his shoulders and walked into his house. It was a very dark day indeed.

"How could he!" shouted Rose. "It was a simple request. A small favour on behalf of another, and he still denied you. I cannot believe this. It is rude, it is inconsiderate, and it is downright selfish. How low it is to deny a man a funeral."

Henry walked silently beside Rose as she ranted on. Dinner had passed by agonizingly slowly as he waited to tell Rose his news. Now, as they walked, he wished that dinner had lasted a while longer, so that he would not have had to tell Rose about Caleb's decision.

"Does he have no care at all for the deceased?" she asked pleadingly. "Surely, he will have pity. He has to have pity. Someone has to do the funeral." Rose was begging now, and Henry hated that Caleb had not accepted the task. How could the man be so cruel?

"I do not know, Rose. He seemed quite determined not to do the funeral, though I can't understand why. He said that it would be a lie before God. I don't understand how that is so, but he is a curate and understands these matters better than we do." Henry shrugged. "Maybe we should do as he says."

Rose's eyes grew big with shock. "So you agree with him!" she exclaimed. "I cannot believe you, Henry. If you agreed with him, why didn't you say so immediately, and I would have gone to speak to Caleb myself?" She turned and began walking much quicker.

"You misunderstand me, Rose," Henry called from where he was stopped on the path. "I do not agree at all with Caleb, but he may be right. I'm just wondering if you think there is a possibility that he might be right, but you obviously don't think so."

Rose slowed again. "No, I don't think that he is right." She let out a sigh. "I guess I feel that I am to blame, because Caleb hates me so much. He is gaining his revenge by not allowing this man his funeral. I will have to talk with him myself."

"I don't know if that will help, Rose. Caleb seemed quite determined. He almost seemed angry when I suggested it. I will talk to him again, but I think it would be better if you waited to speak to him."

Rose thought about this for a moment. "No, no. I have to talk to him. That's the only way. I will speak to him tomorrow at the hospital. He cannot ignore me there. Besides, I will have the support of other nurses as well. All of them will want a proper burial for Mark."

"If that's what you wish," sighed Henry. He still did not think it would be the best course of action, but he would support her. He only feared what would happen tomorrow at the hospital when Rose confronted Caleb. Both persons had quite a temper, and both knew how to speak their minds. Sparks would very likely fly.

"Caleb, could I have a word with you?" Rose asked softly when she saw him the next day at the hospital. "It is a matter of great importance." Caleb looked at her hesitantly but the followed her to a more secluded corner where they wouldn't be as easily disturbed.

"I would like to know why you denied Private Hepton a proper funeral. I talked with Henry yesterday, and he said you refused. Why?" Rose's voice was demanding and angry, and Caleb responded in kind. He tensed up and his voice became stiff and forced.

"I told Henry exactly why I cannot do the funeral. It would be inappropriate and a sin before God. Therefore, I will not be able to do it in good faith."

"Posh, Caleb! You are making that all up, and I resent you for it. It is no sin to hold a funeral for a man you don't know, and you know it. You are just denying Mark because you hate me and you want to cause me pain."

"Don't be silly, Rose. Ask anyone here. It would be inappropriate to hold a funeral for Private Hepton." Miss Cummings just so happened to be passing at that time, and Caleb called out to her. "Now, Miss Cummings, do you think that we should hold a funeral for Private Hepton?"

Miss Cummings looked at Rose with dislike. "I think that it would be very inappropriate for anyone to hold a funeral for a man with no family. It would be much better to bury him and be done with it." She had a smug look on her face as she turned to Rose, who looked at her with stony wariness.

"It is inappropriate for a young woman to spend the night with a man she is not wed to. It is not inappropriate for a funeral to be held for a man without family."

The smug look left Miss Cummings' face, and she sneered at Rose. "Then you are very experienced at the inappropriate, aren't you, Miss Wooden. How many men have you spent the night with now? Let's see. You spent the night with Mr. Hyden when he was ill, and Private Hepton. Two infractions already? My, my, Miss Wooden, that is quite the record."

Rose bit her lip but did not respond.

"That is enough, Miss Cummings," cut in Caleb. "You may go back about your work." Miss Cummings left, and Caleb turned back to Rose. "No matter what you say, Rose, I will not do the funeral for Mr. Hepton. I simply cannot."

Rose stood stiffly. "Fine, I will have a funeral for him on my own. Though I do not know how he will be buried or where, I will make sure that it is done properly." She curtsied slightly and left an angry Caleb sitting in the corner.

The funeral was very simple. Henry enlisted the help of a young man from the town, and they lowered the simple pine casket into the ground in the pasture. Rose spoke a few words over the dead man, but it all felt meaningless. He was already gone.

When she was done, Henry and the young man started throwing dirt over the wooden box, and Rose stood back watching. Each clod of dirt brought a fresh tear to her eye and closed her heart a little more to the cold reality of love.

TWENTY-THREE

ROSE WALKED TO THE HOSPITAL TO WORK, but it seemed wrong. What was there for her? Mark didn't need tending, and there were plenty of other women to care for the other patients. She didn't belong there. She wasn't needed.

She could return to the orphanage and help out with the children there. But Mrs. Jennings was down to only a few children, and they also didn't need her. Sure, she was welcome for a visit every now and then, but otherwise the orphanage was in good order, and she was unneeded.

Rose sighed. Where did she belong? She had already been proposed too twice, but had rejected both men on different grounds. Could she really expect a third proposal in one year? It would be better if she returned early to her aunt in defeat. At least then she would be married off sooner and would have a longer time to adjust to her husband.

But defeat was not her way. She would rather fight it out to the end. She had six months left. She could make it through. She still received frequent letters from John, though those came fewer and farther between as John became enthralled with his work. He no longer had time for a pesky younger cousin. It wasn't his place to care for her.

Uncle Murdoch would gladly care for her, but he was too ill. The last report she had of him stated that he was no longer able to hold a pen in his hand. Such news nearly made Rose weep.

She had been weeping a lot lately. Too many people had died, and Rose hurt. She was angry and hurt. She didn't like to weep, but the tears came every time she was faced with another pain, and the world was full of pain. She searched for a haven from that pain, but she had not yet found it.

Rose walked past the hospital. No one inside would miss her. She walked into the market and looked at the wares that were on sale. It would be Christmas soon, and she wanted to find a gift for Henry. It wasn't the common Christmas tradition to buy gifts, but Rose wanted to do something in return for all that Henry had done for her.

He had been so kind to her, always trying to make things easier. He had helped her with the funeral and comforted her when she cried. She wanted to get something nice for him in return. But what could she get him? He was a rich man, she knew, and her funds were limited. She could make him something. But what could she sew that would be appropriate?

She could make Henry a pair of socks, but that hardly seemed appropriate. What was a young lady supposed to buy a young man as a gift? There were too many rules of decorum that prevented her from giving him all the practical things that she could think of, and all the impractical things were much too expensive.

Rose walked slowly through the market. There was not much on display, as the cold winter weather kept most folks inside, but some trinkets glistened in the sunlight. At one booth there were watches displayed. Some were for men, and others were for women; all were stylishly displayed. Rose took one look at the prices and moved on.

Rose wound her way through the market. She stopped at one stall to look at baubles and another to look at children's toys. She enjoyed the freedom of the day. There was nothing holding her to a particular place or time; there was no appointment to keep, and there was no one telling her she had to do this or that.

Rose sighed contentedly and turned to continue on her way. What she wasn't expecting was to run into the wall-like solidity of a man. She took a step back when the lapel did not retreat, and she looked up into the face of the man towering over her. "Good day, Caleb," she said stiffly.

"How are you, Rose?" he asked in return. Rose didn't know what to say. She had been enjoying herself until he had intruded on her time, but it would be rude of her to inform him of this. She would have to be polite and use tact, if at all possible.

"I am quite well, thank you, but I think that I must be on my way. There are so many things to do." Rose made to leave, but Caleb stopped her.

"May I join you? I have some things to accomplish while I am at the market, and I would greatly enjoy the company. That is, if you don't mind."

Rose cleared her throat and tried again. "We are probably headed in opposite directions. I am going to look for some gloves and a handkerchief for Katy and Mrs. Monks. Surely, you cannot be going in the same direction."

"I believe I am. I am looking for a gift for my housekeeper, Mrs. Meps, and I thought that a handkerchief would do rather nicely, don't you think?"

Rose was getting frustrated. There seemed no way to deter Caleb, and she did not want to insult him. "But I must first stop at the ribbon shop, for I am looking for a ribbon to go with a dress that I will be wearing on Christmas day."

"Then I shall go with you. It is along the way, and I am sure that a single ribbon cannot take so long to decide on."

Rose had had enough. "Why must you be so insistent, Caleb? Can you not see that I do not wish to travel with you? I would much prefer it if you would let me be to myself."

Caleb turned away as if saddened by these words. "Will I ever be able to walk with you again, Rose? I know it may be a little awkward at the moment, but surely we can look past that and be friends."

"It is not that easy, Caleb. For now it is better that you just leave it as it is, and the two of us can go about our own ways."

Caleb looked at her, his eyes pleading. "Why isn't it that easy? Why can't it be that easy? I don't understand. Is it because I didn't do the funeral for Private Hepton? I will do anything I can to remedy that."

"It's more than that, Caleb. If it were just the funeral, I could deal with it, but there are more reasons than that as to why we can never be friends."

"What? What is it that keeps us from being friends? Tell me, so that I can do anything in my power to fix it, because I dearly miss you as my friend."

"Do you really miss me as your friend?" Rose asked, her voice raising slightly. "If you do, I find it odd that you would so quickly forget that when you proposed to me, you hurt me. I don't mean you hurt me internally, but externally. You caused bruises on my arms and pain in them. The bruises were easily mended, but it will take me time to forgive you."

Caleb looked at her with horror smeared across his face. "I did do that, didn't I?" he asked in a small voice. "How could I? How could I have done such a thing?" He turned away, and Rose thought she saw a tear on his cheek. "Forgive me," he said, and then he was gone.

Rose watched, bewildered. Why would Caleb react so to such a charge? He had acted like he really hadn't remembered, as if his mind had told him to forget and he had listened. It was a mystery, and Rose didn't think she would ever understand.

The night was cold and bitter. The wind spat contempt at any who dared to venture into it. Its long sorrowful sighs sent ghastly shivers down the backs of those huddled before crackling fires, snug in the caress of blankets.

One man stepped forth on this bitter night, his hair flapping wildly in the wind, lashing out against the pink of frozen skin of his face. He seemed delirious, or drunk, his steps staggered and uneven. Shudders coursed through his body every second step, and his fuddled mind led him farther from the safety of the town.

He walked deeper into the unsaturated dark of the countryside. No moon guided his way, and the stars were blocked by a mass of unmoving, angry clouds. Roots and loose stones clawed from the ground, causing the drunkard to trip over his already clumsy feet. Every element of weather seemed to detest this man and his journey.

Icy snow dropped from the sky in swirling torments. Not a sound was made but the laboured breathing of the drunken man. Birds had long ago migrated, and all other sane living things were deep within their dens, hiding from winter's knife. The long eerie howl of the wind moaned and whistled through the demented branches of the haunting trees.

With an animal yelp of terrified surprise, the man stumbled to the ground. He rolled for a while in a thin tangle of ice, trying to free himself from terrors that only resided in his head. He moaned with the mewling wind and wretched in the grass beside his hand. He was despicable, contemptible. If only they could see him now.

He pushed his way forward, into the dead pasture and walked toward the frozen dirt of a fairly new grave. There he collapsed in a heap of dirtied clothes and his own vomit. He started to giggle. The laughter mingled with the insanity inside his head. It boiled over the edges of his mental capacity, twisting his face into a horror-wrecked mass.

"If only they could see me now," he shrieked through his giggles. He rolled in the snow beside the grave. His bare hands tore at the earth around it. He threw the dirt in the air and felt it land with separate thuds on his head and arms.

His laughter turned to sobs. Deep horrendous wails escaped from his tortured lungs. "If only they could see me now," he screamed at the wind. "What do you want from me?" he shouted at the sky. For a moment, he dreamed that his petition had reached the heavenly realm, but that was the disillusionment of a drunkard.

"I am nothing," he wailed. "Why do you torture me so? Have I not paid enough? Must I give more? What is there left to give? Should I give my body? My hand?" He took out a knife from his dangling cloak. He pressed the blade to his bared wrist that shook at the heavens. He pressed the blade harder, as if taunting the unquenchable God. A trickle of blood slipped down the contours of his arm, its warm embrace bringing a moment of sanity.

He dropped the knife to the ground and buried his face in his hands. "My hand is not enough? I have already given you all my gold and silver. I have given my life in ministry to you. I have given every last ounce of my body and soul to you. Would it now be better if I were dead?" A groan escaped his chapped lips, and the wind carried it away.

"How come he had peace?" whimpered the man. "What did he do, that he had peace?" The man looked at the grave and moaned. "If only I could be where you are, brother. But you were always better than me. You were always the good one. People knew you would turn out better."

"I want to die," shouted the man to the wind, but the wind did not respond. Its icy fingers swept by, not concerning themselves with the torture of one man's lost, lonely soul. "Why can't I die?" he begged. The knife was once more in his hand. It levelled at his throat, ready to deal a fatal blow. The world held its breath as he made his choice.

The blade shook and trembled in his grasp. Sweat built on his brow where the wind licked it up. Tears froze on the tip of his nose and the cavities of his cheeks. His Adam's apple bobbed with the gentle hiccup of death's tears. Still, the knife held. It refused to leave the throat at which it held vigil, and the hand that possessed it gained no willpower as the war raged on.

His hand tightened on the knife as he made himself ready to go on to the next life. He was pressing harder when the yelp of a stray dog startled him. The hand dropped the knife, and the drunkard cursed the world. What dog would howl on a night like this? What dog would even venture this far from its home?

He groped around, searching for the lost weapon, but he could not find it. He crawled about on his hands and knees, hoping he would find the tool that would end his misery, but it could not be found. Defeated, he lay on top of the grave, and cursed the God who had made him who he was. He cursed the God who had made him the son of a rapist murderer.

"I hate you," he screamed at the sky. "Why did you even make me? You knew I would hurt her. You knew I would kill her. Why didn't you end my life before it was created? Why didn't you stop it all before it could even start? I hate you. You killed Sarah. You killed her because you made me. Why? Why did you make me?!"

The wind gentled and began to whisper. It breezed quietly by in a soft lullaby, its loving voice telling of sweet forgiveness. But the man did not hear. He was asleep in his misery, haunted by dreams of destruction. So much was he tormented that he was unable to hear the gentle whisper, "I love you, Seth."

The church stood silent. The people within didn't speak a word; instead, they watched. The pulpit remained empty. The curate did not occupy his normal spot for a Sunday morning, and the people did not know what to do. Should they wait and hope that he would come, or should they go home?

A constant drip-drop could be heard from the eaves outside, and its continuous pattern set a melody for the time spent waiting for the missing curate. Drip-drop, drip-drop. Still, they waited. Someone in the back sneezed, and a few members jumped at the unexpected noise. A bit of a flutter followed as they settled themselves again. Drip-drop, the noise continued.

Henry sat in the pew next to Rose. He sat with the Monks now every Sunday since he had returned. Before he had sat near the front, because he was Caleb's visitor, but now he was staying at the inn. At this turn of events, he almost wished he had stayed with Caleb, for whatever had befallen him was surely a great mishap for him to miss the service.

The doors at the back burst open, and a haggard Mrs. Meps stumbled in. "He's gone!" she shouted. "I don't know what to do. He was there last night when I left, but now he's gone, vanished. I thought perhaps he might be sick, but he is not in his bed and his covers are untouched." The severity of the message seemed to catch up with the poor lady, and she swooned onto the wooden floor.

Young ladies raced to help the fallen woman. Men jumped from their seats with shouts of outrage. "Something has happened!" shouted one rash young man. "We must go out and find the person who has harmed our minister. It's only just!" His words gained an unnatural cry of acceptance. There seemed no order, only chaos based on supposition.

Henry saw the probability of things getting out of hand. He jumped to the pulpit, and a hush fell as he yelled above the hollers of unsettled men. "Good sirs, it would be rash of us to assume someone has harmed our good friend the Curate. For all we know, he could have become lost in last night's blizzard. Therefore, I suggest we search for him before we go about accusing men of crimes that have not been done."

Good sense seemed to have a calming effect on those present, and many of the men settled back in their seats next to their cowering wives. The women of the town were not used to such rash displays of anger. "What do you suggest we do?" shouted out the young man. "Should we just wait until we learn that our minister is no more?"

His words sparked a ring of tension in the audience, but no one rose from their seats. "What I suggest," replied Henry tersely, "is that we set out a search party to go looking for any souls that may have been lost during last night's storm. If they do not find the curate, then our suppositions will be brought before the authorities, who will better know how to deal with any such crime that may have been committed."

The young man looked at Henry with disgust, but the rest of the audience seemed to agree with him, and a search party was soon formed. The men bundled in their warmest clothes. They formed a sleigh that could carry a man and still slide easily over the snow, and piled it high with extra blankets. The women remained at the church to send up prayers for the missing curate.

Of all the prayers that went up, Rose's were the most earnest. She feared the worst had happened to Caleb, and she had not made her peace with him yet. She would need to tell him that she had forgiven him, but she feared that it was too late.

Henry walked through the snow with the search party. Every now and then someone would call out Caleb's name, but there was never a response. They worked their way into the country, where they found a blurred trail of muddled footprints. Some men took this as a good sign and took off ahead of the group.

Henry stayed with the main group, slowly following the footsteps and listening for Caleb, searching for any sign of him. They were just about in the clearing when they heard a call from ahead saying that they had found him. The group broke out into a run toward a twisted black mass on the fresh white snow.

Caleb lay sick and pale. Red tinges marked his cheeks where ice droplets had formed. His whole figure appeared twisted and deformed under the cloaks that had been mutilated by the winds of the night before. A slight moan escaped his lips.

Gently, Henry lifted him in his arms, trying to warm him while they waited for the sleigh to come with the blankets. He whispered soft reassurance to the man that lay so sick in his arms. "I got lost, on my way home," coughed Caleb. "I was so sick," he wheezed. "So very sick."

"Shhh," Henry whispered. "It is okay now. We have found you, and we will bring you to the warmth very soon. You'll be okay." Caleb's head lulled to the side in Henry's arms, and Henry shook him awake. But Caleb's eyes remained shut. The sleigh came, and Caleb was loaded into its warmth, where he slept soundly.

Henry watched as the contraption slipped slowly out of the clearing. That was when he realized where he stood. The dirt under his feet was freshly turned, and the grave marker was newly made. *Mark Hepton* was carved into the wood, and beside the cross lay a knife.

Henry looked curiously at the out-of-place item. Blood tainted its blade, frozen there for all to see. Slowly, Henry reached forward and picked it up. He would have to ask Caleb about this; he was the only one who would know for sure.

TWENTY-FOUR

ECEMBER 18. THERE WAS ONLY ONE WEEK until Christmas, and she still didn't have a gift for Henry. What could she get him? What would he want? Rose raced around the marketplace, going from store to store trying to find the perfect gift. The only problem was that she didn't know what he would want.

For the past few weeks, the two of them had been spending a lot of time together. They had gone on walks and talked about art and music and life in Emriville and anything else that came to mind. They had shared meals at the Monks' table, and washed many dishes together. At one time, Henry had even taken her and Katy horseback riding. But during all that time, Rose had not figured out what he would like for Christmas, or anything about his life, for that matter.

No mention of his home had been made, and on occasion when it looked like he might open up about his family, he quickly stopped himself, as though to protect a secret. Rose's forehead knotted as she puzzled over the mystery of Henry. Who was he, and why wasn't he telling anyone? She was very certain that he was noble, but no noblemen had been reported missing, so she could not begin to make a conjecture as to what family he came from.

Rose sighed. All in due time she would learn who he was, and she wouldn't push him until he was ready. She turned to look in a shop window. Displayed before her were boxes of chocolates and sweets. A sign above them read, *A Little Sweetness for Your Sweetie.* Rose walked in and considered the price for a moment. It was an odd gift idea, but she was desperate. Henry had mentioned eating fudge during Christmas at home, so perhaps a box of that would do.   The lady at the counter was petite, which seemed at odds with the store. Rose had pictured a robust woman with a large grin who had sampled many of the store's wares, but this lady was kind enough.

Rose took her package and walked outside the store. She was done. She didn't have anything else to worry about, and she was quite content. She blew air out of her mouth and walked toward the Monks' house. Snowflakes danced on their way down to the ground where piles of their relatives rested. Rose smiled softly and slowed her pace.

She walked past the hospital where only a few of the patients still resided. She had heard that Caleb had spent some time there after his night out in the snow, but that was probably rumour. Nothing had proven to be wrong with the curate besides a bit of the flu and a very nasty cough. Still, it was nice to think that the facility was there if needed.

She continued on her way. When she passed the orphanage, Rose couldn't help but stop in. It had been some time since she had last seen Mrs. Jennings, and she greatly missed the company of the older woman. She slipped through the front door and snuck up behind the widow, startling her.

"My goodness, Rose!" she exclaimed when she had calmed herself. "I did not hear you come in, and och, it has been so long. But aren't you a sight for sore eyes. You look more beautiful than ever!"

Rose blushed slightly and returned the compliments.

"Now, don't think I don't miss you. You promised you would come visit me in my loneliness, but I hardly see a speck of you anymore. It's more common for me to see James puttering about. Nice man, he is. He's done cleaned up this whole place. It'll be a lucky lady who gets him, though I think he may already be spoken for, though no one knows it yet. But, anyway, how are you?"

"Forgive me, Mrs. Jennings. I honestly do try to visit more often. It just has been so busy lately. Perhaps I will stop by on Christmas. I doubt I will want to stay cooped up in the house all day, and if you are right about James belonging to a lady already, I doubt he will want to stay long at the Monks' table, though he may feel obliged since I've already asked him."

"Don't be silly, girly," exclaimed Mrs. Jennings. "That whole bit about James already having a lady was just the rambling of an old lonely lady. Silly as I am, I probably just make up these things to keep myself satisfied. Besides, James would be all kinds of a fool if he had any other lady than the one that is set right before him." Mrs. Jennings winked at Rose, who turned red from the insinuations.

"Don't be silly. James has no such feelings for me, and it is just... it's just... nonsense to suggest something like that. Besides, we are of two different classes, him and me. For all we know, he could be a nobleman, or some other rich fellow, and I, I am an orphan. No, such things shouldn't even be suggested!"

"Och, settle yourself down, Rose," soothed Mrs. Jennings. "James is a nice fellow, and don't you ever think that he is out of your league. If anyone ever suggests that, they are lower than you are, and not worth your beauty. I was just thinking how lovely it would be if two nice people, such as James and yourself, could get married. I haven't been to any nice weddings lately, but I'm sure that will be remedied soon. I have heard of three engagements in the past month already."

Rose smiled politely, but she had tuned out the older lady's words. She was deep in thought. What had been the cause of her outburst? Mrs. Jennings' words had been harmless; there was no reason for her to get upset when Mrs. Jennings had suggested that Henry would be a good match for her; yet she had. It just didn't make sense.

Rose's conversation with Mrs. Jennings was short-lived. Mrs. Jennings had a lot of things to do, and Rose needed to return to help with dinner. It was decided that the two would meet on Christmas, and, if he wanted to, James was invited as well. Rose smiled as she walked back to the Monks'. Christmas day was sure to be pleasant.

"Have you got it finished, Hudges?" Henry asked as he slipped into the silversmith's shop. The room was warm and smelled slightly metallic. The walls were lined with silver articles that could be used in daily life, as well as special items that made good gifts for Christmas. Henry would have liked to visit a goldsmith, but the small town of Emriville did not have one, so he supposed silver would have to suffice.

"It's right here in the back, Mr. Hyden. I think you will be impressed with the handwork, sure enough." Henry stepped behind the counter and headed to the back where Hudges, the shopkeeper and smith, waited. The big man looked awkward standing gently polishing a small, intricate piece of silver, but by the way his hands moved, one would think that the article was more precious than the Holy Grail.

Henry leaned over to inspect the piece. What he saw impressed him beyond amazement. What he thought would turn out to be a simple hair clip had turned into a work of art. Tiny flowers wound their way around the prongs of the clip peeking out of crevices and displaying the wonder of fully bloomed roses. It was both delicate and elaborate, a true masterpiece.

Henry grinned. "Very well done, Mr. Hudges. Very well done, indeed. I will have to pay you top dollar for that piece. It's spectacular."

"Oh, shucks, Mr. Hyden," replied Hudges, roughly shoving his hair back from his face to cover his embarrassment. "Now, we agreed on a price already, and I won't take a dollar more than the price we agreed on. You're already paying more than the piece be worth." Henry grinned again. He had forgotten how shy the man was, so unlike what he appeared to be.

"Very well then," replied Henry. "You will just have to accept a little more than what we agreed on as a Christmas gift, for you and the young wife I hear you have. I'm sure you won't be complaining about that."

Hudges grinned, displaying slightly crooked yellow teeth. "No, I suppose I can't go complaining about that, can I, sir? But I will be thanking you kindly for your generosity."

Henry smiled and, taking the clip from Hudges, placed some coins in the outstretched hand and left before Hudges could refuse the money that nearly doubled the price of the small silver clip. Hudges had gone far beyond what he had been asked to do, and Henry wanted to reward him for his excellent handwork.

Henry stepped out onto the cold street. Pulling out his handkerchief, he wrapped the delicate object, placing it in his pocket for safekeeping until tomorrow. He smiled as he thought of tomorrow. He couldn't wait to see what Rose's reaction to the clip would be. If all went well, he would ask Rose if he could court her. Yes, he would court her. It only seemed right to be able to court a woman.

Henry smiled to himself and walked into the inn. That would have to wait until tomorrow.

Christmas day dawned bright and cold. It had snowed during the night, and frost kissed the window panes with icy brilliance. Rose climbed out from under the covers and attempted to dress quickly, before the chill could get into her. It had gotten quite cold that night, and her dress hung stiff on the hanger. She pulled it over her head and raced down the stairs to light the stove. Mr. Monks had beaten her to it.

"Good morning, Rose. Merry Christmas," he said politely. Rose returned the greeting and began to prepare some breakfast. Mrs. Monks and Katy soon joined them. Merry Christmases were wished, but the real desire was to get warm, and both Monks ladies crowded around the oven to warm themselves. Mr. Monks rolled his eyes at the two and returned to his newspaper. Rose bit her lip to try to keep from laughing.

Breakfast was to be simple; a large Christmas dinner had been prepared for after church, and no one wanted to spoil their appetite. It therefore wasn't long before all of the Monks, and Rose included, were ready to head toward the church, where the town waited. Rose smiled as she walked into the crowd. People were in high spirits, and the gaiety seemed to spill over onto all those present. Even Caleb was in a good mood.

As the town clock struck the hour, families spilled into the building and found their seats. A fire crackled in the stove, its warmth filling the room. Caleb went up to the front and led the church in some Christmas carols, and then continued with a brief sermon. After a few more carols, the service was over, and the people were free to return to their festivities.

Rose met Henry in the aisle, and taking her hand, he tucked it under his arm. "I believe it is my duty to escort a certain young Miss to her Christmas dinner," he whispered in her ear.

Rose smiled and retorted, "Is that so? Well then, I think it best you find that young lady, so you can escort her to her dinner and then come join me at the Monks. Unless I am mistaken, you have already promised to share our Christmas dinner, and I will not have you back out now, or there will be far too much turkey left over!"

Henry laughed, and the sound carried through the building. "You know very well, Rose, that I was speaking of escorting you to dinner and I will not have you say no. It is Christmas, after all."

Rose let out a sigh. "I suppose I can allow you to escort me to dinner, but only just this once, because it is Christmas." The two of them laughed together and walked out of the church. If they hadn't been so concerned with the happiness of the day, they might have noticed the eyes of the defeated young curate following them out of the building.

The two continued their walk down the street toward the Monks' house. Mrs. Monks had left immediately after the service to prepare the dinner, and would be waiting at the house for all the company they had invited, which in truth was very little. Henry was coming, along with an elderly couple, the Jenkins, who always went to the Monks' for Christmas. It seemed odd that Mrs. Monks would be stressed over entertaining so few people, but she was not the type to enjoy entertaining, so even a small crowd caused her stress.

"So, how has your Christmas been thus far?" asked Henry.

"Hmm," sighed Rose happily, "I love Christmas. It has to be the best time of the year. People are happy, and they let go of bitter feuds, just for Christmas. It also smells better. I think people purposely reserve pine logs for this day, just so that the whole town can smell delicious, don't you think?"

"Really? I've never noticed," said Henry. "But now that you mention it, I can definitely smell the pine, and it is the most wonderful of smells. At home, on Christmas day, the whole ca—I mean, house—is alive with sounds and smells. It is wonderful. My mother and father spend the day giving out gifts, and at night, there is a ball. It is a large ball, and tables are full of food, so full that the table groans from the weight."

Rose smiled. "It sounds delicious. I would love to see it one day. Is it far from here?" She could hardly believe that Henry was saying so much about his family. She liked it when he spoke of his home; his whole face lit up as if it were a special treat to speak of his loved ones.

"It isn't so far that it is impossible to get to, but far enough that we would be unable to return the same day. I will return there next year. Perhaps you could join me then." Henry looked at her expectantly.

Rose smiled weakly. "Perhaps," she replied, but she did not think it would happen. Instead, all she could think of was the imposing date, and that in a year's time she would be married to who knows who, living under the regret of her aunt. All of a sudden, the air didn't seem as fresh, and the atmosphere as gay. Rose and Henry walked on in silence.

The rest of the day went by nearly undisturbed. Rose and Henry ate an early dinner with the others, then they left to visit with Mrs. Jennings before dark. When they returned, dessert was being served, and they settled in to enjoy the rich custard and sweet apple pie that Mrs. Monks had prepared. When all of this was finished, Mr. Monks and Mr. Jenkins started a game of chess. Mrs. Monks, Mrs. Jenkins, and Katy played cards while Henry and Rose set about doing the dishes.

When the two of them had disappeared, Mrs. Jenkins turned to Mrs. Monks. "Oh, those two do make a sweet pair, wouldn't you agree? And did you see the way he stared at her all dinner? My, my, I dare say that boy is smitten, as he rightfully should be."

Mrs. Monks smiled smartly back at Mrs. Jenkins. "So I am not the only one who has noticed. Well, it is about time someone took interest in that poor girl. You know, her aunt sent her here because she couldn't bear the sight of her. The sweet girl is unwanted where she came from."

"Oh, the poor girl. If that is so, then it is good of Mr. Hyden to look on her the way he does. It will keep another young lady from living off of charity, and a pretty young lady at that. It is amazing that she has not been proposed to already. For a while there, I thought she might be the lucky bride of the curate, but I suppose that wasn't to be so."

"The curate? Honestly, Mrs. Jenkins, you couldn't possibly believe that Mr. Taylor would fall for Rose. Though the two of them would suit very well, I have heard it told that Mr. Taylor wishes to stay a bachelor for all his life, though who ever heard of such a thing?"

"If not the curate, then perhaps that Mark Hepton boy, but then again, the poor lad did die while he was in the hospital, and I hear that he had quite a temper on him."

"Well, there are certainly many men around now for Rose to choose from. Katy was telling me just the other day that there appears to be more men in church than women. Can you believe that? Who would have ever thought that the day would come when there would be more men in Emriville than women?"

"One thing I know for certain," replied Mrs. Jenkins, "is that it certainly does make the whole affair much more complicated for the young women and a lot more difficult for their fathers." Both women agreed on this point and then continued on with their card game. There was plenty of gossip around, and they had just touched the tip of it. Before the night was out, they would cover the Lawson's developmentally delayed child, the odd behaviour of the Cummings girl, and the tidied-up appearance of the orphanage.

The hot water bubbled and frothed as Rose dunked in the dishes, washed them, and handed them over to Henry to dry. The pile was higher than normal due to the number of guests, and the various courses that had been served, but Rose didn't mind; she enjoyed the task. "So, how has your Christmas been, Henry? Has it compared favourably to the ones at home?"

"Hmm," he murmured. "It was nice. Mrs. Monks did a wonderful job with the meal, and there was good company." He turned and looked at her, and she blushed slightly, but he grinned. "I don't think I can compare it to the ones at home, because both nice in their own way, and I wouldn't change anything about either."

Rose nodded slightly and continued with her work. It was cold in the kitchen, and she shivered slightly. Henry put down his dishtowel and walked over to the stove where he stoked the fire. "That should be better," he said. "It is a cold one out today. It's best if you keep the fire going throughout the night."

"That wouldn't be wise," replied Rose. "The stove is old. It would catch fire too easily if no one watched it. It's better to let the fire go out, and use lots of blankets. Besides, I don't imagine any one of us would want to get up in the night to get the fire started again. It is much nicer to lie abed under the covers where it is warm."

Henry groaned. "How do you get up in the morning then? Everything must be frozen if the stove doesn't keep going. Why, I wouldn't be surprised if you had frost hanging on the curtains when you wake up!"

Rose laughed. "Surely you have experienced a cold morning here or there. It is not that big a matter, though I do admit that it takes all of my willpower to get out of bed. It would be much nicer to remain under the covers. But alas, work needs to be done, and someone has to start the stove."

Henry gave her a look of bewilderment, and she laughed at him. He shook his head and the two continued with the dishes. When everything was done, Henry took the tub of water out to the back and dumped it. He then returned to the kitchen to find Rose frowning at her fingers. "What's the matter?" he asked.

"Nothing really," she said, still frowning. "I just hate it when my hands wrinkle like that from the water. It looks horrendous, I think." She gave her hand a little wave as if to end the conversation, but Henry took a hold of it.

A snicker escaped before he could help himself, and Rose quickly pulled her hand away. "I told you they look horrendous when they are all wrinkled. I don't understand it. The water feels so nice on the hands, but as soon as my hands have had enough, it is like they sour up and go all wrinkly."

Henry laughed aloud. Rose scowled at him. "I'm sorry, Rose. It's just that you reminded me of my childhood." She still stood glaring at him, so Henry thought that he should explain. "When I was younger, I hated when my fingers would go all wrinkly in the bath, and I called it pruning." Henry reached out and took Rose's hands. "My mother thought it was cute when I told her that the water pruned my hands, and she would always take my hands in hers, just like this, and kiss them and send me to bed anyway." Henry stooped a little and gently kissed each of Rose's hands.

Rose blushed slightly and without thinking replied, "Am I supposed to go to bed now?" Henry burst out laughing, and Rose joined in. It had been a good day, and they both overflowed with the high spirits that tended to come with Christmas.

"Wait here," said Rose. "I have something for you upstairs." Henry nodded, and Rose ran off to her room upstairs. Packed in her trunk, she found the box of fudge that she had carefully wrapped in a handkerchief that she had made for him. The handkerchief was intricately embroidered, but it did not have any initials like most handkerchiefs these days had because she could not be sure what Henry's initials were. Instead, she had stitched a sword in the corner, and though she had tried to make it look like Henry's sword, it looked much more like the one she had upstairs.

When she came back downstairs into the kitchen, she suddenly felt shy. What if Henry didn't like it? What if he found it childish, or worse, feminine? But there was no way around it now. She had told him that she had something for him, so slowly she handed the box over saying, "I hope you like it."

Slowly Henry traced the stitching on the handkerchief. He followed the outside boarder into the corner that had the sword. He ran a finger over the tiny weapon and let out a low whistle. "That is amazing. It is very beautiful and well crafted, thank you." He smiled at Rose, who blushed.

"The handkerchief was just something to wrap what's inside. You need to open that up." Rose watched silently as Henry slowly unwrapped the box of fudge, and she rejoiced silently as his eyes lit up with pleasure at the sight of the simple sweet. "I remembered that you said something about liking fudge at Christmas, so I thought that you might like a box now."

Henry stood there looking at her, and Rose felt slightly self-conscious. She turned to walk to the parlour where the Monks and the Jenkins were playing games. "Would you like to go on a walk with me?" Henry asked politely. "I know it is cold, but it is such a beautiful night."

"That sounds wonderful," Rose said, smiling. "Just let me get my coat and tell the Monks where we're going. They will be wondering what's taking us so long with the dishes." Again she turned, and this time she disappeared through the door.

After stopping by the parlour, Rose raced to the front hall where her wraps waited. She nearly flew back to the kitchen where Henry stood waiting in his coat. He held out his arm, and the two dipped out the back door into the cold dark night.

Rose breathed in the crisp clean air, scented only by the pine-wood smoke drifting from every chimney in town. Red tipped her nose and her cheeks where the cold wind touched, and her dress clung to her boots where the snow had made it wet. Everything was silent except for the quiet puffs of air coming from her and Henry.

They walked for quite some time before the silence was broken. "You know," started Henry, "the only thing that I miss about Christmas at home is the couples dance that there always was."

Rose stiffened. Was it possible that Henry was thinking about a girl he had waiting for him at home?

"I never liked the dance before," he continued. "But if you were there with me—" He stopped and turned toward her. "—I would be asking you to dance that dance with me, as well as every other dance that evening."

Rose blushed and turned away. "But we are not at your home, and it is unlikely that shall ever happen, so it is best that we enjoy what we have now, instead of ruining the night by thinking of what-ifs."

Henry sighed, and they continued walking.

"May I be allowed just one what-if, for the moment?" Henry asked. "I promise you that it will not ruin the evening." He looked at her with such sincerity that Rose could not help but give in, and Henry proceeded. "What if... what if we danced together, right here outside? Then I would not miss the ball at home, and I could dance every dance of the evening with you."

Rose stopped in her tracks. "But–but there is no music!" Rose exclaimed. "What would we dance to? And it is cold, and there are no other couples; how then could we dance?"

"I will hum," replied Henry. "And there are dances that do not require a line of people, but rather only two. Would you like me to show you such a dance?" Henry held out his hand, but Rose turned her back to him.

"I am well aware of such dances, Mr. Hyden, and I even know the steps to a few, but there is a reason they have not become popular. They are not much enjoyed, and they are far too intimate for mere acquaintances to participate in."

"But you do know some of these dances?" asked Henry. "If they are too intimate for mere acquaintances, then how do you know of them? Have you danced them with a man you considered more than an acquaintance?" Henry prodded.

Rose hugged herself. "My father taught them to me. He and my mother learned them long ago, and because my father was a robust type of character and very cheerful, he would often sweep me around the parlour in a dance. He is the only person I have danced such a dance with, and I will not dance them again unless they are with a person I consider more than an acquaintance."

Henry sighed. He reached into his coat pocket and pulled out the hair clip. He stared at it for a while, then, slowly, gently, he reached out to Rose. She turned around slowly to face him, and he held up the hair clip for her to see. He lifted it up and placed it softly in her hair where it shone delicately in the moonlight.

Rose looked up at him with wide innocent eyes. Her lower lip trembled uncertainly. She bit it and turned away. Henry touched her cheek gently. "Rose," he whispered, "I would very much like to be more than an acquaintance." His hand slipped from her cheek to her hand, and the two began to dance.

TWENTY-FIVE

THE NEW YEAR CAME WITH VERY LITTLE ENCOURAGEMENT, and January nearly passed without notice. By the time February arrived, Rose was ready to get outside and vent some steam. Too often, she spent her nights cooped up in the Monks' house. Sure, it was fine playing cards and chess, and it was really nice when Henry came over, but he was the very reason she needed to vent.

For one more chilly evening, Rose put up with the card games, but when she got a chance, she slipped into some warmer loose-fitting garments, grabbed her sword, and left the house to those who slept. Snow covered the pasture, but that was all right. It would test her endurance to muck about in snow this deep. Setting her mask in place, Rose took a ready stance and began to fight her invisible opponent.

THE MASK

Snow swished about her feet, and some of it melted, causing her garments to get wet, but she hardly noticed. She set forth with a vengeance, trying to relieve the pressure that had accumulated during the winter months. Her legs started to burn, but she fought on, determined to beat out all her unresolved issues. And when her legs finally gave out, she sank onto the rock, panting and thinking.

Who was Henry? Why did he seem to like her so much? Of course, she knew him as Mr. Hyden, and she knew that he wanted to court her, but what was beneath that? She knew that he was a noble. Everything about him spoke of his noble birth. Why others could not see that, she did not know. The very air about him spoke of the confidence of a king. It really was a sight to see.

Rose sighed. She had watched him carefully for the past month or so. He was well liked wherever he went. He was charismatic and charming, and she was a fool if she thought that he could really care about her. Sure, he said that he cared for her, and it appeared as though he did, but there was no way that a man such as he could care for an orphan. It defied all social norms.

Besides, if he did care for her, she would have to dissuade him. It was unlikely that his parents, whoever they were, would allow him to marry her, and he deserved better than her anyway. Henry deserved someone who could love him. Rose could never love him. It was impossible, no matter how good looking and wonderful he was. She had sworn off love. It hurt far too much.

No, she would have to dissuade him, but she didn't know how. She thought of Christmas night. The air had been fresh and marvellous, and the snow had been crisp beneath their feet. The whole

him? Had he done something to anger her? What could it possibly have been?

They washed dishes together like normal, and when everything was put away, Henry made to remedy things. He took hold of Rose's hands, and kissed them gently. She turned from him, but did not pull away. "Rose, I do not know why you are angry, but I will do anything in my power to mend whatever damage has been done."

At this, Rose pulled away, but Henry pushed on. "Would you go on a walk with me?" Rose looked up at him fearfully. Those eyes, which Henry had earlier been reminiscing about, bore into him, displaying a whirlwind of emotion that was so quickly cut off that he couldn't even begin to comprehend them. He began to fear that Rose would not go for a walk with him, when she nodded.

The two walked out into the cold air. It wasn't as cold as December had been, but it was still cold enough for snow to reside on the ground. They began to walk, and Henry kept up idle chatter to help Rose relax. It didn't really work. She remained stiff and hesitant, so Henry decided to jump into the heart of the matter.

"Rose," he began, "what have I done that you act this way toward me? You must have a reason. Please tell me."

The night fell silent, and they continued to walk. After what seemed like ages in Henry's mind, Rose asked, "What do you care?"

Henry smiled slightly to himself in triumph. He didn't care how much the question hurt him, as long as she was talking to him. "Don't you know, lass?" he asked in a playful, teasing voice. "It matters to me what you are feeling."

"But why does it matter?" asked Rose sternly, and somewhat angrily. "Why do you care if I am angry or upset?"

Henry had not been expecting this, but he calmly took Rose's hands and made her face him. "Rose, it matters to me what you are feeling because I care for you deeply, and if you are hurting, I would like to change that, just because I care."

Rose pulled away, and a knot puckered her brow. "But that doesn't even make sense. How can you care for me? It defies all social normalcy, and you know it! What would your parents think, or other people of your status for that matter, if they heard you speaking such to me?"

Henry let out an exasperated sigh. "Is that what this is about, Rose? Are you trying to dissuade me because you think something as trifling as social status would keep me from caring for you?"

Rose looked at him. "You are noble. I am an orphan. I am nothing but a charity case, an educated servant, in the eyes of society. I have no dowry, no social standing to offer you. There is no possible way that you could care for me, and if you really do at this moment, it is only a flirting with the unknown. There is no possible way that you could care for me more than that, because as soon as you go home to wherever you live, you will see how I do not fit into your life. Then you will realize that I am right, and that you don't really care for me at all."

Henry let out a low growl of frustration from deep in his throat. "Don't you understand, Rose? I left my home because I could not find a woman that could possibly fit in my life. I left with my father's blessing to find a woman who is not of my 'social standard,' but who has a heart that lives up to this standard, whether she be peasant, educated, or middle class. You have this heart and more!"

"How can you be so sure?" Rose whispered.

"I don't know," replied Henry. "I can't tell you how I know. All I know is that when I picture my life from here on in, it is with you by my side, along with a passel of kids and possibly a dog or two."

Rose couldn't suppress the giggle that climbed up her throat. It was infectious, and soon Henry was laughing as well. "Do you really picture kids and a dog?" Rose asked.

Henry smiled. "Lots of kids, and a Great Dane or two."

"Those dogs are huge!" exclaimed Rose. "They could eat a man whole!"

"Well then, perhaps we will have to get a terrier of sorts for the kids."

Rose laughed. Then, in a more serious tone, she said to Henry, "I can't be all that you think I am. I don't think I will be a very good wife, and Henry, you deserve someone so much more than me."

"Shhh," calmed Henry. "How about we don't worry about that. For now, let me just court you, and in May I will bring this up again, if it is even pertinent. So, until May, let us just be two young people who have a general interest in the other. Do you think you can live with that?"

Rose sighed. It was a dangerous gamble to agree to this, but it was not a promise to be held to. She could easily slip out of it, and by May her aunt would be making wedding arrangements for her anyway. Rose smiled and slipped her hand into the crook of

Henry's arm. "How do we go about being two young people with only general interests in each other?"

Henry smiled. "Well," he said, "for starters, you allow me to come for dinner once a week, and once a week only. We will wash dishes together, and every other week we will play cards with the Monks. On the weeks not taken up with card playing, we will go out for walks, to talk and enjoy each other's company. When we meet in the market, you should allow me to carry your parcels, and on Sundays, we should share warm greetings."

Rose laughed. "You sound as if you have experience with this sort of thing. How many women have you had a general interest in anyway?"

Henry smiled coyly. "A number less than two, and greater than nil, and you are closely associated with the one."

"You're insufferable!" exclaimed Rose, giving Henry a gentle shove.

"Is this how you plan on starting our general interest in one another?" asked Henry with feigned indignity. The two laughed with each other and continued their walk. They had a lot to talk about and much nonsense to cover before the evening was over, and Henry didn't want to waste a minute of it.

Katy sighed as she looked out on the two shadowy figures that walked about the yard. It was so unfair. Why was it that Rose could have all the men chasing after her, while she was stuck with only scrawny, little Joshua? He was repulsive. It wasn't that he was ugly, or unkept, it was just that he was so, so... young! He was barely a year older than Katy, yet he seemed to believe that it was possible she might like him.

No, she couldn't like him, especially when there were men around as handsome as the curate, or even Mr. Hyden. Joshua would just have to find another girl, or maybe he could wait a few years. It only seemed natural that he would wait before even considering a bride.

Katy turned on the couch and let out a huffy breath. Bother! Life was so unfair. She longed for the day that a man would hold her in his arms and whisper sweet nothings in her ear. Her friend, May, had told her about a man who had spoken such to her at one of the balls, and Katy had burned with jealousy. May wasn't even that pretty!

Wouldn't it be so romantic if a man could sweep her around a ballroom whispering in her ear and sharing secrets that no one else would understand? The thought sent butterflies up her throat until reality cut in. What was she thinking? She couldn't dance! She was a horrible dancer. Oh, Rose had tried to teach her, but her feet just wouldn't obey the right command, and on more than one occasion, she had stepped on the foot of a suitor.

No, the man who would win her heart would come bearing gifts of gold and silver. Wouldn't it be splendid to marry a rich man that decked her in gold and took her out to balls where people stared and gawked at her beauty and riches? The very idea of it sent shivers down her back. She had seen the clip that James had given Rose, and she decided that the man who would marry her would have to give her something just as spectacular.

There was also another option for her husband; one unthinkable, but oh so wonderful option for her husband. Wouldn't it be the most romantic thing if her husband was the most respected and sought after man in the entire town? Who could fill that bill other than the curate himself?

Katy closed her eyes in a dream of the handsome Mr. Taylor. Caleb was his name. She had heard Rose using it, and she repeated it to herself a hundred times over to get the feel of it on her tongue. Then there had been his surname. Taylor. She had written it out over and over on scraps of paper. Katy Taylor. It had a ring to it, and it looked wonderful written down. She would know because every time she wrote down Taylor, it was preceded by her own name.

How she dreamed of becoming the minister's wife. But she could tell no one. Once she had made the mistake of telling May about her desire to marry Caleb, and that had only ended in disaster. She would not make that mistake again. If she was left to it, she would spend the rest of her days dreaming about the handsome curate who could do no wrong.

She wondered what it would be like to kiss him. May said she had kissed a boy, and it had been wet, but Katy doubted that. May had made it sound like a disgusting ordeal that women had to put up with in order to please their men, but Katy was sure that it could only be spectacular. The only man she had ever kissed was her father—on the cheek, but she had dreamed of what it would be like to be kissed on the lips for ages.

The door to the parlour creaked open, startling Katy out of her reverie. Rose slipped in, a gentle grin on her face. James followed and said his goodbyes, saying that he would be back in a week's time. Katy glowered at them. It was evident that James was smitten with Rose, and it just wasn't fair.

The rest of the evening was spent in silence. Rose tried to engage Katy in a game of cards, but she was feeling too bitter to play a game, so she headed upstairs to her room. When Rose came up later, she buried her face under the covers and pretended to be asleep.

She listened as Rose sighed and began her normal rituals before bed. When the room fell unusually silent, Katy looked up to see what the matter was. Rose stood by the dresser running a finger over the hair clip that James had given her. Her face was lined with worry, and she seemed in a way scared.

At that moment, she turned and saw Katy staring at her. She smiled slightly. "It is a beautiful hair clip, is it not?"

Katy nodded, not sure what to say.

"He is a nice man, Mr. Hyden is, but how I don't understand him. He is far beyond me." Katy was shocked. Rose didn't understand Mr. Hyden? How could that be? They spent most of their time together. By this time, they should be reading each other's thoughts and finishing the other's sentence.

"It is scary," said Rose. "I don't know what to think of it all." She blew out the candle and slipped under the covers. Katy sat blinking in the dark and quiet. "But I guess," continued Rose, "it'll be your turn soon, Katy, and you'll understand what I am saying."

Katy hesitated, then in a shaky voice she asked, "Has he kissed you yet?"

Rose burst out laughing, and Katy didn't understand why. "No, Katy," she said, "Mr. Hyden has not kissed me yet, except on the hand. Though I can't say that I really want to be kissed on the lips... I hear that it is a wet affair."

Katy let out a frustrated stream of air between her lips, then the two girls dissolved into giggling that lasted the rest of the night.

TWENTY-SIX

JOSH WAS GETTING A LOT BIGGER. That was all that Rose could think about as she looked at the young man who stood before her. It was their first lesson after the winter weather, and the cold March winds still bit during the late hours of night. Rose looked up at her pupil, who now towered over her. If she wasn't careful, he would soon be able to beat her, and that was a scary thought.

She wasn't afraid of Josh. He was gentle and kind and he would never hurt anyone intentionally. What scared her most was their bargain. Josh had begun to wonder who was teaching him to fight, and Rose had told him that if he ever beat her in a match, she would remove her mask for him to see his instructor. This thought terrified her.

Josh was smart. He was catching onto the lessons quickly, and he was becoming quicker. Rose was impressed with his skills, and she knew he could show up any of the young men that resided in the village. Perhaps she could break off with him before he became any better. In this way, she would protect her identity as well as make it easier to leave Josh. She would, after all, have to leave within two months anyway. She bit her lip. That wouldn't be fair to Josh. She would just have to hold her own for two more months.

She lifted her sword to encourage Josh to take a ready pose, and the two began to duel. They fought harder and harder as the time went on, with neither of them gaining the advantage. Rose feinted to the left and went to disarm him, but Josh was ready with a counterattack, and the mere force of his blow sent the sword flying from Rose's hand. Josh looked stunned at what had happened, but Rose didn't give him a chance to think. Before he could react, she sent a foot into his hand and a quick sweep under his legs. Afterward, he lay sprawled on the ground. When he reached for his sword, she stepped on his hand, pinning him to the ground. He looked at her with wide-eyed terror.

Slowly Rose regained her breath. That had been too close. She would have to be much more careful in the future. She looked down at Josh, who looked up at the faceless master. "Never," she said raggedly, "never be caught off guard. People will often fight with more than their sword, and it is better that you fight with all tools offered to you." Josh nodded his head, and Rose sent him on his way. She would have to do something quick, or she would be revealing to the whole town what a scandalous person she really was.

King James Arden looked down at his son's letter and smiled. It was full of talk of a specific young lady that he couldn't wait to meet. Rose Wooden sounded like the perfect daughter-in-law. She was intelligent and beautiful. At least, that was what Henry said, and her social manners were above those of an average commoner. What he liked most about her was that she had his son totally and completely smitten.

Yes, this was exactly what he had hoped to accomplish with his son leaving the castle. Perhaps in two months time he would be handing the crown down to his son, and he would be free to relax and enjoy his kingdom. It would be a dream to walk down the streets and not have to worry about whether the taxes were too high, or if justice was being done. True, all these things would still weigh on his mind, but now he would be able to enjoy the smiles more. He would be able to look every person in the eye, knowing that he had done his best for them, and he would be content.

James looked at the letter again. There was only one thing that troubled him. Henry had not made one mention of the girl's faith. He had stated that she regularly attended services, but he had never stated whether or not she had taken the faith as her own. He would have to ask Henry about this in his next letter, for it could cause a lot of problems if she was not a Christian.

The king pushed this thought aside and began to put a picture together of his son's love. She was very short, with auburn hair he had said, and she had bright eyes. She was an orphan, which hopefully meant she would be more willing to become part of their family, but in the end that would have to be seen. She was stubborn, a perfect match for his stubborn son.

James laughed out loud. Rose was perfect. For him, May could not come soon enough. He only hoped that Henry wouldn't mess it up. A flower such as the Rose he described did not appear every day, and it would be a terrible loss for his son if anything were to happen to her.

Rose looked at the Monks' family Bible and read the words again. Inwardly she cringed. It just wasn't fair what the verse suggested, and she in no way wanted to live by it. She looked at the verse in 1 Peter 2 just one more time to make sure they still read the same way. "Submit yourselves for the Lord's sake to every authority instituted among men: whether to the king, as the supreme authority, or the governors, who are sent by him to punish those who do wrong and to commend those who do right."

It wasn't the part about doing right that bothered her. In truth, the only thing that bothered her was the fact that she was to submit to the king. This king did not deserve her submission. In fact, the king did not deserve to be in authority at all, yet the Lord still called her to submit. Rose scowled. It just wasn't right. How was she supposed to submit to a murderer?

In her mind, Rose could picture her aunt yelling at her uncle. It had been the day after she had arrived, and she had accidentally spilled the milk. Her aunt was peeved to say the least, and she had shouted at her husband to do something about the dolt of a child that the law had left them with.

Uncle Murdoch had not been too happy with Aunt Agatha for calling her a dolt, but he had let her rail on and on. Finally, he had become fed up with his wife and yelled back. This was the first and only time that Rose saw her uncle yell. "If you want someone to blame," he shouted, "blame the king, for it's his blasted war that killed Aaron and eventually your sister. I am sick and tired of hearing your moaning about Rose, and I don't want to hear any more of it."

That was the day that the battle between Rose and her aunt had started. Aunt Agatha refused to acknowledge her for one whole week, and she was forced to care for her own necessities, such as a morning toilet and daily cleansing. She would have gone without food as well, had it not been for Uncle Murdoch and John who forced her to eat at mealtimes.

From that time on, Rose refused to acknowledge the king. Why should she acknowledge the man who had killed her father? She would much rather die than have to go about at his beck and call, but seeing as she was an orphan who lived almost a week's journey from the castle, it was unlikely that she would ever see the king, so her vow of contempt was easily kept.

Again, Rose scowled at the verse in front of her. It was clear that with such a verse present in the Bible, she would have to get rid of her dislike, but she really didn't want to. She pondered this for a while and came to a conclusion. She would keep her vow for the time being. After all, every change in attitude or behaviour took some time. There was no use trying to rush the process. If there ever came a time that she must submit to the king, she would deal with it then, but for now, she would let her anger fade slowly.

Henry sat in his room staring at the calendar. The days were passing quickly, and May would soon be upon them. May, the month of promise for him. It was the month that he was going to marry Rose. He was determined. He had told Rose that he would wait until May to bring the subject of matrimony up, and he would wait that long, and that long only. In fact, he planned to propose on the first of May.

Henry dug into his pocket and pulled out a ring. It had been his mother's ring, and she had given it to him to give to the woman he wished to marry. This would be the ring that would grace the hand of his gentle, loving Rose. It was a beautiful ring. It held only one stone, but that one stone was a large blood-red ruby that sparkled when hit by the sun just right. It was a ring that would befit a queen—his queen.

Henry played with the ring, running it back and forth between his fingers, thinking of the girl who would wear it. He loved her, of that he was certain. What other emotion could it be that made him smile with just the mention of her name, or made him giddy as a school boy at the thought of visiting her? Yup, there was no doubt. He was far past smitten. He loved the girl.

From the sounds of his father's letters, there would be no objection to her either. There might be a small uproar from the ladies of the court who would be quite hurt that they were not chosen to marry the Prince. But ultimately, not many people objected to nobles marrying middle-class commoners, as long as it did not lower the status of any other person. Of course, marrying Rose would not heighten Henry's status, but it could in no way do him harm, as he was the direct heir of his father. There could be no objections to him taking the position of king, and not many people would dare question his choice in a wife, especially after they met her.

Henry had no fears in regards to status. He knew Rose would be able to play the part of Queen better than most ladies of the court, and she would be a better helpmate to the king than any other woman alive. She would probably even make a better addition to the household, because she was very likeable, and she would not look down upon anyone because of their position in life. Rose was the perfect fit.

Henry continued to smile as he thought of her. He looked at the calendar again. It was March twentieth. In just over a month, he would be the happiest man alive. He couldn't wait for the day when he would take Rose home as his wife.

Rose smiled as she took the letters from Miss Mede. Most of the post was for the Monks, but she was hoping that she might come across a letter from her cousin this week. It had been quite some time since she had heard from him. She flipped through the letters, reading to whom they were addressed, and soon she came to the bottom of the pile where she found a note addressed to her. As she had hoped, the letter was from her cousin.

It seemed unwise to open the letter in the street, so Rose tucked the letter with the other envelopes into her reticule and began the walk home. It was cold outside even for a spring day, and Rose wondered if they would get a late snow, though the farmers of the area said otherwise. Most predicted that they would experience true warmth with the beginning of the next week. Rose hoped so; she didn't like the cold.

When she arrived home, Rose placed the letters on the table and made her way up the stairs to where she could read her letter in privacy. She sat down on her bed and looked at her cousin's lettering. To her it seemed abnormally messy and sporadic. This abnormality sent a shiver down her spine, and she began to fear the worst. She opened the letter and began to read the few short sentences.

> *My Dearest Cousin,*
>
> *I don't know how to say this other than bluntly. My father has passed away, and you need to come home. I don't know how to arrange this, but the funeral will wait for your arrival. Please come quickly.*
>
> *With love,*
> *John*

A tear slid down Rose's cheek, dropping onto the paper and smudging the ink. Rose allowed it to sink in, marking all the bitterness that welled up inside her. Why now? Why her uncle? There were plenty of evil men out there. Why did her uncle have to be the one to die? He was only fifty-six. He had committed his life to his family and to God. Why then did God abandon him?

Rose gently placed the letter beside her on the bed. Tears welled up in her eyes and spilled their sorrow over the contours of her face. She did not weep in long sorrowful wails. Instead, she allowed her very soul to cry out in wet, silent shudders that shook the foundation of her being.

She didn't know how long she had been sitting there, or how long the river of tears flowed, but in good time they ceased. A new determination stole over her, one that guarded her heart and gave her strength enough to persevere through this. Slowly she stood, and with an indignant lift of her head, she bit her lip, wiped her eyes, and walked out of the room.

Mrs. Monks looked at her and her sad eyes and right away her motherly instincts kicked in. She ran over and wrapped her arms around her, dragging her over to a couch and forcing her to sit down. Once seated, she cooed over Rose, asking her what the matter was. Rose stiffened slightly and handed her the letter.

Mrs. Monks took one look at the letter and began to wail. Rose gathered the distraught woman in her arms and held her as she mourned the loss of her ever beloved brother. The whole time Rose held her, she ranted on about the necessity of her being there, and that if she had been there, none of this would ever have happened. After all, his good for nothing wife didn't care for him. Rose had to bite her lip to keep from laughing at this point.

By the time the woman was done wailing, the whole Monks family had been informed of the news, and Mr. Monks had already looked into a way of transportation to Thespane. Not until later that afternoon did he conclude that it would be impossible for him to make the journey, and it was in no way reasonable for two or three young ladies to travel without a chaperone. It was in this distracted state that Mr. Hyden happened to walk in on them.

"What do you mean, it cannot be done?" asked Rose as Henry knocked at the door. Katy went to answer it. She tried to dissuade Mr. Hyden from coming in, but he insisted upon seeing Rose.

"It is quite simply this, Rose. I have business here that must be attended to. If I do not stay, I will lose my job, and then my whole family will be without a home. If I have to choose between keeping my home and going to a funeral, I would much rather keep my home," replied Mr. Monks calmly.

"Fine," returned Rose. "Then let me go with Mrs. Monks. It is not that inappropriate. Women travel together all the time. It is becoming a popular trend throughout Samaya."

"I will not have it," said Mr. Monks a little bit angrily. "I do not deem it appropriate, so it will not occur."

"If your wife will not go, then I will go alone!" Rose was near yelling. "I will not miss my uncle's funeral because shallow rules of society deem it inappropriate for women to travel without a male chaperone. It's barbaric and cruel!"

"I agree with Rose," Henry cut in.

Mr. Monks turned to Henry and began to sputter. "You of all people think that it is wise for Rose to travel alone to Thespane? I would have thought that you would be against such radical thinking and want to protect the decency…"

"Don't get me wrong," continued Henry. "I don't want to see Rose travelling by herself, but if it were the only way for her to get to her uncle's funeral, I would understand it completely. Seeing as it is not the only way to the funeral, I do not think there is any need in worrying about it."

"What do you mean, it is not the only solution? There is no way I can leave Emriville within the near future, and there is no other male who can accompany them as a chaperone. What other way do you suggest she attend the funeral?" Mr. Monks sounded a bit miffed at being undermined by the younger man.

"I believe you have too quickly vetoed one of your options. There is still a male chaperone willing to accompany your wife and Miss Wooden to the funeral if you would allow it. And they are ready to go at any time pleasurable to you. They even have a carriage ready and waiting."

"Who is this man?" asked Mr. Monks.

Mr. Hyden smiled and gave a slight bow. "Yours truly," he stated. "To be perfectly honest, I stopped by to inform Rose that I would be gone for the next week or so on business in Thespane. Upon arriving, I discovered your dilemma, and I thought it best that I offer my services."

Mr. Monks gave him a look that lacked trust. "That seems unnaturally convenient. How can I be sure that I can trust you with

Miss Wooden? After all, you are courting her. It may look rather suspicious if you are her means of transportation to her uncle's funeral, don't you think?"

Henry gave a slight chuckle. "Mr. Monks, I believe you have a slight case of worrying too much. I believe that your wife would appreciate being able to go to her brother's funeral, and I promise you that I will not go anywhere with Rose without her present. Does that satisfy your conscience?"

Mr. Monks let out a small grunt. "It's far from satisfying my conscience, but you have proven to be an honourable man. Besides, I fear that if I do not let you be chaperone to this journey, Rose will take off on her own and find her own way to Thespane. No, I think this is a much better arrangement than the latter." He let out a sigh as if to give it all an air of hopelessness.

Henry smiled. "Thank you, Mr. Monks. I believe the only question now is, when would you ladies like to leave?"

"I can be ready within the hour," stated Rose bluntly.

"My, oh my!" exclaimed Mrs. Monks. "That will never do, dear Rose. There is much too much to do. We will need at least till tomorrow morning to prepare. I will have to get my dresses organized, and I will have to find a nice black dress as well, which will be difficult to produce in such a short time. I will need a parasol and a fan and a...."

Rose tuned out Mrs. Monks' voice and turned to Henry. "We will be ready tomorrow morning by ten. I will be sure of this." Henry nodded his head and turned to leave. Rose grabbed his arm and he turned to face her.

Tears began to well in her eyes. "Thank you, Henry," she whispered. "Thank you so much." He knew she had noted his bluff.

TWENTY-SEVEN

THE CARRIAGE RATTLED AND SHOOK as the miles of endless road flew beneath the wheels. Henry bounced to and fro on the seat and tried not to grunt as the driver flew over a particularly large pothole. He now knew why his father refused to ride in a carriage. Such contraptions were death traps only to be condemned. Unfortunately for him, he had chosen to ride with two women, and it would have been inappropriate for them to take just horses, so there he sat in the carriage.

The journey really wasn't all that bad. Henry thought of it as a chance to spend some time with Rose. They had five days together to spend in the close confines of a carriage. The only downfall to this was the additional close proximity of Mrs. Monks. She was not an unpleasant lady to be around, but Henry could think of better things to do with his time than listen to the older lady prattle on about stitching and dresses and other such feminine concerns.

Rose spent her time stitching, so Henry wiled away the hours watching Rose work. If worse came to worst, his horse was tethered behind the carriage waiting for him to ride.

On the fourth day, their routine finally changed. They were drawing near to Thespane, and Rose was getting anxious. She could no longer work on her stitching. Instead, she spent many hours staring out the window at the passing scenery. Mrs. Monks also began to act differently. As they drew closer to her hometown, she became nostalgic and began to tell stories of her childhood. One particular story was of her brother and herself, and by the time she was done the telling of it, she was weeping because the memory of poor Murdoch was just too much to bear. Henry handed her his handkerchief.

Rose turned away from the window and allowed Mrs. Monks to cry into her shoulder. Henry didn't know how long this lasted, but what seemed like ages later, the old woman finally hiccupped and fell into a deep slumber. Rose patted her head. "There, there," she whispered, and she gently rested Mrs. Monks on the bench. This being done, there wasn't much room left for Rose, so Henry moved over and made room for her beside himself. Rose was hesitant, but she soon complied.

When she had settled herself, Henry whispered, "How are you?"

She let out a sigh and looked out the window. "I am tired, I suppose," she replied. "It is a long trip back to Thespane, and I had not realized that it would be this long before I could be with my family."

"Is that all that troubles you?" Henry asked. "Or is there something more that keeps you so taciturn?"

"I am also quite anxious to see my cousin again. It has been quite some time since we have been able to converse, and I miss him terribly." Rose turned back to the window and the conversation ended for quite some time before she asked, "Why did you volunteer to take us to Thespane when I know that carriages have to be your least favourite mode of transportation?"

"I suppose I volunteered because I believe everyone has the right to attend the funeral of a loved one. Besides, I feared that if I didn't volunteer, you would find some other means to get there, and I doubt I would be able to close my eyes the entire time you would be gone for fear that something would happen to you," replied Henry.

"I guess that makes sense. But what are you going to tell Mrs. Monks when she finds out that you actually don't have any business in Thespane? She won't be too pleased with you, you know."

"That is exactly why I don't plan on having her find out. I brought my horse along so that for one day I can disappear and say I was about business in the town. I will spend that entire time enjoying nature and the seat of a good horse." Henry smiled at Rose, and she gave a sly smile back.

"Is that what you did the last time you had 'business' to attend to? I really am starting to wonder about you, Henry. I'm beginning to think that you aren't noble at all; you are just a regular old truant."

Henry burst out laughing, and Rose jabbed him in the stomach with her elbow, when Mrs. Monks began to wake up. The two held their breath as she settled back into the cushion on the seat. Slowly Rose let the air out between her lips. "That was close," whispered Henry.

"Much too close for comfort," replied Rose. "I don't know what I would do if I had to listen to any more quips and advice about stitching. For a while there, I thought I was about to go crazy."

Henry snickered softly. "I thought that was all young women talked about these days. I mean, what could possibly be more important than how the ball is coming along, how handsome the curate is going to look in his formal wear, and how hard it is to stitch a French knot?" Rose's giggle encouraged Henry to continue on. "Honestly, Rose, I believe you are the only intelligent woman I have had the pleasure of talking to, besides my mother."

"You must be jesting. There are plenty of intelligent women out there. Just because they talk about stitching and such doesn't mean they don't have a brain. And I can hardly say that I blame those who are without knowledge. Look at the society that we grow up in. Women are treated as bargaining chips. If you have a beautiful daughter, you can trade her for a better position in life. Why bother with giving them brains when they have beauty?"

"That is a valid point, but then why not educate a beautiful girl so that she is at least bearable for a man to marry? There is no use marrying someone if she can't do anything but stitch," replied Henry.

"Men don't look for wives with brains. How embarrassing would it be if their wives ended up being smarter than they? Women are meant to be the submissive sex. Giving a woman an education would be like handing her the rights to rule over man." Rose spat out the words bitterly as if they seared her tongue.

"I see. I think that our country is making a grave mistake. It is very possible that we are stunting the growth of society by doing this. What happens if a woman has wisdom that surpasses that of a normal being and can add to society, but she is not given an education and cannot therefore discover this gift that she has? Women should at least be given the chance at an elementary education."

Rose looked at him slightly shocked. "Are you serious? You aren't just trying to appease me? You actually believe as I do?"

Henry furrowed his brow and looked at her. "Why wouldn't I be serious? Yes, I can understand why some men might not wish to have an educated wife, but we owe it to society to teach our children—both boys and girls."

Rose smiled, but then a shadow fell across her face. "It would be wonderful if this could happen, but unfortunately we will never see the day."

"Why not?" asked Henry.

Rose looked at him sadly. "No matter how much we believe this, we are only two out of thousands and millions. Even if this bill is brought before the people, it will never pass because women don't have the right to vote, and men don't want change."

"Hmm, that does bring about a predicament, doesn't it?" replied Henry. "Perhaps I can see what I can do."

Rose smiled at him again. "Don't bother yourself with this, Henry. Though I would like to see this change someday, I am content for now to see that I am not the only one who feels this way. All in due time, it will happen."

Rose turned her head to once again look out the window.

Henry sighed and leaned back into the seat. In a few more hours, they would be in Thespane. He shivered with the thought of it. For when they reached Thespane, they would also reach Rose's family. He would have to meet them, and the thought of it scared him ever so slightly.

Rose was jerked awake by the sudden lurch of the carriage. She caught herself just before she went sprawling on the floor, but not before she knocked heads with Henry, who had also been sleeping. He let out a grunt and Rose tried to fight back the squeak that wanted to squeeze past her teeth.

Mrs. Monks also awoke. She looked at the two of them curiously and then glared at their proximity. "Quick, Rose," she said. "Move yourself over here. It is highly inappropriate that you sit there by Mr. Hyden by yourself. What would your aunt say if she saw the two of you so close? Oh, she would be horrified with me for allowing such a thing. And who knows what you were up to while I slept? Such a horrible chaperone I've been."

Rose gave Henry a look as Mrs. Monks prattled on about the indecency of sharing a carriage with a single male. It would have been much better if they hadn't gone at all. Henry laughed when Rose rolled her eyes, and Mrs. Monks gave him a look that even the bravest would cower at. He apologized profusely.

Rose looked out the window, and her heart began to beat a little quicker. There was the mercantile, and the inn. The post office was next, and in another few minutes they would be pulling up in front of her aunt and uncle's home. She bit her lip as the excitement grew. She would get to see John again, and she couldn't wait.

Soon the carriage began to slow. A large, white, imposing building stood before them, and before anyone could react, Rose was out of the carriage and onto the front walk. The front door burst open, and a large man flew down the steps, sweeping Rose up into his arms.

Henry stood back in jealousy as Rose and her cousin swirled round and round. John had tears in his eyes, and Rose was laughing lightly. Finally, he put her down, and Henry walked toward them. "Mr. Hyden," she said, "this is my cousin John Borden. John, this is my good friend Mr. James Hyden." The two men shook hands and studied each other.

"It is nice to finally meet the man that I have heard so much about," said John politely. "Please, come in, James and meet the rest of the family that has come. I fear it is very little, seeing as both my mother and my father's families have had many deaths at young ages. But I believe you will find that we are not lacking in friends."

"Thank you. I will join you shortly, but I believe there is a lady waiting in the carriage who will need you to escort her in, and I have a horse that needs tending to, if you wouldn't mind telling me where I could house him." Rose let out a little squeal and raced toward the carriage. Slowly she helped Mrs. Monks out, who complained of being forgotten about. Rose tried to soothe her, but nothing seemed to work.

"I believe my aunt should be fine as soon as she finds my mother. Perhaps it would be best if I allowed Rose to bring her in, and I will show you to the stables."

Henry complied, and the two men made their way to the carriage where luggage was being unloaded. Henry loosed his horse and followed John as he led the way to the back of the house.

"I believe I owe you a thank you for escorting my cousin and aunt here so quickly. I did not want my cousin to miss my father's funeral." John bit his lip and shook his head before he continued. "The two of them were very close."

"It was really no trouble for me," replied Henry. "I have a day's worth of business in Thespane, and I was making my way here anyhow. It did not bother me in any way to travel with company."

"No, I suppose it would be much more amusing to travel with my aunt than to be by one's self. I am sure her talk about stitching kept you much occupied. Or perhaps she entertained you with stories about her childhood." There was a glint in John's eyes that

Henry almost missed, but when he saw it, he burst into laughter which was soon echoed by John's.

"It is so good to see you again, Agatha," Mrs. Monks said when she first saw Rose's aunt. "It has been much too long. We must visit more often. And now, poor Murdoch has passed on, and we will have even less reason to visit. It is so tragic." Aunt Agatha nodded her agreement, and Rose slipped away before she could be tied down to a conversation she would much rather not be a part of.

She walked out of the room and headed toward the kitchen where she knew she would find the cook in desperate need of help. As she passed a window looking out into the back, she heard laughter. When she looked, she saw Henry and John laughing like two school boys who had become fast friends. She smiled to herself. She had known they would get along.

In the kitchen, Nancy, the cook, was bustling about with pots of various scrumptious dishes. Rose tiptoed behind her and poked her lightly in the sides. The startled cook flung her wooden spoon into the air and spun around on the spot to see who had dared enter her domain. "Ach, my dear Rose, such a blessing to see you!" she exclaimed when she realized who had startled her. She wrapped her arms around the young girl and squeezed tight. "It's a pity that you had to come back for a funeral."

Rose sighed. "It is better to come back for a funeral than not to come back at all. I have missed you all terribly. I don't know how I

389

would have lasted through the year without coming to see you again. It is bad enough not being able to see you."

"Ach!" Nancy dabbed at the dampness in her eyes. "They don't feed you enough where you're staying. Look! You're skin and bones. Go over there on that stool and eat. Then you can help me here. For there are far too many people in this house for me to try to feed on my own." Rose laughed and scooted over toward the stool. She helped herself to a bowl of hot stew and began to eat.

She took her time enjoying the flavours and absorbing the general warmth of the room. It had been a long time since she had felt this comfortable in a house, and she enjoyed every minute of it.

She was just cleaning out the last drops of stew from the bottom of the bowl when it hit her. "Nancy," she said, "where is my uncle?" She needed to say her last goodbyes before they laid him to rest. It was only fair that she got the chance to do that.

Nancy bit her lip and tried to avoid the question, but Rose was persistent. Finally she submitted. "I don't know what to say, Rose. We tried to wait for you, but it just took too long, and the body wasn't lasting. We had the funeral a couple of days ago. Everyone is planning to leave tomorrow morning."

At first, Rose didn't respond. How was she supposed to respond? She had missed her uncle's funeral. Could the world be any more unjust? "Where did you bury him?" she asked softly.

"Where he always wanted to be laid to rest," whispered Nancy.

Rose placed her bowl in a tub of dishes and walked toward the door. It was warm out, so she didn't bother with a wrap. Instead, she just walked. The meadow was quite full of flowers, and the earth was damp and soft. The oak tree stuck out of the middle, like a beacon for the lost. Slowly, Rose walked toward it.

Beneath the tree lay a fresh mound of dirt. There was no marking of the grave except for the fresh earth. It would take at least a couple more weeks before a tombstone could be brought in. Dead leaves were scattered across the ground where they rotted. Dark green covered the tree in a blanket of life and new buds. Everything about the meadow was a contradiction.

It seemed unfair that so much death could reside where life was meant to be. "You know," she whispered softly, "you were right. You said you probably wouldn't see me marry, and you were right." Her voice began to rise as she fought back tears.

"I suppose you are wondering what is taking me so long to get married. It's not that I'm not trying; I would have married Caleb, but to tell you the truth, he scares me. I know, you are probably watching me now and think that I am silly. There is no reason to be afraid of a minister. He is a man after God's own heart, after all.

"Then there was Colonel Jasper. You know, I don't think I ever learned his first name. He was gentle and sweet, but he wouldn't marry me because I didn't love him back. Was it wrong of me to tell him the truth? If I hadn't, you would have seen me marry. It wouldn't have been that horrible to be married to him. He is a good man.

"And then there is Henry. Everyone knows him as James, but I know the truth. He is a noble on the run. What he is running from, I haven't got a clue. He is a good man. He is kind and considerate. He has a sense of humour, and he is very good at fighting with a sword. He is a true follower of Christ, and he is everything that you wanted me to have in a man. You would have liked him a lot, Uncle Murdoch, but I guess you know that already.

"You are probably wondering why I haven't married him already if he is such a wonderful man. Does it make sense to you that it scares me to marry anyone, especially if they care for me? I guess it wouldn't, because Aunt Agatha never loved you. But what would happen to him if we got married and then I died? How could I bear to put him through that pain?

"I guess I worry too much. He hasn't even proposed to me. We are what he calls 'general acquaintances.' It is his way of saying that he is courting me, but he doesn't want to put any pressure on me to have to think beyond that. I like him for that. He is always thinking of ways to make me comfortable."

Rose bit her lip before she could go on. "I miss you a lot," she whispered between tears. "Why can't you be here when I need you the most?" A tear slipped down her cheek. "I'm sorry that I wasn't at your funeral. I tried to get here as fast as I could. I really did." She wiped her eyes and continued. "I don't know how to say goodbye to you. All I want to do is hold onto you forever and ever, but the earth is already in the way."

She picked up a handful of dirt and sifted it through her hands. "I remember mom's and dad's funerals. I just stood there, and I felt so cold inside. You were there. You stood beside me, and you placed your hands on my shoulders. I remember you squeezed them gently, and then I couldn't hold my tears in any longer. I know it seems kind of silly that such a small action could have made me come undone, but it did."

Rose inhaled deeply. The scent of earth and spring filled her senses. "I guess I should go. People will be wondering where I am, and I should speak with everyone before they leave tomorrow. It looks like you had a large crowd turn out. It just means you are well loved."

Rose stood and looked down on the grave. "Goodbye, Uncle Murdoch. I will miss you so, so much." She kissed her hand and placed it gently on the dirt that she pictured was right above his head. Then, with tears streaming down her cheeks, she walked toward the house.

TWENTY-EIGHT

AGATHA GLARED AT THE YOUNG MAN who had intruded upon her property. James Hyden was a very unwelcome addition to their party, but propriety said that she should board him. So, grudgingly, she had made up a bed for him on the uppermost floor. She would not have him anywhere near her if possible.

She did not hate him because of any detestable trait that he carried, but rather for one detestable action he had committed. He had had the audacity to fall in love with her niece, and Agatha hated him for that. He would ruin everything that she had planned. If he proposed, she lost, and it would all be over. No, something must be done. He must not have any more contact with Rose if at all possible.

All of a sudden, Mr. Hyden turned and stared at her. She glanced downward and pretended to be in deep mourning. Deep mourning? Pah! Who could mourn over a man like Murdoch? She had been counting the days until he would die. He had been a weak man, and that was how she had been able to persuade him to file his land in her name. She was not going to be left without when he died. She had heard too many stories of elderly widows who thought their sons would take care of them when their husbands died, but the poor unfortunate souls were greatly mistaken. As soon as their old geezers hit the grave, they were out in the streets.

She didn't have much pity for these unfortunate ones. In her mind's eye, it was their own fault. They should have seen it coming and had the intelligence to do something about it. Or they could at least have had the decency to die before their husbands did.

Mr. Hyden shook his head, as if wakening from a stupor, and left the room. Agatha sighed and quit her pretence. In some ways she wished she had been able to go first. It really was quite depressing having to wear black for the next year. She would rejoice on the day that she could again dress in something a little bit fashionable.

The door banged shut and she caught a glimpse of Rose slipping up the stairs. She made her way over to cut her off. "Rose," she called, "I would have a word with you."

Rose looked at her a bit startled, but she then hardened her eyes and followed.

Rose had been a weak child when they had first gotten her. So tiny and fragile, Agatha had detested her. She was nothing like that now, but Agatha still hated her. She was pretty and young, and she looked far too much like her mother for Agatha ever to care for her. And she had her father's eyes, which haunted her.

They stepped into a side room. "I have been thinking," Agatha began. "I think it would be best if you did not return to Emriville. The year is almost up, and it is unlikely that you will find a husband in that time. Why don't you remain here? You could marry the curate, and that would be the end of that. It would be better for everyone. After all, the curate isn't getting any younger."

"You may be right, Aunt Agatha," Rose said stiffly. "But you gave me a year, and I plan on taking up that entire year. Besides, who would travel back to Emriville with Mrs. Monks if I did not return? And most of my things still remain there."

"Don't be silly. Mrs. Monks is a married woman. She can travel back with Mr. Hyden unattended, and the rest of your belongings can be shipped down. I'm sure that it really won't be such a huge problem," replied Agatha sweetly.

"I was promised a year," stated Rose, "and I plan on using my entire year."

Agatha stiffened. "Fine, have it your way, but if the curate dies before you make it back, do not think it will be any better for you. I will win in the end."

Rose turned and walked out of the room. She did not look behind her. She just kept walking. John sat outside the door skimming through a book. Rose tapped him softly on the shoulder and kept walking by. He looked up slightly from his book to acknowledge her before he continued reading, and she walked on.

The meadow was different that night. It had the same flowers and the same night sky, but they both avoided the tree. They didn't want to acknowledge that the grave rested so close to where they fought.

Rose beat on John with a fury. She was angry, and she wanted to get it out of her system, but it seemed she was only getting angrier. John fought back just as hard. He was tired, and just for a while, he wanted to let it all go, so the two went at it for quite some time before John called a halt.

Rose collapsed into the grass to try and catch her breath. John settled himself beside her. "You are getting quite good at this, my cousin," he stated. "You must have been practising while you were away."

Rose lifted her mask and looked at him. "I have been giving lessons to a young man who wished to know how to fight. He has kept me on my toes lately."

John let out a groan. "How can you be giving lessons unless he already knows your identity, Rose? Didn't I tell you never to reveal to someone that you know how to fence? It could be the death of you someday if you're not careful."

"He doesn't know who I am. I wear my mask, and we fence. My voice must be muffled enough by the mask to make me sound like a man, or people are blinded by their own opinions that a woman cannot fight. Either way, he does not know that I am a woman. My reputation is safe."

"Perhaps you shouldn't go out with your sword anymore," John suggested. "It would be much safer if you remained out of harm's way. I mean, what will you ever use a sword for, and my goodness, what would happen to your reputation if someone found out?"

"Someone already has found out," Rose stated nonchalantly.

"What?!" exclaimed John. "What do you mean, someone has already found out? Do you mean to say that your reputation is already ruined in Emriville?"

"Seriously, John, use some common sense." Rose gave him a look of disgust. "I persuaded the person that it would be in his best interest not to speak about my 'special talent.' The man has since left town, and I highly doubt that I will ever see him again."

"How can you be so sure?" asked John hesitantly.

"Well, first I challenged him to a sword fight, and when I beat him, I told him to either leave town or I would deprive him of something that is of great value to him," Rose stated bluntly.

"What do you mean?" asked John.

Rose shot him another disgusted look. "I gave him the choice of either leaving town or losing his manhood."

John let out a yelp and jumped to his feet. "That's it!" he shouted as he grabbed the sword from Rose's hand. "Such talk is far too inappropriate. I should never have taught you to fight. You are beginning to sound like a man! Honestly, Rose!"

"Well, what do you expect of me?" she shouted at him. "Maybe I should just be a man. Maybe I should do away with dresses. I could disguise myself, and sign up for the army. Perhaps I would win medals, or better yet, I would die in battle."

"Quit it!" John shouted back. "Quit talking like that."

"But why?" Rose asked. "Why should I not speak like this? Why shouldn't I become a man when as a woman I am thrown around like a wasted piece of garbage? Do you know how lonely that is?" Tears began to pour down her face, and John pulled her into an embrace.

"Ach, Rose. Take it easy now," he whispered. "There, there. You're all right." Rose hiccupped into his shirt, and a small shudder ran down her spine. "Shh," John hushed. "Now, tell me, what has got you so upset?"

Rose sighed and wiped her eyes. "Your mother has suggested that I stay and marry the curate. She had to rub in the fact that he might not be around by the end of my year, and that it could get worse for me if I didn't marry him now."

John bit back the pool of curses that wanted to spill out of his mouth. "That won't happen. I promise you, Rose," he whispered. "Besides, you will probably be married before my mother has a chance to choose for you."

Rose let out a gentle harrumph. "I don't know if you know this, John, but I have already turned down two proposals. It is highly unlikely that a third one will come my way. Can you imagine? Three proposals in one year! The very thought is preposterous."

"Well," commented John, "I wouldn't put it past the dashing Mr. Hyden. Anyone can see that he is beyond smitten with you. I wouldn't be surprised if you got a proposal from him within the

"I'll look into that," said John. "There's no loss in asking. Besides, I've wanted to make a trip to Silidon for quite some time now. Maybe I'll stop by the palace. Supposedly they have some job openings there. The Prince is to become king soon, you know. The only question is, who is to be the queen?" he added with good humour.

Henry tensed a little, but then shrugged it off. "It was good to meet you. You are a good man, John." The two men embraced like old friends; then John went about helping Rose and Mrs. Monks with the remainder of their luggage. Mrs. Monks was quite perplexed, because her bag had been placed much too precariously on the top of the carriage. Any bump or rut in the road could easily knock it off.

Mrs. Borden took this time to come up and speak with Henry. "They make a beautiful couple, don't you think," she whispered. Henry tried to follow her gaze, but all he could see was John helping Rose with her bag.

"What do you mean?" he asked.

"Well, Rose and John, of course. Why do you think I had to send Rose away for a year? The two of them were falling for each other, and it was highly inappropriate that they were in the same building. I thought that after a year of separation, they could marry with no scandal arising out of it. I thought perhaps that Rose would want to stay and marry John this week, but she has decided to give him time to grieve his father's death. She is such a sweet girl."

"Are you telling me that Rose and John are engaged to be married?" asked Henry. He turned to look at Mrs. Borden, to see if she was telling the truth, but her lips remained turned in an easy smile.

"Didn't you know that?" asked Mrs. Borden with seeming innocence. "I thought you knew. Well, it's a good thing you know now, because I wouldn't want you getting the wrong impression of her. I can't wait to have her as my daughter-in-law."

"I'm sure that will be just lovely for you," replied Henry tersely. "Please excuse me, but I must help with our preparations." With that, he disappeared behind the carriage.

The trip home was miserable for Henry. He spent most of his time trying to ignore Mrs. Monks as she prattled on and on about her visit, and when this did not satisfy her, she would speak of her brother and sometimes spend her time weeping. While she wept, Henry glared at Rose, who sat across from him. When Rose tried to start a conversation with him, he cut it short, and she glared back at him. The rest of the journey was stiff and awkward, and by the time they reached Emriville, only Mrs. Monks was satisfied.

When they reached the Monks' home, Henry helped them unload their belongings, then went to make a quick escape, but Rose would have none of it. She stopped him before he reached the carriage, and very nearly demanded that he talk with her. As soon as they were out of sight, she railed on him. "What is the matter with you?" she demanded. "Why in the world did you have to make the trip back so miserable?"

Henry tried to hold in his anger, but he couldn't keep himself from shouting. "Why am I angry? Do you honestly not know?

Surely, you didn't think that your secret would stay safe after I met your family. Is this all a big game to you, Rose? See how many men you can get to propose to you before the year is out? Was that your plan?"

"What are you talking about?" Rose shouted back. Henry had been the one who didn't want to talk, who ignored her on the entire ride home, and here he was blaming her? Something was completely out of sorts.

"You, Rose!" he shouted. "I'm talking about you being engaged to your cousin and not telling anyone." Rose's mouth gaped, and Henry continued on at a lower decibel. "What was I to you, that you couldn't tell me you were already engaged? Was I just a game, an idle passing of the time? Was I just there to add pleasure to your charmed life?"

Rose went cold. "Charmed life?" she asked evenly. "Do you think it is a charmed life when both your mother and your father die when you are only ten? Do you think it is a charmed life to have everyone you love die or move away? Do you think it is a charmed life to grow up in a house where your only mother figure hates the sight of you and will punish you just because your eyes are green?" Rose glared at him.

"I don't have a charmed life!" she shouted. "If I had a charmed life, my uncle wouldn't be dead, and you certainly wouldn't be accusing me of being engaged to my cousin! Honestly, Henry, where did you come up with this? I am not engaged, and if you ever accuse me of toying with another's emotions…" Slowly she shook her head and walked away. Henry stood there and watched her leave, not exactly sure what had just taken place.

Rose raced up the stairs to her room where she slammed the door and began to take deep steadying breaths. "Can I see?" asked Katy as she bolted from her bed in the corner to where Rose stood. "Come on, you have to show me," she begged.

"What are you talking about, Katy?" Rose asked. "What is it that you want to see?"

Katy rolled her eyes and grabbed her left hand. "Hey," she said, "it's not here. Where did you put your ring?"

Rose was starting to get frustrated. "What ring, Katy?" she asked. "I don't have a ring."

Katy let out an exaggerated sigh. "Your engagement ring, silly. Of course you didn't have a ring before the trip, but everyone assumed that you and James would get engaged over the weeks that you were gone."

Rose let out a groan. "I'm sorry, Katy. But James and I made an agreement not to talk about engagements until the month of May. Besides, I hardly doubt that he will propose now. We got into an argument. He is not too happy with me, and I am not too happy with him."

"Don't be silly," said Katy. "Everyone fights every now and then. I'll bet anything that he'll be over here tonight asking your forgiveness. And have you looked at a calendar recently? It's already the second of May."

Henry looked at the calendar and then again at the ring in his hand. He had been stupid. She wasn't engaged, and he had been a fool to believe her aunt. Now he had wasted an entire day and gotten into a fight with her. It was hard to say if she would forgive him. If he were the swearing type, there were a few choice words that came to mind that may have been appropriate for his own stupidity.

Henry stuffed the ring in his pocket said a little prayer, and hoped for the best. Perhaps she was feeling forgiving today. If not, he would go to her again tomorrow, and the next day, and the next day. He would keep begging for her forgiveness, day in and day out, until she consented, because if she didn't forgive him, he didn't know how he would cope.

It was a cool spring night as he stepped out into the air. He shivered slightly, but pressed on. Rose didn't answer the door. It was Katy. She called for Rose, and Henry couldn't be certain, but he thought he heard her say, "I told you so." Rose didn't want to talk, but she consented to a walk around the back pasture.

"I don't know where to start," began Henry, "but I would really like to ask for your forgiveness. I know there is no excuse for my actions, but I would like to try to explain myself." When Rose didn't respond, Henry ploughed on. "You see, before we left, I was given some false information that you and your cousin were engaged. I was hurt and confused, and I didn't know what to think, so I didn't think, and for that I am greatly sorry." He stopped, not quite sure where to go from there.

"Why did you believe it?" Rose asked quietly. "Don't you know me better than that by now?"

"Yes, I do!" exclaimed Henry. "I do know you a lot better than that, but I wasn't thinking, and I forgot about everything else except how hurt I would be if you were truly engaged to your cousin."

"What does it matter to you?"

Henry turned to Rose. He looked deep into her eyes and just stood there for a moment. "Don't you know?" he asked softly. "I love you, Rose. I love you more than life itself." He bent down and gently kissed her lips. He longed to kiss her again, but he counted himself blessed for not being slapped the first time.

Rose looked up at him. Her lower lip trembled, a temptation that he knew he must resist. Slowly she turned her head down. "Why?" she whispered so softly that Henry almost missed it.

Placing his fingers lightly under her chin, he tilted her head until she looked him in the eye. "I love you because of who you are. You are the first person I think of every morning. You make me smile when my day has been rough. You challenge me. You encourage me. You give me hope. But most of all, I love you because you hold my heart, and where you go my heart must follow."

Slowly Henry knelt on one knee. Taking her hand, he kissed it softly. "Will you, Rose Wooden, do me the honour of becoming my wife?" Slowly, Rose nodded her head. A smile bloomed across her face as she vocalized her answer. Henry let out a whoop, and getting up off his knees, he pulled her into his arms and kissed her soundly. When he finally let go, Rose giggled slightly and Henry dug into his pocket to find the ring. Taking her left hand, he slipped the ring on her finger.

"It's beautiful," Rose whispered.

Henry kissed her on the cheek. "It was my mother's, but she wanted me to pass it on down to my wife."

"Won't she miss it?" Rose asked.

"Not likely," replied Henry. "I am wondering, though, when would you like to announce our engagement? I was thinking we could go tell the Monks now and then tell everyone we see tomorrow. How does that sound to you?"

Rose burst out laughing. "You can't be serious!" she exclaimed. "No. Though I like your suggestion, I believe it is tradition here to try to keep it a secret until the next Sunday when it is announced in the church. That leaves us a couple of days to keep this a secret."

Henry let out a slight groan. "I was afraid you might say that. But that is why I brought a chain," he said, pulling out a gold chain from his other pocket, "so that you can still wear the ring until Sunday."

Rose laughed. She slipped the ring off her finger, and after it was on the chain, she allowed Henry to tie the clasp at the back of her neck. A shiver ran down her spine as his hand brushed her neck. "There," he said. Rose hid the ring under her blouse, then Henry took her hand and they walked back toward the house. Rose didn't know how she would keep this a secret from Katy, but she would find a way, as long as she could keep the silly grin from her face.

TWENTY-NINE

KEEPING THE SECRET FROM KATY had been surprisingly easy. Rose smiled politely at her when she came in from walking with Henry. She told her that they had made up, and that she was very glad they had. Katy was gullible enough to believe that that was the extent of the story.

It wasn't quite so easy to keep the news from the good people of Emriville the next day. While she walked into town, she nodded at people and smiled. One young man gave her a goofy smile back, and Rose realized that she had been a little too exuberant in her greeting. She bit her tongue and tried to keep herself from laughing as she made her way to the post office.

Miss Mede hardly took notice of her giddy behaviour. She handed Rose a stack of letters and informed her that she had one from her cousin near the bottom of the stack. Rose thanked her profusely and immediately left to see what this letter could be about. If it was in fact from John, he would have had to send it nearly immediately after they had left, but Rose was certain he had been leaving to visit the palace at that time. Impatience wore at her, and she decided to open it where she stood in the road.

> *Dear cousin,*
>
> *As you may know, immediately after you left, I found myself heading toward Silidon in the hopes of claiming a grant from the king. I am sending you this letter now from a post just outside the king's castle. The post is much faster here, and I fear that this letter may reach Emriville long before you even arrive.*
>
> *Forgive me. I am tarrying in my message because I do not know whether my news will bring joy or sorrow. For starters, I must warn you not to share the contents of this letter with any other soul. I am already putting my honour on the line by telling you, but seeing as the matter greatly affects you, I deemed it necessary.*
>
> *When I entered into Silidon, I immediately made my way toward the king's palace. I wished to see about a position opening up on the king's staff, namely in the judicial area. A young lass directed me to where I should apply in the palace, but I must have taken a wrong turn, for I found myself standing outside the door where the king was speaking with one of his chief advisors.*

I could clearly hear what they were saying. They were speaking of the Prince, Henry Arden. The king mentioned that he missed his son and was counting the days until he came home and introduced his new fiancée. The advisor asked if the king knew the name of the girl, and the king replied that she was a lass by the name of Rose.

This took me by surprise, but what startled me more was when the advisor next asked if this girl knew the Prince for whom he was or if she still believed him to be the man James Hyden. I must have gasped, for the king turned and saw me through the crack in the door. From there, the story is unimportant. I was sworn to secrecy and so on and so forth. What really matters is this: James Hyden is Henry Arden, the Prince.

Please tell me you knew of this, Rose. Because I am terrified for the poor boy if you are just learning this news. Promise me not to be rash. You have been favoured by the Prince. Remember that.

As always,

Your loving cousin,

John

Rose inhaled deeply, trying to calm herself. This was a mistake, a farce. Someone was playing a trick on her. Surely, this could not be true. She continued to tell herself this, but it didn't seem to stick. Why would someone make this up? What good could possibly come of it? Was someone trying to break her and Henry up?

Rose could only think of one person who would do that. The thought of him made her angry. She made a face at the thought of speaking with him, but it needed to be done. Tucking the letter in her reticule, she picked up her skirts slightly and stomped off to find the curate.

Caleb had just been sitting down to an afternoon tea when he heard the banging on the door. Slowly he got up to answer the door, all the while bemoaning his life as a minister. What a horrid job to have to respond to the beck and call of everyone's demands. Calmly he opened the door.

He had to look twice to make sure his vision was true. Rose stood on his step, a look of pure fury twisted her face. With forced politeness, she asked, "May I come in?" Caleb opened the door wider and watched as she waltzed past.

In the parlour, Rose took a seat on his chair and made herself comfortable. He took the chair across from her and waited for her to start the conversation. She glared at him, as if demanding that he speak first, but he refused. She had been the one to knock, and she would be the one to talk. There was going to be no way around that.

Finally, Rose complied. "Who is Henry?" she asked.

So she had finally figured it out. "He is the Prince of Samaya," Caleb replied evenly. "I wondered how long it would take you to figure it out."

Rose glared at him.

"How do you know for sure that he is the Prince?" she demanded.

"Look, Rose," Caleb said, "he showed me a letter signed and sealed by his father. He showed me the signet ring of the king. If he isn't the Prince, he's a mighty good fraud."

Rose's face paled dramatically, and Caleb worried she would swoon. He tried to think of something to say to calm her.

"What is it about that fact that bothers you, Rose?" he asked.

A muscle twitched in her jaw, and colour returned to her cheeks. "Nothing," she said. "Nothing about him being the Prince bothers me, except, maybe for the fact that he neglected to tell me."

"Oh, I see," said Caleb without thinking. "You are afraid that you won't be accepted into court because your status is so much lower than that of the Prince's. Did he propose to you, Rose? Is that why you are so worried?"

"Is that what you think, Caleb?" Rose spat. "You think that my status is lower than his?" She got up from the couch and headed toward the door. Fire turned her eyes into mottled stones. She glared once more at him. "Now I know why I could never marry you." With that, she walked out of the door.

Rose paced back and forth in front of her bed. Caleb had done nothing but confuse her. Was Henry the Prince, or wasn't he? How was she to know? She hated him if he was. But did she love him if he wasn't? What if he was the Prince; what would she do? What could she do? She had already accepted his proposal. Was there any way to undo that?

Rose lashed out at the things around her. How could she have been so blind? It was all there in front of her. First there had been the boots. Then there had been the incessant talking about court and court affairs. At Christmas he had spoken of a feast. What a fool she was. Who other than a king would hold a feast at Christmas?

But what if he wasn't the Prince? What if Caleb was trying to get her to break off her engagement with Henry? Would he really do that? He was the curate, for mercy's sake. What kind of curate would do that?

All afternoon Rose punished herself. Sometimes she would accuse Caleb and hate him. Other times she would accuse Henry and hate him even more. Every time she changed her mind, she would rejoice in the fact that she had come to a conclusion only to find another argument that proved her wrong. It wasn't until late that night that she came up with a solution.

Once Katy's breath came in deep huffs, Rose slipped out of bed. Donning a pair of inexpressibles and her mask, she took up her sword and headed out of the room. What better way to determine the truth than to go straight to the source? She made her way toward the inn. When she arrived, she realized her plan was muddled. She had not recognized that the keepers would lock up at night. If she couldn't get into Henry's room, there was no use in coming.

She turned to leave, and that was when she saw him. He stood by the livery leading a horse into the stables. His sword swung lazily at his side. She watched him enter the building. Then, taking up a position outside the door, she waited. It wasn't long before he again stepped out into the darkness. Quickly and quietly, Rose unsheathed her sword and pressed the tip gently against Henry's throat. "Drop your sword belt and kick it behind you. Do as I say and you won't get hurt."

Henry felt the cold tip of the sword on his throat. Slowly he placed his hands on his sword belt, unbuckled it, and dropped it to the ground. As he kicked it behind him, he asked, "What do you want? My money is in the inn. Seeing as it is late, I will probably be stuck in the stables for the night, but if a reward is needed to save my life, I offer you my sword. Take it and be content." The blade lifted from his neck, and Henry turned just in time to see the stranger bend down to pick up his sword.

His assailant was quite peculiar. The would-be thief was rather small and dressed all in white. His face was covered in an odd mask, but his motions were fluent and graceful. Henry knew he should be fighting for his sword, but it seemed a small trifle. If this man needed the money, let him have the sword. It was easily replaced.

Henry turned to walk back into the stables. "Stop!" the masked man demanded as he placed the blade back against Henry's neck. "I am not done with you yet. You will do as I say. For starters, you will walk down the street and make a left hand turn."

Henry had to bite his lip to keep himself from laughing. Was this man serious? Did he actually think he would accomplish anything by this? He had Henry's curiosity, so Henry walked. It wasn't long before he realized that he was being led to the back pasture where he had met Josh. This realization brought back memories of that night. Josh had told him about the masked sword master. If what Josh said about this sword master was true, the masked man that now led him could be that master.

Henry began to sweat.

When they reached the centre of the pasture, the masked man ordered him to turn around. Slowly, Henry obeyed. When he faced his captor, he was thrown his sword and told to take a ready stance. Henry complied and readied himself for battle.

He had never fought in an actual battle, but he had trained with the best fencers in all of Samaya, and they had taught him well. He had also trained with some of the best men in his father's army. He was ready for this, whatever this might be.

The masked man made the first move. He unleashed fury with a series of well-aimed attacks meant to disarm his opponent. Henry blocked these easily as he began to get into the flow of the fight. He moved gracefully. At first he fought defensively, trying to gauge what this man could do, determining his strengths and weaknesses. When Henry realized that his strengths were many, and his weaknesses very few, he began to fight in earnest.

They danced like this for some time. Their bodies flowed back and forth, blocking and thrusting. If Henry did not consider this a fight for his life, he would have thought the motion beautiful.

They wore on each other, breaking down defences until only the true soul of the person fought. Henry lunged forward, but his attempt was blocked, and he felt his sword flying from his hand. Before he could react, he felt his feet sweep out from under him, and the tip of a sword again at the base of his neck.

"Who are you?" screamed the man through clenched teeth.

Henry stuttered. What was he supposed to say? What would this man do if he realized that he was the Prince? "I am James Hyden," stated Henry.

"Liar!" his assailant shouted. "Tell me! Who are you?"

Henry fought back the terror that longed to take his common sense. He took as deep a breath as he could with the sword at his throat and replied again, "I am James Hyden."

"Quit lying," the man accused as he pressed the sword a little harder. Henry felt a trickle of blood slip down his throat.

"I am," he whispered, "Prince Henry Arden of Samaya. Does that satisfy you?"

"Why?" wailed the man. "Why did you lie?"

Henry was helpless to answer. What was he supposed to say? He had lied so that he could find a wife? He had lied so that for once he could live a somewhat normal life? He had lied so that he could have some fun before he was to take on the responsibilities of the crown?

Henry sat motionless. The man reached to his own throat and tore at a chain that hung there. He looked at it once; then, turning a blank masked face at Henry, he whispered, "Hate makes you do things that you will always regret." Slowly he dropped the chain on Henry's chest where it landed with a thud, and he turned to walk away.

Henry looked at the chain and saw the ring: Rose's ring. Terror filled his heart. What had happened to Rose? What had that man done to his love, his fiancée? Rage blinded him as he grabbed his sword from the ground, and swinging it in a high arch, he impaled the retreating stranger through his right shoulder blade.

The masked face whimpered softly and collapsed to the ground. Henry pulled out his sword, dropped it to the ground, and began to claw at the mask. "Show yourself," he demanded. "Show me the coward that does his dirty work behind a mask. He is no man, but a worm."

The mask slipped off and Henry yelped as layers of thick auburn hair spilled out. Rose's face was white. Sweat droplets formed on her forehead. Silent gasps of pain came out of her mouth. Henry crawled toward her. Gathering her in his arms, he tried to stop the bleeding. Her wound seeped life all over his jacket, its rich red paint the sign of lost vitality. Tears dropped off the end of Henry's nose as he stroked her hair.

"Why, Rose, why?" he asked continually.

Slowly, desperately, she grabbed his hand to get him to listen. "I needed to know the truth," she whispered. "I needed to know who you are."

"Then why like this?" Henry begged. "Why with swords and blades? Why didn't you ask me, love? I would have told you. I would have given you answers."

"Because," cried Rose, "if you were the Prince, I hated you." Tears streamed from her eyes, but she was incapable of wiping them away. Gently Henry rubbed his thumb along her cheek.

"Then why didn't you kill me?" he asked. "Better my life than yours any day."

"I couldn't," wept Rose. Henry feared the pain was becoming too unbearable.

"Why?" he asked one more time.

"Because," she whispered, "you were also Henry, and I loved you." Henry stood and carried her in his arms. She was so light. How could he have been so blind not to see that she was a lady? Her loose-fitting garb barely hid her curves, and her other very feminine features. Henry beat on himself as he went to find help. It didn't take long for Rose to pass out from the pain.

The closest house was only about a hundred metres away. Henry would have run to the door except for the fragile luggage he held in his arms. He reached the door at an agonizingly slow pace, and before he could knock, the door swung open. Colonel Jasper stood before him, fully dressed. Henry's mouth dropped open, and he took a step back.

419

"Oh, don't look so flabbergasted," shouted the colonel. "I've learned enough from war not to sleep when danger is around. I heard the two of you traipsing to the pasture and had sense enough to watch what would happen. Bring her upstairs. There is a bed waiting. I was just about to get some bandages."

Henry shut his mouth and swallowed. "Who are you?" he asked.

"I am your father's aid." At Henry's blank look, Jasper continued, "The king sent me to look after you and Rose, and if we don't hurry up, I may not be able to help you." Stepping into the house, Henry allowed the colonel to take control. He placed Rose gently on the soft mattress provided and waited helplessly. What was he supposed to do? How was he supposed to help her when she already looked dead? He started to brush back her hair and sooth her, whispering to her.

The door banged open and the colonel walked in with a pale-faced maid. The maid was carrying tattered sheets that would supply the bandages. She looked as if she might be sick. "Highness, I need you to go into the next room. There is a set of clothes and a pitcher of water sitting out. Clean yourself off, and throw your old clothes into the fire. After you have done that, I want you to ride to the Monks' and tell them that something dreadful has happened to Rose and that they must come right away. Whatever you do, don't tell them what happened tonight."

Henry nodded mutely. He didn't want to leave Rose, but neither did he want to see her die. He was about to leave when he saw Jasper lean over the bed and start to tear at the sleeve of Rose's shirt. "What do you think you are doing?" hollered Henry. He lunged at the man who easily caught him and held him back.

"Honestly, Your Highness, you are going to have to leave. I need to be able to get to the wound, then Miss Jansen here will help me dress it. There is no other way for me to reach the wound than to remove part of Miss Wooden's shirt. Now, go clean yourself up. You stink."

Furious now, Henry stormed into the other room, cleaned himself off, and headed toward the Monks'. He banged on their door until finally a very befuddled Mr. Monks opened it. "It's Rose," Henry stated. "Something bad has happened. You and Mrs. Monks should come immediately. I will wait here while you prepare yourself." Mr. Monks stood there in bewilderment, not sure what to do. "Go, I say, go!" growled Henry, and gave the man a slight push to send him on his way.

Jasper leaned over the inert body, willing her to live, willing her to be strong again. He pressed a cloth into the wound, replacing it every now and then as each one filled with blood. He worked methodically from much experience on the battlefield, cleaning wounds and stitching them up as best could be done.

He did the best he could with Rose's wound, then placing a bandage on either side of her shoulder, he rolled her so that no pressure was put on the wound. He stepped back to observe his handiwork. Rose was very pale. The bloody sheets provided a dark contrast for her death-coloured skin. Her chest rose and fell ever so slightly with shallow empty breaths. He would need help changing her sheets.

He bent down and brushed a hair from her face. She let out a silent moan. He hushed her softly, and taking a damp cloth began to clean off the blood that had smeared on her cheek.

There was a knock on the door, and Miss Jansen went to answer it. The Monks bustled up the stairs and burst into the room. Katy and Mrs. Monks let out shrieks of horror. Mrs. Monks fainted before he could order them out of the room. Mr. Monks still looked slightly confused, and Henry looked spent. Miss Jansen, with the help of Katy, dragged Mrs. Monks out of the room, while he and the Prince changed the sheets.

"What happened?" rasped Mr. Monks.

Henry looked about to answer, but Jasper cut in before he had a chance. "No one knows but herself. She is just fortunate that Mr. Hyden came by in time to save her life."

Mr. Monks nodded slightly, but Henry looked angry. "I need some air," he whispered. Then he disappeared from the room. Later, when Colonel Jasper went to search for him, he was nowhere to be found. He had taken his things from his room at the inn and left.

THIRTY

HENRY RODE HARD INTO THE NIGHT. He didn't stop; he just kept riding. He longed for home. He longed for comfort. How he wished he could curl up into his mother's arms and weep. *My God, my God,* his soul wept. *What have I done?* The hoof beats of the horse matched the rhythm of his pounding heart.

Day in and day out he travelled like this, only stopping to rest when his horse demanded it. With this steady pace, he arrived at home at the dawn of the third day. He slid from the back of the horse in front of the palace and watched as it walked toward the stables. It would get cared for there. He walked like an old man up the front steps and heaved on the heavy oak doors.

The sound of his trampling about must have awakened the entire palace, for by the time he made it through the doors, the front entrance was filled with people. He had only enough time to look at all the startled faces before he collapsed on the ground from exhaustion.

When he came to, he was resting on an overly soft bed that encompassed nearly the same amount of area as a small house. When he looked around, he saw the expensive furniture and all the rich colours of the room. For that instant, he was able to forget all that had happened. He rolled on his side and let out a groan. He closed and opened his eyes slowly.

In the far corner of the room sat a sword. When he saw it, he jumped from his bed and tried to get as far away from it as possible. Tears misted the corners of his eyes. This couldn't be true. This was one big joke. Someone was playing games with him. He crept forward and touched the weapon. Sure enough, it wasn't his. The sword belonged to Rose.

He stepped away from it again. In his rush to leave Emriville, he must have grabbed the wrong sword. Now he was left with a weapon that would haunt him for the rest of his life.

The door creaked open, and his mother stepped in. She walked over to him and pulled him into her arms. Gently, she rested his head against her shoulder. "It's not your weapon," she whispered. "Do you want to talk about how you acquired a weapon that does not belong to you?" Henry shook his head slightly. How could he tell his parents what he had done? He was a murderer, and they should loathe him.

"Supper is in half an hour," she continued. "Your father expects you there, so you'd better clean yourself up." She kissed him on the cheek then was gone.

Henry sat there. He didn't want to move. Why should he move? There was nothing left for him. All he had loved was gone. Rose was dead. She had to be dead. Her wound was too deep. There was no way she could survive that. He had wounded her, and now she was dead. It was all his fault. He was a murderer.

He didn't know how long he sat there for, but it didn't seem long before the door creaked open and his father came into his room. He sat down on the bed beside Henry and, grabbing his shoulder, gave him a half embrace. Together the two of them stared at the sword. Finally, his father spoke. "What happened to Rose, son?" he asked.

"I don't want to talk about it," whispered Henry hoarsely. He pulled out of his father's embrace.

"What happened to Rose, Henry?" his father persisted. Henry stood and began to pace. He didn't want to answer; he didn't want to tell about the horrible person he was. Why did his father insist upon knowing? The truth was better left unspoken.

"Henry ..." His father spoke his name with authority. It reminded him of the many times his father had reprimanded him when he was younger. His father had always used that voice. It was always gentle but firm. It was a voice that spoke of his love even though it hurt him to punish his son.

"I killed her," he whispered so softly, it was barely audible. "With my own hands, I killed her." Tears streamed down his face, and his father gathered him in his arms. He soothed his son as he wept, and slowly the whole story burst forth.

When Henry was done, he and his father sat across from each other on a set of chairs. "She might not be dead, son," James stated. "I have seen many battle wounds, and it is very possible that she can survive a stab to the shoulder, even if she did lose a lot of blood."

Henry shook his head. "Even if she did survive, she could never forgive me. I wronged her more than just physically. Ha! I was a coward. I ran from her when she needed me most because I was too afraid to face her if she did come through, and too terrified of what a funeral might do to me. No, she needs someone far better than me."

The king sat thoughtfully for a bit, and then asked, "What I don't understand is why she was so upset by who you are. Most women would rejoice to learn that they are engaged to the Prince. Why didn't Rose share the same sentiments?"

"Don't you see?" Henry asked. "It is not that I am a Prince that bothers her. I lied to her. I gained her trust, and then threw it away when my identity was revealed. How do you think Mother would feel if you told her that you really weren't who you said you were? She would loathe you, and you know it."

"That may be so, but you said that Rose knew you were noble; therefore, the deception wasn't that great. Surely, there must be another reason for her anger." Henry didn't respond. There was nothing more to say. "Another thing," said the king. "How was it that such a slight girl, as you described her, could disarm my fully grown son? Quite honestly, I am amazed."

Henry looked at him, shocked that he would say such a thing. The king laughed at his son's expression. "Come," he said. "Dinner is waiting, and we have guests. I am sure that you will enjoy their company."

Kayla Beton waited in the palace's sitting room. Her parents sat beside her and conversed freely with the queen. The king had recently left to go handle some matters of importance. Dinner would be served when the king returned and, hopefully, the Prince would be with him.

It had been rumoured that the Prince had returned from a long excursion about foreign lands. Where he went exactly was unknown. It was all really a big secret. Some said he was in Isbetan working out a peace treaty, while others said he was securing a wife among the Calidions. Some ventured to say that he was travelling about their own country, searching for a wife among the peasants. Of course, the last suggestion had little merit, seeing as no Prince would willingly marry a peasant when so many beautiful young ladies waited for him at court, namely herself.

The herald walked in and announced both the Prince and the king, and everyone stood to greet their Sovereign Majesties. Kayla curtsied deeply, then smiled coyly at the Prince from under pretty eyelashes. He acknowledged her, then he walked to his mother. Taking her hand, he stooped and kissed it. She looked at him curiously, but he just smiled. The king took Kayla's mother's arm, so

Kayla was left to be escorted to dinner by her father. She was furious, but she refused to show it.

When seated, Kayla was given a place of honour across from the Prince. She relished in the fact that she would be able to talk with him all evening. As the meal began, Kayla began to talk. "Highness," she started, "you have been long away from the palace. What sort of business could grasp your attention for so long?"

The Prince pondered this for a while, then stated, "I have been about my own country, and I have been learning how to be a king. I stopped in various villages, and in a small town along the way, I learned that the best way to be a king is to show compassion. We are all trying to make our way through life, and no matter our station, we all need compassion from those around us to succeed."

"Whatever is that supposed to mean?" asked Kayla, though she didn't care one bit about the garbage he had just fed her. She only cared that she kept his attention long enough for him to take notice of her. How else was she to become Queen?

"It means," continued Henry, "that I must not look at people's station and label them as insufficient. Instead, I must look at what they have to offer this country and help them grow in a manner where they will bless the nation in their own particular way. Being king should not be about elevating my rank, but the rank of those around me."

"But," Kayla pushed on, "not everyone can be noble."

"No, not everyone can, but that doesn't mean we can't strive for equality and rights for all people. Really, there isn't much difference between a young lady of the court and a young peasant lady. Many of their characteristics are the same. For example, both of these ladies are searching for a husband who will not lower their rank in life, but will also provide a house for them to live in. It is the same way with young men."

"Surely, you wouldn't put someone such as me in a group with the likes of a peasant girl!" exclaimed Kayla. "Such a suggestion is preposterous." Henry's eyes glazed over, and he chose not to respond to the lady sitting across from him. It was silly trying to persuade her of what he believed. She was much too self-absorbed to really care.

Instead, Henry turned his attention toward his father, who was having a conversation with Sir Beton about the state of the economy. It was a rather dry conversation, but Sir Beton was so deeply steeped in economics that the king indulged him with conversation on the topic. Henry enjoyed the rather mundane distraction that it brought.

Kayla tried to resume their conversation, but he ignored her to the best of his ability. He wasn't impolite; he was just blunt and to the point. By the time the dessert course had come around, Miss Beton still had not gotten the point. This frustrated Henry so much that when the guests retired to the parlour for the entertainment, he excused himself and made his way toward the kitchen. There he could at least have five minutes to clear his head.

The kitchen was rather dead. The cook had finished his task for the day, and only the scullery maid worked on cleaning up. She was stooped over a steaming basin washing the dishes when Henry walked in. To say she was startled would be an understatement. It wasn't very common that one of the royal members made their way into the kitchen. The poor maid didn't know what to do with herself. She pulled her hands out of the water and tried to dry them while she dipped into a deep curtsy. The spilled water made the floor rather slippery, and the maid soon found herself on the floor in a pile of embarrassment.

Henry raced to the lass's side, and helping her back onto her feet he cleaned up the mess on the floor and began to wash the dishes. She began to object, but Henry demanded that she start drying. Not knowing if it was proper to object to such an order, she took up a cloth and began to dry the dishes.

There were piles to be washed. The servants had just finished eating, and there were also all the cooking utensils and various other assortments of tools to be washed. By the time Henry was done, his hands were wrinkled beyond recognition. He made a face at them. "My hands are pruned," he stated.

The maid nodded. "I'm sorry, Your Highness," she started smoothly. "I should have warned you, or at least taken the task of washing the dishes myself. There was no need for you to help me, and it won't happen again."

Henry looked at the young girl. She was probably only twelve or thirteen. "What is your favourite sweet to bake?" asked Henry quietly.

Henry saw her eyes light up, but they quickly dulled as she said, "I cannot say, Your Highness. I am not a cook yet, so I cannot make any good sweets. Someday I will be a cook, but until then I'm just a scullery maid."

"Not a cook?" questioned Henry. "But surely everyone has a favourite sweet to make. I'm not a cook, and I have a favourite. Do you want to make it with me?"

The girl looked at him with a quizzical frown, but she nodded her head. "Good," said Henry. "I haven't made these in a while, so perhaps you will have to help me remember some of the ingredients." The girl's eyes widened, but she nodded, so Henry began. He got her to find a bowl, and then he started listing ingredients.

The maid soon caught onto the fact that they were making sugar cookies and began helping him find the right ingredients. Every now and then, Henry would forget an ingredient and his little protégé would fill it in. By the time the batter was mixed, they were laughing, and the counter was covered with flour and extra bits of this and that.

Henry had just taken a slick of dough when the kitchen door opened, and his mother walked in along with the Betons. The scullery maid, whom Henry discovered was named Leah, backed up and gave a lopsided curtsy. She looked nervously at the mess on the counter and the mess on the front of her dress. Henry did the same with his clothes and had to fight back laughter at his own appearance.

"What have we here?" his mother asked. "Henry," she said, "I thought you were going to join us again once you attended to some matters. When you didn't return, I thought something had happened to you. We ladies decided to search you out to make sure you were not lost in the palace after being gone so long."

There was no denying his mother was smarter than most. She had found a way to keep the ladies entertained and the absence of her son a mere joke instead of the rude behaviour it actually was. Henry gave her an appreciative smile. "Forgive me, Mother," he said. "I was on my way back when I happened upon the kitchen and was distracted by the urge to make some cookies. Fortunately, young Leah was here, and she helped me remember the ingredients, so now all that is left to do is bake them."

The queen gave him a look, so he continued. "Leah is going to be a cook. Perhaps she could help us bake them, and then we can all enjoy a mouthful of sweetness before the Betons must depart."

Lady Beton clapped her hands together gleefully. "How delightful!" she exclaimed. "That is the most marvellous suggestion I have heard. I'm sure Kayla would agree. She does adore cookies." Kayla wrinkled her nose at the sight of the cookie dough, but she agreed with her mother, so with a little encouragement from Henry, little Leah stepped forward and began to show them all how to bake the delicacies.

It wasn't long before the smell drifted down the hall to where the men were drinking their whisky. The scent enticed them, and they soon found the source in the kitchen with all the women and Henry. "Nothing like the scent of food to capture a man's attention," quipped Lady Beton, and they all allowed themselves to laugh a little.

In what seemed like minutes, the cookies were finished, and everyone found a seat. Henry pulled up a chair beside him for Leah to sit in. She didn't want to at first, but Henry soothed her enough so that she took a spot next to him. Once seated, she moved the seat as close as she dared toward him in an attempt to sit farther away from Sir Beton, who was an imposing figure on her right.

She reached for the plate of cookies to serve everyone, but Henry reached it before her. Holding the plate in both his hands, he extended it toward her and offered her the first cookie. She looked up at him with wide eyes and pulled one from the centre of the tray. She then waited to eat it while Henry served all the others. After he had taken his first bite, she dug in.

King James smiled as he bit into the cookie. "Mmm," he said, "we must have a very talented baker among us, for these cookies are delicious; the best I have ever had." The others joined in speaking the praises of the cookie and the young girl who had made them. Leah was blushing, but her whole face glowed in the delight of it. Henry didn't think the day could have gone any better for her.

As the cookies were finished up, Henry looked around the kitchen at the mess. If he left it as it was, little Leah would be staying up late to clean up the mess by herself. It would be better that he humble himself and help her. "Well," began Henry, "those dishes aren't going to clean themselves." Leah jumped from her seat and began racing around collecting plates. "Hold it, Leah," Henry called. "I was just going to say that I will wash the dishes, if you dry them."

She looked at him, a bit confused. "But your hands will get pruned," she stated, but quickly covered her mouth when she realized others had heard her.

Henry started to laugh. "I suppose they will, won't they? Oh well. As long as you promise not to laugh, I think I can handle that. Do you promise?" She nodded her head solemnly and Henry began to get the water ready.

Kayla looked at him in mute shock. How could a prince lower himself to the position of a scullery maid? What was he thinking? She was just about to turn away from him when her mother caught her attention. "Help him," she hissed. Kayla glared at her, then taking up a cloth she stood next to the filthy serving girl and began to dry dishes.

She plastered a smile on her face and said, "It is so nice to work at these little tasks, don't you think? It keeps the heart satisfied to do something such as this for someone who is lower than yourself—especially when the task is so easily far below your status."

Henry gave her a smouldering look. All he could think of when he saw her with the towel was how Rose looked washing the dishes, not because she had to, but because it was in her nature to do something for others. Rose and Kayla were exact opposites. Rose was kind and considerate. She did not consider station, but she looked on everyone with equality. Kayla was self-absorbed and childish, and Henry loathed her because of that. "I don't find washing dishes below my status," he stated. "The only thing that is below me is a lack of honour. I will do my best not to fall to that."

They washed the rest of the dishes in silence, and by the time they were done, it was time for the Betons to leave. But they did not leave empty-handed. The king assured them that there would be a ball within the month, and that they would be invited.

Henry again sat in his room. It was late, and he should be sleeping, but the mention of the ball had him wide awake. He got up and went to pace out in the hall. He hadn't been out there long when he was joined by his father. Together they walked in silence.

"I lost," stated Henry. "I didn't find a wife in the time I was gone. So, who will you have me marry? Miss Beton is amiable enough." Henry tried to hide the bitterness in his voice but failed.

"Don't be silly," replied the king. "I wouldn't allow you to marry Miss Beton. She's much too selfish. She's enough to drive any man mad. No, I won't force you to marry anyone."

"What about the ball then?" asked Henry. "Why have you planned a ball if not to announce who I will be wed to?"

"Do I really need a reason to have a ball?" asked the king. "I simply thought it might be nice to have a ball to welcome you home, as well as to announce my resignation as king. After this year is out, I will no longer hold the crown."

"So you don't wish me to be your heir? I have failed you, and now you will name another to the throne. Very well then. I know I don't deserve it." Henry turned his face away from his father. Shame burned his cheeks and seared the back of his eyes.

"Bother, Henry, is that what you think? Do you think I would disown you based on an accident? You need to stop blaming yourself, or all that Rose did for you will go to waste. At the ball, I am going to name you as heir, and if anyone challenges it, I will make a motion that the Prince need not to be wed in order to take the throne as long as he can provide a suitable heir in some form or fashion, and you can."

Henry looked at his father, shocked. "You would go through such trouble for me?" he asked. "But we made a deal. I promised to wed after a year's time. If I had not chosen my own wife by then, you would choose one for me."

The king thought for a moment. "I think that this is my choice for a bride for you. Your people will be your bride, and you will care for them as much as you would care for your own wife. But as far as I am concerned, you still have ten days to find a wife on your own."

"There is no possible way that I will find a woman that I could love in that time. As much as I wish it weren't true, my heart belongs to Rose and her alone, and I killed her. I will never be able to forgive myself for that, and I will no longer be able to love another unless she sets my heart free."

"Give it time, Henry," said his father. "That is all I can say. Just give it some time. As for now, it is best that you head to bed. You have a busy week ahead of you. People will want to speak with you and learn about your travels. It will be best if you are well rested." Taking Henry by the shoulders, the king led him to his room. Sleep would have to carry him the rest of the night.

THIRTY-ONE

WHEN ROSE AWOKE, IT WAS TO THE SEARING pain in her shoulder. She ached all over. She felt as if she had been dropped off the side of a cliff and left to die. She rolled onto her back and gasped when her shoulder hit the mattress. Instantly someone was by her side, soothing her and telling her to take it easy.

Slowly she opened her eyes to the brilliance of the room. The first person she saw was a worried Colonel Jasper peering down at her. She didn't know why, but she tried to smile at him. It only seemed polite. The smile came out a grimace as a spasm of pain seared through her shoulder. She stifled a scream as the pain washed over her.

The pain soon passed, and Rose was able to breathe again. "Where am I?" she asked softly.

"Do you not remember?" the colonel asked. "You are in one of the spare bedrooms in my home. You are recovering from an injury to the shoulder received from a sword. The Prince brought you here."

At the mention of Henry, all memory came back to Rose. She remembered the night and the horrible truth that was revealed to her. She remembered the anguish and the pain. "He must hate me," she whispered. "I need to ask his forgiveness."

She tried to get up from the bed, but both the pain and the colonel kept her in place. "I don't think that is possible, Rose," stated Colonel Jasper. "The Prince left later that night. He is probably halfway to Silidon by now."

Rose started to tremble. How could she have been so stupid? Henry had only been kind to her, and she had repaid his kindness with evil. No wonder he had run. "What have you told the others? They must be wondering why I am in such rough shape."

"I told them nothing, but I suggest you say that you were set on by thieves who wished to do you harm. Henry just happened to come along and saved you, but not before one of the scoundrels stuck you. When they ask what you were doing outside, you should say that you and Henry had gotten into an argument, and that you couldn't sleep, so you went for a walk outside."

Rose smiled. She hadn't thought that the colonel would be that cunning, but he was, and her honour was still intact because of that. The smile soon faded. "You must loathe me. I'm not what I appear to be to many people. I fight with a sword; I walk about in the night. I am everything a young lady shouldn't be. For goodness sakes, I even gave lessons to a young man on how to fight."

"I don't loathe you," replied Jasper. "I've known about the fencing lessons from the very beginning. I saw you practice with the young Joshua. You have quite a talent, and I wasn't surprised one bit when you beat the Prince. I think you took him by surprise, though. He has never been tested before."

Rose grew silent. She worried the corner of her blanket. "I need to write him," she stated. "He deserves to know the truth." She looked up at him. "Will you help me? Can you scribe what I say to you? Henry needs to know; otherwise he might spend his whole life blaming himself. I don't care if he hates me, as long as he doesn't hate himself."

Colonel Jasper nodded. "I can do that, on one condition. You need to visit with the Monks while I gather some writing supplies. If you can make it through that, then I will scribe the letter for you." Rose nodded, and the colonel headed off. The Monks bustled into Rose's room, and he feared he had made a bad decision, but when he came back with the writing supplies, Rose was in good health and smiling.

He sent the Monks away, and then he took up a place beside Rose's bed where he could easily hear her and write what she had him write. It wasn't long before they began.

Dear Henry,

I am probably the last person you want to receive a letter from, but I needed the chance to explain my-

self to you, and to reassure you of my health. I am well on the way to mends, but my heart aches because I know I have done you wrong. There is no way to justify my actions, but I think it is best that I explain them by telling you a little about myself. You see, it all started when I was ten.

My father was off at war. He was a conscripted soldier, but he was due home any day. His term was to be finished within another two weeks. Both my mother and I were looking forward to seeing him again. I was especially looking forward to him coming home, because I hoped that if he came home, my mother would get better. She had been ill for the past month and spent most of her time in bed.

One day, while the doctor was tending to my mother, a message came from the battlefield saying that my father had died. I took the message because my mother was too ill, but I really didn't understand it. I thought that all those confusing words simply meant that my father was sick in the hospital, but I was too afraid of what would happen to my mother if I showed her, so I kept it a secret.

Two weeks later, my mother passed away. I was angry. I thought the doctor was lying and that she was just sleeping. Then they placed her in that awful casket as I watched. My nurse mentioned contacting my father, but she didn't know how to do such a thing. I hoped the letter would help, so I showed it to her. I can still remember the look of pity on her face as she took the letter and showed it to the doctor. That was when my fate was decided.

I was sent to live with my uncle and my aunt. Really, it was the best situation for me. I was an orphan that could be well cared for by my family. The only mistake in sending me there was that my aunt loathed me. She did all she could to make my life miserable, and I learned to retaliate. I became self-sufficient. I didn't need my aunt, and I would avoid her as much as possible. This worked for a long, long time.

Perhaps you are wondering why this even matters, and I guess this may not be pertinent, except for one fact. When I had first arrived at my aunt and uncle's, I was miserable. My aunt loathed me, and I loathed her. One day as she was complaining to my uncle about me, he said that if she wanted someone to blame for her troubles, she should blame the king, because it was the king who had started the war, and if he hadn't done such a thing, my father would still be alive, and I would not be an orphan.

That was the last of the conversation that I heard. The rest didn't matter. I was angry, confused, and hurt. I blamed the king. Uncle Murdoch had said it himself. It was the king's fault that my parents were dead. *From that point on, I loathed the royal family. I hated them because they had taken everything from me and given nothing back. I wanted to hurt them as they had hurt me.*

I realize now that I was wrong, but Henry, please forgive me for being so foolish. If you cannot, then do not blame me, for I was a child, and I was so alone. Most of all, do not blame yourself, for I do not blame you. You did not know it was I who hid behind the mask. I was too much of a coward to face you without it.

You have changed me, Henry, and I will never forget you. I will always love you, though I know you will probably soon forget about me. You will be a great king someday, for your heart is great. I suspect I will be hearing your praise until my dying days, and I will not discourage it. Instead, I will take part in honouring my king.

I do not know if you were told, but I was given a year to find a husband. That year is almost up. My aunt will soon have me married off to the curate in Thespane. I know that I will always live with the regret of my situation. Don't live with the same regret in your life, Henry. You are worth far more than that.

Always live the life that matters to others. Give them your love and compassion. Show the world the man that I know you are. Find a wife who loves you as you deserve, and rule this nation with justice and mercy. As for me, I will remain yours always.

Rose

Tears rolled down Rose's face as she finished speaking. "Do you think it will do?" she asked sadly. Colonel Jasper nodded. "Do you think he will forgive me?" Rose asked.

The colonel sighed. "I don't know," he said. "I really don't know. The Prince is a man of honour. Perhaps he will forgive you. But I think the greater question is, will he be able to forgive himself?"

"He will," whispered Rose. "In time, he will." She closed her eyes, and it looked as if she slept. Colonel Jasper went about cleaning up the paper and posting the letter. He was about to leave the room when he heard Rose whisper, "Do you think God will forgive me?"

A sad smile crossed his face as he looked at the small figure on the bed. "Always, Rose," he said. "Always." He left the room and headed toward the post. He had a letter for Rose's cousin John. John would want to come immediately. He also had his own letter for the king. He would want to know how the young Rose was doing.

Henry read and reread the letter. It wasn't in Rose's hand, but that was easy enough to explain. She wouldn't have been able to write with her shoulder hurt. It would have to have been scribed by another. Henry wondered who the scribe was. Perhaps it was Katy. She would hate the royal family then as well. Or perhaps it was Caleb. It was very possible that the curate was comforting the lady in her time of distress.

No matter who had written the letter, Henry hated it. He hated what it revealed about Rose, he hated that he was angry with her, and most of all he hated that he no longer knew what to feel. He still loved her more than anything in the world, but she had hurt him. Then again, he had also hurt her. But she had hurt him worse, hadn't she? She in a clear mind had attacked him with a sword simply because he was the Prince.

Henry let out a sigh of frustration. As a habit, he turned to his diary and began to flip through the pages. He didn't read anything; he was far too distracted by his thoughts. But the sound and smell of the moving pages provided a small comfort. When he came to a loose piece of paper, he stopped and pulled it out. He read, *What are you willing to give up for love?*

Henry fiddled with the paper. He read it and reread it, and tried to come up with an answer, but none was forthcoming. He stuck the paper in his pocket and decided to think about it later. There was going to be no answer now. Besides, he had to say goodbye to his father. His father was leaving on business and wouldn't be back for another week and a half to two weeks. It was only right to wish him farewell.

He met his mother in the front lobby. His father was pulling on a pair of riding gloves. He looked very stately even in a simple riding smock. When he was ready, he kissed his wife goodbye, and he shook his son's hand. "The palace is in your hands while I am gone," he said. Henry nodded. Then, the King was off. Henry looked around the room at all the faces of the servants. Soon the palace would always be in his hands. The thought of it scared him.

By the time John reached Emriville, Rose had fallen into a fever. Her temperature was quite high, and it was very rare that she was lucid. Most of the time, she slipped in and out of consciousness, only eating when broth was trickled down her throat. Her eyes were dull, and she had lost weight. The wound on her arm flamed bright red. Jasper feared that it would kill her.

When John arrived, he spent day in and day out by her side. He bathed her when the fever burned too hot, and he provided quilts when she shivered. When John was exhausted, Colonel Jasper took over. The two of them watched over her and cared for her so much that the town began to call them her men. Of course they only meant it kindly, but when the king rode into town and asked about a Miss Wooden, he was told she was with her men, and he was quite taken aback.

He immediately rode to Jasper's house, where he found the two Monks women sitting in the kitchen preparing a meal. Both of them stood when they saw him. "How may I help you?" asked Mrs. Monks politely.

The king smiled politely. "My name is Henry Hyden, and I was hoping you could tell me where a Miss Wooden would be. I am also looking for a Colonel Jasper. If you know where he might be, I would be greatly in your debt."

"That's easy enough," spouted Katy. "You'll find them both upstairs in the bedroom on the right. Just make your way on up. I'm sure Colonel Jasper will be glad to see you."

King James nodded his thanks and flew up the stairs. What was Jasper thinking spending time in the girl's room unchaperoned? Such a thing was ludicrous. The king knocked softly on the suggested door and heard a quiet, "Come in."

Jasper sat beside a pale Miss Wooden, dabbing at her forehead. His brow wrinkled in deep thought, as if he was trying to remember something. On the other side of the young lady paced a young man. The young man he had seen at the palace. The one who had overheard him speaking of his son. It really was a small world.

"What's this I hear in town about Miss Wooden and her men? I have heard about it all over town. I had to fly all the way over here to find out if it was real. I must say that I am astounded to see there is some truth in the saying."

Colonel Jasper didn't look up. Instead, he began rubbing his forehead, willing a thought to come forward. "If that is all you came for," said the colonel, "you may as well leave. This patient will not be getting any better with people gawking over her all the time. She needs her peace."

The king laughed. "Colonel Jasper," he said, "will you not look to see who has come to visit you?" The colonel looked up from where he was staring and startled to his feet. He bowed deeply. The young man on the other side of the bed also seemed to come out of his reverie, and followed the colonel's lead.

"Your Highness," said the colonel, "forgive me. I did not know it was you. We have had so many people come to see the beautiful Miss Wooden that I have tried to deter them as best I can. As you can see, she is in a lot worse state than when I first wrote to you about her welfare."

The king stepped further into the room. He gave the colonel a reassuring nod, then turned to the young man. "You, sir," he said. "Your name is John, is it not?"

"Yes sir," he replied. "I met Your Majesty in the palace a few weeks ago. I had accidentally overheard a conversation about your son, Prince Henry. You swore me to secrecy, and now I must confess something to you." John's face was long and sorrowful, but his words were sincere. "I didn't keep my vow, Your Highness. I told my cousin, because she was the one you spoke of when you said your son was in love. I couldn't allow her to walk into that blindly, and I fear now I may have killed her."

"I have heard too many people blame themselves for a death that has not yet occurred," stated the king bluntly. "First my son came home and said he had killed his love. Then I get a letter from Jasper here saying that Rose blames herself for all that has occurred, and now you, John, you say you have killed your cousin. Who is to blame next? Should I blame myself? After all, I did kill her father, didn't I?"

John looked at the king, his mouth agape. How was he supposed to respond to that? What was the right thing to tell the king in this instance? All he could manage was a soft, "Oh." He didn't know what else to say.

"As far as I am concerned," continued the king, "no one is to blame. We are all at fault. We all neglected our duties to each other, and therefore we can all be blamed for what occurred. But blame does not help Rose any. What she needs is good care, and as soon as she is healthy enough, we will be transporting her to Silidon where she will receive top medical attention. Until then, the two of you will refer to me as Henry Hyden. I figure it is only suiting."

"Yes, Your Highness," the two citizens said in unison.

"Now," said the king, "where can I get something to eat?"

John and Jasper looked at each other. Jasper rolled his eyes and John snickered slightly. Once a king, always a king, and this king was hungry. It was best that they feed him immediately.

The number of Rose's men increased that day, for the king thought it his duty to take up a role by her bed. Seeing as there were three of them, the men decided that they would take up shifts. It only seemed to make sense. That way, they could all be well rested and fed, and Rose would be well looked after.

During one of the king's shifts, the young lady decided to wake up. There is nothing odder than waking up to a stranger's face.

Rose peered up at the king, and he looked down on her. She blinked a few times, trying to clear her vision, but the stranger never disappeared. "Who are you?" she finally croaked.

"Well," the stranger replied, "the Monks know me as Mr. Henry Hyden, but your cousin and Colonel Jasper always call me Your Highness, no matter how much I insist they call me James. They are good men, you know. In fact, the three of us are considered *your* men, because we have been keeping constant vigil over you while you were ill. Can you imagine that?"

"Can I have some water?" whispered Rose. She was still a bit confused as to who stood over her, and who her men were. The stranger didn't seem to be making any sense at all.

"Certainly, certainly," he said. "I can very easily do that for you. Just wait one minute. John will be wanting to talk to you as well, but I think he is sleeping right now. I will have to see. I'll be right back." He disappeared through the door, and Rose was left to wonder who the strange man was.

She wasn't left for long. Within seconds, John burst through the door and raced toward her side. He embraced her gently, avoiding her shoulder though it screamed at her anyway. She bit her lip and tried to ignore it. "I'm sorry," she whispered to John. "I should have known better."

John shushed her and gave her a kiss on the cheek. The strange man entered again with a pitcher of water. "John," she nudged him, "who is that?"

John laughed softly. "That, my dear cousin, is the king, come to make sure you are all right. I believe he has every intention of bringing you back to the palace as soon as possible to make sure you are all right, and also to make sure his son doesn't grow taciturn in his longing for you."

Rose blushed. "Henry won't ever forgive me, and besides, I have gone over my year most likely by now, and your mother has the right to marry me off to the curate. We had a bargain."

John looked at her sadly. "I don't think there will be any problem with that, Rose," he said. "I've taken over the family property. Mother thought she had control of it, but Father had changed his will, after all. When she was told this, she was quite furious and she refused to speak to me. I haven't heard her speak for nearly a month. She just putters about the house without saying a word."

"Oh," Rose said. "Henry still won't forgive me."

"Let's not worry about that right now," said John. The king handed Rose a cup of water, and John helped her drink it. Before she was finished, her eyelids began to droop, and John laid her down to rest. By the morning she would be ready to talk, and he would be able to convince her of what was best.

Josh knocked at the door. He didn't know what he would say if it was the truth, but he had to know for sure. In his hands, he held a mask. It was his teacher's mask. He had found it out in the pasture. It was the same pasture where he had always practised, and it was the same pasture that Rose Wooden had been injured in.

The door opened, and Colonel Jasper looked at him. "I," stuttered Josh, "I was hoping that I could see Miss Wooden. If it would be okay." The colonel looked him up and down and Josh began to sweat.

"Only for a little while, and only because she is driving everyone else crazy. You can go up and see her." The colonel let him in, and Josh stepped hesitantly over the threshold. He was directed to a room upstairs where a young woman could be heard arguing about something or other and two men trying to convince her of a different opinion.

Josh knocked, and the voices silenced. He was beckoned in. As he had predicted, two men glared down at Miss Wooden, and she glared stubbornly up at them from her place on the bed. When he walked in, she looked up and her face lit up. "Josh!" she exclaimed. When his face fell, she realized her mistake.

He held up the mask and handed it to her. "I guess it is true then," he said. "You are the knight. I guess I should have known you were a girl. You're smaller than any man I know. It was dumb of me to think that you were a man in the first place."

"A lot of people made that mistake," said Rose softly. "I'm only sorry that you had to find out the truth this way. I was hoping you would have been able to unmask me yourself someday. You were getting mighty close. You almost got me that one day."

Josh nodded slightly. "I guess I'll have to find another teacher," he said. "But I really don't know who." The room fell into silence. It was the first silence it had heard all day.

"You know, Josh," said Rose. "I bet that John here will know someone who can teach you. He's the one who taught me most of what I know. How about he finds you someone to work with, and maybe that will stop him badgering me? He's bound and determined that I'm going to head to the palace with the king tomorrow, but I'm sure and certain that only bad can come of that. Perhaps if you get him off my case, I can convince him otherwise."

"Why don't you want to go to the palace? Wouldn't that be a good place to go right now?" Josh asked.

"I don't know, Josh," said Rose. "You remember Mr. Hyden?" she asked. "Well, he was actually the Prince, and I hurt him real bad, and now if I go to the palace, I'm afraid he will still be angry with me."

"I suppose that could be a problem," said Josh. "But we all have to stand up to our fears sometime, don't we? And it is only just to give the Prince a chance, isn't it? You always told me to make sure I'm just in my actions. Isn't it your turn to be just to the Prince?"

"I guess that's the truth." Rose thought for a moment. "I'll go on one condition," she said. "You have to promise me that you will look out for Katy. She thinks she loves the curate and I'm afraid she is going to do something silly. Do you think you could look out for her for me?"

Josh smiled. "I'll be happy to look after Miss Monks. I don't know if she will be too pleased about it, but I'll keep my eye on her. She is awful pretty." Rose smiled, and Colonel Jasper stuck his head in the room.

"It's time to go," he said to Josh. "Miss Wooden needs her rest. She has a long trip ahead of her, whether she likes it or not." Josh gave her a smile and stepped out the door. Rose chuckled softly and sank farther into the bed. She got tired far too easily these days. She didn't know how she would last all the way to Silidon. By God's grace alone, that was for sure.

THIRTY-TWO

T HE CARRIAGE JOSTLED AND BUMPED, up and down, up and
down. Rose held her stomach in an attempt to hold back the
nausea. Perhaps taking this trip wasn't such a good idea. Her
shoulder went from burning to itching. This would have been
enough on its own, but the dear Lord deemed it necessary to add
to her misery the lopsided churning of her stomach and the constant drumming of her brain pounding against her temples.

Of course, her misery was her own fault, and she could not
blame God, but that would not keep her from petitioning for the
end of it all. No matter how long she prayed, the carriage still
rolled on. Pace after pace, the horses plodded toward their home in
Silidon. Only a few more miles, Rose kept telling herself, only a few
more endless miles.

To pass the time, Rose decided to observe her host. The king
sat regally. It sounded a bit cliché even to Rose's own ears, but

there was no other way to describe his upright posture and square shoulders. He looked every bit the king he was, even though he was clad in the garb of a common merchant.

Do I still hate him? Rose asked herself as she stared across at the king. Had she ever really hated him? She had once pictured a day when she would meet the king and deliver to him the same harm he had delivered to her father, but she could no longer find that resentment. All she could find was a hollow sadness. There was no more loathing. There was only an emptiness, a void.

In the past few days, Rose had gotten to know the king. He was kind, charitable, and compassionate. There was no mark of a murderer, as she had always pictured. His eyes were soft and warm. In fact, everything about the King's appearance contradicted what Rose had previously pictured, making it impossible to hate him.

Rose sighed and turned to look out the window. It was time to let go of the past. Her father had been gone for over eight years, and there was no use holding onto him anymore. She tried to picture his face, but couldn't see it. She tried to remember what it had been like to dance with him around the kitchen, but all she could remember was what it had felt like to dance with Henry. A tear rolled down her cheek as she tried to remember her father's voice, his laughter, his anything. But it was all gone.

She lifted her hand to wipe her face. The pain in her shoulder caused more tears to come to her eyes, but Rose refused to call out. She leaned her head back against the seat. "Goodbye, Daddy," she whispered. The words were final, convicting. She had moved on, and it was finished. Sitting up straight, she realized that the king was watching her.

"Is everything all right?" he asked.

John, who had been sleeping, woke up at these words and stared at Rose, waiting for an answer. She nodded, but neither man was satisfied. The look of concern on their faces caused Rose to laugh slightly.

"I'm fine," she said. "I'm only a little tired, and I moved my arm a bit too far. I'll be all right."

The king sent a look to John and the two seemed to agree. "We'll stop earlier today. There is no rush in getting to Silidon. Besides, the horses could use the break," stated John. There was no room for argument in his voice, but that didn't keep Rose from rolling her eyes. She was fine, but leave it to John not to believe her.

They stopped at a small inn in the next town. John didn't allow Rose to walk. Instead, before she had a chance to protest, he scooped her up in his arms and carried her to an open table in the lounge. If she had been feeling better, she might have put up a fuss, but her stomach roiled, so she decided not to fight it.

The night was long and hard. The mattress was uncomfortable and lumpy. No matter what position she tried, Rose found that there was one lump or another poking into her shoulder, her side, or any of her other body parts. She spent the entire night tossing and turning, trying to get comfortable. By the time morning came, she was less rested, and her stomach turned at the thought of food.

Her chaperones looked at her worriedly when she did not eat, but they were soon on the road, and it was forgotten.

The days passed much the same. They spent the mornings in the carriage bouncing down the road. By mid-afternoon, Rose would be exhausted, and John and King James would deem it necessary to stop for the night. Each night was worse than the previous one, and Rose felt her illness slipping back. She longed for them to be done with travelling, but with the short days, it was taking them quite a while to reach their destination.

On the third such day, the small entourage met up with some trouble. They were stopped at a small town eating an early lunch when the king was recognized by a young soldier returned from the war. The group had intended to pass as a family, for if the king could not conceal his identity, they were all in danger. This danger did not threaten their lives, but rather it threatened their reputations. For it was unseemly for the king to be travelling with a young lady and her male cousin.

The young soldier ran up to the king, shouting, "Your Highness!" The king tried to hide himself, but it was no use; the soldier was determined. He pushed through the crowd toward the monarch, striving for a chance to converse with his sovereign away from the battlegrounds. He came up to the small group and looked slightly confused.

Rose took advantage of his stutter. "Papa," she said to the king, "do you know this man? He seems to have mistaken you for someone else." She slid her hand into the crook of King James' arm and leaned toward him a little. He patted her hand slightly.

The soldier looked at the king, a bit bewildered. "I'm sorry, sir," he said. "I could have sworn you looked exactly like the king back there. My mistake, sir." He looked at Rose, and grinned. He bowed to her, then to King James, and walked away. The three of them slowly exhaled and returned to their lunches. They would have to be more careful. As they neared Silidon, more people would begin to recognize their sovereign, and they couldn't risk being discovered.

The dawn of the seventh day brought nothing but drear. The sky was overcast and the clouds wept fat teardrops, each one sounding a gentle *splick* on the carriage roof. John had carried Rose out to the carriage and she hadn't objected. Her whole body ached, and she could no longer pretend she was in good health. Her fever was back and she shivered in the humid confines of the carriage.

This would be their last day on the road. They would not stop early. Instead, they would travel the rest of the way to Silidon, no matter how long it took. The risk of someone recognizing the king was just too great from here on out, and not a single member of the party wished to take that risk.

The day dragged on. Rose fell in and out of a feverish sleep, and the king and John watched her closely, not knowing what to do. They tried to comfort her, but there wasn't much comfort to be offered when a carriage wheel slipped into a rut, and the whole riding contraption shuddered. The most effective tool they had was prayer, and pray they did. On and on, as dawn turned to day, and day turned to dusk.

THE MASK

It was nearly the next morning by the time they reached the palace gates. The horses picked up their pace with the stable in sight and made their way to the back. The king lifted Rose from the seat where she slumbered fitfully. John followed close behind. A maid was awakened from her night's sleep an hour early to attend to making a bed for the feverish woman, and another was woken to find the proper garments for their guest.

Once Rose was attended to, James was able to turn his attention toward his other guest. Not much was needed besides a bed. The luggage would be gathered later on in the morning. James let out a sigh and headed for bed himself. It had been a long time since he had been home, and he much preferred his own bed to the lumpy beds at the inns. All conscious thought left him as soon as his head hit the pillow.

Rose felt herself being lifted from the carriage and carried into a building. It didn't smell like an inn, so she knew they must have arrived. She floated about in the arms of her supporter. She heard him whisper to the maids and relaxed a little when she was settled into a bed. That was what a bed was supposed to feel like. Feather down conformed to her body and eased the aches out of her joints.

She felt the gentle tug as the maid removed her dirtied clothes, and she let out a slight moan of pain when she tugged a little too hard on her wounded shoulder. She heard the maid gasp when she saw the wound that was most likely festered and bleeding again.

The woman soon recovered and moved quickly, pulling a soft cotton shift over Rose's head.

Thick blankets tucked her in; then Rose was left to sleep. Exhaustion took hold of her body and pulled her deeper away from consciousness. It wasn't until late the next afternoon that she awakened, and then only because her stomach demanded to be fed. She propped herself up and looked around her.

The bed that she lay on was massive. There was room enough on it for four of her. Drapes hung from two windows, blocking out the daylight. A chair stood in the corner decorated by a dress, aired and ready for her use. She went over to inspect it.

It was an old dress, but pretty nonetheless. It had a coat of dark green, and a striped skirt that would trail at least a foot behind her. Slowly and carefully, she pulled it up to her body to measure it against herself. If she were healthy, it would most likely fit perfectly, but seeing as she had not eaten well for the past few days, it would probably hang. She tried it on, only to discover her assumptions to be correct.

It would have to do. Taking a step toward the door, she opened it and stepped out into the hall. For a moment, light-headedness stole over her, and she needed to lean on the door-frame to catch her balance. A little less confidently, she set off down the hall in search of food.

Each step cost her. She wasn't near as well as she had thought. Her stomach ached from hunger, and pain shot up and down her arm with every slight motion. She tried to ignore this and kept pushing on. Servants in the hall acknowledged her with slight bows, and she nodded, not sure how else to respond. The corridors were endless and she felt as if she was travelling in circles. She made a move to turn around the next corner when she saw him.

The morning had been long. Henry's father had returned, which meant there were social events to tend to. The Betons had come again. It was hard to ignore the vivacious Kayla, who did everything in her power to capture his attention. The ball was coming up, and rumour had it that he would choose his wife there. How they all would be shocked when he refused to marry. He expected some of the women to be angry, and perhaps some fathers as well, but he would live through it.

As the afternoon crept up, Henry was finally left to himself. He took a breath of air to relax the stiffness in his back. Thoughts swarmed his head, and he closed his eyes, trying to forget. The harder he tried, the faster the memories flooded his mind. First there was her laughter. Rich and sweet. He could listen to it for years and not tire of it. Then her smile. It bewitched him, taking his breath away.

But most vivid of all memories was the dance. How could he forget how she had felt in his arms? How she moved with him through the garden though no music played? Such a thing was unforgettable.

He rubbed his eyes and groaned. He must forget. She hated him, and he had every right to hate her. She had destroyed him, taking everything good in him and holding it in her grasp. If only she would let him go. If only he could see her one more time. He longed for her, yet he loathed her. His head spun from the contradiction that was his heart.

He fumbled his way out back to the woodshed. An axe stood stuck in a log. He picked it up and began to swing. Piece after piece splintered on the ground around him. Sweat dripped off his forehead, and his shoulders began to ache, but he pushed himself harder and harder. He thought of her smile. *Swoomthud.* He thought of her laugh. *Swoomthud.* He thought of the dance. *Swoomthud.*

He was out of logs. Frustrated, he dug the axe into the ground and headed back toward the palace. His whole body reeked of sweat and dirt, and he didn't feel any better. So much was built up inside, he wished he could scream, but that would never do. People were already questioning the odd behaviour of the Prince. Screaming would only compound their worry.

He stomped through the halls toward his chamber. He turned the corner and stopped.

She was standing there right by his door. Her face was pale and drawn. She looked as if she was about to faint. His mind was playing tricks on him. It had to be a trick. Slowly, he reached out and touched her face. It was warm and wet. She was crying. "Rose?" Henry whispered softly.

She turned away. "Your father brought me. Apparently, Colonel Jasper was a friend of his sent to look out for you. He sent a letter to your father about what happened." She stopped and looked down at her hands, which hung uselessly at her sides. "I'm so sorry, Henry. I'm just so sorry."

He didn't know how to respond. What was he supposed to say to the woman he loved, yet hated? "You know the conversation we had, and you asked me what I would be willing to give up for love? I was stupid and ignorant back then. I said I would be willing to give up everything, even my own life. I now realize it is different and harder than that."

Rose nodded and rocked a little on her feet. It was all over. Henry couldn't forgive her. He had pretty much just said that straight out. She bit her lip to keep more tears from coming. She felt sick and lightheaded and wished she hadn't emerged from her room.

"You see," continued Henry, "when you fought me that night, I thought I had killed you. I hated myself. I hated that I had been the coward and waited till your back was turned. I hated that I had been responsible for my love's death, and I no longer felt worthy as a Prince. When I got your letter, that all changed.

"I no longer hated myself, you see, but I thought I hated you. You hurt me. You terrorized my thoughts and filled my head whether I slept or woke. I hated that you held my heart, and you refused to let it go. I vowed to myself that I would never marry. You were to wed another, and I could not willingly give myself to someone whom I could never love. I loathed you, yet I loved you.

"I promised myself that if I ever saw you again, I would turn the other way. It would be easier that way. I would not have to remind myself of my love for you, and I would allow my hate to grow until it overpowered my love. But now you are here, and I find that I cannot turn away."

Rose watched Henry. His steady gaze met hers, and he did not turn away. She was the first to break eye contact. She fiddled with her thumbs. She couldn't think. She couldn't move. "So, where do we go from here?" she asked quietly.

Henry smiled. "You know, I have asked that question a million times these past few weeks, and it isn't until now that I have found an answer." He stepped toward her and lifted her chin so she had to look at him. "Rose, no matter how much you hurt me, I cannot continue hating you. For love, I am willing to forgive you if you will forgive me. It still hurts that you would detest my family so much, but if you could look past that and say you will become my wife, I would be the happiest man alive."

Rose felt herself leaning against Henry as her light-headedness became too much. He wrapped his arms around her, and she cried gently into his shoulder. "When we fought," she whispered, "I was a child. All I could see was my need for revenge. I was hurt and lost. I missed my father, and I was angry. I thought I hated your father. I thought…" Rose paused to think for a while.

"I used to think that if I could just get revenge, my heart wouldn't ache so much. But when I met you, I began to forget. I forgot about the war and about death. I forgot what it was like to live with my aunt under her oppression. I even began to forget my father. I no longer thought about his smile and his laugh. I could hardly remember what his face looked like. I was happy for the first time in so long.

"Then I discovered who you were. I was angry, hurt, betrayed. I wanted you to pay because you were the king's son. I thought that if something happened to you, I would have my revenge because the king would know what I had gone through. I thought that in a fight, either I would kill you or you would kill me and it would be over.

"As we fought, I let my anger lead me. It made me strong and kept the sword in my hand. Then you were on the ground. I asked you your name, and you said it so defiantly that I knew I couldn't kill you. I loved you, for all the insanity of it. I knew you would hate me, so I did the one thing that I thought made sense. I gave you back your ring."

Henry held her a little bit tighter. He kissed the top of her head and rubbed large circles on her back. Rose closed her eyes as she continued. "After I sent you my letter, I became very sick. It was an infection that caused a fever. I think I may have almost died. When I woke, your father was looking down at me. He was much different than I had pictured him.

"Anyway, he convinced me to come here. I didn't want to. I fought it, tooth and nail. Josh ended up being the one who persuaded me. He is the boy you fenced with the one night when I was late for his lesson." Henry nodded that he remembered the boy. Rose smiled as she thought of the two fencing together. It really had been a marvellous sight.

"The way was rough and long, and I had a lot of time to think. I realized that I had never hated your father, not really. Now the part of me that hurt so much is gone, but what's left is empty."

Rose's words died off, and the two of them stood there holding each other. The silence soothed them, and mended any of the hurt that still remained.

"Do you remember the second question you asked me that day?" asked Henry.

Rose looked up at him. "What do you mean?"

"You asked me," continued Henry, "why God would choose to love when he knew that it would cost him so much." Henry smiled at her. "Your question bothered me so much, I wrote it down and stuck it in my diary. I found it again the other day, and I think I have an answer."

Rose tilted her head up and listened as Henry went on. "You see, God didn't consider the cost when he sent his Son. There were only two things that he considered: love and justice. God is just, so he couldn't ignore the penalty, but he is also love, and he couldn't ignore that part of his being either. So God did the only thing that he could do to satisfy both justice and love. He sent his Son."

Rose nodded her head. It made sense. "I pray," said Henry, "that God will give me the wisdom and the capacity to love as he loved. And I hope that you will be there to share in that love for the rest of my days, till death does us part."

Rose leaned against Henry, stood on her tiptoes, and kissed him boldly on the lips. Smiling up at him, she replied, "Only on one condition." Henry looked at her with a questioning grin on his face. "You carry me to find food. I'm famished, and I don't think my legs will carry me all the way around the palace. I seem to be a little off balance the past few days."

Henry laughed. He scooped her up in his arms and returned her kiss. "That, my dear," he said, "I think I can do." Then slowly and gently he made his way down the hall, his head next to hers, whispering secrets of a life to come.